ANDY REMIC

Twilight of the Dragons

BOOK II OF THE BLOOD DRAGON EMPIRE

ANGRY
ROBOT

ANGRY ROBOT
A member of the Osprey Group

Lace Market House,
54-56 High Pavement,
Nottingham
NG1 1HW
UK

www.angryrobotbooks.com
twitter.com/angryrobotbooks
Quite a lot of killing

An Angry Robot paperback original 2016

Cover by Lee Gibbons.
Set in Meridien by Epub Services.

Distributed in the United States by Penguin Random House, Inc., New York.

ISBN 978 0 85766 457 0
Ebook ISBN 978 0 85766 458 7

Printed in the United States of America

9 8 7 6 5 4 3 2 1

*Twilight of the Dragons is
dedicated to Marie Vedat*

Prologue
KILLING TIME

The band struck up a merry tune from a low wooden bandstand, with musicians playing happy fluttering notes on flutes, strumming lyres with vigour, and one woman, a ferret-faced baker with wild curly red hair which bounced in time to her efforts, hammering out a fantastical beat on several wide drums of cowhide. Banners and flags fluttered in the chilly breeze up and down Pig Market Street in the small, country village of Vanda, deep in the heart of Vagandrak.

Children ran down the hard mud road, giggling and shouting, playing games of *Kiss Catch, Beat the Rat* and *Stab the Leper*, whilst the men gathered around the ale tent with serious faces and bushy beards, tankards clasped to chests or balanced on rounded bellies. Their womenfolk either danced before the band on the paved, stone square, skirts held above their knees and faces ruddy with exertion, merriment and the cold weather, or huddled in groups, tongues wagging in earnest as they gestured towards other gossiping housewives.

Little Annie clutched her doll to her chest and watched the bigger children play. Little Annie had a sweet, round face, long, blonde hair woven into plaits that nearly reached her waist. Her red cardigan and red battered shoes added a splash of colour to the late winter drabness as her large green eyes followed a group of girls who were running with a glossy, pink streamer.

Little Annie wanted to play with the bigger girls so much it made her want to cry, but she didn't have the courage to approach them – she was far too shy – and so she stood with tears filling her eyes, chewing her lip, and hoping.

Then, a miracle!

One of the girls peeled away from the group and jogged to Little Annie. She bent a little, and smiled a warm, friendly smile. "I know you. You're Little Annie. My mother's just started working in the wool barn with your mother."

Little Annie nodded.

"I'm Chalina. It's nice to meet you."

"It's… nice… to meet you," said Little Annie, licking her lips nervously, eyes wide.

"Do you want to come and play?"

"That would be fun."

Chalina took Little Annie's hand, and within minutes they were running together, laughing, their footsteps matching the rhythm of the band as they ran as fast as they could, as fast as the wind, the glossy pink streamer undulating like the ripples of a moving snake. They stopped, panting, halfway down the street. The music was distant now, as was the rumble of talk and laughter which merged into a low undertone that formed the aural backbone of the friendly gathering.

Little Annie was looking back towards the crowd, a little nervous at being away from the village centre and her house and her mother.

"Do you want to run with the ribbon?"

Little Annie's eyes went wide. "Could I?"

"Yes, yes! Of course you can!"

"Fabulous," said Little Annie, eyes shining, wet lips wide as she took the crimped end of the ribbon in her free hand, and thought, *you are the best friend I've ever had, you are wonderful, Chalina*, and she knew, *knew* deep in her heart that this new friend was a friend for life!

"Come on, back to the village square."

They set off, and Chalina ran ahead now, looking back, giggling at Little Annie's simple pleasure, her laughter and her shining eyes. But even as she ran, Chalina's eyes narrowed and her face changed, but Little Annie was having too much fun to notice, caught up in her own fun game, in her own little world.

A dark shape seemed to fill the end of the street, coming in low and fast from over the rolling hills of surrounding countryside. Chalina caught a sudden vision that made her stumble and fall, rolling on the muddy road, scrambling onto her back and staring straight ahead, past the still-giggling form of Little Annie, at the… at the *dragon* which swept towards them.

There was a *whump,* and suddenly Little Annie was gone, and a warm wind rushed over Chalina who rolled and turned, in time to see the black dragon lift sharply, huge tail covered with black spines whipping neatly as the beast climbed steeply with Little Annie in its mouth. There came a distant *crunch* and two severed arms and two severed legs came tumbling down out of the sky, to land with quad *thumps* amidst the shocked, suddenly motionless group of dancing women.

One hand still held the doll, twisted in a bloody, torn piece of ribbon.

Blood pattered down like rain, and a woman began to scream.

"Dragon!" bellowed one man, and ales were tossed aside as men ran for houses and weapons. High above, Volak rolled, lazy and huge, and then slowly came to the end of the climb where she hung for a moment, impossibly suspended, like a bead of blood on the tip of a blade, balanced, refusing to obey the laws of physics. And then reality kicked in, and Volak tipped and her snout dropped towards the ground, tail whipping in a vicious arc, cracking through the sky as the villagers scattered beneath her and she powered down towards these pink-skinned *insects.* Many scattered. Some had returned with bows. Arrows whizzed up towards her, several clattering from her black, iron-like scales. And suddenly her wings smashed the air, her head reared up and she landed on the stone square, rippling the ground and cracking the paving slabs. More arrows screeched along Volak's scales, and her head dropped to ground level, neck moving like a snake as her eyes narrowed and her gaze swung around, analysing the villagers before her.

"Ants," she hissed, tongue flickering, flames curling around her elongated black snout. Then she laughed, and the villagers started to run.

Volak took a deep breath, her chest glowed, and with a squeal, a superheated blast of fire roared out.

Reeka the Merchant, chunky, receding hair, his face crisscrossed with worry lines, sat back on the silk cushions of his carriage and tried not to think about the fast approaching darkness.

They should have reached Woodhaven long before dusk, but a broken carriage wheel had set them back two hours, and now the darkness had crept over the forest, and Woodhaven seemed like a distant, unachievable sanctuary.

A horse whinnied, and Reeka jumped, sweat gleaming on his balding pate, his fingers clenching and unclenching in the soft wool blanket that covered his knees to ward off the evening chill.

The carriage lurched from side to side, creaking. Boza and Dull, the driver and bodyguard, had taken far too long to change that broken wheel. *Damn them! They have caused me unnecessary risk!*

Reeka frowned, mind ticking over, but not that quickly. Despite being relatively wealthy through a series of fluke maritime transactions, Reeka was not the brightest candle in the room, and unfortunately, was not bright enough to realise his own lack of illumination.

Slowly, the carriage ground to a halt. There was a *crack* as the right wheel rested on a fallen branch.

"Boza? Dull? Why have we stopped?" Reeka's voice was wavery, nasal, almost feminine.

"Er, boss," said Dull, "better step out here."

"Step out *there*?" Reeka could hardly disguise his disgust. *What? Step out into the dark? Into the cold? Into the fucking forest? Has the man lost his brain? Dull by name, dullard by nature.*

"Er. Yeah, boss. We got a problem."

"What kind of problem?"

"I kinda gots to show yer."

"Huff." He actually *said* the word huff. "Very well. If I must. If you insist. But it better be very bloody important because I'm very bloody unhappy, and it's all your fault, for taking so long with the bloody carriage wheel…"

Reeka stepped down from the carriage, wrapping his blanket around his shoulders and not, immediately, looking up. A horse stamped, smoke drifting from nostrils.

"Er, boss."

Reeka looked up. Into the grinning faces of ten forest bandits, who had levelled crossbows, rugged attire, and an air of menace that sent shivers quivering up and down Reeka the Merchant's entire body. He felt his bollocks retract into marbles, as quite commonly happened, and his mouth was suddenly too dry to speak.

The silence, and lack of movement, was deeply unnerving.

"Wh… wh… what do… do… you want?" Reeka licked his lips. Fear was not something he was used to dealing with, and deal with it badly he did.

One bandit stepped forward; he was a handsome chap, with a cheeky grin that said, *I know when I've got you by the balls*, and he rested his crossbow against his thigh, lifted his chin, thinking for a moment, and said, in a slow, sardonic drawl, "Stand and deliver. Your money, or your life."

Reeka, Boza and Dull were naked, tied together with harsh hemp rope, and squirming as only three naked men could squirm in an attempt to not touch one another's nakedness.

"You shall be fired for this," snorted Reeka, eventually, watching the bandits open one of his chests and cackle at the silken finery they found within.

One bandit danced around the road with a pair of Reeka's lacy underwear on his head, making sexual grunting noises and grabbing his groin. "Oooh, I'm Reeka, the Lord of the Manor, want to touch my silky pants and the gold coin that lies within?" The others laughed. Reeka reddened.

"Stop that! Stop that, I say!"

They ignored him.

"Fire me for what?" Dull was annoyed. Annoyed he'd been taken prisoner, annoyed he was naked, but even more annoyed that he was pressed up against Reeka's naked flesh and the plump merchant's penis occasionally brushed against his leg. "Come on, you fucking fat prick, what you gonna fire me for?"

Reeka reddened more. *Prick* was an old playground nickname he thought he had long left behind. Dull couldn't have known about Reeka's tortured childhood, but the barb shot straight to his heart and stuck there, quivering.

"How... how... how dare you!" Reeka was fuming. His penis pressed hard against Dull. Dull frowned. Dull was deeply annoyed. Dull didn't want Reeka's maggot sliming down his leg. It made Dull want to beat Reeka's head repeatedly against the ground until he didn't move no more.

"I dare," growled Dull, dropping from anger to danger in one swift pendulum swing.

The bandits, who had now ravaged their way through all six chests, were in fine merriment. Many had pulled on Reeka's ridiculous wardrobe, and were parading around, pretending to be gentry. Many crossbows were leant against trees.

Dull's eyes narrowed, and his fingers found a knot. He twisted left. A fully loaded triple-shot Steir & Moorheim leant against a tree, stock gleaming black and dangerous. If, *if* he could just get to that weapon, he'd unleash a chaos amongst these fucking forest bandits like they'd never fucking seen in a lifetime.

Reeka shifted, moaning incomprehensibly, and his penis slid along Dull's buttock.

"Keep your fucking prick to yourself, you disgusting... *prick*," he snarled.

Reeka was shivering, and simply nodded.

Dull felt the knot fall open under his fingers. The bandits were still dancing around. They had red wine now, sloshing in tankards, and it looked like they were making a party out of Reeka the Merchant's misfortune.

"Right," said Dull, cracking his knuckles, and suddenly rose, leaping left, grabbing the Steir & Moorheim and cocking it with a solid-sounding *thud*. "Right, youse bastards." One bandit turned – and was punched backwards from his feet, a black bolt in his throat, spewing blood down Reeka's fine crimson silk pantaloons. He scrabbled for a while and various drunken bandits turned and stared at Dull, but more importantly, stared at the Steir & Moorheim.

"Er... " said Reeka, covering his eyes.

"Who's fucking next?" growled Dull, face pale in the moonlight spilling from on high between distant branches.

Drunk bandits stared at him, mouths open at this sudden reversal.

There was a *whump*, and Dull was gone.

The Steir & Moorheim clattered to the forest trail.

"By the Seven Sisters," muttered Reeka, looking around him suddenly.

A screech rent the air, high pitched, feral, alien, *dragon*.

Everybody froze, and then suddenly started to run. Fire seemed to blossom from nowhere, an inferno; trees went up in an instant to become roaring totems of surging fire, and the forest was no longer a forest, but a rendition of the Chaos Halls where everything, and everybody, burned...

Men and horses screamed as they were eaten by fire.

The air was filled with the stench of scorched meat.

Reeka, miraculously freed from Boza when a random blast of dragon fire scorched the ropes and ignited the unfortunate driver, sending him sprinting and wobbling into the forest, his very skin and fat on fire, had crawled along the path away from the many fires, and was busy praying to a God he didn't believe in for a miracle that couldn't happen.

There was a *thump*. The ground shook.

Reeka slowly looked up.

A *dragon* stood on the forest road before him, and was swaying slightly, as if hypnotised. It was dark silver in colour, scales appearing to be made of metal, and its head had two huge horns. But the eyes – the eyes were black slits, and with a *jump* Reeka realised they were fixed on him.

"Wh… what do you want?"

A long, low hiss ejected on streams of steam.

"Can… can you speak, *monster*? Or are you just a dumb beast intent on murder?"

Kranesh chuckled, lowered her head, and stared hard at Reeka the Merchant. "You are cocky, for such a feeble sack of maggoty shit," she said, and gave a slow, lazy blink.

Reeka swallowed, and urine ran down his leg.

"What do you want, Hell Beast?"

"Revenge," said Kranesh, and leaning forward slowly, delicately tore off Reeka's head. The corpse hit the ground, twitching and squirming, blood spraying from the neck stump until the body was empty, the life was gone, and Reeka the Merchant was no more.

Deep in the forest, there came a clatter.

Kranesh grinned. "More fresh meat," she murmured, and moved forward, the strength of her bulk and mass toppling trees as she pursued the surviving forest bandit deep, deep down into the bowels of the Furnace.

Sergeant Dunda and Lieutenant Filligorse stood on a low hill, watching the winter sun rise slowly from behind the jagged mountain peaks. Mist crawled across the uneven ground, skeins curling around upthrust boulders, as the dawn light painted purple streaks through the clouds and from the distance came the thump of marching boots.

"I hope this display is better than last time," said Filligorse, his voice a little nasal, his watery blue eyes narrowed against the bright light.

"The lads have been working hard, lieutenant," growled Dunda, and rubbed at his beard before turning to the bugler. "Gahi, sound the charge."

Gahi lifted the bugle, and gave three short blasts.

The heavily armoured infantry units broke into a charge, coming into view. Their boots thundered, plate mail clanking.

"Explain your formation, sergeant."

Dunda coughed. "A hundred and fifty on left and right wings, hundred centre, hundred reserves."

"Jolly good. Bugler, sound a halt, followed by weak centre."

The bugler gave a series of blasts and the five hundred Vagandrak soldiers, steel bright and glinting in the dawn sunlight, stopped with well-measured precision, and the centre units retreated, twenty peeling from each side to reinforce the left and right wings. The idea was that a weak centre would invite an enemy attack, and the wings would curl around to encompass the enemy from three sides, crushing them.

Boots stamped to attention, and silence drifted across the plain.

"They are better, much better," observed Filligorse.

Dunda made a low growling sound, but said nothing. He fought hard against wanting to punch the lieutenant on the nose.

Mist curled around boots, and the soldiers waited with military patience, hands on sword hilts, heads high, backs straight. Although these were not veterans, not battle-tested, they still presented themselves well, had trained hard under Dunda's expertise... after all, he *was* a veteran. He had survived the Second Mud-Orc War. He was revered and highly respected by the men.

Dunda marched forward without a word to the lieutenant, to stand before his beloved units. He puffed out his chest proudly, and beamed a smile. "You done me proud, lads," he said, voice rumbling out across their motionless ranks. "Now, what we're going to do is have a little bit of a run." Where once there would have been groans, now there was simple acceptance. And that was a small miracle in itself; running in full armour was no pleasure at all.

Dunda looked back at the lieutenant. The man had a slightly pained expression on his face. Dunda grinned and scratched his chin once more... but then frowned, because there was something in the sky. *An eagle? But Gods, it was big. A Golden Eagle?* He squinted again, then turned to the white peaks, a saw blade across the horizon. It was feasible. They were within range...

Then there came a distant *thump*, as of some great object slapping the air, and the object accelerated with impossible speed. Dunda felt his mouth drop open, something that hadn't happened since he manned the walls of Desekra Fortress.

"By the Seven Sisters..." he said, and felt a sudden ripple of fear course through the armoured men behind him.

"What is it?" Lieutenant Filligorse was saying. "What's the matter with you lot?"

And then he turned, in time to see what looked like a *brass dragon* speeding towards him, wings outstretched, their edges lined with spikes, scales gleaming with reflected sunlight, eyes black and slanted and narrowed... and fixed on him.

His muscles tensed.

"Oh no," he managed.

Then Moraxx opened her jaws, and grabbed him from the hilltop like a man plucking a lollipop from a child. She soared above the arranged infantry, and every head turned, following her silent passing. Silent, until she bit down, and spat out Filligorse on a short jet of fire.

The two halves of his scorched body hit the ground

amidst the infantry, and many leapt back, noses wrinkling
at the stench of half-cooked human flesh.

"Right, you fuckers!" screamed Dunda, and suddenly
the men leapt back to attention. "Seems we have a fucking
dragon who wants to have a fight. Those with short-range
crossbows, load and fire on my command..." Dunda was
watching the beast circle, a wide, lazy arc and his brow
furrowed at the sheer scale of the beast, the sheer, inherent
power...

Moraxx came in on a silent glide, head outstretched,
dark, slitted, malevolent eyes gleaming with intelligence.
Dunda screamed a command, and bolts lashed through the
air, a dark hail... and they watched with open mouths as
Moraxx dipped one wing, dropped under the bolts, then
suddenly accelerated towards the armoured infantry,
landing in their midst with a *crash* that sent men toppling
like armoured skittles. Her tail lashed out, sending twenty
soldiers screaming into comrades, their plate armour
buckling. Bodies pulped inside metal as soldiers *merged* with
friends to form broken heaps of severed limbs and crushed
flesh. Moraxx roared, but the Vagandrak infantry charged,
swords hacking at her scales, at her legs. She turned in the
midst of the melee with lazy contempt and lowered her
head. Her chest glowed, snout opened, and fire roared from
the furnace of her throat and fire glands... men screamed,
as armour became suddenly superheated and they cooked
inside their metal prisons, flesh pink and steaming, skin
curling like fried pig, until eyes popped and knees collapsed
and the scorched armour held their cooked bodies together,
boiled live like lobsters in a pot, fried in their own juices
and body fat, which ran clear from the legs of armour as a
hundred men lay sizzling.

Moraxx started to lash out, marching amongst the
soldiers. Swords hacked at her, but long claws like polearms
punched out, cutting soldiers in two.

Sergeant Dunda ran up behind Moraxx, his huge paws
swinging a double-headed battle axe that smashed into her

flanks, dislodging several scales. Again he struck, and again, until suddenly Moraxx whirled on him and, in the blink of an eye, he was in her jaws. Gasping, he dropped his axe and grabbed her snout, trying to force her jaws apart, trying to ease the terrible pressure which crushed him. Moraxx shook her head, Dunda's limbs flailing like a doll, and then she bit deep and cut him in half, spitting out the two halves of corpse like a dog ejecting a rotten bone.

She breathed deep, black eyes glinting, burning corpses sending glints of orange bouncing from her scales. The remaining soldiers had retreated, gathered into a unit. There were perhaps fifty left. They held a ragtag assortment of weapons, and remembering their training, they formed into a wedge, shields lifted for protection, trying to ignore the feeble cries of so many half-cooked comrades who steamed like burned pig slabs on a fire rock.

"Charge!" came the cry.

Moraxx inhaled: there came the whisper of her fire glands, and a stream of flames erupted, engulfing the charging unit of soldiers, blasting them backwards, into a heap, into a mass of one, where flesh cooked and blackened, bodies thrashing and trembling, hot fat running. The fire continued, changing from yellow to blue to pure white as it streamed from the wyrm's jaws, illuminating her black cruel eyes as she strode forwards… and plate armour finally melted, and the whole unit of Vagandrak infantry became one mass of molten steel and flesh that ran from a mound to a puddle on this, its final resting place.

Moraxx stopped, fire whispered, and suddenly a strange silence fell like ash.

She turned her head and, with a slap of her wings, leapt into the sky and was soon a black dot on the horizon.

The Cock

The insanity of violence and bloodshed which followed, well, it all started because of cock.

It was to be a heroes' pub crawl around some of the less salubrious slum-quarter establishments of Vagan, capital city of Vagandrak. It would feature renowned and decadent drinking dens such as The Fighting Cocks, The Cock Horse, The One-Legged Cock, The Big Cock and, simply and amusingly, The Cock. These were hard and harsh working men's taverns. Soldiers' taverns. Fighters' taverns. Women of nobility and money, with babies suckling on enlarged teats, did their best to avoid such rough and ready dives.

It was called *The Five Cock Race*, and one, if so inclined, was expected to drink five tankards of ale per establishment in the shortest time-frame possible. There was a reason why *The Five Cock Race* contained no establishment named The Upstanding Cock. That was a Vagandrak drinking joke.

And there was Beetrax, Beetrax of the Axe, his ginger beard bushy and hardly combed at all, his laugh uproaringly infectious and booming across the tavern, making men and women of lesser fibre look away with a shake of the head and a narrowed frown or scowl.

Three taverns in three hours, they'd managed. Fifteen ales in. Beetrax was what could only be described as generously oiled. "Come on you lank bastards, it's fucking time for something fucking stronger! Landlord! Bring out the whiskey barrel!" He roared with laughter and punched the tabletop, making cups and flagons jump.

The landlord narrowed his eyes, and his fist tightened around the helve secreted beneath the bar. "Listen. I think you've had enough, son," he said, words trembling only a little, much to his credit. Beetrax did this to people.

Beetrax scowled, then suddenly grinned, showing a chipped tooth. "No problem!" he boomed, and slapped Dake on the back, forcing the man's face into his frothing ale.

"For the love of the Holy Mother!" spluttered Dake, pushing himself backwards and scowling, but Beetrax simply laughed again and slapped him once more, harder this time.

A singer crooned in the corner, his voice a gentle lullaby.

Men and women drank and laughed and sang.

It was going well, as these things often do. Humour was good. Humour was high! Until Rodrake Ritch, a small and normally innocuous portly guardsman from Wall 4 of Desekra Fortress, decided to get out his cock and dangle it in front of all the ladies present. It was his party trick. His personal comedy. His *special move, baby.*

Some gasped, some laughed, some covered their eyes; but most just shook their heads. Rodrake Ritch was renowned for drinking too much and getting his tackle out. It was a miracle nobody had done anything about it before, including chopping off, with a large knife, the aforementioned set of dangling ridiculousness.

"Oy, Ritch," said Beetrax, uneasily. Somehow, the fun seemed to be trickling out of the evening.

"Yeah?" beamed Rodrake, his round face the gawping, grinning face of a thousand village idiots in a thousand idiot villages throughout the land.

"Put your dick away," said Dake, his face losing its humour. "Nobody wants to see it, mate. Trust me on this."

"But it's great!" said Rodrake, and gave his little member a circular twirl.

"Yeah, but it's not great you're showing it to my woman," snapped Dake.

"Oooooh, listen to the tooucshy man!" slurred Ritch.

Dake started forward out of his seat, but Beetrax placed a hand against Dake's chest. "Best let me handle this, lad. You're all wound up because your pretty girl is here, being forced to stare at… at *that*." He pulled a face full of distaste, and put out his tongue for a moment, as if he'd brought up a bit of sick.

Beetrax stood, and squared up to Rodrake Ritch, which was quite a sight, because Beetrax was one big, brutal motherfucker, and Ritch was portly and small, and happily, drunkenly oblivious to his impending pummelling by fists the size of shovels. It was an amazing mental state to acquire for a man so readily willing to produce his cock in front of other men's wives. One would have thought he'd learnt a lesson sooner.

"Listen, son. Now. This is the way it is. There's a lot of people here, and a lot of people who have their woman present. Now, no man likes his woman looking at another man's cock. It's just not right. And any man who wants to get his cock out and parade it around, well, he's not fucking right in the head, either. So what I suggest is this. Put your cock away in your trews, and I'll think about *not* knocking out your teeth in front of all these good folk who have only come out for fun and a few drinks. How does that sound?"

"Wahey!" Ritch swung his cock around once more. Some men, it would appear, had a death wish. Rodrake Ritch, however, had a *cock wish*.

"Best let me handle this, lad," muttered Dake, from just in earshot. Beetrax felt himself flushing red and he frowned.

"All right, Roddie. I've had enough of your cock. Put it away now – that's fair warning. Or I'll be forced to thump you."

Ritch wiggled his penis some more, oblivious to the retching of the crowd.

"So be it," growled Beetrax, and punched him full in the

face, a straight hard right that sent Rodrake Ritch staggering backwards, cascading stools and tables crashing around him, until he landed on his back, a tooth on his chest, and blood on his chin.

"Well done," said Dake.

"That fucking showed him," nodded Beetrax.

"That. Is. My. Brother." The words were like the rumble of an earthquake. They were like the destruction of stars. They were *the end* of the world, so deep was their resonance. And they also explained why most present had been willing to put up with the little cock.

Beetrax turned, slowly, to face a chest. A broad chest. A *very* broad chest. He looked up. And *up*. And Beetrax was *big*. Which made this motherfucker *huge*.

"So what?"

"My brother!" growled and rumbled the human mountain, thumping his chest with one fist, and glaring at Beetrax with crossed eyes, as his purple tongue protruded like a cow's that continually licked at its lips. His face was a crisscross of scars. Most of his teeth were missing. And Gods, he stank like a sewer. Worse. Like ten corpses in a sewer being eaten by corpse rats with dysentery.

"And your name is?"

The punch hit Beetrax on the nose, sent him reeling backwards, where he sat down on his arse and banged his skull against the bar. He shook his head, stunned for a moment, blood leaking from his nostrils as Rodrake Ritch lay on the tavern floor, giggling, his flaccid penis limp against his trews like a tiny maggot waiting to be hooked on a line.

Dake leapt on the man-mountain's back, arms around his throat in a stranglehold, and the man began to spin until Dake was tossed aside. The man staggered a little, dizzy from his own exertions, as Dake rolled into a table.

"Anybody else want a fucking go?" boomed the man.

Beetrax hit him with a stool, splintering the wood, and dropping him to one knee. Beetrax stared at the broken stool. Then at Rodrake's brother. Gods, the man had a hard head! So he hit him again, sending the huge bastard crashing sideways.

"Better get out of here," muttered Dake.

Laughing, Beetrax nodded, and gesturing to his friends to follow, they ran for it, out into the rain, down the slippery cobbles, back towards The Fighting Cocks, with Beetrax cackling like a demon, and shouting, "These are great days, Dake, great days we're living in! We're happy brothers, and things will never be the same again, you mark my words!"

"Things will never be the same again," muttered Dake Tillamandil Mandasar, as he followed Beetrax through the narrow stone tunnel, eyes fixed on the broad axeman's back. Nobody spoke. The roof of the tunnel was abnormally high, and above lay thin diagonal lodes of silver and gold, web traceries of glittering metal encased in black granite, trapped within the embrace of the mountain.

She's dead, he thought, for the thousandth time.

I cannot believe she is dead.

Things will never, ever, ever be the same again.

His loss hit him like a hammer blow to the head. Like a sledgehammer to the heart, crushing him with its ferocity.

There was a pressure inside Dake's skull, like a huge hand had grabbed his brain and was squeezing itself into a fist. Crushing him with pressure. Breaking his thoughts, his dreams, his memories.

She's dead, he thought, and tears welled in his eyes, rolling down his cheeks. *Jonti is dead.* His throat throbbed with pain, razor-scraped. His heart beat fast, thundering in his chest. And once more he considered following her, chasing her down the dark corridors of pain and into a well of death from which he could never return. He thought of the slender dagger in his boot. He could stop. Kneel down. Pull out the blade, hold the tip to his breast – one short, powerful thrust. Through the heart. He'd be dead in seconds... and then he'd see her again. Be with her again.

Entwined with her beauty for an eternity.

He closed his eyes, boots thudding along, matching the rhythm of Beetrax before him...

Jonti Tal was standing in a field of golden corn. The sky was the colour of topaz, deep, rich, more beautiful than any painting. She was slim, athletic, her long brown hair flowing to one side under the caress of the wind. The corn wavered, giving off a soft rustling sound, rhythmical, in tune with the breeze, nature, the planet. And then she smiled, and her radiance dazzled Dake, almost blinded him with its stunning beauty; almost poleaxed him with the love which emanated from that intense and majestic gaze.

Jonti's hand reached out. She was wearing a gauzy blouse of white, and the sleeves were long and flowing, edged in white lace. The garment exaggerated her movement, her gesture of welcome, her invitation for Dake to join her, be with her, walk with her, smell her skin, taste her, kiss her... He moved forward, automatically, a cog in a machine unable to halt his own progress. Her smile broadened, if that was even possible, and the world smelled good and fresh and *alive*. Reaching her, Dake took Jonti's hand. Her delicate skin was warm and soft. He could feel various pads of hard skin from the wielding of her sword, and he smiled at the memory.

"You must come to me," she said, voice a low purr.

"Yes."

"Will you stay with me?"

"Yes," he said, cheeks wet with tears. "I will stay with you, forever."

"Good. Because I miss you. I miss you terribly, Dake. I remember all the good times, the happy times, the best times. I am so sad we will never have children, my dear, my love, my lord. Heartbroken. So come to me, and we can live *another* life right here, in this golden place."

Dake rubbed the tears from his cheeks, and lifted his head up, back straightening, as the impact of the decision took hold.

"I will come to you," he said, and opened his eyes back in the gloomy tunnel deep down in the mines of the Harborym Dwarves, as deep down as any human had ever travelled, and certainly not in the capacity of being a free man.

Dake coughed. Readied himself to kneel, grab his dagger, plunge it into his breast...

"You all right, laddie?" boomed Beetrax, wheeling suddenly and leering close, large bearded face within inches of Dake. Dake could see crumbs of dwarven bread in Beetrax's beard. And a piece of cheese.

"Y- Yes," he stuttered, shocked by the suddenness of the big axeman's movement. *Damn. It was almost like he bloody knew...* "Get your bloody beard out of my face! Man, you still have half your lunch in it!"

Beetrax glowered at him for a few moments, shifted his axe which he currently carried across his back, and cracked his knuckles. Then, quietly, so the others up ahead couldn't hear, Beetrax said, "I know how you feel, Dake. I know how much you're hurting. Just remember, I'm here for you. Remember, we're *all* here for you."

"I know," said Dake, in a voice so feeble he couldn't believe it had come out of his own mouth. "But... Jonti dying, dying like that; it's broken me, Axeman. I feel crumbled and dead inside. I feel hollow, like a fire has raged through me, burning away every last ounce of life."

"I can't take away the hurt, lad, but I'm telling you from experience... it'll get better. The pain will lessen. You've just to keep those good memories with you, hold onto them like a drowning man clutching a log. Or you'll drown, and I'm damned if I'm stripping off my trews and jumping in after you with my cock swinging in the freezing bloody air!" He rumbled slow laughter, and glanced down the tunnel where the others had halted, and were waiting. Lillith tilted her head to one side in question. Beetrax gave a curt nod and turned back to Dake. "Come on. Your friends are waiting. And we're all counting on you to see this thing through. We *need* you Dake. We need our Sword Champion."

Dake nodded, and slapped Beetrax on the shoulder. "Thanks, brother."

"Anytime, brother."

In silence, they continued their march.

They'd found a small, circular side-cave, possibly used as some kind of restroom for dwarf miners. It had a brazier burning in the centre, an evil black iron thing that wouldn't have been out of place in a torture chamber. Coals were glowing, but there was no sign of any dwarves, any life. The heat was most welcome.

"This is a good place to halt," said Lillith. "Easy to defend."

"I'm ready to drop," said Beetrax, mumbling several curses. "I know I look like I'm indestructible, but I'm fucking *not*. Can somebody else please take first watch because I can't guarantee you any sort of wakefulness."

"I'll do it," said Talon, and dropped his pack. "Any dwarves come down that tunnel, they'll get a shaft down their throat. Bastards." He smiled, with a nasty glint in his eye.

Beetrax nodded, and glanced sideways at Dake, who remained silent, and then looked over to Lillith. Unspoken words passed between them and Lillith gave a narrow smile.

We'll all look out for him, that smile said. *We'll protect him, down here, in the mines of the Harborym Dwarves.*

Dake dreamed.

He stood at the altar of the *Blessed Church of the Seventh Holy Mother*, boots so shiny he could see his face in them, handlebar moustache neatly waxed, hair combed back and slick with oil. His regimental uniform was pressed to perfection, and he wore a ceremonial sword at his hip, a sword that had been passed down through all the Lords of the House of Emerald. It was truly priceless.

In front of the altar, petals had been strewn down the aisle, and the church was filled with smartly dressed friends and relatives, all talking in hushed whispers. Candles burned, perhaps a hundred in total, giving the whole scene a beautiful ambience; the air glowed, and was heady with incense.

Dake twitched, looking back down the aisle, then back to the altar.

"Don't worry," rumbled Beetrax, looking hot and bothered in his starched shirt and neatly pressed black jacket. He looked so out of place in a uniform it wasn't even funny, and he constantly shifted and wriggled, tugging at his cuffs and collars, his (for once) waxed and neatly combed beard not its usual bush, contrasted nicely with the deep black of his military dress.

"Worry?" Dake met his gaze. "I'm not worried."

Beetrax boomed out a laugh, and slapped Dake on the back. The laugh reverberated around the stone interior, and there came a rush of buzzing disapproval from many present. "Well, you could have fooled me, you dickhead!"

"*Beetrax, please*, no bad language in here. It's the *Blessed Church of the Seventh Holy Mother!* Have some respect!"

"I lost my respect for religion a long time back," Beetrax growled, frowning, eyebrows moving together. "The day my dad died, I realised it was all a farce. God? The Holy Mother? The Seven Sisters? Don't make me puke. They're all in it for the money, *your* money, *my* money, *our* money, it's all about bloody money!"

"*Shh!*" Dake actually stamped his boot. "This is hardly the time or the place! Shut your stupid fat mouth!"

Beetrax shrugged, nonplussed. "All I'm saying, right, is that your bride will *definitely* turn up. I've seen the way she looks at you, mate. No sitting at home bloody weeping, wondering whether or not she loves you, wondering whether or not to stand you up at the altar! Oh no. No massive embarrassment and unforgiveable humiliation for *you*, Dake my lad."

"*Shut up!*"

Gentle music tinkled from a large, curved, brass harp by

the doorway, made to sing under the fluttering fingers of a delicate elfin maiden. Jonti Tal stepped through the breach, head to foot in white, her dress flowing, her brown hair full of flowers.

Dake gasped audibly.

Beetrax kicked him on the shin.

"What did you bloody do that for?" scowled Dake, eyes narrowed at the huge axeman.

"Just keeping it real, lad. Keeping your feet on the ground."

"Well... *don't!*"

Jonti was walked down the aisle by her father, an old army sergeant with neat uniform, ramrod spine and stiff upper lip. They stopped beside Dake and Beetrax, and Jonti's father smiled kindly, and said, "Look after her, son. Or I'll break every finger you possess," before retiring to the rough-sawn bench with his other daughters, and never once bending from above his arthritic hips.

"Great," muttered Dake, then watched as Jonti lifted her delicate veil.

She smiled at him, in radiance.

He beamed back, like a hopeless fool in love.

The priest stepped forward, smiled, and said, "Let us begin."

They drank, they danced, they kissed, lost in their own little world, a bubble in which only Dake and Jonti existed. Her lips were sweeter than a peach. She smelled like summer flowers, her skin softer than the most delicate of feathers.

They looked deep into one another's eyes, transfixed.

"I love you more than life," she said.

"And I you."

"I'll love you forever, Dake."

"I know, my sweet. And I'll love you until the stars go out."

She snuggled her head against his chest. "Let's grow old together. Let's die together."

"Yes, my sweet," he said, burying his face in her hair. "*Let us die together*," he whispered.

And in his sleep, Dake wept.

Talon touched Beetrax's shoulder, and he grunted, looking up.

"You all right, Axeman?"

"Aye. I am that." He yawned. "You're looking... fine. How do you manage without sleep?"

Talon shrugged. "I think I've finally found an equilibrium. Mentally. We have a mission to carry out. We get in, out, and then the fuck out of this fucking nightmare. And to be honest, after coming down here, sleep is something I rarely *need*."

Beetrax nodded.

"Do you miss the outside, Trax?"

"I do, lad. I miss the mountains."

"I miss the fresh air! A breeze on my face. Trees. Birdsong. How do they do it? How do they live in this pit?"

"It's just wrong, ain't it?"

There was a pause. Beetrax stood, and faced Talon. "I meant to say. You did well back there. During all that shit. All that violence."

Talon shrugged. "It's what we're good at, isn't it?" He smiled. "Killing, I mean. What we're trained for."

Trax nodded. "I can't remember a time when it wasn't."

Talon moved away, to a stone bench, and tried to get comfortable. But in truth, and despite his words, exhaustion was his mistress, and despite the hard ridges digging into his spine and knees, in only a couple of minutes he was asleep...

Beetrax moved to the head of the tunnel, and seated himself, brow furrowed, eyes narrowed, heavy battleaxe in both scarred hands.

"Fucking dwarves," he muttered, and his words were laced with poison.

He looked back over his shoulder. Everybody was sleeping. Snoring.

Beetrax gave a nod, and gripped his axe tighter.

I'll protect you.

I won't take no shit.

Any dwarves come, they get an axe between the eyes.

But between the reality of the world, and the chemistry of exhaustion, Beetrax was just like any other human. He was prone to the laws of his basic physiology. Two hours of sleep were nothing and slowly, tenderly, Beetrax's eyes drooped. He sat there, leaning on his brutal chipped axe, and the demon sleep gently took him, and spirited him away...

"Ka kash!"

"Ko karim kek jo kash! Be quiet, cunt!"

"What is it?"

"Up ahead. An overlander. With a big fucking kresh axe!"

"Fucking slaves. They need to die."

"Shh. Carefully now. It'll be easier if we don't wake him. He looks... handy. Not like the worms we are used to."

Nods.

Boots trod softly, as the dwarf killing party advanced on the sleeping, snoring figure of Beetrax...

The Cathedral of Eternal Hate

The dwarf was stocky, and yet if anybody had been present to observe him, watching him kneel at the altar, they would have realised he was also... *twisted*. Broken. His back was hunched, the result of a historic tunnel collapse in which he'd been trapped for days, spine broken, and after his miraculous rescue, the injury had slowly healed and yet... healed *wrong*. This resulted in Skalg, First Cardinal of the Church of Hate, suffering intense pain during pretty much every waking hour when not under the influence of tryakka or lillimuth or the golden petal. Here and now, however, in the Iron Vaults deep beneath the Cathedral of Eternal Hate, core and pillar and cornerstone of the Church of Hate, shrine to their doctrine, containing the Holy Library and protected pages from the Scriptures of the Church of Hate, as penned by the Great Dwarf Lords themselves, so Skalg was enamoured with something other than drugs flowing through his veins, or lingering like gas in his lungs. Here, and now, Skalg was infused with *religion* and he was high on *belief*.

The altar was a huge, twisted, carved iron beast, with spikes and curves and angles, with absolutely no symmetry at all because it was a symbol of power and a symbol of chaos, a core concept which ran through every page of the Scriptures of Hate, like virgin blood once ran like wine in the cups of the Great Dwarf Lords, Gods of the Harborym

Dwarves and the original creators of the Dragon Engine.

"Now gone, now broken," said Skalg, and tears wet his cheeks. And although *belief* in his faith ran strong through his every atom, so *disbelief* in the escaped dragons, Volak, Kranesh and Moraxx, peppered Skalg's fractured, jumping mind like randomly fired crossbow quarrels puncturing his skull from a hundred misguided Educators.

Stop, came the word, and with it, came calm.

Skalg looked down. Before his kneeling form, on a cushion of black velvet, were the three Dragon Heads – fist-sized, colourless jewels said to contain the remains of the Great Dwarf Lords themselves. Despite being clear, each jewel had facets and faults, layers and internal markings. When light shone through them, it changed, moved, bounced, diffused, split, each second moving and shifting and changing, always unpredictable, constantly unreadable.

Skalg took a deep breath, pain tingling at the edge of his hunched, broken back, and his eyes narrowed as he thought about the escaped dragons. *How? How did it happen? What fool set free the minds from Wyrmblood?*

And he knew the answer, instinctively. The dragons themselves had somehow ushered a victim to the tower where the minds had been trapped, imprisoned, with what promise Skalg could not even imagine. But what he did know was that now, the three great wyrms were free, and superbly pissed off. They would wreak havoc through the Five Havens, through Janya, the highest underground city which traditionally housed the poorest of the dwarves, usually the lowliest mine workers, criminals, the unemployed; next came Keelokkos, where dwarves of self-awarded self-importance lived in the meagre abodes purchased with their lowly incomes. Third down the descending hierarchy of wealth and prestige was Sokkam, a place of modest spires and iron bridges, of plain arched walkways and cobbled streets, with confined streets and black stone houses built high and narrow, stepping out until they nearly touched in the higher reaches. Fourth came Vistata, and now, *now* the architecture became grand, with soaring carved bridges of stone and iron, with broad decorated walkways containing ornate iron trees and sculpted iron flowers, and sprawling residences of the wealthy. But only in Zvolga, home of the Iron Palace, the Cathedral of Eternal Hate and a thousand other magnificent civic and public buildings where only the *truly* wealthy could afford to live in luxury, only in Zvolga could one truly walk with head held high and know, *fucking know* you'd scrambled down through the mountain and up the hierarchy and actually *done something* with your life.

Skalg was one such dwarf. From mine digger to broken invalid to church apprentice, Skalg had worked and betrayed and killed and sucked and fucked his way up the church hierarchy, fuelled by his pain and crippled back, driven on by purest hate, the true diviner and motivator for one in the church. Yes, Skalg had progressed at a rate of promotion never before seen in the Five Havens, and would probably never be seen again.

Zvolga. *Ahhh, sweet Zvolga.* His city, his birthright, the place of his home and the most grand of his churches – now burned and smashed by the vengeful bitch dragons on their way up to the surface to first punish the world of men, and then, the fear sinking in, when the days had turned into weeks and months of terror, waiting for them to return and finish the job. And yes, then they would return, and Skalg knew the Harborym Dwarves did not have the might, the tools nor the magick to resist them.

"O Great Dwarf Lords, it is I, Skalg, First Cardinal of the Church of Hate, and I am here to seek your counsel!"

Silence.

Skalg opened one eye and stared at the Dragon Heads. Light pulsed gently through them from the candles lining the altar. A cool breeze crept across the floor like an invisible mist. Skalg breathed, and could see his breath like... like dragon smoke.

"O Great Dwarf Lords, I beseech thee, speak to me in this hour of need! The mighty wyrms, Volak, Kranesh and

Moraxx, whom you captured and imprisoned many years ago, whose city of Wyrmblood you destroyed, cast to the flames, crushed under the mountain, they have escaped, and I need your ancient wisdom."

Again, silence.

Candlelight pulsed.

Frustration started to gnaw through Skalg's mind, which began to jump in terror, flitting fast from one problem to the next to the next to the next, until fetid images piled up like a deck of cards, all overlaying one another, a rough-shuffled pack of abstract problems which he could not solve. He felt fear, not personal physical fear, although Skalg was privy to such personal doubts on occasion, but sheer terror at the plight of the *church*, and the possibility of the dragons destroying the churches, and even the Cathedral of the Church of Hate itself. More importantly, he felt the fear of *losing his position as First Cardinal*. The death of King Irlax, Skalg's direct opponent in the power play of Crown and Church in the Five Havens, had left the playing field wide open for Skalg's utter dominance. He'd won! The Church had won! And then the fucking dragons had awoken and spoilt it all!

Skalg chewed his lips.

"O Great Dwarf Lords," he intoned, and stared at the Dragon Heads. He thought, not for the first time or the hundredth time, that *maybe* this was a pile of donkey shit, *maybe* the Great Dwarf Lords were just a construction to keep the Harborym Dwarfs in check, *maybe* it had been dwarves, not gods, who had tamed the mountain, tamed the dragons, and built The Dragon Engine. Just *maybe*.

"O Great Dwarf Lords," he said, throat raw now, eyes itchy and full of frustration tears, "O Great Dwarf Lords, stop these fucking dragons from burning down my world, stop them taking away my churches and houses and Wardens and Educators. Help me put these fucking disgusting wyrms back in their cage…"

There was a *thrum*, a pulse of power that surged through

the chamber. If Skalg had been standing, he would have lost his footing, but kneeling, he pitched sideways, one hand shooting out to steady himself and as a result sending a spear of pain through his hunched back. He screamed, a short sharp sound of animal pain, but the scream was cut off when his eyes fixed on the Dragon Heads.

They were vibrating. Jiggling against their black velvet cushion.

Skalg lay there, staring at them, his mouth dry, piss leaking through his trews. He waited for something terrible to happen, for some great energy to rip through him, destroying him utterly, or for some dragon to rip the roof off the chamber and bite him in two. In shame, he soiled himself, and a rancid reek wafted up from his dirtied undergarments.

"I curse you!" he screamed suddenly, and waved his fist from his lying position. "The mountain fucking gives and the mountain fucking takes away! Well, all it did was fucking take from me in that bastard mine collapse! Look at me! Look what a feeble cripple I have become." And he wept, lay there for a long time, the jewels – priceless before him, and yet unable to cure his ailments – vibrating against velvet.

Slowly, the vibrations, the rumbling, the feeling of pressure inside Skalg's skull – they all stopped.

He lay there, wet, dirty, tears on his bearded cheeks.

That it has come to this, he thought. *I am a disgrace to the dwarves*.

No, said a voice inside his head. And it was at once magical and all-enveloping.

No?

You have been our champion for many a decade. Just because you have a broken, crippled, weak, pathetic shell worthy of nothing, like the lowest and most pointless worm, wriggling through the dirt and the shit, useless to everybody, useless even to the lowest scum and whore and criminal, this has *not* halted your ambition, your drive, and your prosperity. You have done well for yourself, Cardinal Skalg. Very well indeed. You have gone from strength to strength. Increased your power. Killed your enemies. Taken what you wanted. Climbed to the top of the shit pile. And, Cardinal Skalg, First Cardinal of the Church of Hate, we have been watching you.

You have?

We have.

Why would you watch me?

Because we are the Great Dwarf Lords, and we do what the fuck we want.

Skalg swallowed. One could not argue with that.

You, er, you imprisoned the great dragons? Built the Dragon Engine?

We did.

Er, I'm sorry to tell you this, but things have happened. I don't know how, but the dragons retrieved their minds. They broke out of the pits. They have… escaped.

Yes. We know this. That's why we're talking to you.

To me? Skalg got a very, very bad feeling, all of a sudden, deep down in the pit of his stomach. It spread like acid, like wildfire, erupting from his innermost being and reaching out in all directions, like strands from a spider's web. Fear followed, and Skalg felt his mouth was suddenly very dry, his mind numb, pounding but numb, and all he wanted to do was get away from this place; to flee. Because, instinctively, he knew something *bad* was going to happen, and it was going to happen to *him*, and life would never be the same again.

What could you possibly want from me? I am a cripple, weak, worthless. A worm, you said! Yes, a worm! A worm in the dirt and the shit.

And yet the most powerful worm in the Five Havens, said the voice, like a very cool lullaby.

Ahh.

Skalg. We are your gods. The gods of the Harborym Dwarves. The escape of the three dragons, Volak, Moraxx

and Kranesh poses a very big problem for us. For all of us.
For you. And for every dwarf on this planet.

Skalg did not want to ask the question. But he did
anyway.

Why?

You must come with us.

Where?

No more questions. Do you agree?

Skalg wanted to say no. He wanted to *scream* no. He
wanted to climb to his feet and hobble as fast as his broken
body would allow, up the stairs, out of the Cathedral of
Hate, away, away from the dwarves, away from everything
because this, *this* was a moment of reckoning, a moment
he knew would ultimately lead to his downfall. He felt
it, in his very bones. After everything he'd done, after
all the shit he'd been through, after all the murders and
the back-stabbing, after all the whispering and assassins
and violence, here, now, he was being called upon by the
fucking gods to do the right fucking thing. And he could
not bear it.

Do you agree?

There was an urgency there. But something more. An
impatience. The Great Dwarf Lords were not used to being
fucked around. Not even by the First Cardinal of the Church
of Hate, and after the death of King Irlax, now the mostly
singly powerful individual in the realm of the Harborym
Dwarves.

*What happens if I do not? I don't mean to sound rude, I'm
sorry, truly I am, but I'm very frightened. Running the Church is
one thing, but being asked to… what, recapture the dragons? Save
the world? That's best left for heroes – dwarves with stout hearts
and strong axe arms. Me, I'm a broken waste of space… I would be
no good for you, O Great Dwarf Lords.*

There came a pause. A very long pause.

Do you agree?

"What happens if I don't?" he squeaked.

The Dragon Heads will bathe you in Holy Fire and your

death will take a thousand years.

Skalg considered this. He tilted his head. As if obeying some unspoken command, the Dragon Heads grew warm before him. Heat bathed him. It felt like a gentle warning. Skalg swallowed.

"Yes," he whispered.

The Dragon Heads grew even warmer, and brightness spilled from their faceted interiors. It flickered around the chamber, shooting beams of light and heat that spun, and danced and coalesced. Skalg cringed in terror, cowering down on that cold stone floor, cowering in upon himself, making himself as small a target as possible – as if that would matter. He was like some bearded, distorted embryo. And still the Dragon Heads spun, and light fell from them, like light from a million stars. And the heat became hot, too hot to bear, and Skalg started to scream curses and obscenities, howling at the Great Dwarf Lords for they were going to kill him, murder him like the backstabbing bastards they were. Heat washed over Skalg, and he wailed like a newborn baby, and covered his eyes, and sniffed in his own shit-stink, and he was a bastard, he was a wretch, and he hoped that death would be quick...

The jewels spun on their velvet cushions, and a noise came, a high-pitched shrilling like a million insects trying to break free. Skalg covered his ears and soiled himself again, feeling the shame as warmth spread across his buttocks and down one leg.

"Do it!" he screamed. "Fucking do it! End it! Kill me now!"

The light and the heat grew, until the chamber was nothing but a vision of pure bright white.

And then it was done. The light died. A cool breeze drifted through the chamber.

Darkness crept back in.

The Dragon Heads spun to a stop. They were no longer bright and beautiful. They were dark, and filled with an oozing, evil oil.

A scent of hot metal hung in the air.

There was a tiny scratching sound, like a nail dragged across slate.

And Skalg vanished.

Skalg floated through a million dreams, like a swimmer through a lake of black oil. Voices called to him, some he recognised, like his mother, and a lover he had murdered, but many he did not know. And then the words became clearer, and he realised they were shouting at him, screaming at him, accusing him...

Fucking dirty bastard cripple...

Abuser, abuser of women, abuser of children...

You raped me, I will see you burn in the pit, I will see your eyes torn out by crows, I will see your cock chewed off by rabid hounds...

How could you do this to me, Skalg? Your own mother? How could you leave me to die, not visit me when I suffered on my deathbed; how could you let me die alone, my son? How could you let me die alone and unloved?

"I didn't!" he screamed. "I didn't do those things!"

And yet he knew that he had, and shame burned him, not just his face, but deep down to his core.

You took my money and had me beaten to death, spoke a different voice. An old man, this time.

You murdered my husband, then forced me into your bed before having me killed for my inheritance. You bastard. You fucking bastard's bastard. Have you no soul? Have you no pity? Is the only thing you care about — money, and power, and ejaculation? I will see you hang, you dirty little scabby cunt.

You went to the Ministers. You told them lies about me. I was summoned to their offices, like some cur, some criminal, tried and convicted without any investigation. They believed honest do-good Skalg, for his track record was clean, but really he was snake in the grass, a dirty back-stabbing poisoner, a dwarf with his finger on the trigger of an evil, loaded crossbow just waiting to stab me in the back, take the right shot, the killing shot... well, I will get my revenge, Skalg, you hypocritical little shit, you twisted and corrupt piece of fucking rancid offal, I will get my revenge on you... I will see your lovers burn, see your children turned to dust... now, or in the next life, or in the next...

"Stop, please, I beseech you!" Skalg tore at his hair. Tore at his purple robes. His mind felt fractured. As if he was going to implode. He could take no more. And just at the moment of his greatest madness, when the pain and the confusion climaxed, a calming voice touched his mind.

"Shhh," soothed the voice. "You have to learn to zone out the *zyigs*."

"Zyigs?"

"Lost and broken spirits from your past. They may exist, they may not. They may be figments of your imagination, or lost souls looking for retribution. One thing is for sure – you must zone out the voices, or they will certainly turn you insane."

"But... but they know things!" wailed Skalg.

"That only you know? Yes. Which is why they may be a manifestation of your guilt."

You took my daughter. Took her from my home. You promised her power and wealth and respect. You took her to your bed, you fucking whore bastard, and you raped her, for she was enamoured of your power. Then when she turned on you, you dropped her from your monstrous tower. I will hunt you down, hunchback, and I will use a saw to cut through your hump and your spine. I will cut you in half, you fucking evil little cunt.

My father came to pray at the Cathedral of Hate. But he was not important enough to kiss your arse, O mighty Skalg. So you had him removed, and your Church Wardens beat him on the steps of the cathedral. And he died there from a fractured skull. I hope the Great Dwarf Lords burn you in a Chaos Hall of their own devising...

I loved you. You were my best friend. You were like a brother. And yet you turned on me. You reported me to the authorities. You stabbed me in the back, you evil shit-sucking motherfucking maggot. I trusted you. I thought you were my friend. And yet you spilled your diarrheic filth like sewer shit from your filthy lips. One

day I will find you, and I will kill you for betraying me like you did.
One day I will find you, First Cardinal Skalg.

Skalg.

Yes?

I am Kokar. Remember that name.

Why? Why should I remember your name? You're just like all
the other cunts…

No. I am Kokar. I am special. You murdered my daughter. You
dropped her from your fucking tower. And I will never, ever stop
hunting you, you pointless, worthless, useless fucking cripple…

"No more, no more, no more," he whimpered, hands
over his ears, no longer swimming through the oil of dreams,
but sinking, sinking, deeper and into darkness. Then hands
grasped him, and lifted him, and the zyigs seemed to drift
away, their complaints and rants and hate and loathing
drifting like a stray leaf on an ocean current.

Skalg went limp, like a dead fish…

And then everything faded to black.

Skalg awoke, face down against black hard rock. He
stared at the rock for a long time. It was jagged, like it had
been quarried, and was lined with tiny lodes of precious
metal. He was cold, and realised his body was shivering.
The pain through his humped back, his twisted spine, was
considerable, and he gritted his teeth for a long time, trying
to will the pain away. But as usual, as always happened in
these situations, the pain remained. Got worse, in fact. As if
the God of Pain was mocking him. As usual.

"Bastard," he muttered. "Son of a fucking mule." He
wondered what had happened, and remembered bad
dreams, first about the Great Dwarf Lords insulting him,
then about ghosts of his past inflicting insults and threats.
He shivered. "You've done a lot of bad things, Skalg," he
murmured to himself, and shame burned his cheeks beneath
his beard. "You've hurt a lot of good people. You done a
lot of… *evil* things on your way to becoming First Cardinal
of the Church of Hate." He shuddered, remembering the

accusing voices – *feeling* their hate, a force so real and painful that it stabbed him like a silver blade right down to his core.

"But… where am I now?"

He rolled onto his back with a grunt, and looked up at a black sky. He was outside. *Outside.* And with a shudder, and emitting a tiny whimper, he realised there were no stars. Like all dwarves, Skalg hated the outside, despised the concept of being "overground", as much as a fish hated being stranded on a beach. Dwarves were *born* to be underground. It was in their bones, like it was in the bedrock of the mountain. But he *knew* about the night sky, he *knew* about stars. He'd seen pictures in books. Here, there were none.

"What kind of place is this?" he wondered out loud, and exhaled, watching his cold breath stream like smoke. "Where am I?"

"You are in a special place," said a small child dwarf, who stood near him. The child had silver skin and was naked. He looked… unreal. Not a thing of flesh and blood, but a being, something *created* by something which had only *heard about* flesh and blood. An organic construction.

The child stood, staring at Skalg. "You were brought here. By the Great Dwarf Lords. I am their servant, Mokasta. I am here to help you, and to administer the challenges. Now get up."

"Challenges? What challenges?"

Grunting, Skalg managed to get to one knee, then wobbled slightly, pain coursing through him. He cursed in a variety of languages, and tried to rise, grunting, sweat standing out on his brow, his lips puffing, until he placed both hands on one knee and tried to lever himself up. He failed.

Mokasta stepped forward, and looked down with eyes like small black pebbles. His skin shone silver, as if under moonlight. His face held a perfect serenity, and his head tilted to one side.

"You struggle?"

"Of course I bloody struggle!"

"Would you like me to help you?"

"What do you think, genius?" growled Skalg.

"There is no need for animosity here. Soon, you will be begging me for help."

"You reckon?"

Mokasta held out his small hand, and the fingernails were black. Not the black of injury or dried blood, but gloss black, like the beady eyes of a carrion crow on a battlefield, unwinding entrails from a rancid corpse.

Skalg took the hand. The grip was incredibly strong, and Mokasta lifted Skalg easily to his feet. The hunchback stood there, glaring at the little boy, who simply turned and started walking across the undulating black rock. Skalg followed, limping, one arm hanging slightly lower than the other, and only now did he look around himself properly.

The landscape of rock stretched off in all directions, a relatively flat plain, and they were surrounded by savage, saw-toothed mountains. They towered high into the obsidian heavens, impossibly big, but strangely without snow at their summits.

Skalg suddenly realised there was no breeze, no circulation of air whatsoever. The air was cool, however, and his breath steamed as he struggled after the small boy, his panting accelerating as his heart rate increased. Unused to any physical activity, and with a lifestyle filled with unwilling women, rich red meat and Ushgak Red, Skalg's stamina was far from being anywhere near adequate.

"Where are we going?" wheezed the First Cardinal, as Mokasta started to pull away. Followed by, "Slow down, will you? Can't you see that walking is difficult for me?"

"We are going to that mountain, there." Mokasta pointed towards an evil-looking vast tower of rock, a shearing upthrust mountain like a giant, inverted tooth, sheer and terrifying to observe. "They call it the Demon's Cradle."

Skalg eyed the huge mountain warily, and continued to hobble after Mokasta.

"Oy, lad. What will we do when we reach the foot?" He

stumbled suddenly, and cursed loudly as a narrow streak of pain like molten lava shot down through his twisted back, and speared him through the pelvis. Urine leaked out as he lost some bladder control for a few moments. He coughed and spat.

"We are not going to the foot of the Demon's Cradle."

"Eh?"

"We are climbing to the summit."

Skalg stopped dead, and it took a few moments for Mokasta to also halt, when he became gradually aware of Skalg's lack of perambulation.

"What the fuck does that mean?"

Those dark eyes surveyed him. "You called upon the Great Dwarf Lords. They answered your call, Skalg. Being First Cardinal of the Church of Hate required some considerable effort on your part, but now the Great Dwarf Lords have answered you – the first in a thousand years – and you must further prove yourself worthy of their patronage."

"By climbing a mountain?" scowled Skalg.

"It is not merely the climbing of a mountain," said Mokasta, and gave a sly smile, an image that looked wrong on the small boy's face; it was too advanced, too adult, too *knowledgeable*. "It is an honour to be challenged by the Great Dwarf Lords themselves. Is this not so?"

"But... but I'm a physical wreck!" wailed Skalg. "I am crippled! I'm in constant agony! I suffer so much I spend many nights on the verge of passing out, or insanity, or both. Can you not see what a fucking physical disgrace I am to the dwarves?"

Mokasta trotted a little closer. He placed his hands behind his back. And that round silver moon face peered up at Skalg. Softly, he said, "And that is why this challenge will make you so much more worthy than your able-bodied peers."

Mokasta moved to a small mound of boulders, which led to a slope of scree, and then a jagged, ascending ridge like the spikes on the spine of a great wyrm. "I will meet you at the top," he said, then turned and leapt from boulder to boulder, scrambling up the slope.

Skalg stared for a long minute, then limped forward, cursing. He climbed onto the first boulder, breaking a fingernail and frothing in anger. Then he stepped gingerly from rock to rock, aware that a single slip, a misplaced step, could break an ankle or pop a knee joint. For several minutes Skalg trod gingerly across the boulders, then stood at the foot of the scree slope. He looked up, and sweat stung his eyes. Pain crawled down his hump and spine something horrid.

Taking a deep breath, and with tears in his eyes, Skalg began the impossible ascent.

The Deeper Halls

Beetrax groaned. Shit. Fuck. Cold. Stone tunnels. The flickering edges of a candle burning low.

And he realised. He was sleeping on guard duty.

Sergeant Kalka. That evil old crippled bastard. "Any of you fucks sleep on guard duty, I'll have you whipped a hundred fucking times! It's cunts like that who get their best mates killed." And yet – and *yet* exhaustion was not something you could control. It wasn't an on/off switch. You didn't decide it. It fucking *infected* you. It decided *you*.

Fuck, he said again, internally, lifting his axe and staring at his dulled, muted, distorted reflection in the chipped and battered blades. *We're here. In the dwarf mines. And I wish I was somewhere else. Anywhere else. Preferably with brandy and a pork slab sandwich. Maybe a bit of apple sauce on the side.*

Maudlin, and filled with a sudden desolation that blew through his soul like a demon wind through a desecrated tomb, Beetrax wondered when this horse shit would ever, ever be over...

His eyes stared into the dull metal reflections of his axe blades. They were hazy. In those axe-blade reflections he could determine no detail, no definition, just blurred representations of what he was in reality. The thought saddened him. *Is this what my life has become? Trapped in a fucking dwarf mine with no hope of survival, of getting out alive? Of ever breathing fresh air again?*

The sound came to him. A tiny skitter of stone on stone. A minute pebble kicked. A shard of gravel raking over rough-stone tunnel floor.

Beetrax did not move, did not flinch, did not tense. He continued to stare into his dulled, lifeless, blurred-eye reflection as his senses suddenly screamed and the hackles rose on the back of his neck. He heard the sword hissing towards his head, *oh how did those fucking bastards get so close without him realising?* and threw himself sideways, axe lashing out in a sudden sideways movement that half cut the dwarf's leg mid-thigh. The dwarf collapsed like a battered sack of donkey shit, suddenly screaming, sword dropped with a clang, clutching at his half-severed leg as blood pumped out, and flooded that tiny compartment of hewn stone corridor.

Beetrax's head came up, eyes narrowing at the five remaining dwarves in the tunnel, and lifting his axe, he whacked it down through the screaming dwarf's head, silencing his cries and cutting the head almost in half like a ripe melon, sliced from eyeball to opposite jawline.

"Any other cunt want to die?" he growled, as he felt the rage swelling within him, a rage so raw and basic and primeval he knew he had no control, no sanity, but did not fucking care anyway. It washed over him like a tidal wave of blood from an extinct race, and the dwarves spread out as much as they could, which was only two wide in the tunnel, as Beetrax simply growled, baring his teeth in a snarl, and attacked.

The two lead dwarves had axes. One deflected Beetrax's overhead swing, but collapsed when his boot stomped his kneecap, breaking his leg in half, folding it back at the knee with a brittle *snap* like deadwood on a fire. In instinct, Trax shifted a thumb's breadth, as the second dwarf's axe whistled past his ear, skimming his shoulder but bouncing free. With no space to wield his weapon properly, Beetrax stepped forward, kicked the dwarf in the balls, and as the stocky warrior went down, stamped on his skull with a sickening crunch. The dwarf lay there, blood leaking out of his nostrils, head caved in.

"Come on!" screamed Beetrax, axe in both hands. "Fucking come on, I say!" he bellowed as all the hate, all the anger, all the fucking frustration welled up within him, a pan of water hitting the boil, a fucking volcano filling up with a payload of molten lava and ejecting it with a scream that blew rock and ash a thousand miles in every direction.

The next two dwarves paused, sickened by what they had seen. But the one behind pushed forward. He was almost as wide as he was tall, barrel-chested, his armour and helmet battered, burned and broken, his face carved with battle scars, his beard growing in strange directions due to the carved scar flesh beneath.

"Come on then," he growled, black eyes glittering, "you fucking pale worm from over the mountains, you fucking grease stain on the honour of our Harborym ancestors."

Beetrax leapt forward, as did the dwarf, and their axes clashed, bounced away, clashed again. Beetrax's weapon sent a shower of sparks from the wall, then cut sideways at neck height. But the dwarf was moving, ducking, and his own weapon came up, cutting the cloth of Beetrax's tattered shirt and missing impaling his chin by a hair's breadth.

They both took a step back, acknowledging the other.

"I'm here, Trax," came Dake's voice. Beetrax heard the slither of oiled steel.

"No. I got this."

"You think so, you fat, pompous, southern cunt?" growled the dwarf, brutal jaw hardly able to handle the Vagandrak tongue. But he grinned, and his eyes sparkled dark and evil, and he gripped his axe in powerful hands and braced his shoulders and got ready to kill.

"Fucking show me, midget," snarled Beetrax, baring his teeth, and the two warriors leapt at one another. Axes clashed, three times, four times, smashing from one another, smashing from the walls in showers of sparks. The dwarf kicked Beetrax in the stomach, Beetrax grunted, went down on one knee, threw a left straight into the dwarf's groin and staggered back.

"I see you only got a pussy in there," growled Beetrax.

"No, it's just my cock is harder than yours."

Beetrax launched forward, and their axes locked. They strained against one another, and although Beetrax was a huge warrior, incredibly powerful, the dwarf held his own, grunting, broad shoulders braced, a heritage of mine-working and sledgehammer-wielding giving him prodigious strength; boots scrabbled on the rough carved stone, and their faces came to within inches of one another.

"You fucking stink," said Beetrax.

"And you're an ugly southern streak of piss."

"At least my mother didn't have a whore's cunny fish-breath like you!"

The dwarf made a squawking sound, and pushed harder. He slammed his head into Beetrax's face, hammering the warrior back, and their axes clattered to the stone tunnel as they grappled. The dwarf had a low centre of gravity which gave him an advantage. He dragged Beetrax to the ground and they rolled around for a few moments, punching one another, headbutting, time and time again. Beetrax reached down and grabbed the dwarf between the legs. He let out a squeal, high-pitched and feminine. Beetrax crushed as hard as he could, every ounce of energy he had, with memories of his own previous torture in the cock area fuelling his rage.

"Stop stop stop!" screamed the dwarf.

With his free hand, as they squirmed on the tunnel floor, Beetrax reached down and pulled a knife from his boot. With the dwarf's crushed balls in one hand, he lifted the blade and plunged it into the dwarf's eye.

Blood fountained, drenching Beetrax, turning him into a demon.

The dwarf squirmed for a while, and they continued to roll around as Beetrax held him tight, waiting for him to die.

Then he slumped, and was still. Beetrax untangled himself, and pulled free the dagger from the bloodied eye-socket, and dragged himself to his feet. Two dwarves still stood in the tunnel, fixed with fear, and Beetrax grinned at them with bloodied teeth, face a crimson mask.

"Class," said Talon, stepping forward, brushing back his long hair. "Could you have even produced more blood?"

"I didn't see you fucking stepping in, pal!"

The remaining two dwarves turned and started to sprint down the short tunnel. Talon unhooked his bow, knocked an arrow, and fired. It took the left dwarf in the nape of the neck, slamming him stumbling into a fast-forward run until he fell on his face, which cut grooves through his flesh.

Talon looked sideways at Beetrax. "Am I earning my bread now?"

"There's one left, cock-head."

Talon drew, fletch to cheek, and fired. The arrow hissed, rotating, and punched the dwarf in the back. He hit the stone floor and started to scream, reaching around, trying to pull the shaft out, legs kicking. Then he went suddenly limp, but continued to scream like a man on fire.

Talon had severed his spine.

"Savage," said Beetrax, quietly.

"But now we've got him for questioning, yes?"

Beetrax looked at Talon. And smiled. "Neat. Remind me never to cross you. Or at least, never to turn my fucking back on you."

Talon unstrung his bow. He smiled, but it was a cold and unfriendly smile. The smile of a man who had made his peace with God and the Seven Sisters, and was happy to settle down in his grave.

"You remember that, Axeman," he whispered.

"You can't do this," said Lillith.

They'd dragged the dwarf back to the chamber, and propped him up, like a limp eel, like a half-slaughtered lamb, on a stone bench. He was weeping, tears running down his cheeks and into his beard, staining his leather jerkin. His eyes darted around swiftly, in fear, surveying Beetrax, Lillith, Dake, Talon, Sakora and finally Jael.

When he saw Jael, despite his tears, despite the fact his hands were like flopping fish on the bench, he gave a narrow smile.

"Krakka's bitch," he spat, and spit drooled from the corner of his mouth.

Beetrax frowned, and leaning forward, slapped the dwarf hard, knocking his head from right to left, and cracking his skull against the wall.

"You'll talk."

"I won't, southern scum."

"Talk, or I'll saw off your legs."

The dwarf looking into Beetrax's eyes, observed his blood-caked face, and remembered the spectacle with the warrior dwarf back in the tunnel. His breathing was fast and shallow. Beetrax worried he didn't have long left to live.

"What do you want to know?"

"You were hunting us?"

"No."

"How did you find us then?"

"We were in a side mine when you passed. We heard you clattering about like fucking amateurs." The dwarf smiled then, but his face was torn with pain. A little blood drooled from his mouth and stained his beard.

"You sure you weren't hunting us?" Beetrax slapped him again, a hard, open-handed slap that rocked the dwarf's head against the rock. He sat, stunned, and then blinked a few times regaining his senses.

"No. Why would we?"

"You tell me."

"But you *were* in the mines, weren't you? I saw you. With Krakka."

"Well, I killed that cunt."

"Yes. I was surprised. You were only saved because Cardinal Skalg needed your help."

Beetrax frowned. "How do you know that?"

"It was the talk. In the mines. After you were betrayed."

"What the fuck does that mean?"

"You were betrayed. One of your group was helping Krakka. He told them about your escape plan – with the cauldron. That's why there were a hundred dwarves on hand with primed crossbows. You didn't think it was a coincidence, did you?"

Dake leant forward. "He's lying."

"Why would I?" The dwarf cackled, blood dribbling down his chin. "You know I speak the truth. You know there was no reason for those bastards to be there, fully armed, waiting for you to make your escape attempt."

Beetrax rubbed his beard.

"Who was it?"

The dwarf grinned. His eyes shifted, past Beetrax. Beetrax turned.

Jael was backing away, his face pale, looking as if he might puke any second.

"You?"

"No," said Jael, and the young lad stumbled.

Beetrax frowned. "You told Krakka about our escape plans? After we rescued you from those forest bandits? After we saved you from certain death? After I tried to teach you the secrets of the axe? After we fucking *helped you*."

"It wasn't my fault!" wailed Jael, and turned to run, but Lillith was there, and he fell into her arms, buried his head in her bosom, and started to weep, dropping to one knee. "It wasn't my fault," he wailed.

Beetrax stood, slowly, like a lumbering bear. He gripped his axe tight.

"No," said Dake, grabbing Beetrax's arm. Beetrax pushed him aside as if he were broken branch, a leaf in the wind. Dake fell against the wall and collapsed. Beetrax strode forward, face forming into a maelstrom of violent thunderstorms.

"You betrayed us?" he said, reaching forward.

"No," hissed Lillith, slapping his hand away. But still Beetrax came on.

"You fucking *betrayed us*?"

"I didn't mean to," Jael said, mumbling from Lillith's bosom.

"How the *fuck* did you not *mean to*?"

"I was forced!"

"How?"

"By Krakka. The Slave Warden."

"*How*?"

"He threatened to torture me."

Beetrax stood, staring in disbelief at Jael. Then he spat on the stone. "He fucking had us *all* tortured, you whining little cunt. We all went through weeks of agony. And you squealed like a whiny, back-stabbing little piglet."

Beetrax turned and strode back to the paralysed dwarf. His axe sang out, a song of death, and cut the dwarf's head from his shoulders. The head rolled down the corridor vomiting blood.

"No," hissed Lillith. "Stop!"

Beetrax pointed with his bloodied axe blades. His words were so filled with emotion and disgust he could hardly speak. "Jael – lad – if you *ever* come near me again, I will surely kill you."

Jael nodded, and hid in Lillith's embrace.

The group travelled in silence for what felt like weeks. With the death of Jonti-Tal, and now this revelation over Jael's betrayal, their morale was seeping away faster than water from a battered sieve.

They trudged through what seemed like endless mine tunnels, always heading down, always alert for the sounds of dwarves, be they miners or soldiers. But for a long while they saw nobody. The mines felt abandoned, which was ironic, as it was this status of barrenness which had attracted the heroes, and certainly Beetrax, in the first place. What had he said during Dake and Jonti's anniversary party, when he had first sprung his plan on them?

"It's a map that leads to the Five Havens, the five dwarf cities under the Karamakkos Peaks. They were once ruled by the Great Dwarf Lords who mined untold wealth – I'm talking oceans of jewels, warehouses full of gold coin, lakes of molten silver! Enough to buy you a lifetime of whores, Falanor brandy and Hakeesh weed! … The point is, the Harborym are long gone, extinct for ten thousand years, the Five Havens lost to the knowledge and thoughts of us mere mortal men. But all that treasure is still there, waiting for some hardy adventurer types to trot along and fill their pockets, and maybe even a few wheelbarrows, with an orgy of sparkling loot."

"I hate to piss on your fire, Beetrax," said Dake, frowning, "but unless you hadn't noticed, we're all affluent to the point of decadence. That's what being Vagandrak's Best Kept War Heroes did for our pockets. Why then, in the name of the Holy Mother, would we want to risk life and limb climbing mountains, fighting rock demons, and delving into long forgotten underground pits probably better left to the psychopathically demented Rock Fairies and all their little golems? Hmm?"

"Because of the three Dragon Heads," said Beetrax, eyes glinting. "Tell them, Lillith."

"The Dragon Heads were colourless jewels found deep, deep beneath the mountains. It was discovered they had incredible healing powers – they could bring a man back from the brink of death; they could heal massive, open wounds, making flesh run together like molten wax; they could cure plagues and cancers and other diseases we couldn't even dream of. They are referred to in the Scriptures of the Church of Hate with reverence, as if they were bestowed on the Great Dwarf Lords by the Mountain Gods themselves. Indeed, it is the Dragon Heads that gave the Great Dwarf Lords their dominion and kingship."

Beetrax gave a sardonic smile, his boots scuffing against rock. So much for his fucking plan! They'd not even *infiltrated* the bloody Harborym mines, instead being attacked by one of Orlana the Changer's *splice*, a deformed and mutated creature, a horrific blend of man and horse.

After an avalanche, the group had been captured by
dwarves, or more precisely, Krakka the Slave Warden, an
evil bastard who hated humans and set about torturing
their group. With their wills broken, or so Krakka believed,
they had been set to work in the mines. They soon planned
and executed an escape, with Beetrax killing Krakka in the
process, and had then faced death due to Jael's betrayal – a
death which would have been certain, if Skalg, First Cardinal
of the Church of Hate, hadn't caught wind of their existence
and decided he had a better use for these overlander slaves,
these *heroes* of Vagandrak: namely, the assassination of King
Irlax, royal thorn in Skalg's side.

Beetrax went over the events in his mind, again and
again, wondering how things could have turned out
different, how they could have avoided capture, how they
could have evaded torture. He touched his testicles gingerly
as he walked, remembering the man who had tortured him,
remembering the *Ball Cracker*, a machine he had become
intimate with during his days of "fun". Trax's face turned
crimson with fury. His fists clenched involuntarily. And then
he thought about Val. Val, the twisted bastard dwarf who
had raped his love, his life, Lillith. Raped her repeatedly.
Beetrax knew it in his soul, although had never had the
nerve or lack of compassion to *come right out and ask it*. But
to Trax, it was as plain as day, written on gentle Lillith's
face, an agony of emotional scars etched into her skin as
a metallurgist etches patterns onto copper. Beetrax felt his
fury rise another notch. And another. If the day came when
he ever got to confront Val – well, that would be a reckoning
worth watching.

Beetrax took deep breaths, and Lillith came up beside
him, looked up at him, smiled, her serene face filling him
with a splinter of peace. He smiled back, but she could read
his eyes and could sense his fury. Her fingers clenched his
bicep, and that hold said, *be at peace, my love; be calm, my love;
be as one with me, my love.*

Beetrax tried. Oh, by the Seven Sisters, he tried.

But sometimes, being filled with fury was the right place to be.

Seeing Lillith's concern, he tried to think of better times, older times, wiser times. And he regressed. He plodded down that stone corridor in the shit-hole that was under the mountain, and he looked at Lillith's face, and he *remembered...*

His room in Vagan was spartan, for Beetrax was not the kind of man to hoard crap. He had a large, broad bed, rough-cut pine table and chairs, and various cushions which had been a gift from Lillith when she first saw how uncomfortable his room had been. There was a rug, also a gift from Lillith, and a vase of dried flowers, again, from Lillith. Beetrax was an axeman, military, serious for the majority of the time. As he would put it, he had little time for flowers and girl shit.

However, on this particular evening, Beetrax had excelled himself for one so unmeasured in the art of seduction. Not that seduction was his aim, far from it. This was a mission of forgiveness. Him, begging forgiveness, from her. For being a horse dick. Again.

He didn't remember how the argument started, but he'd been drunk, again, and belligerent, again, and finally, aggressive, again. They'd been in The Fighting Cocks, but the argument spilled out onto the cobbles with Dek wagging his finger and proclaiming things like,

She's right, you know. The woman is always right.

You'll regret it in the morning, old horse.

Better crawl back to your room now; it'll look worse in the morning, I promise you, mate.

To which Beetrax had proffered many scowls and various hand gestures only understood by mud-orcs and those who killed them.

Lillith had raged at him in the street, as he swayed, after several flagons of wine too many, scowling, and reacting to aggression with the only way he knew how – more aggression. Beetrax had never backed down from a fight in his life. All his scars were on his face, arms, chest and thighs. He always faced his enemies, and was happy to cleave them from crown to bollocks with a hefty axe strike. And yet, and *yet* now he was facing the biggest threat of any man's life: an angry lover.

"You think you can treat me like this, say those things to me in front of your friends, and walk away? You think I'll forget it all, just roll over like a sweet little lady and let you hurl abuse and make jokes at my expense? Well fuck you, Beetrax. Fuck you."

"No, fuck you!" he bellowed, and pointed in her face.

She smacked his hand out of the way.

"But you know the worst thing, you useless piece of horse dung? It's the comments about *him*."

"Him?"

"*Him.*"

"Oh. Him. That cunt. Well, why not go running back to him? He'll lap you up like cream. He'll suckle your nipples like a squealing piglet. He still wants you, Lillith... I can sense it. In my bones. He wants you back, and he thinks I'm just some big stupid oaf, oh yeah, just a soldier, just a killer, uneducated, whilst he's a fucking *officer ooooh a fucking officer*, well go back to him, I don't fucking care anymore, you made it plain you think I'm stupid and uncouth, just a brute with an axe, that's why I said those things I said, did what I did, because you're laughing at me, Lillith, I can see it in your fucking *eyes*. Go back to him. He'll open his arms and welcome you, drink you down like fine wine, stick his little tongue between your legs and ooh how you'll moan in pleasure, just like the old days... "

The slap rang out like a broken bottle against an unprotected skull. Beetrax rolled with it, and in truth, it had little power, nothing he couldn't suck up in the blink of an eye and with a cheeky grin. But it was more the *act*, because Lillith had never struck him. *Never.* But she had now. And he didn't know whether to cry or to fight.

"How dare you," she said, trembling with rage. "How

dare you speak to me like that!"

"Well, I'm dumb, ain't I?" he mumbled, but his rage was gone, and the alcohol had made his mind foggy, and he wondered in the midst of his sudden abject misery how the *fuck* he could climb out of the pit he'd just fallen into.

"Beetrax. I never, ever want to see you again."

She turned, and walked away, disappearing into the darkness of the, ironically, foggy Vagan street. Beetrax stared after her, face cherry red, wondering what he should do. Should he chase after her? Pursue her? Endure more slaps? Should he give her time to calm down, then approach her with his mumbled apologies? Or should he... go back into The Fighting Cocks and continue to get fucking wasted?

Beetrax would be the first to admit, he was not the brightest firebrand in Vagandrak.

So he turned, frowned at the grinning faces peering at him from the doorway, and entered the yellow warmth of The Fighting Cocks Public Tavern.

Five days, it had been. Five long, lonely, cold days waiting for Lillith. She did not knock on his door with her usual bustling, cheery greeting, bringing him a basket of cheese and bread and cured meats from the market.

No.

She did not appear. Beetrax paced the floorboards, fists clenching and unclenching, wondering what the hell he should do. Should he take her flowers? Declare his undying love? Apologise? Write her a letter? What? *What?*

The morning after the argument, he'd awoken with a pounding head, and distant memories of slaps and screams. It had taken the whole day, with sweet hot coffee, lots of buttered bread, and several gallons of water to clear not just his churning belly, but his churning mind. Images flickered back to him, one by one by one, and with each image he groaned, and slapped himself in the face, and chewed on his lip, and considered what a colossal insulting vulgar horse dick he'd really been.

And the sad thing?

It hadn't been the first time.

He was an idiot. He freely admitted it.

"I'm an idiot," he groaned to Dake, clutching a tankard of ale and staring forlornly across the quiet innards of The Fighting Cocks. Afternoon sunlight painted lines across the boards. The landlord wiped dirty tankards with a dirty rag, and eyed Beetrax uneasily.

"Listen," said Dake, looking over his shoulder to make sure *his own wife* could not hear. "What you have to do, mate, is grovel. You have to beg. You have to say it's all your fault. Then she'll say some of it was her fault. Then you'll find some common ground, and you'll hug and kiss and cry, then have the most amazing sex you've ever had. Hey!" He beamed and slapped Beetrax on the back, making him choke on his ale. "Been there, done it loads of times."

"No, Dake, you fucking dog, this is it! She's left me. I fucked it up. I might as well go tie a rope and hang myself from the rafters."

"Don't be silly." Dake put on his serious face. "Me and Jonti, right, we've been together for years. You think in all that time I haven't got drunk and said stupid things? You think I haven't danced with the wrong woman in the wrong way to the wrong tune? That was an icy cold walk back to the house, followed by an even icier sleep in the summer house at the bottom of the garden." He shook his head. "Anyways. What I'm trying to say, Trax, is that we all fuck up. Men is men is men. We get drunk and say stupid shit. Our women, they fall out with us, and half the time we're that fucking emotionally backward we don't even know what it was we said that done the damage! But the art, my boy, the *art* is how we repair the damage after we do the stupid shit in the first place. You get me?"

"Eh?"

"It's all about your apology, Beetrax. It is inevitable, in any relationship, that you will fuck it up. That's a given. It's written in the Scrolls of the Seven Sisters. *Thou shalt fuck it up, wept the virgin Salander.* Just trust me on this one, old horse. But, *but,* what matters is what happens next!"

Dake beamed. He was a little drunk.

"And what happens next?"

"What do you think happens next?"

"Er. I knock on her door? I take her flowers?"

"No, you fucking dolt, you lump of rancid horse excrement, you have to make her *believe* you love her again. I mean, I'm sure you do. But you have to show your feminine side."

Beetrax's voice hardened. "My feminine side?" he said.

"Yeah, baby, your fucking feminine side."

Beetrax deflated. "I don't think I have one," he said. "Maybe I could ask Talon?"

"No no, listen. I'll teach you."

"You'll teach me to have a feminine side?"

"No, horse dick... I'll teach you how to get her back."

And so, armed with Dake's sage counsel, Beetrax had gone shopping. Now, Beetrax the Axeman was not an axeman to go shopping lightly, and so he took his axe. This wasn't well received at the market, and he was certainly *remembered*, especially after threatening to cut a market trader in half for inappropriate comments about the *size of his axe*, but all in all, it went smoothly, if embarrassingly for Beetrax, and he returned to his room and penned a short note, which read:

> *Lillith. My love. My life.*
> *Please come to my room tonight.*
> *I have writ you a letter.*
>
> *Love,*
> *Trax. X*

He sent it with an urchin for a copper piece. Then went to work transforming his simple axeman's room...

•••

Lillith stood outside the door, frowning. She took a deep breath and went to knock, but the door opened and Beetrax stood, in his cleanest trews, with a new black shirt that, actually, if Lillith thought about it, looked quite good on him. He smiled apprehensively. Lillith smiled back, although there was pain there.

"I wasn't going to come," she said.

"I didn't expect you to," he said, wretchedly.

"I... I just thought, I *knew*, I had to hear what you had to say. Before we... you know. Never saw one another again. Before we took a bow, and left the stage, you know?"

"All your friends think I'm no good," said Beetrax, and clenched his teeth.

"It's not that. It's just... the drinking. The fighting. And then you turn on me. I can't take it anymore, Trax. I can't take the uncertainty. And I know we think we're in love," he looked at her hard, then, "but you have to know, if this isn't love, then it's over, because nothing lasts forever."

"Look. Just. Come in. Please."

Lillith stepped across the threshold. And, if truth be told, she was stunned.

The walls were hung with drapes, red, gauzy drapes that gave the room an intimate warmth. Candles burned. *Many* candles burned. And Lillith knew Beetrax was not the type of man to light a candle. Drink a whiskey flagon? Yes. Buy candles and arrange them romantically and light them? No.

"You expecting somebody, Beetrax?" she said, her voice low and husky.

"Er. Yes. You."

"I know. You dolt. Is that a new comfort couch?"

"Yes. Took three of us to carry it up the stairs. I hurt my back."

"Mmm."

Beetrax looked sheepishly around. "You like red, right?" he said.

"I love red."

"And, and, I lit thirteen candles. You like thirteen, right?"

"I *love* thirteen. It's my favourite number."

"Yes. I remember."

They stood there, staring at one another in the candlelight. Beetrax wanted to rush over, to take hold of her, to pick her up, to crush her, to love her, but he did not, he could not. Because he'd been a dick. And he'd fucked it up. Like he always fucked it up.

"I have cooked," he said.

"You have? What?"

"It's, er, slivers of Randa fish on a bed of rice, salad and peppers. Then I razored some cheese shavings over the top. With a touch of garlic. And salt. Er…"

"Sounds divine," said Lillith. "Shall we go in? Sit? Eat?"

"You want to stay?"

"Yes."

"Why?"

"I want to read your letter."

"Ah," said Beetrax.

Lillith looked crestfallen. "You mean, you haven't writ the letter you said you'd writ?"

"No. I writ it all right."

"So are you going to give it to me?"

"I'm just a little… embarrassed." He stood there, like a small schoolboy who'd forgotten his homework. Lillith decided to take pity on him. He was obviously making an effort. The biggest effort he'd ever made. Which for Beetrax, was quite something.

"Take me through," she said, again, her voice low and husky.

Beetrax reached out, took Lillith's hand, and led her through the main room to the kitchen. Here, he had actually put a *tablecloth* on the table, and lit more candles. Lillith's keen eye counted thirteen. He'd also bought a few small statues, which he'd put on a shelf. Hell, he'd *erected* a shelf. And then put his new statues on it. Lillith squinted. They looked like clay renditions of fairies. She pursed her lips into a smile, imagining Beetrax, with his axe, buying fairy statues at the market. Now *that* she would have paid good coin to witness.

"I like what you've done," she said, finally.

"Really?"

"Yes."

"I done it all for you."

"I know, Trax. I know."

He pulled out a chair, and she sat. The plates were already on the table. To Beetrax's credit, the food smelled damned good. And Lillith was hungry. She hadn't eaten for five days. She'd been too busy crying.

"First, I'd like to see the letter."

"Ahh."

"Please?" She looked at him, and tears rolled down her cheeks.

"I'll get it," rumbled the big axeman.

He disappeared and re-emerged, handing her the folded paper, his fingers shaking.

"Are you all right, Trax?"

"Not really," he said, and sat down and poured himself a goblet of Vagan Red. He sipped it. She noted him sipping. Sipping, as opposed to swigging.

She opened the page. There, with several crossings out, a couple of inkblots, and a lot of love, was Beetrax's letter:

I wanted to apologise in writing. I'm sorry. I am a horse's dick. I'm sorry I said those things about you. I'm sorry I was horrible to you. I absolutely do not care about a man you used to see, and I know I moan about him, but I can read the love in your eyes like bright candleflames, and I know I mean everything to you, like you mean everything to me, and so I am sorry I mentioned his name and got angry about him. It will never happen again.

On reflection, I realise I am frightened. I am frightened of losing you. I know you are too good for me, I know I am uncouth and vulgar at times, I know I am not always the best companion, especially for a smart and edqucated woman like you, but I love you so much, and yet I treat you abominabally. I fear you will leave me, And so my fear turns to darkness. And then I am a horse dick. And then you do leave me.

Lillith.

I love you. You are my white witch. You are my sanity. You once said that I shine, and you reflect, but you are so so so wrong. More and more and more, you shine and I reflect. You are the sun, I am the moon. I am your willing servant. I am your slave. I am caught in your orbit. And without you, my sun, I could not exist.

I trust you. I love you. I want to be with you, always.

You are my molten tears, Lillith.

You are my beating heart.

You are birdsong.

You are the surf gently sighing up the shingle.

You are my muse, Lillith.

Please.

Please never stop loving me.

Because I will love you until the stars go out.

Yours.

Trax. xxx

She looked at him. He looked at her. She stood. He stood. They moved together. They pressed together. His great arms encircled her, and her arms encircled his waist. He leant down to her, but did not kiss her. He looked into her eyes.

"I love you," he said.

"I know," she said.

"I want to be with you," he said.

"I know," she said.

"You are everything to me," he said.

"I know," she said.

And then she reached up, standing on tip-toes, and she kissed him, and he melted into her, and he knew that everything would be well with the world.

•••

Talon had taken the lead, and he kept his bow strung at all times. He felt maudlin, a great sadness within him. He had loved Jonti-Tal, in his own way; not as a woman he craved for sex, no, but as a soul sister. They used to call her *The Ghost*, for she'd been deadly with a blade. Now, she was just dead, and this horrific event had rocked Talon to his very core.

Of course, on the walls of Desekra, he'd seen many a comrade fall. But during those insane days of blood and steel and death, Talon, Beetrax, Sakora, Dake, Lillith, Jonti-Tal, they'd formed an almost unbreakable unit. They'd become brothers and sisters, not just of flesh, but of bone and blood and fucking *soul*. The sort of bonds that could not break. The sort of bonds which could only be severed by… *death*.

And Talon realised his complacency. They'd been hard fuckers, fighters to the core, practically invincible. And Talon, for one, had started to believe their own ego… until they faced down the splice, and been captured by the dwarves. Beaten, fucked up, tortured; Talon's nerve, his beliefs, had been irretrievably wounded.

He lifted his bow a little. And he realised there was a tremor to his hand. His lips were dry. Mouth dry. Fear darted like a moth inside his brain. *What if they met more dwarves? What if he fired his arrow, and missed? What if the bastards captured him again, captured them all again, and the beatings began, and the torture returned?* Talon had been invincible on the walls of Desekra Fortress. But down here, he had come to realise his own mortality, underlined in blood by the savage and untimely death of Jonti-Tal.

We will all die, he realised, as his morale spiralled downwards.

We will be destroyed.

What are we doing? Where are we going? Why are we not trying to escape?

He stopped at a junction of tunnels, and listened, head tilting to one side. There was a strange sound. A kind of metallic *thrumming*. Then it stopped. Talon frowned, and realised his palms were sweating. He wiped them on his trews.

They'd had their chance. After the dragons broke free and tore the roof off the palace, Skalg, in some ways their *saviour*, had kept to his part of the bargain. Kill Irlax the King, and they would have their freedom. But ironically, they didn't kill the king, and still got their freedom, but then chose not to accept it. They had decided to *do the right thing*, as fucking heroes always should.

He smiled sardonically. And realised, with a bitter taste, that Beetrax had been right.

What had Lillith said?

You don't understand, these great wyrms, these creatures of Wyrmblood – it says in the Scriptures of the Church of Hate that once they ruled the world. All races were slaves beneath them. Men, dwarves and elves.

Aye? What has that got to do with us?

They're free, Trax. They will seek to re-establish their Empire.

You reckon?

Oh, I am certain.

Well, correct me if I'm wrong here, but there's only three of 'em, yeah? How can you establish an empire if there's only three of you?

That's what we're going to find out.

So now they were on a mission to find the dragons, find the city of Wyrmblood, unravel what the hell was going on. And for what? To save men? The people of Vagandrak? The fucking *dwarves*?

Talon gave a little shake of his head, and held up his hand. Behind, the group stopped. Dake came up beside him.

"A problem?"

"I heard something. Something… odd."

"Clink of armour odd? Dwarven voice odd?"

"No." Talon frowned. Then looked hard at Dake. "Are you with this? I mean, this mission? To find Wyrmblood?"

Dake shrugged. "If I'm honest, Tal, I'm beyond giving a fuck. Jonti is gone. My life is over."

Talon gave a nod. He knew how Dake felt. Talon felt

pretty despondent himself.

"I just wonder..." he said.

"Yeah?" Dake looked at him quizzically.

Talon shrugged. "It doesn't matter."

They moved on down the tunnel, and several times Talon heard the sound. Each time it seemed to increase in intensity, making him frown harder and harder. He knocked a shaft to his bow, and seeing the action, Beetrax and the others loosened weapons, wondering what it was Talon had detected.

The tunnel suddenly ended, emerging onto a platform of smooth black granite. Beyond the elevated platform was a tunnel, with tracks, and the adventurers remembered their journey with Skalg, First Cardinal of the Church of Hate, on the underground carriage system.

Now, however, there was no steam, no hissing, no clanking. Because the dragons had escaped. The train system's source of motivation had been unleashed, and with the wyrms' escape came mining immobility.

Talon knelt at the junction of tunnel and granite platform. He listened, and waited, and tuned in. *What had he heard? What the fuck had he heard?*

And it came again. A vibration through the great chains which had once powered this mining train system.

It thrummed, a metal song, then faded.

"What is it?" said Sakora, coming forward with Lillith. "What can you hear?"

"The chains. They keep vibrating."

"Is that strange?" said Lillith, peering through the gloom.

Talon nodded. "With the dragons gone, the source of energy vanished, and the trains should be totally immobile."

"Maybe it's the wind, lad," grinned Beetrax. "Wobbling the chains, like."

"No. No wind could shift those. They weigh more than a building, I'd wager."

"What, then?" said Dake.

It came again, more violent this time. The chain started

to vibrate, and they could see it, shimmying, singing almost. Only this time, not only did the chain vibrate, the whole platform started to shake. It was gentle, but they felt it beneath their boots. Lillith put out her hand and steadied herself against the tunnel wall. Beetrax grasped his axe tightly. Dake frowned. Talon licked his lips.

Gradually, the tremble faded.

"Mine collapse?" suggested Dake.

"Earthquake?" said Beetrax.

Silence fell like ash as these concepts sank in.

Nobody wanted to be buried alive.

"I don't like it," said Beetrax.

"Come on," said Lillith. "Let's follow the track. These things will only lead to major areas of the mines."

"I think we're doing the wrong thing," said Beetrax, slowly.

They all looked at him.

"We have to find out what's happening," said Lillith, voice gentle.

"Why?" said Trax, uneasily. "If that was an earthquake, and it happens down here, we're proper fucked."

"I don't believe it was," said Lillith, closing her eyes, and touching the rock wall. "I believe the mountain is stable. These mines have existed for thousands of years. Why would it change now?"

"Because of the random chaos of nature?" offered Talon, and Lillith gave him a pained look.

"Come on," said Dake. "We're wasting time. If we're going to find this dragon city, the faster we find it, the faster we can leave. Right? I, for one, am sick of the Harborym Dwarves. I want to see the daylight before I die. I want to breathe the scent of a forest. I want to see people again. My kind of people." He moved to the edge of the platform, and dropped down into the chasm. The iron rails were polished silver with use, the rest of the track grime-smeared and littered with pebbles, rocks and old black oil. At the centre of the track, suspended at waist height, was a thick chain –

about the width of a dwarf's thigh. Dake peered up ahead, through the half-light, and could see a series of stationary carriages. Made of timber, they had iron wheels, and were smeared with dust, oil and thick grease.

The others followed, one by one, climbing down into the cutting and standing there, breathing in stone dust, old oil, grease and scorched iron.

"This feels dangerous," said Sakora, warily.

"What happens if the carriages start to move?" said Dake.

"How can they?" reasoned Lillith. "The dragons have gone."

Again, the ground seemed to tremble beneath their feet. Just a modest vibration, but enough to make them exchange glances.

"Let's get this done," said Beetrax, and strode ahead, away from the platform and deeper into the long, dark tunnel ahead.

The others followed, feeling sick to their stomachs.

Behind them, the thick chain vibrated, chiming, like some deformed musical instrument playing a lament for these poor Vagandrak heroes caught here, in this pit of eternal chaos; this living hell.

Deep, deep, deep underground, down a narrow passage which led from an obsolete, long-forgotten mine, through a series of five heavy, locked, foot-thick iron doors, there was a chamber. It had once been an excavation, and had only one entrance – and one way of getting out. Krakka, the former Slave Warden, had been aware of its existence – he had to have been, because on occasion he met one of the dwarf engineers who worked there. This was a place commissioned by the late King Irlax, and not one dwarf in the Five Havens knew about its existence, not even Skalg, First Cardinal of the Church of Hate. *Especially* not Skalg – because this had been intended as a scientific experiment in order to create a weapon Irlax could use against his enemies, of whom Skalg was numbered one.

The chamber was quite large, with a high vaulted ceiling, and completely rough-hewn. Lit by oil lamps, it contained row after row of steel benching, littered with medical instruments, vials, test tubes, beakers, syringes, scalpels and a thousand other objects required by the dwarves to conduct this, their *experiment*.

Fifteen dwarves had been commissioned by King Irlax for this project after the discovery of a certain artefact in this very chamber. This artefact sat against the far wall, on a low plinth, protected by an iron and glass cage, with three locks down one side of the casing. Alongside this plinth stood huge iron flasks, three to either side, each one twice as tall as a dwarf and serviced by portable iron steps. Beneath the flasks, a huge section of rock had been excavated and replaced by thick iron mesh – for drainage. The workers wore black aprons and leather gloves. They were serious-looking dwarves, many greying, all with dour expressions and nervous eyes. They barely spoke, simply went about their business, communicating only to share ideas or compounds or results. Brought together by King Irlax nearly ten years previous, they were the foremost minds of the Harborym dwarves, consisting of chemists, biologists, and doctors, two of whom had been struck off and condemned to death by hanging for their crimes against the Harborym. The final dwarf, the one in charge of the experiments, liked to call himself a *warlock*. He had spent many years above ground in the world of men, studying in their libraries, discovering and purchasing forbidden texts using the seemingly unlimited supply of gold offered by Irlax for such a purpose. This dwarf was named Movak, again, a criminal who had been condemned to death for crimes against the Church of Hate – crimes involving Equiem magick. He considered himself an authority, and had mastered several of the dark arts. It was Movak who had given inception to the plan funded by King Irlax.

"Gregor, seal the flask, ready for the final burn."

Gregor nodded, and did so. The huge vertical rods

slotted into place, and Gregor stepped away, somewhat
nervously, as if they might explode. Which, in reality, they
might. Gregor glanced at Movak, and was annoyed to see
not a flicker of emotion decorated the dwarf's face. He was
oblivious to pain and fear. He was like a machine, unafraid
of death, and what lay beyond.

"It is done."

"I can see that."

*Well, fuck you, you sanctimonious old cunt, why don't you
fucking do it yourself, then?* But he said nothing. He smiled.
The smile of somebody who wants to take your position and
is happy to see you die in the process.

They stood, waiting, watching. As they had a hundred
times before.

As they had a *thousand* times before.

And it always went the same.

The twisted, merged, magick-infused subject *died*. It did
not grow. It *died*.

Only...

Not this time.

In the flask, the liquid bubbled. Only it was more than
just a liquid. It was a life source. It was a cocktail of nutrients
and enzymes carefully balanced to help in the creation of
life. New life. It was a very special kind of amniotic fluid.

"It's working," said Gregor, voice hushed in awe.

"Shh!" snapped Movak, and scowled. He moved forward,
a few teetering steps, and began a series of invocations
designed to accelerate and stabilise the process. The other
engineers watched Movak, and took a step back as dark
smoke started to pour from his mouth.

Gregor swallowed, and wished, suddenly, he was
somewhere else. Or at least back with the family he loved...
a family being kept in the Ruby Dungeon by King Irlax, in
case Gregor decided in any way to not comply.

"Get back," said Movak, his voice curiously low, and
slow, and husky. Smoke drifted from his nostrils.

Everything descended into silence.

And this, the thousandth experiment they had worked on over the years, went silent also.

Gregor shivered. This wasn't usual. Usually, the blend of embryos began to scream, or thrashed about, kicking the inside of the flask in acute agony, banging themselves around in a convulsing death dance, before, ultimately, smashing their own tiny skulls open on the inside of the iron chamber.

This time, it was different.

Gregor stepped forward.

"I can hear it breathing," he said.

Movak nodded, and gestured for Gregor to step back. The other engineers looked on with stark, drawn faces. If this thing *worked* they were guaranteed not just wealth, but a return ticket to their families. To see their children again after so many years locked away in this dungeon laboratory. To see their families who had been imprisoned by Irlax as insurance policies. The *bastard*.

A curious silence descended on the laboratory. Each dwarf tilted their head slightly, listening. And they *could* hear it. It was in Flask Three. Their creation. A creature, forged from different genetic materials and *grown*. They would set it loose in the Five Havens, and it would wreak havoc. It would be an abomination and they would blame it on the Church of Hate.

"Open Flask Three," Movak said.

Warily, Gregor stepped forward and slid open the locking rods. As the third slid up, so fluid began to leak from the edges of the flask. As the fourth slid up, the trickle turned to a flood, and on the fifth the flask door swung open and a gush spilled out the contents. Gregor leapt back, but his boots and apron were drenched. He frowned. He heard gasps behind him. And then he looked up.

Gregor's eyes went wide.

It was like nothing he could ever have imagined.

The creature was huge, twice the size of any dwarf, and almost cubic in proportions, with the huge thick arms of a dwarf, powerful legs and a solid, thick torso. But there the similarities to dwarf-kind ended. The head was a twisted, elongated muzzle, with thick ridges running from nostrils to crown. The face was pulled out, fangs bared like a rabid dog, and black eyes blinked, as the creature stared at its creators. A tail whipped, with a gleaming razor spear at its tip. It growled, low and threatening.

"Holy fuck," said Gregor, taking in the mottled green and black flesh, the scales that ran in random spirals across the creature's skin, but most of all, at the flames which flickered at its glowing nostrils. Samples taken from the discovered *artefact*, from the section of dead dragon embryo they had found, had been synthesised with various unborn dwarf babies – to create this. A monster.

And, it had to be said, Movak's inspiration – Orlana's *splice* – could be seen clearly in the magick and flesh construction.

Gregor took a step back, but the beast leapt forward, squealing, thick fingers, which ended in claws, grabbing Gregor. That long muzzle opened wide, and clamped over Gregor's head, razor fangs shearing through half his skull, leaving a cross-section of bone, muscle and a neatly sliced-through brain. Gregor's lower face remained, although cut at a slight angle, and the lips quivered before the dwarf scientist dropped as if his limbs were fluid. The creature screamed again, lifting its muzzle, spitting out the half-head, and wailing to the ceiling as if in the throes of some terrible torture.

Movak, who had been frozen by the vision of the abomination they'd created, suddenly bellowed, "Get the weapons!" and turned to sprint for his unloaded crossbow… the beast simultaneously lowering its head, dark eyes glowing, and taking in a deep, loaded breath.

A stream of fire lashed out, hitting Movak in the back, lifting him up, smashing him across the chamber and pulverising him against the rough rock wall, where the fire continued to stream and splash, roaring, incinerating, until there was nothing left of Movak but ash…

Grak, Movak's second-in-command, turned slowly and gestured to the engineer nearest the door.

"Lock it," he said, voice trembling with fear. "This beast must *never*..." but flames engulfed him, and he started to scream, and the beast stomped towards him, powerful hands reaching out, grasping him, and hurling him across the laboratory, sending a bench and a hundred instruments and vials and beakers crashing to the rocky ground.

The dwarves turned to run... as the engineered hybrid went about its killing.

Talon stopped.

"What is it?" said Beetrax, eyes narrowing.

"I heard something." Talon's voice was soft. He looked sideways at Sakora, who gave a nod.

"I heard it too."

"Bloody hell, you two are jumping at shadows!" growled Beetrax, gripping his axe tight.

Jael shivered. "I have a bad feeling about this."

"Nobody asked you, lad."

"There!" Talon held up a finger, but this time he did not have to bring attention to the sound, for the wail, the *scream*, was louder this time. There came a distant cracking sound, then a pounding, as of a fist on iron.

"Er," said Beetrax. "I don't like the sound of that."

They listened.

"It sounds mighty pissed off, whatever it is," said Talon, drawing an arrow and fondling it gently.

"Maybe if we head down that tunnel there?" Beetrax pointed.

"I agree," said Lillith, and her face darkened, eyes closing. "There is something up ahead. Something created by the dark arts of Equiem magick."

"Can we fight it?" scowled Beetrax.

Lillith shook her head, and now her eyes held nothing but fear as she looked remotely into the creature's dark and twisted soul. "No, my love. This time, we run."

The Tower

Volak flapped her great, scaled wings, ascending in lazy spirals until the land of Vagandrak spread out before her, a huge tapestry of fields and villages, forests and lakes. Mountains bordered to north and south, ice-capped and sparkling under weak sunlight. Sunlight also shone dully across her black, overlapping scales, as her spread wings stretched out, rigid now, like hammered iron, and she started to glide. Her wide wings contained razor-sharp spikes at each wingtip; perfect killing implements. Needles ran down her spine to the end of her tail, whipping gently, ending in a large triangular spike which gleamed. And in an ancient face, a demon face from history and myth and nightmares, above a long tapering snout filled with black fangs, and below horns which sprouted from her head amidst scales, sat her narrowed, slanted, gleaming black eyes. And Volak's eyes saw... they saw the present, and they saw the *past*.

My Empire.

Volak drifted, as if in a dream, with flames curling around her fangs. Her eyes looked down at the rivers and forests and villages, and yet these she did not see. She witnessed her memories, vivid as molten gold shining in her mind, bright as the fire with which her and her kin had rid the land of the pestilence known as *man* and *dwarf* and *elf*.

In her waking dream, she saw the sky filled with a thousand dragons, each clan sporting different coloured scales. But Volak was Queen, her clan the eldest, most powerful, the rightful leaders of Wyrmblood by heritage and fire and violence.

A thousand dragons surged through the skies, dropping in tight formations, and from a distance the races on the face of the world must have thought them a swarm of birds, or a cluster of launched arrows. Until they fell, dropping from copper-bruised skies at terrific speeds, jaws opening, screams wailing like some terrible song, followed by jets and washes of billowing flame… Civilians ran in their thousands, flocking down the streets, abandoning market stalls and carts and whatever business had seemed *so important* just a few seconds before. Bodies were picked up in streamers of howling fire, tossed blackened down streets which glowed, as talons smashed through stones and buildings and joists and roofs, sending debris flying, demolishing walls which crumbled to crush screaming men and women and children and babes in prams in the streets below. A thousand dragons attacked the city, and as Volak watched dreamily from above, wings still outstretched, replaying the glorious moment, so the roars and the fire and the screams all combined to create a beautiful symphony of slaughter which spun like woven silk through her mind, causing a harmony which she found ecstatic.

She blinked, and below forests rustled under a gentle breeze, sunlight gleamed silver crescents on the lapping shores of inland lakes, a unit of cavalry cantered in the hills to the north of Vagan, their silver spears sparkling with a hundred razor-sharp tips.

But no music. No symphony. No screams.

I want my Empire back, she thought, still dreamily, still remembering the glorious genocide; *I want to hear your screams, I want to see rivers of bubbling human fat running down the gutters of your burning, broken cities, I want your kings to bow down at my claws so I can chew off their pompous, self-righteous heads… I want my world back, for myself, and my offspring to follow.*

She roared, coming out of her dream state, and powered her wings, slamming across the sky like a dark shooting star towards the single tallest structure in the entire land of Vagandrak.

The Tower of the Moon.

The Tower of the Moon had been commissioned by King Yoon after a spate of drunken orgies and was, quite simply, the tallest tower ever built. From the flat summit, on which Yoon conducted weekly parties, one could see clear across the distant Pass of Splintered Bones, through the valleys of the Mountains of Skarandos, and deep into the lands of Zakora, the Three Deserts. The stone for the tower had been mined in the White Lion Mountains to the north of Vagandrak, and even more mined from the heart of the Mountains of Skarandos to the south. The tower had been the masterpiece, or folly, of Yoon's Chief Engineer, Isvander, a tortured and troubled man, who during the build firmly believed he'd been given a poisoned chalice. After all, it was near impossible to please King Yoon who was, to all intents and purposes, insane. In private circles, in hushed whispers, the vast, glorious, impressive, gleaming white structure was not referred to as the Tower of the Moon. It was known simply as Isvander's Tomb, or even just *The Tomb*. The structure which had led to Isvander's eventual suicide.

Now, the evening sun painted the tower a glorious deep orange. The tower's shadow fell like an accusatory finger that wound its way around across the city of Vagan, accusing the population of allowing a lunatic like Yoon to build such a monstrosity at, it was said, the cost of seventeen hundred lives. And that didn't include the ex-lovers Yoon had hurled from the various stages of completed summit during intervals in the tower's completion.

The summit was flat, paved white, with a deep, sunken bath which could accommodate forty with ease. Trays of sweet meats, brandy and Vagandrak red floated serenely across the pool, bobbing when somebody entered or left the water from the wide, curved white stone steps. The water was heated by a clever brass engine in the room below, so that a gentle curl of steam always seemed to hover across the surface, like a baby dragon's smoke.

On this fine evening, Princess Emilia Ladine, niece to King Yoon, reclined naked amidst the steaming waters, her wrists and arms adorned with numerous priceless bangles and bracelets, her face filled with serenity as she watched a couple copulate a few feet before her, moaning and groaning, licking and kissing and rubbing, their faces twisted in pleasure which she found at once fascinating and humorous. Emilia began to giggle. And when Emilia giggled, so her fifty-or-so entourage of lackeys and sycophants also giggled, despite not really understanding what Emilia found so amusing. She flopped a hand outwards, as the two lovers paused, turning towards her, confused a little at her behaviour. They must have conveyed a question in their looks, because the princess wet her lips a little, fluttered her long, dark eyelashes, and said, "Oh, don't let me stop you, please continue. It's just that… you reminded me of my father." She giggled again. Around her, splashing in the pool, and seated on loungers scattered across the white paving stones, fifty giggles echoed in a subtle parody.

"More wine," said the princess.

A muscular, tanned man with a military-grade haircut and chiselled good looks fine enough to make any court lady swoon, swam across to Emilia, and reaching for the tray – which bobbed a scant six inches from her own bobbing breasts – lifted a silver goblet and deposited it in the princess' flopping hand, pale and white and so reminiscent of a dying, panting fish.

"Oh, thank you, Geraldo, you are such a moonbeam." She sipped delicately, spilling a few droplets, probably because this was her eighth goblet and the drinking of wine had taken up most of the day.

"A moonbeam, why, thank you, princess."

"A pleashure," she slurred, and fluttered her eyelashes again. Then she blinked and stared harder at Geraldo. "You have a very fine physique, Geraldo," she said appreciatively, and gave a pout, a perfect pout, a perfect pink pout that had won the wallets, if not the hearts, of many a suitor.

"Why, thank you, Your Highness."

She giggled again, and wiped her lips with the back of her hand, removing a little froth of wine bubbles. "May one ask, my dear, where you managed to achieve such a mus... such a musc... such a good shape."

"I was in the army, Highness. Five years in the infantry." Geraldo spoke the words carefully, for he had told her on numerous occasions in the past, including once that very morning, but Princess Emilia Ladine was extremely adept at not retaining information, especially about anybody whom she didn't consider more important than a chicken.

She seemed to look at him for the first time, and gave a little purr. "Really?" she said. "So, lots of running, and wrestling, and sword play?"

Geraldo nodded, distracted for a moment by a game of bat and ball occurring just a few feet away between two young men, both naked, their long dark oiled hair leaving rainbow trails in the water of the rooftop pool.

"Fabulous," she said, and rested her chin on one fist. "Truly, fabulous." She fluttered her eyelashes again, and sipped her wine. She seemed suddenly *less* drunk and *more* predatory. Then she frowned. "May I ask, Geraldo, how you went from being a soldier in my uncle's army to being naked in my pool?"

Geraldo gave a strangled little cough. He glanced around. "One of your... *lady friends* spied me whilst I was on parade. She requested that I be dismissed from the king's guard and re-employed here as your... as your..."

"Yes?"

"As your butler," said Geraldo, voice perfectly even, eyes staring straight ahead with the same stare he'd used whilst being bellowed at by a staff sergeant. "I open your carriage door. I close your carriage door. I bring you trays of drinks. I feed you sweetmeats. Sometimes, I even cook your evening meals." He lowered his gaze, so that he stared straight into the princess' emerald eyes. "It's a real challenge," he said, without any hint of irony.

Emilia flipped her other hand, and tilted her head. Her long blonde curls bobbed across the water in what she imagined was a massively seductive posture. Nearby, a naked man on a stool deftly tuned a lyre, then started to croon a love ballad. The sun painted orange whorls across the lapping water. Distantly, the city buzzed, a muffled backdrop to the real business of royal hedonism.

Geraldo could sense what was coming. Married, with two young daughters, he wanted no part in this pantomime, and deeply resented this mindless goldfish of a woman who had, indirectly but by her royal edict, had him forcibly ejected from the military – the love of his life – and sentenced, *sentenced,* to an eternity of pointlessness. And yet he could not go against a direct order of King Yoon. It would not only cost him his own life, but that of his family.

And so he gritted his teeth.

"It's funny," crooned Emilia, and sat up a little, slopping wine into the water, "But I feel a little chill, and so I think I shall retire to the royal tent for a lie down. Geraldo, would you please accompany me with my goblet and a fresh flask of chilled wine."

"Yes, Your Highness," said Geraldo, and taking the proffered damp limp hand, helped Princess Emilia Ladine to stand, resplendent in her gold bangles and nothing else, and then to step daintily up the steps, emerging dripping and radiant from the pool whereupon a maid rushed forward and draped a luminous floating chiffon robe around her pale shoulders, hiding nothing of her sexuality. Then she linked arms with a dazed Geraldo, and guided him to the extravagant tent which had been erected to one side of the platform roof near the fancy, carved marble barriers.

The tent was perhaps twenty feet square, and contained a bed, silk blankets, a brazier, and a large, elaborate, carved-oak drinks cabinet which had taken ten men, a league of rope and nearly a week to haul to the top of the tower on an elaborate pulley system. The rich tent fabric was red and gold and glossy, and rich, with more gold, as befitted a princess, and especially a *beautiful* princess of King Yoon's lineage. Incense was burning, and this incensed Geraldo who was, to all intents and purposes, an honourable outdoor man who would rather keep Emilia's rancid stink and drugs from his system.

Oh no, he thought. *I knew this day might come. That I might have to make choices. But how do I wriggle out of this donkey shit? How do I get away from the insane bitch who's suddenly taken a liking to me?*

Emilia ducked through the tent flaps, practically dragging Geraldo with her. Once inside, she turned, and smiled at him, droopy, drug-infused eyelids fluttering, and started making slobbering kisses as Geraldo strained backwards.

"Come to your princess, there's a good boy," said Emilia, closing her eyes and tugging him towards the bed.

"Wait, wait, Your Highness!"

Finally recognising the panic in his voice, her eyes opened and she fixed him with a quizzical stare. "Yes, Geraldo? What is the matter? What could *possibly* be of urgency *now,* in this moment of our most intimate intimacy?"

Geraldo coughed. "Look. Princess. I'm sorry. I'm a married man. I have two beautiful young daughters. I'm employed here as a butler, and I respect you as a princess, I really do, but I am an honourable man. I *was* a military man, and I don't think it's *right for me to come* to your bed."

Princess Emilia Ladine considered this, then slipped the chiffon robe from her shoulders, where it tumbled lazily, erotically, to the floor. She licked her lips. Her eyes were dreamy with drugs.

"I am royalty. You will do as I say." She started to rub her hands up and down her body, swaying her hips, and moved backwards again, to recline naked and glistening on the silk sheets of the bed. "Come here, boy."

"Please, Princess, I cannot do this..."

"Come here, or I will tell my uncle to have you beheaded.

Publicly. And I will ensure your pretty little wife and pretty little daughters are there to witness the spectacle."

Geraldo lowered his eyes, and shuffled forward to stand beside the bed. *Oh no. It's happened. She's finally going to force me to entertain her sexually, like I've seen so many other poor bastards endure...*

Emilia touched herself between her legs. She groaned.

"Come," she said, face cracking into a sculpted smile, "I want to witness your succulent tongue, I want to be orally stimulated by you, I wish to feel your tongue, down here, tickling and tasting, licking and sucking and flicking; I want you to come here and make *me* come..." and she frowned suddenly, pointing to his limp penis, "and *do something* about that, make it hard, immediately, or I'll..."

"I can't just *make it hard,*" snapped Geraldo, anger suddenly getting the better of him. Five years of hardcore manoeuvres on mock battlefields, beaten by swords, skewered by capped spears, punched in the ribs during unarmed combat – to end up *here.* "I'm not a fucking machine!"

Emilia gasped. "Oh my. Oh by the gods! By the Seven Sisters! I cannot believe you feel no sexual attraction towards me, *your little princess,* for I am perfect in every way! I've had a hundred lovers, each one desperate to lick and suckle my perfect pert breasts, each one eager to kiss my sweet mouth, each one desperate to thrust his manhood inside me and bring me squealing to a pinnacle of perfect writhing pleasure... *how dare you not get a hard cock and pleasure me...*"

Geraldo coughed, looking down again. Now he was really fucked. Or not.

Emilia climbed onto her hands and knees, the dreamy drug state evaporating as righteous anger took hold. Her face changed, from sweet, pampered and powdered pooch, to a mask of anger which turned her into something ugly and horrific. Rage swam through her face like piranhas through blood-infested waters. Her eyes narrowed and an accusing finger lifted, pointing at Geraldo.

"You... you are going to fucking *hang*..." she said.

"But... Your Highness!"

"Guards! Guards!" she squealed.

There came a *whump*. Emilia's hair streamed behind her and she blinked, ten times in rapid succession, simply not understanding what she was seeing, or indeed, what had happened. She could see the pool, shimmering with crimson sunlight. Her entourage of sycophants were running around, apparently, in circles, screaming and knocking over goblets of fine wine. But, but, *but* she suddenly realised the *tent* had gone. And so had Geraldo.

"Geraldo?" she said, voice tiny.

There came a distant crack, a pause, a sound like rainfall, and then the upper half of Geraldo's torso slammed onto the white flags before Emilia. From the broken waist trailed streamers of tendon and tattered muscle, and from the layers of meat and fat poked a broken hip, sheared away, jagged, stark white, and twitching.

Emilia took a rapid succession of panting breaths, then screamed, screamed for help, screamed for guards, but everybody was running around in a panic like chickens in a hutch when a fox digs his way in.

Emilia lifted her hand to her head, touching her fingers to her forehead, and swooned, toppling back on the silk sheets, now speckled with Geraldo's blood. She waited for some attendance. When none came, she opened her eyes to see a dark shadow flit across the sky, wheel, and dive. It approached so fast Emilia let out a gasp, and when it landed, the whole tower shook as claws gouged long grooves through the white stone flags, cracking some, breaking others, ripping up more so they exploded in a shower of shattered stone, which whirred across the tower top causing several bludgeoned injuries.

The *dragon* came to a halt, and its tail whipped out, connecting with ten of Emilia's wailing entourage and sending them spinning away like skittles, where they bounced from the roof of the Tower of the Moon, and wailed a long way down into tumbling oblivion.

The dragon turned, lazily, with utter contempt, and dark eyes fixed on Emilia. Slowly, the head lowered. Lips curled back. And the dragon *grinned*.

"I am a princess!" squeaked Emilia, shuffling backwards, face a rictus of terror. "Princess Emilia. I have royal blood! I am the niece of King Yoon, you know. I have rights, you know."

Flames curled around Volak's lips, and her grin widened. Those dark eyes bore through Emilia's soul.

"You are a princess, you say?" came Volak's powerful, musical rumble. "I am impressed!"

"You are?" came the tiny squeak, as Emilia's bladder suddenly weakened and urine stained the silk sheets.

"Yes! However."

"However?"

"You are a princess. But I am the queen," said Volak, eyes narrowing, "and this is my world now. Do you know what happens to enemy royalty when a royal throne is usurped?"

Emilia was shaking too much to reply.

Volak smiled, showing far too many fangs. "They burn," she said, and gave a tiny exhalation of fire which ignited Emilia and the bed on which she trembled. For a moment there was no response as her hair went up in flames and her skin started to blacken, then she leapt off the bed, hands flapping, a wail erupting from flame-charred lips, and in a blind panic ran, slamming into the low barrier which surrounded the roof of the Tower of the Moon, to flip neatly over the side.

The slap of imploding flesh and compacting bones came much, much later.

Volak turned, to see possibly ten remaining sycophants, frozen in various naked poses, in what could possibly have been considered a comedy tableaux, if they hadn't been about to burn.

Volak smiled at them.

A young man screamed.

Fire howled across the platform, as Volak *sang*...

Engineered

"It's getting closer."

Beetrax halted, and looked at Talon, then Lillith, and finally, Dake.

"It's following us, ain't it?"

Talon gave a single nod, and aimed down the tunnel. A cool breeze blew, chilling the group, and making Talon's long hair drift gently in the airflow.

A wail spun out again, a long and lonely ululation, a sound of pain, and terror, and ultimately, despair.

"It sounds hurt," said Lillith, slowly.

"I wish it'd hurry up and die, then," snapped Beetrax.

"That's beneath you, Trax."

"Sorry," he mumbled.

The wail went up again, closer. They heard several crunching sounds, and more thumps.

"We're going to have to fight," said Talon.

"Not here," snapped Beetrax. "We need somewhere better to defend."

"Come on."

They started to jog, and the corridor sloped down, the rough, rocky floor spiralled with rainbow colours of spilled oil. The tunnel opened into a chamber filled with a myriad of engineering objects. There was a row of perhaps twenty mining carts, several on rails which then led off into adjoining tunnels, before disappearing in the darkness.

There were two carts on their sides, with missing wheels and sections of undercarriage cut free. This was obviously some kind of repair shop.

A collection of oil-filled barrels stood next to one shed, together with piles of ropes and chains. There were racks of mining tools along one far wall, and a large well, its circular wall fashioned from stones cut from the chamber. Next to where they entered were various wooden scaffolds, which towered up to their right, perhaps twenty to thirty feet in height.

"A good place to fight?" said Talon.

Beetrax nodded. "You get up there on that scaffold, lad. I'll stand here with Dake, and lure it into the open, and whatever it is emerges from that tunnel, you shower it with arrows, all right? And, er, you girls better go hide behind the shed. And take Jael with you, the spineless little fucker."

"I can fight," said Jael, quietly, but Beetrax ignored him.

"Hide behind the shed?" Sakora snarled at Beetrax. "What are you, some kind of idiot?" She pulled free two knives, and scowled at him. "I could kick your arse any time, fat man. Just name the place and time."

Beetrax grinned. "That's more like it," he said, and moved to a space before the tunnel opening. He rolled his neck and shoulders, and readied his axe, then watched Talon climb the scaffold, taking precise care with each hand and foot hold.

"You climb that scaffold like old people fuck," he said.

Talon stopped, turned, and frowned. "Feel free to climb up it yourself, you sarcastic old goat. I don't like heights, all right?"

"Now, now, don't be like that. I was simply observing that if you moved any fucking slower, the fight might be over before you even get the chance to loose off a single arrow."

"If you didn't keep *interrupting my concentration*, then maybe I'd actually get to the top of this pile of shit."

Beetrax swore in several different languages, including

mud-orc, and faced the tunnel, and waited. Sakora stood to his left, loosening up, and Lillith moved back, her face filled with apprehension.

Something bad is coming, she realised. *Something... old. Something changed by the magick of the Elders; the magick of Equiem*. She shuddered, and delved down deep inside herself, searching her repertoire, her internal library of white spells, magick used for healing and cures. There were hundreds. But deep down, past the layers of civility, through clouds of spiritual fog which *protected* her, there were dark spells, tangled tails of Equiem magick. She had once taken an oath to never, ever use them... for to use dark Equiem was to give away a part of one's soul, a little bit at a time. Every time you used the dark arts, they infected you, ate away at you, gradually transforming a person from good to evil – until you stood in a place where you no longer had any control, and were completely lost. Eventually, Equiem took away your humanity. Even casting a single spell would send Lillith on a dark road towards the Chaos Halls.

"Beetrax?"

"Yes, Lil?" He was eyeing Talon as he reached the top of the scaffold, and peered over the edge, tentatively, as if frightened he might fall. Beetrax tutted, shaking his head.

"Whatever comes through that tunnel opening, kill it."

Beetrax frowned. "You've changed your tune."

"Just do it!"

"All right, all right!" He twirled his axe in a figure of eight, a blur of steel, blades hissing. "Kill it. I got it." He stood, shoulders braced, and waited, eyes narrowing. Dake stood slightly to one side, out of range of Beetrax's blades; he didn't want them in the back of the head by accident.

A cool breeze drifted from the tunnel opening. Behind, from some far section of the chamber, water dripped. There came a creaking sound from one of the shacks, and Beetrax turned around once more, the hackles rising on the back of his neck. Something felt wrong. Out of place.

"It's the dark arts," whispered Lillith.

Beetrax shrugged, and faced the gloomy hole of the tunnel.

The sounds had stopped. Silence oozed from the dark hole like black honey, and Beetrax shivered.

"You ready up there, archer?"

"I am, axeman."

"You'll watch my back, right?"

"Have I ever let you down?"

"When you do, I'll be dead, that's for sure."

"Trust me, Trax."

Beetrax nodded, and his humour had gone, as he prepared to fight. Something was coming, he could feel it, as unstoppable as the seasons, as terrifying as nature. And then it was there. It halted within the depths of the tunnel, its breathing slow-paced and husky. Then there came a flowering of flame, just for an instant, which blossomed like the opening petals of a dark rose, before it withered and died, the rose crumbling to ash.

"What the fuck is that?" said Sakora, breathing deeply, calming herself.

"Not quite sure," said Beetrax. "But it'll die just like any other bastard."

"It's studying us," said Lillith, carefully. "It is a monster, but it's intelligent."

"Why doesn't it attack?"

"I don't know," said Lillith. "But it *has* been tracking us. It has our scent in its nostrils."

They waited, watching the beast in the darkness.

And then it stepped forward, slowly, into the light.

"By the Seven Sisters," said Lillith, taking another step back.

Flames flickered around the strange, twisted dragon snout. Black eyes glittered, watching them, as its tail whipped backwards and forwards like an angry cat, the speared tip glinting, razor sharp, whining through the air.

Beetrax acknowledged this, and was about to charge, when flames rumbled around the creature's grinning maw.

"Er, it has fire," said Beetrax, through clenched teeth, out the side of his mouth.

Sakora nodded, dumbly. She had never seen anything quite like it. Well, *she had*, but Orlana's splice had been a completely different proposition. This was… this was horrific beyond anything she'd ever witnessed.

"You are one ugly motherfucker," snapped Beetrax, and his words snapped the spell. The beast let out a sudden, high-pitched wail and charged, thundering forward, black and green scales glinting, legs stomping, tail whipping about.

Beetrax watched, carefully, then his eyes flickered to Talon.

A shaft hissed through the gloom, smashing into the creature's back, making it rear its head, screaming, as Beetrax stepped to one side and his axe slashed out. A blade was *deflected* by scales in a shower of sparks, and the creature slammed passed, as Sakora danced backwards and the tail came around, slashing in a horizontal arc that crashed into Beetrax at midriff height, doubling him over and sending him flying across the rocky floor, face purple, gasping for breath, axe clattering off to one side. Dake ran in, sword raised, eyes hard, but a second swipe of the beast's tail lashed out, cracking him around the head and sending him rolling, to slam against a stack of old wooden crates. He rose for a moment, but then slumped to the ground, stunned, clutching his head where blood trickled from a savage wound in his cheek, and from his nose.

Sakora leapt at the beast, and a blast of flames sent her skipping away, knives glinting, eyes wide, attack forgotten as the heat scorched her eyebrows and hands.

The beast turned, panting, and glittering eyes fixed on Lillith.

Lillith took a step back, her voice a gasp, spells suddenly forgotten under that Equiem-born gaze.

Beetrax had got to his knees, then his feet, but he was too far away…

An arrow flashed, hitting the creature behind one ear before deflecting, and whining off across the chamber. A second arrow followed, punching into the creature's back, just below the shoulder blade. The point went between scales and bit deep, with a solid *thunk* of steel in flesh. The beast grunted, and turned away from Lillith, and looked up at Talon on the scaffold.

Sakora leapt onto its back, a dagger flashing down, but it grated against dragon scales. A thick-fingered hand sporting long, dangerous claws reached back, plucked Sakora from its back – holding her suspended and dangling for a moment – and then launched her across the chamber, where she hit an upturned mine cart, folded around it with a grunt of pain, and lay still, a broken doll.

Talon fired another arrow, but the creature side-stepped, and it skimmed from its twisted dragon head.

The beast grinned, took a deep breath, and a stream of fire blasted across the chamber, hitting the scaffolding, and igniting the wood.

Talon squawked.

Beetrax charged, axe slashing out, but a back-handed swipe sent him rolling across the floor, to hit the wall of the shack. Dust and pieces of wood rained down on him, making him sneeze violently, and sag, as several huge chunks of wood thundered down onto his skull, and unconsciousness threatened him with a dark dropping veil.

The beast charged at the scaffold, and Talon fired two, three, four arrows which glanced away. A fifth shaft hit the creature in the eye, but it didn't even slow, smashing into the lower struts of scaffold which groaned, and twisted, and sagged. Talon slipped, and grabbed a support, as the whole structure groaned again, moving to one side in its entirety, flailing like a dying dancer on ice.

"Fuck!" screamed Talon, as flames roared around him and he dropped his bow. "Trax! Sakora!"

But he could see Sakora. She was out of the game.

Dake was unconscious, blood under his face.

And Beetrax sat, like a drunkard in the gutter, shaking his head, wondering what had hit him.

Talon's eyes, reflecting the glow of roaring fire, met with Lillith's. The heat was rising fast now, and his boots were burning.

Help me, said his eyes.

Lillith sighed, her face filled with sorrow.

I cannot, said her eyes. *I cannot access the dark arts… or my soul will surely be gone…*

And so Talon waited to burn, as the creature smashed and broke and slashed at the scaffold, the only narrow, collapsing barrier between Talon and fire and death.

We're all going to die, he realised, and desolation filled his soul.

We're never going home again.

Iron Wolves

Trista was tall, elegant, and incredibly beautiful. She wore a stunning green silk ballgown, which billowed out from her waist in a globe reinforced by wires to keep the shape. It sparkled with glittering sequins. Her shoes were a glossy green to match, exclusive items made to measure by Hitchkins of Drakerath. She wore a gold watch on one wrist, which shone with inset precious stones, and a diamond bracelet on the other, which sparkled as it caught the firelight from various flickering brands.

Trista's face had high cheekbones and nobility, cheeks flushed pink, lips painted with just the right pastel shade of green; her earrings glittered with yet more diamonds set in molten tears of silver. Her luscious blonde hair was piled atop her head, curls stacked and skilfully interwoven to add a foot in height to her already tall, athletic frame.

Music was playing.

It was a wedding march.

Trista stepped across the stone flags, heels clacking, and paused by a column at the rear of the church. The ceremony was in progress, the bride in white, the groom and his best man in dark grey. She clutched flowers. He clutched his own hands. They made a perfect couple. They were beautiful, and happy, and Trista could smell the stench of their perfection.

"Beautiful people," she muttered.

A grey-haired old lady turned from the back pew and frowned at her.

Trista shrugged, lifted her glass of wine, and sipped, sighting on the perfect couple with their perfect lives and perfect minds and perfect jobs and perfect marriage, and she felt the hate coursing through her veins.

"Those fucking bastards," she whispered. The old woman turned again, and tutted, scowling. "It'll never last." Trista wiped away a tear and took another sip.

The newly wedded, how fucking sweet, their lives perfect. They are lucky beyond belief. They have a long bright sparkling future ahead of them. They will consummate the marriage and she will carry his seed and they'll have a plump bouncing baby girl, soon followed by a golden haired utterly perfect beautiful little brother. And the world will be so right for them. Their future will be an everlasting fucking dream.

The grey-haired old woman stood up, and turned towards her. Trista felt a secret blade emerge from up the sleeve of her ballgown, and appear, concealed, in her fist.

But...

But maybe their future won't be so perfect after all. Maybe he'll be out drinking, laughing with his friends, and end up in a savage bar brawl. Maybe he'll get stabbed in the guts, lie bleeding in the gutter, calling for his lovely new wife. But he'll die, and bleed everywhere like a spear-stuck pig, and where will she be then, I wonder? Will she move to his best friend, slip into his bed, between his sheets, like some whore at the sign of a silver coin? He'll touch her, as her husband used to touch her, and she'll sigh and coo, and they'll fuck, him sliding in and out, in and out, her cunt wet with her eagerness. How sick, how crass, we're all just fucking animals, there's no faith, no honour, no nobility, no fucking loyalty. We're all whores. All fucking whores. And every whore deserves to die...

The grey-haired old woman was close now. Her mouth had opened, and suddenly her eyes dropped and saw the blade, glinting orange with firelight. Trista recognised the signs of an impending scream, and she tensed, ready to move fast...

"There you are," rumbled Dek, stepping from behind a pillar, his hand on her shoulder. The blade flashed, a reaction, instinct, and a tiny droplet of blood appeared under one of Dek's eyes.

He stared hard at her.

"You've been watching me?"

"I've been watching you," he agreed. Dek's eyes shifted from Trista's face, to the grey-haired old woman. Quietly, he growled, "Go sit down if you know what's good for you." Then he grinned.

"What have I become?" whispered Trista, going from absolute anger to sudden deflation in one heartbeat.

"You're just troubled," smiled Dek. "Like the rest of us. But you're getting better. I know you're getting better."

"I'm a monster," she said, and her tears wet Dek's shoulder.

"You're no monster," he said, hugging her tight. "You have your reasons. I know that. But you *are* improving."

"How? How the fuck am I improving?" she hissed.

Dek nodded, to where the bride and groom were kissing. People cheered and threw fruit and confetti.

"Because they're still alive," he said. "Now come on. Come with me. We have a job to do."

Trista nodded, and took Dek's rough, calloused hand, and allowed him to lead her from the church.

On the way out, he reached up, and touched the nick, his finger coming away with blood. He smiled, a grim smile, and stepped with Trista out into the light.

Dek drained the wine flagon in one, belched, and launched it at the flagstones where it shattered into a hundred jagged pieces. He clenched and unclenched his fists, brows furrowed, battered, broken features clearly annoyed as he digested the words he'd just endured. One half-stitched wound below his eye had opened, and slowly disgorged beads of blood that left a trail like crimson tears down his face.

The landlord stepped over, and pointed. "None of that, son," he said.

Dek stared at him, and went to rise, but Trista reached out, her palm against the brutal pugilist's shoulder, pushing him back down.

"We'll pay for it," she said.

"By fuck we will," growled Dek, scowling.

"Dek?"

He met Trista's cool, unnerving gaze, and looked away. She was incredibly beautiful, her cheeks flushed pink, lips painted, diamond earrings glittering with reflection from the open, roaring fire; her head was piled high with luscious blonde curls, her teeth white and perfect and often smiling. And yet, *and yet* here was possibly one of the few people in the whole of Vagandrak, Dek would not broker an argument with. You did *not* fuck with Trista. Trista was a simple and brutal incarnation of knife-death.

"Yeah? Well? Tell him. Tell that fat, dumb, drunk bastard to close his mouth, or I'll knock out his few remaining teeth. He just won't let it go, Tris. Just won't fucking let it go, week after week, every time I think *that's it, he's moved past it*, he just brings it up again like a bad coin. I'm sick of it. Sick to my bones."

Trista leaned close. "I know, Dek. But we've been through hard times. You know that. It's just Narnok's... *way*, his way of getting over it."

"Getting over what I did?"

"Yes. And the rest. The torture which followed. The facial scarring. That bastard Xander putting out his eye with acid. It's like, like *you* are his pressure release valve. Without you, I'm not sure what he'd do. It's almost like you've became his reason to live, to fight, and to hate."

"Well, I'm fucking sick of it," complained Dek.

He looked up, tattooed fists clenching again as Narnok half-staggered across the busy tavern. The Fighting Cocks was crowded on this late afternoon. It was the day following Labourers' Pay Day, and Vagandrak was awash with ditch diggers, stone breakers, builders, cesspit cleaners, all eager to enjoy their single day off. Usually with a generous measure of alcohol thrown in.

Narnok.

The giant axeman sat, and his stool creaked. His face was a nightmare mask of crisscrossed scars. One eye was a milky white, obviously blind, and he had thick-banded tattoos, many of them military in origin, up his wide arms and across his neck.

He grabbed his tankard, and downed the dregs, then belched. He rubbed his hand through his beard, then turned his good eye on Dek, and surveyed the shattered flagon.

"You have an accident?"

"No."

"What's wrong with you?" Narnok scowled.

"Leave it," said Trista, and glanced across to Mola, who was asleep on one arm, drunk and useless. Mola was snoring. Trista kicked him hard on the shin under the table, but the snoring simply changed pitch and tone.

"It's you, ain't it?" scowled Dek, unable to help himself. "Same fucking moan, same fucking argument. All the fucking time, it's all I fucking hear, you banging on about Katuna and how I, well, you know…"

"Fucked her."

"See, there you go again…"

"You fucked my wife, Dek. What do you want me to do? Forget about it?" rumbled the huge axeman, and now he'd flushed red with anger and Trista sighed because she could see the argument, and possibly the fight, the eternal fight, looming large and very real. She noted that Narnok had shifted slightly, and was leaning more towards his double-headed axe, butterfly blades on the flagstones, haft against the wall. "You want me to forget that your stupid, battered mouth closed around her nipples, suckling away like a greedy babe at its mother? Perhaps you'd like me to ignore your hand on her quim, fingers sliding inside, that's my wife, Dek, *my fucking wife*, and you had your fingers inside her cunt-honey." His temper was rising incrementally. "So, Dek, my old friend, my old chum, you want me to forget you sliding your cock inside her greased quim, do you? Pounding away at her, like some sailor at the docks with a cheap whore? You want me to FORGET IT?"

They both surged to their feet, jaws clenched, fists cracking, heads slamming together as they stared and stared hard, deep into one another's souls.

"Let it go, brother," said Dek. "Or by the gods, I'll fucking pound you to the dirt."

"I'd like to see you try."

They froze. Trista had risen, a shining, silver, razor-sharp knife in each hand. Blades touched throats. Her words were calm, and measured, and soft, and sweet, but her eyes were raging. Inside her soul, there was a furnace that would never go out.

"I love you both," she said, ejected on sweet breath, and with a smile that could break a million hearts. "And you know I would never kill you. But I swear, if you do not cease this foolishness, I will cut you. Both of you. Deep and bad. Not enough to kill, but enough to make you *wish* you were dead."

Slowly, Dek and Narnok backed away, still scowling, faces like a summer thunderstorm. They sank to their stools.

"Well, it's him, ain't it, Tris," grumbled Dek.

"If he hadn't done it, I couldn't complain about it," moaned Narnok.

"Shut up!" hissed Trista. "He'll be here soon, and he needs our help, and what's he going to think if this is the sight he's presented with? He's an *Iron Wolf*, by the Seven Sisters. Have some decorum for a brother, will you?"

Dek nodded, and picked up another wine flagon, taking a hefty swig.

Narnok rubbed his beard, and belched. "Remind me again who he is?"

Trista sighed. "Kareem Maff. Fought at Desekra against the mud-orcs. Kiki knew him. Spoke very highly of him.

Said he had a demon in his soul."

"Well, I don't remember no Maff fucker," said Narnok, scowling, and taking a heavy drink of ale.

"I do," said Dek, quietly. "He was a dangerous motherfucker. Dark skin, big bushy beard. Sergeants kept ordering him to shave it off, but he refused. Did ninety days in military prison, still wouldn't shave that fucking beard off. They sent in three Staffs to do it for him, and he broke their noses and cheek bones. Good lad. Salt of the earth."

"Did you fight him in the Pits?"

Dek shook his head. "No. He was more… moral than that. Wouldn't fight for money. Only to the death." Dek looked up. "So don't piss him off, all right?"

"I have no need to pick a fight with this man," growled Narnok. "After all. He didn't shag my wife." He gave a narrow smile with thin, scarred lips.

"You see, Tris?" moaned Dek. "See what I have to put up with?"

At that point the door to The Fighting Cocks opened, and Kareem Maff stepped in. He was over six feet tall, massively broad, and carried himself like a natural athlete, a warrior. His dark eyes swept the tavern and most turned away under that dark, intense gaze. Then he spotted Trista, and his face cracked into a smile, and he moved across the tavern in much the same way as a galleon glides through a collection of bobbing, useless rowing boats.

"Trista!" He held out his hand, and she shook, her small, white fingers engulfed by fists easily as big as Dek's.

He surveyed Narnok and Dek coolly, not fazed in the slightest by their size, demeanour, oozing menace or reputation. He grinned then, a full-teeth grin, and sat down. The stool creaked.

"You're as big as I remember," said Trista, and gave a little flutter of her eyelids.

Kareem beamed. "Well, that's a very nice thing to say, Trista. You're certainly as beautiful as I remember…"

Dek leant forward. "What the fuck is this? Have you

come to lick pussy or is there a fucking reason for your visit?"

Kareem eyed Dek up and down, face slowly dropping into a frown. "Hey. Friend. I have a problem, and came here to talk to Trista about said problem. I don't need no broken-toothed simpleton interjecting on the conversation. Now, if you don't like me and Tris smiling at one another, I suggest you *fuck off* and find a whorehouse." He smiled. "Somewhere they like to pander to your kind."

Dek kicked back, but Narnok grabbed him. With momentum and power, Dek dragged Narnok halfway down the table.

"What the fuck does that mean?" snarled Dek. "*My fucking kind*?"

"Calm down, calm down," beamed Narnok, still holding a flagon.

Kareem shrugged, and looked at Trista. "I thought you said they were cool?"

"No." She pursed her pretty lips. "I said they were headstrong, and a little insane, but salt of the earth and usually willing to help a fellow Iron Wolf. Especially one who fought on the walls of Desekra."

Kareem nodded, and stood, stool scraping. He eyed Dek, gaze narrowing. "You're quick to anger, my friend," he said. "So I'll be saying goodbye. I didn't realise my brothers would be such a prickly fucking bunch. I ain't come here to fight. I came here for help. Because I need it and I thought my Iron Wolf brothers would be the ones to turn to in, like, my times of trouble."

Narnok scrabbled to his feet, and moved forward. "Listen, lad," he said, and belched. "Don't pay much attention to Dek, he's a fucking horse dick on occasion, and if I didn't love him like a brother, I would have chopped him from crown to bloody bollocks with yonder axe." He nodded in a vague direction of his ill-abused weapon. "Look, lad, sit down, tell us your problem, we'll help you if we can." He forced a smile, and patted Kareem on the shoulder.

Slowly, Kareem sat. He frowned a little, and glanced at Dek.

"It's all right," said Dek, scowling at Narnok, "Narn is right. We'll help if we can."

Kareem took a deep breath. "I have a problem. And it's not your normal kind of problem that can be sorted by cracking a few skulls."

"Well, you look handy enough for that, lad," said Narnok.

Mola snored in the corner, head now back against the stone wall, dead to the world. Or as close to death as alcohol would allow.

"Go on."

"Well, it concerns the Red Thumb Gang."

"Ahh," said Narnok.

"Ahh," said Dek.

"We know those bastards pretty well," smiled Trista, sipping daintily at a goblet of wine. As a rule she did not drink, she could not stand to lose control, and recognised inherently that to be a warrior, one had to retain one's senses at all times. Not that it stopped Narnok and Dek. But then, that's why they had considerably fewer teeth than Trista.

"I hate those bastards," muttered Narnok. "You know why they're called the Red Thumb Gang?" Kareem nodded, but Narnok, fuelled by pride and ale, continued anyway. "When they murder some poor, unfortunate bastard, they leave a bloody thumb print in the middle of his – or her – forehead."

"I am aware of this," said Kareem gently, looking to Trista, who shrugged, as if to say, *he's going to say what he's going to say, there's no stopping the drunk old bastard when he's on a roll. Better just let him get it out of his system, like piss into a piss trough. When he needs to go, he needs to go.*

"Red Thumbs. Bah! Think they rule every criminal activity in every city from here to the other pissing side of Vagandrak. Think they control the Honey-leaf in Drakerath, the whores in Zaret, illegal sorcery in Katarok... but we showed them, didn't we Mola? Eh? Eh, Mola? Remember that thing with the Elf-rats?"

Mola continued to snore.

"Anyway," interjected Trista, "please, Kareem, tell us your problem. Something to do with money, I presume? It would appear it's very easy to get into financial... difficulties with the Red Thumb Gang. And once you're in their pocket, you fucking *stay* in their pocket, if you know what I mean."

"Money?" Kareem gave a small laugh. "If only it were that simple."

"Go on," said Narnok.

"I fell in love," said Kareem, looking down at the rough-sawn wooden planks of the drinking bench. "I said it would never happen. I always said I was a military man, fighting was in my blood, I'd never succumb to a bloody woman's magical charms... that's what I always swore. But I did. I fell. And I fell hard."

"How's that a problem?" rumbled Dek.

"Well," said Kareem, scratching his whiskers, "have you heard of Debanezeer Salt?"

"Red Thumb overlord," growled Dek. "Got his name because he'd decapitate his enemies, cut their heads right off, scoop out their brains, and fill their empty heads with salt. He'd have them, upside down, lining the drive to his big house on the outskirts of Vagan. I knocked some of his teeth out, once." Dek grinned. "Nearly started a fucking war."

"And you're *still alive*?"

Dek winked. "I don't kill easy, son. And luckily, he was drunk. Too drunk to remember my ugly mug, so he must have been pissed! Anyways. What did you do? Shag his wife?"

Narnok reddened, and scowled at Dek. "You just can't let that sort of thing lie, can you?" he snapped.

"No, no," said Dek, "I didn't mean anything like that, didn't mean nothing by it. I was making an observation, is all."

"Yeah, but you couldn't say it different, could you? Had to say *shag his wife*. Just like you shagged mine."

"Don't fucking start again, Narn."

"Guys, guys," said Trista. "Focus? Kareem? Problem? Red Thumb Gang? *Remember*?"

Grumbling, the two Iron Wolves subsided, and Kareem continued. "Debanezeer Salt. Scum of the earth. Human offal waiting to shuffle off this mortal coil. Well. He has a few sons. And he has a daughter."

"Ah," said Trista, nodding in understanding.

"Met her at a dance. Beautiful, charming, funny, we laughed all night. What a woman. Said I'd never fall in love. Well, I did. We ran like idiots through the city, drinking, laughing, loving. For weeks. Ignored the world. I've never had so much fun in my entire life. I've never been so happy. Then one night, I'm relaxing by my fire, I love a good fire, a big fired stacked up with logs I've chopped with my own hands, like, and there's a knock at the door. I'm a bit mellow. Been on the old spirits, my brother imports them from the east; so I'm pretty oiled, and I open the door and these three big bruisers bustle in. Now, I'm not a man to start trouble, but three big fuckers coming into *my* comfy living space. So I broke a few jaws, sent them running. An hour later, ten of the cunts turn up. So we have a bit of a scuffle, but some bastard hits me from behind with a helve. Down I go. Wake up hanging from Suicide Bridge in the Scourge, watching the dark waters toiling underneath me, black like ink. I'm groggy from the pick-axe handle, but I'm switched on enough to make out Debanezeer Salt. Big, big, ponderous fat lump of horse shit. Waddles over, leers down at me, gives me some fucking lecture about befouling his pure daughter and all that shite. Then they hoist me up, slap me around a bit, break both my thumbs, and tell me if I ever go near her again I'll be dead Kareem."

He sat back, frowning.

"So... you love this woman?" said Narnok.

"With all my heart."

"No chance of you, you know, finding another fish in the fish pond, like?"

Kareem stared hard at Narnok. "I don't think so," he said.

"So you need to convince this Salt guy that you're a good man, somebody worthy to take his daughter's hand in marriage. Am I right?"

"Yes," said Kareem.

"But he's a murderous psychopath who scoops out brains and fills hollow heads with salt? And uses them as lawn decoration?"

"That'd be it," said Kareem.

Dek thought about this. "I think you're pretty fucked, lad," he said.

Mola continued to snore, a rumbling backdrop like that of a gentle earthquake.

"You know what I suggest?" said Narnok.

"What?"

"Marry her in secret. And run away together. If she loves you as much as you think she does, then fuck everybody else. Fuck them all. You go for it, bloody kidnap her, fast horses, dead of night and all that. Dead romantic. I'll come give you some backup, if you like."

"I was hoping for a more diplomatic solution," said Kareem. "One that meant I could still live in Vagan, with my true love. Live a normal life. Have fun, raise children, watch them grow into men. You know. A *normal life*. Not on the run like some criminal, hunted by criminals. Always watching my back. That's no life, Narnok."

"Hmm," said Narnok.

"Trista?" Kareem's eyes were pleading.

"Don't ask her," rumbled Dek. "She's a psycho when it comes to weddings. She has a certain… history… with brides and grooms."

"*Dek!*" snapped Trista, eyes wide, face flushing red. Fury was suddenly her mistress and they all realised she'd palmed a blade. It gleamed by the light of the fire in the hearth, and the candles that circulated the room on silver candelabra, flames flickering like serpent fangs. "*I cannot fucking believe you just said that*!" Her knuckles were white around the shaft. The tip of the steel trembled, just a little.

"Sorry, Trista," mumbled Dek. "I wasn't thinking proper."

"Yeah, well, you never do," said Narnok with a thunderous scowl. "That's why you upset Trista here, and I think you deserve that blade in your belly, by the way. And that's why you did what you did."

"Did what I did?" Dek's voice was murderously low.

"That thing you did. With my wife."

"I don't know what you mean, Narnok. Better spell it out, letter by fucking letter."

"That *sexual act* you did."

"You mean, when I, like, fucked your wife?"

"That's right, when you fucked my wife."

"Well, she fucking enjoyed it!"

"Not as much as I'm going to enjoy *this*!"

"What?"

Narnok slammed a sudden left hook at Dek, who swayed back, years in the Fighting Pits kicking in and fuelling his instincts by a will to survive... and win money. Lots of money. Narnok howled and leapt forward, crashing into Dek and they both tumbled backwards, taking the table and all the drinks with them. Kareem and Trista leapt away from the upended table and flowing ale and wine, whilst Mola continued to snore in the corner, oblivious to the mayhem kicking off.

Dek grabbed Narnok in a head-lock, but Narnok was big, and mightily strong, and he threw off Dek's warrior embrace and swung another punch, but Dek was moving, clawing his way to his feet to stand, swaying, the worse for wear for so much ale and wine.

"Don't do this, Narn!" he roared.

"Not in here!" screeched the landlady, running forward and placing herself between the two large men. "You fuckers are not breaking up my bar *again*. Now my husband might be a spineless wheelbarrow of horse shit, and yes, I know you're hiding behind the bar you useless sack of turds, but *you two fuckers* are going to take this outside or by all the gods and the Seven Sisters and by all the fucking demons in the Chaos Halls, I'm going to call the City Watch and have you locked up for a fucking week. *Then* I'll pay a goodly sum to bribe the Watch to make sure the Thumbs look after you during your stay. I am *so sick of your fighting and damaging my premises. Now get the fuck out!*"

It was quite an outburst from such a little woman. But it worked. Especially on Dek.

Dek had possessed an inordinate amount of respect for his mum, and so he could not help but obey the majority of women he met. He simply *could not help himself.* Women, to Dek, were on a plinth beside the gods. They were to be trusted and respected and honoured. Woe betide any man Dek caught laying a finger on a woman. Dek would break that finger. Then hand, arm, shoulder and neck.

"Come on," he rumbled. "I'm going out for a piss."

"Not with me, you're not," growled Narnok.

"Well, use the fucking ladies' then. You've certainly grown a pussy these last few months."

Dek stumbled towards the Fighting Cocks' exit. Everybody moved out of his way. *Everybody.* You did not fuck with Dek the Pit Fighter unless you wanted a broken jaw. And a few broken ribs. Maybe a broken leg.

But before he reached the exit, the heavy oak-plank door was flung open, and six large, armed men squeezed through the portal. Muscles bulged, faces gleamed with sweat, eyes were narrowed. They were an ugly bunch, and even an idiot could see they meant trouble; they oozed fight from every stinking pore.

Dek halted, sobering fast, and checked out these newcomers. Behind him, he heard a hissed intake of breath. Narnok, who'd been about to follow Dek out, reached for his axe, sat on a creaking stool, and gently laid the weapon across his knees.

"A ripe bunch," muttered Trista.

Narnok nodded. "Wake Mola."

"I know these fuckers," said Kareem, and his hands curled into fists. "They're Red Thumb. Work down the docks for Salt." And even as Kareem finished the sentence a ponderous man squeezed through the doorway. Has was a fat man, but tall, maybe six feet and five, and one could see why some might underestimate him. His belly flopped into rolls, his thighs were like tree trunks, and a great udder hung under his chin, wobbling with every movement, every gesture, like some kind of distended chicken giblet. But Narnok, Dek, even Trista, could see *beyond* the excesses of pork pie and fried potatoes, rich cream and sugared fancies; they could see the *strength* which formed the trunk of the man. Yes, he was fat. But he was a solid motherfucker, if ever they'd seen one.

Salt surveyed the inner workings of The Fighting Cocks as one might survey something nasty they'd trod in down in the Scregs. He was dressed in bright fabrics, a mixture of tweeds, with ruffs and scarves, with colours and country greens; it was a random mishmash that only the crazy or the heavily protected could have pulled off in Vagan. Most men would have been laughed out of the room. But one sight of this massive gentlemen with his odd dress sense and six heavies caused the feisty landlady to head behind the bar, joining her cowering husband and putting any future breakages down to experience.

"Ahem," said Salt, dramatically, looking straight through Dek as if the pit fighter was a simple *inconsequence*, and settling his small black eyes on a face as ripe as any ham joint, on Kareem.

Kareem went pale, face tightening, lips pursing, head dropping a little as if to say, *oh shit, oh no, why me, why now?* "There's always somebody wants to stick their nose into your life," he muttered, "always somebody wants to stab you in the back." He stood, fists clenching and unclenching.

Debanezeer Salt sauntered across the tavern's main room as if he owned it, brushing past Dek like a petal on the wind

brushes against a tree. Only, as Salt passed, in happy fat
ignorance, so Dek reached out behind himself, scowling,
grabbed Salt's ridiculous jacket, and tugged.

Salt teetered backwards, and sat suddenly on the boards
with a *thump*. Somebody laughed. The six bodyguards
bristled, and one rushed forward towards Dek, face crimson
in anger, lips snarling and spitting.

Dek's straight left split the man's lip, his right hook
broke his jaw, and an uppercut elbow sent him spinning
backwards where his blood washed the floorboards. He
scattered tables on his way down, where he stayed down.

Dek lifted his head, and suddenly Narnok was standing
behind him, axe in both fists, beard bristling something
horrid. And behind Narnok came Trista and Kareem. Trista
held two blades, and Kareem had drawn a short sword
which he brandished in his swarthy fists. Mola snored in
the corner.

"You see," said Dek, turning and looking down at Salt, "if
there's something I can't fucking stand, it's being ignored,
brushed aside like I'm some little fucking girl with spots and
a funny skirt and hair in pigtails."

"Do... do you know who I... *am*?" Apoplectic rage.

Dek squatted, and looked into Salt's face. "Yeah, cunt.
Red Thumb. Debasleazy Twat, or something. Can't say I
give a fuck. Now, do you know who *I am*, because I was
skewering fucking mud-orcs through the eyeballs and
sending a hundred corpses a day to the Chaos Halls whilst
you were sat in your pantry stuffing juicy pies down your
fucking throat. My name's Dek. You might have heard of
me."

Salt gave a chuckle. "Yes. Yes, I've heard of you. And you
might think you're the hard man of the Fighting Pits, but
I've got fifty like you all willing to die for me."

"I'm not willing to die for you," said Dek. He grinned, a
particularly nasty grin. "But I'm certainly willing to kill for
you. Or more precisely. You."

"Wait, wait!" said Kareem, coming forward. "Dek, please,

help Debanezeer stand." Grumbling, Dek did so, grunting and straining at the immense weight. Salt brushed himself down, and looked around the group, then back to his bodyguards, including the unconscious one bloodying the boards. He made a mental note to fire him. Then amended it. Fuck it. The bastard would be fed to the dogs.

"Kareem Maff." Salt smiled, but the smile was with his lips, not his eyes.

"Yes."

"I am confused."

"How so?"

"I thought we'd made an agreement. That you would leave Vagan forever, and leave my daughter Tatanya alone, or I would have my men do unspeakable things to you. And then you would die. I thought it a particularly simple concept to grasp."

"I love her," said Kareem, teeth clenching.

"You love Tatanya?"

"Yes."

"Then leave. And cause her no more heartache. I will not stand for it. I am a respected businessman in these parts, and you have taken my young sweetheart away from me… no, I won't allow it. Leave, Kareem; leave or die."

"Look," said Narnok, stepping forward, and Salt glanced down at the axe.

"Narnok the Axeman?" said Salt.

"That's me," said Narnok with a grin, bristling, happy his reputation had preceded him.

"You smell worse than they say."

"Eh?"

Debanezeer Salt smiled, and his men were shuffling forward so that Dek turned, and scowled, and they stopped. "Gentlemen. And ladies." Salt tipped a wink to Trista. Then suddenly hoisted an uppercut that caught Narnok by surprise, lifting the axeman into the air and sending him sprawling backwards, his sheer weight and flailing size sending Trista and Kareem crashing to the floor. Dek whirled on him, and Salt lifted his fists. "Come on, Dek. Let's see what you've got, you ugly fucking son of a whore."

Dek lifted his fists. Glanced at Salt's men. Scowled.

"You really want to fight me, fat man? I'll fucking eat you!"

The left straight skimmed past Dek's ear, a fast punch he'd hardly seen coming. It was followed by a right, that he blocked, a few jabs, then a thundering right hook that dropped Dek and left him sitting there, feeling like he'd been hit by a sledgehammer.

Salt straightened his jacket as his men came forward. More had entered The Fighting Cocks. And these carried loaded crossbows. There were fifteen, maybe twenty. It was a crowd of muscle. An orgy of weaponry.

And it all seemed to happen so fast…

"You see," said Salt, bending to whisper his intimacy in Dek's ear. "All you see is a fat old man before you. And yes, I have partaken of the pie and the wine flagon these last ten years. But in my fucking day I was champion of the Fighting Pits. Ask your little friend Weasel. He knows my name."

Groggy, Dek swayed where he sat, like a drunkard; a Honey-leaf abuser.

"Surprised, motherfucker?"

Dek groaned.

Salt leaned even closer. "Your little friend here, Kareem, came to you to see if you could *persuade me* to let my only daughter bed him, like a fucking whore. What drugs is he on? What fucking continent? And you, oh yes, the *Iron Wolves*, so hard of reputation, you thought you could stand against the Red Thumb Gang?" He laughed, a sickly, mocking laugh. "All I can say, is… "

Dek grabbed his head, headbutted him with force, breaking his nose, headbutted him another four times, then dragged him into a bear-hug. Crossbows wavered, but Salt's men could not shoot, for their master's huge body lay astride Dek like some bloated lover as Dek headbutted and punched. He reached down, grabbed Salt's bollocks, and squeezed hard. Salt screamed like a woman.

"Tell your men to lay down their weapons."

"Never! I'd rather die!"

"Or be a eunuch?"

"Lay down your weapons!" screeched Salt.

"Fuck that," said one big bodyguard, and triggered a bolt. It whined across the tavern, skimming Kareem's ear, drawing blood. Kareem touched his raped earlobe, frowned, and leapt at the man, launching a ferocious onslaught of punches which battered the large man backwards until his back whacked against the bar, at which point the feisty landlady reared behind him with a flagon of wine and smashed it over his head. But still he didn't go down, until Kareem took several backward steps, ran and leapt, both boots connecting with the man's jaw. Down he went, crashing *through* the bar, splintering the wood, and tangled up with Kareem and broken shards of flagon. Kareem kept punching. It was all he could think to do.

Trista launched herself at the bodyguards. There came several clicks and *whines* but like a ghost she danced through the enemy, small knives slashing left and right, no killing blows, not yet, but opening arms and legs and chest muscles, more than enough to sting, enough to slice muscle, sever a few tendons, disabling but not life threatening... and all the time she imagined the men to be wearing smart formal wedding attire, a white rose in their buttonholes, their boots polished and shining, and she screamed, "You bastards, you dirty fucking cheating bastards," as they dropped to their knees, wondering what hit them, wondering how she'd dodged crossbow bolts and carved open their flesh with fruit knives like a dancer in a dream of death.

Narnok was not so forgiving. He didn't like being punched. He particularly didn't like uppercuts. And he certainly didn't like being laid out on his back like a stranded kipper by a fat man with no dress sense and a name so stupid it belonged in a poetry pamphlet. His axe sang. There came a crunch. A head sailed across the tavern, spinning, pissing droplets of blood in its wake.

A sudden hiatus, a hush, descended on the tavern. A seriousness. A bar fight was one thing. But severed heads?

"Come on, you fuckers!" roared Narnok, brandishing his bloodied axe, as more of Salt's bodyguards piled into the tavern and one frightened customer backed into a flagon, knocking it over. Whiskey flowed over a wooden bench, and onto the floorboards beside the roaring fire. An ember, drifting gently, touched down. There was a soft *whoosh* as flames journeyed along the fireboards and onto the fire-dried bench, which started to burn. The fight slammed forward, punches and kicks, thrown stools and smashed tables. A man staggered past with a blade in his eye. Trista followed him, coolly, and retrieved her dagger with a *schlup*.

"You'll see your bitch in hell," she said, eyes glazed, lips moist, tears wetting her cheeks. Bottles smashed, crossbow bolts whined, and Debaneeer Salt crawled through the sudden mayhem, trying to find the door.

He came up against some legs. They wore boots. They were thick, but not like his own, like barrels of pig offal, but heavy with muscle. He looked up. It was Kareem. A bottle sailed past his head. A stool crashed to one side. Smoke billowed through the tavern. The ambience changed, for fire had taken hold of various benches and tables, and climbed to the rafters, cackling. The roof began to burn, fire screeching like a live creature, a demon in a cage as the fury quickly escalated.

"Ahh. Kareem."

"You dirty, miserable bastard."

"What do you mean?"

"My only guilt is to love your daughter. But you come here and threaten me with death." Kareem's eyes held a wild dark gleam. There was a flicker of madness there: a man pushed too far. His back against the wall. Shit out of luck and with no fucking options. And what happened when you pushed a man? Pushed him to the brink of the mountain ridge? To the precipice beyond?

There was only one way to fall.

And if you're going to fall, then you fucking take your enemies with you...

Kareem's boot found Salt's head, and he stamped down, and down, and down, bludgeoning the man into unconsciousness. Then he wiped the back of his hand across his mouth, and spat at the father of the woman he loved. He gazed around, a dreaming man in the midst of a tsunami. Fire roared through The Fighting Cocks. Men brawled, and fought with knives and swords. Stools and tables were smashed, and bottles sailed through the air. What had been a peaceful drinking establishment was now a riot.

Something hissed, and whistled, and howled through the roof. Thick plumes of smoke charged in waves through the fighting throng, so that the brawlers suddenly forgot their issues, clutching at stinging eyes, burning hair, demon-licked clothes. One stocky man went up in flames, screaming suddenly, clutching his face and burning hair with burning hands, and another, as an act of empathy, threw a tankard over the man... only it was full of spirits, and more fire screamed up towards the burning rafters...

The brawl forgotten, everybody staggered for the door, and there was a sudden bitter fight to *get the fuck out*. The door was pretty much kicked from its hinges. Smoke poured out of The Fighting Cocks as men and women and drunks staggered onto the cobbles. The roof went up with a *boom*. Sparks fluttered up into the heavens. Smoke billowed high in the sky, pulsing in great rhythms like some great, black heartbeat.

Narnok staggered out, and dropped to his knees, choking up vomit onto the cobbles in the courtyard. He choked, and coughed, his one good eye red-rimmed and streaming. Dek came out behind him, hands on knees, taking great gulps of air, fresh air, *oxygen*.

"Did somebody get Mola?" choked Narnok.

Trista emerged, supporting the narrow but heavy compact weight of Mola. Through the shouts and roar of

burning timbers, a great cacophony set up as three huge
dogs came pounding across the cobbles. They were all ugly
brutes, scarred and vicious and brutal, bordering on rabies,
crossed with wolfhounds, their eyes crazy, their coats tufted,
their bodies scarred from numerous fights.

"Down," murmured Mola. "Down, bitches."

Still the dogs barked and yammered, until Mola gathered
himself into some semblance of consciousness and bellowed,
"Duke! Sarge! Thrasher! DOWN YOU FUCKERS!" upon
which they obeyed their master, and lay, heads on paws,
licking their fur, chewing at one another, and snapping at
sparking embers that were falling all around like muted
fireflies, their eyes fixed on their one true love, their one
and only, Mola. Their Master.

Kareem staggered out, and behind him he dragged the
titanic and unconscious bulk of Salt. Kareem dumped him
down, the man's head slapping off the cobbles like a steak
on a block, and he looked around, face smudged with soot,
eyes narrowed, then looking back at the burning building.

"What the *fuck* happened in there?"

"Come on, lad," gestured Narnok, still choking. "Come
over here in the fresh air. And why did you bring that dead
cunt out?"

"Because he would have died," said Kareem, meeting
Narnok's gaze.

"And?"

"He would have died in there."

Narnok fixed on Kareem a brutal look, with only one eye
and the savage scars marring his face. "And?" he said.

"You want him to die?"

"Natural causes, ain't it?" rumbled Narnok, and lifted his
axe, resting it against his shoulder. "Some men, well, they
deserve to live. But other cunts?" He fixed Kareem with a
beady eye again. "They deserve to fucking burn."

"He's the father of my true love."

"And?"

"I couldn't let him burn," said Kareem, and his mighty

shoulders slumped a little. "Maybe it's a weakness."

"It's not a weakness, son," said Dek, placing his hand on Kareem's shoulder. "Is humanity, is what it is."

"What do you know of fucking humanity?" said Narnok, kneeling on the cobbles, drool pooling from his jaws.

"I know enough," said Dek, eyes hard.

"What? You pulp men into gristle in the Fighting Pits."

"So?"

"*So*, you break their spines."

"Doesn't mean I don't have no soul."

"You don't think of their souls when you break them over your knee and take their fucking monies."

"Look, Narn, stop fucking with me."

"Why? You think because The Cocks is burning to the ground I've forgotten about your injustice?"

"Here we go again."

"Meaning?"

"You'll never let it lie."

"Let what lie, Dek?"

"Fuck off."

There came a roar as part of The Fighting Cocks' roof collapsed. Sparks rioted into the evening sky. Beyond, the sun was dropping low over the horizon, casting a deep red glow over every building, every wall, every cobble.

The fire burned, crackling through wood and thatch.

Men and women stood on the cobbles, stunned, staring upwards.

And then, through the pulsing waves of smoke, there came a song. It was long, and haunting, and beautiful. It reminded one of long-lost lovers, dreams of hate, of lives that might have been, of world's end, of dead children, of dying babes, of long hard regrets, of dying, of death. It came through the smoke, through the world, beautiful, and terrifying, and eternal.

"What is that?" said Trista, dropping to her knees.

"Music," said Dek, rubbing his red-rimmed eyes.

"It's beautiful," said Kareem.

"It's death," said Narnok, and staggered, pointing. "Look!"
And they looked.

Through heavy coils of surging smoke, black and grey and pulsing like oiled snakes, they could see *Isvander's Folly*. The Tower of the Moon. Glimpsed in shadow. Glimpsed through smoke. Glimpsed as the blood-red sun set beyond the world.

"What am I looking at?" said Dek, tilting his head, battered face crushed into confusion.

"There's something up there," said Narnok.

"*What* could be up there?" whispered Trista, and even though her voice was low, it cut through the smoke, the fire, the confusion, like a razor blade.

They all stood, staring.

There was a shape. A dark shape. Atop the tower.

Salt suddenly coughed, and was born into consciousness. He writhed around for a bit, but the men and women on the cobbles ignored him. They knew he was Red Thumb, but recently the populace had turned. Whereas *once* the Red Thumb Gang had been seen as saviours, robbing from the rich to give to the poor, recently, *recently* perception had started to shift. They were no longer social terrorists intent on saving the world. Now they were seen as what they were. Criminals out to fill their own pockets. Which was why, in his hour of need, Salt found nobody willing to help.

He sat up, and snorted blood and snot onto the cobbles. He scowled, looking around, trying to catch somebody's eye. None gave it. He got to his hands and knees, and wobbled to his feet.

"You! Kareem!"

"Fuck off."

"What's wrong with you all? What are you staring at?"

"We're enjoying the smoke, idiot," drawled Dek.

Salt turned, and squinted, and focussed. Salt had good eyes. *Very* good eyes. He might have been fat, and decadent, and *evil*, but his eyesight was impeccable. Better than anybody he had ever met.

"The Tower of the Moon," he said, words a murmur.

"Give the man a chocolate," snapped Narnok.

Salt chuckled. "Do you know what you're looking at?"

Dek, Narnok, Kareem, Mola and Trista turned and stared at him. Hard. He felt the animosity of their gathered looks and cringed.

"I meant, do you comprehend what you see?"

"It's a fucking *tower*," snapped Trista, and a blade appeared in her hand.

"No," said Salt, his voice dropping low. "*Look.*"

And they looked.

And they frowned.

And slowly, *slowly*, an impossible reality started to sink in.

"It's a *dragon*," said Debanezeer Salt.

"Horse fucking *shit*," said Narnok.

They stared.

The song filtered down, coming through clouds and layers of smoke. It was beautiful. It was deadly.

The shape, the body, the *creature*, lifted from the summit of the Tower of the Moon, and there came a *whump* as heavy wings abused the air. The creature described an arc, then dropped towards the burning carcass of The Fighting Cocks.

"What's it doing?" murmured Narnok, scowling.

And the dragon turned, and fell, and glided in silence. A terrible silence.

They watched it. Like some huge bird.

"I'm confused," frowned Trista.

"Don't be," said Salt, a strange look on his face, and he hit the ground and covered his head.

Everybody looked at him.

"What the fuck's wrong with him?" scowled Kareem.

The dragon came screaming through the smoke. It was a perverse act. The Fighting Cocks was already burning, already destroyed. This was an act, as if to say, *you call that fire? I'll show you.*

Fire screamed from the dragon, a scream like a stabbed baby, and consumed the walls, the roof, the timbers, the cobbles. The tavern went up like a fish-oil soaked bonfire, and there came *cracks* as wings beat the air again and the dragon flashed low overhead, tail whipping out, smashing the high chimney. Bricks tumbled down, bouncing on cobbles and men and women, who screamed and cried and wailed.

A brick bounced from Dek's arm and he got up, scowling. "A fucking *dragon*!" he hissed.

"That's not good," said Narnok, scratching his tufted beard.

"Show me something that is!" snorted Dek, and drew his short sword.

"You think that's going to work?" wailed Salt, still on hands and knees, arms covering his head as he peered up with terrified eyes. "You think you can use a simple sword against a great wyrm?"

Dek smiled, a long, low, lazy smile; like a lizard.

"I don't know, mate," he said. "But I'm going to fucking try."

Hunt

The underground lake lapped softly at the rough stone shore. It was like an ocean of spilled tears, he thought. Like a well of agony, trickled from the five cities above. And, when he thought about her, tears came to *his* narrow, slightly slanted eyes. He loved her, he realised, in his own strange way. And it *was* a strange way. A strange kind of love.

He remembered touching her face, her soft, olive skin, perfect under his rough, calloused miner's fingers which shamed him to his heart. Her dark hair was a cascade of thick woven strands which fell down her back to her waist, she had deep black eyes, pools of ink into which he could dive, could fall, tumble down end over end for an eternity... fall, until she loved him, or until he died. For without her love, death was all he craved.

But more than anything, it was her scent. She was exotic, strange, natural, and drove him wild. He remembered, painful memories, pushing his face close to her neck, smelling her skin, her femininity, inhaling her like some crazy drug which sent his mind spiralling out of control. Her hands were on him, strong, forceful, but he was stronger, and he pushed her back to the blankets of the cold cell floor in the depths, the heart, of the mountain; and he inhaled her like the heady smoke of the Honey-leaf.

Stuttering images crashed through Val's mind as he *remembered*, as he considered the woman from over the mountains, the lady of Vagandrak, whom he had claimed, whom he had taken for his own. Yes, he loved her, he realised, in his own way. As much as anything he had felt which resembled love. Admittedly, he realised forcing himself upon her, causing her pain, was not in itself an act of love, but he believed with enough understanding, enough nurturing, she would come to understand him, and ultimately come to love him in return.

Or she would die.

Val breathed deeply, and lifted his head to face the gathered throng. Newly appointed as Slave Warden of the mines, reports had come in thick and fast after the three great wyrms had escaped from their imprisonment in the Dragon Engine. The reports also told of Skalg, First Cardinal of the Church of Hate, and his plot to assassinate King Irlax. But worst of all, there had been sightings, reports of the Vagandrak "heroes" and their further descent into the mines in search of the fabled city of Wyrmblood. Or so the rumour went.

What do you want? thought Val, idly, as he surveyed the motley crew before him. Here were the toughest, the nastiest, the hardest, the *elite* of the dwarves to serve under the Royal Guard and the Church Guard. And they had been sent to him. To protect the city of Wyrmblood... if it existed.

If. Such a little word.

So. *What do you want? Foreigners. Aliens. Why head deep under my mountain, when you could have followed the destruction of the three dragons, upwards through the Five Havens, to freedom, back to your own land? Your own world? Your own fucking kind?*

It didn't make sense.

Unless... they *knew* something.

He frowned, mind ticking.

"Slave Warden?"

Val jerked, coming out of his reverie. At the forefront of his mind floated the face of Lillith. With her, he had been given a gift. A silver spoon. And he was damned if he going to let this opportunity slip through his coarse-skinned fingers.

"Yes… " he squinted, trying to remember the hulking warrior's name. It slid away. "Yes, my friend? What concerns you?"

"We are awaiting your instruction."

"I am considering all options," said Val, and gave a narrow smile which sat badly on his narrow face.

The gathered men and women, all warriors, all fighters, surveyed Val. Recent subordinate of Krakka, the original Slave Warden killed by Beetrax the Axeman, Val was tall and slim for a dwarf, not carrying the broad, stocky shoulders so renowned in his species. A treachery of genetics had left him with features that bred a natural mistrust in his fellow dwarves, and he wore a close-cut beard in an attempt to hide what, he was continually reminded, resembled a weak chin. His eyes were black and emotionless, like a doll's, and his quick movements spoke that *here* was the master of the knife in the back, the brass knuckle-duster, and a droplet of poison dribbled onto panting lips as one slept. Val did not appear a warrior, and yet he'd achieved his considerable and advanced position by *some* means. Every dwarf present respected that intrinsic warning, and awaited his words with patience.

Except for one woman.

Like Val, she was slim for a dwarf, even a female, and taller than tradition would suggest was healthy. She had straight black hair to her shoulders, a narrow, pointed face, dark eyes like pits of evil, and a very, very pale complexion; pasty, like a tub of solidified human fat. Her facial expression was a natural sneer, a snarl of mockery showing just a few pointed teeth, and she always appeared to be looking down her narrow nose in disgust at the rancid specimen who cowered before her – no matter who that should be. She wore plain black leather armour, scuffed and battered, showing a history of violence. She had no breasts to speak of, again, a jolt against dwarf tradition, or what was considered "feminine", and only a few spider-leg black whiskers poked from her chin, rather than the soft

pelt which adorned many a buxom, sexy female dwarf's
face. But, despite her apparent delicacy of stature, nobody
fucked with this dwarf who'd made a very real name for
herself, fighting her way free of the Pits of Yrkseer, possibly
one of the most violent slums in all the Five Havens. The
fact her face still carried no scars was testament to her skill
and ferocity in battle. And, of course, the art of stabbing
somebody in the back.

This was Crayline Hew, with the inherited title of
Hewardaline de Slathor – or *The Slime of Heward*. It was a
title of which she was incredibly proud. And you did not
fuck with Crayline Hew, in any way, unless you wanted to
wake up dead – with a poisoned skewer injected through
your liver.

The group of hardened dwarves drifted silently apart as
she approached the front, and the troubled figure of Val,
who was scratching his beard and trying to formulate a
plan more complex than *wander around the mines looking for
the intruders*. And he was hampered by constant visions of
Lillith, her naked, pale limbs, her soft dark skin, her wails
of pain...

"Val, Slave Warden, may I have a word in private?"

Crayline's voice was high-pitched, almost nasal, coupled
with a dangerous glint in her passionless eyes, and a vast
array of knives and other, more esoteric, implements
arraigned around her various belts.

Val was about to say *no, of course not you fucking idiot, I'm
attempting to formulate a plan here* when he caught her eye.
Recognition fluttered across his features like a shivering
butterfly. He recognised Crayline Hew. *Everybody* recognised
Crayline Hew.

"Yes, yes," he muttered, and gestured to an area
away from the underground lake, which drew his eye,
lapping against the sloping rough stone, its gentle sound
a mockery to his ears, not just saying his name, but
laughing at his frustration for his lost love, the barbarian
woman, Lillith.

Out of earshot, Crayline touched Val's arm, stopping him. He frowned. He was aware of the control movement. *She* was in control, and he did not like that. He looked into her face, and gave a little shudder. Here was evil personified, if ever he had seen it.

Crayline smiled. Or at least, tried to smile. It was the kind of smile a snow wolf gives to a wounded rabbit before chewing through its throat, eating the flesh and sucking on the brittle bones.

"Crayline Hew, I believe?"

"Yes. Formerly of Irlax's Guard, before I was… *persuaded* to leave. Personal problems, you understand."

Val smiled coldly, noting the easy way Crayline omitted the title *King*.

"So. Is there something on your mind?" he asked, a little too briskly.

Crayline nodded. A smile spread across her face like a pool of blood across a frozen lake. "It strikes me, *Slave Warden*, that you need a deputy."

"A deputy?"

"Somebody to help you with those difficult decisions. Somebody who, for example, may have had decades of experience hunting traitors through the Five Havens and executing them. Somebody, it might be said, who has an understanding of the criminal mind."

"I'm not sure I believe in a second in command," said Val, frowning, lips tight.

"But you were Krakka's second? When he was Slave Warden?"

"Yes… yes, but that was different."

"How so?"

Val looked into her eyes. Then he relaxed. *Oh. So that's how it's going to be, bitch.* He smiled. "Let's say I do need some help. I expect you are putting yourself forward for the position?"

"Of course not," said Crayline smoothly. "But what you have out there is a hardcore bunch of mercenary *cunts*," she savoured the word, as she might a fine Vagandrak red, rolling it seductively around her tongue, "and who better to control the *cunts* than the biggest cunt of them all?"

She smiled.

Val swallowed.

"That would be me, of course," she said, as if to clear any confusion.

"Of course, Crayline. Of course! Cunts. Big cunt. Biggest cunt. Controlling the other cunts."

Crayline nodded, without any flicker of any emotion. "And, of *course*, I'd be watching *your* back on this *very* important mission on which we are about to embark. The mission down to Wyrmblood, if I am not mistaken."

Val stared at her. "How could you know that?"

Crayline smiled. "The biggest cunt always has her sources," she smiled, showing her pointed teeth.

Val led Crayline back to the group. She stood slightly behind him, to the left, hand on the hilt of a long dagger, notched in many places and quite obviously displaying a chequered history of entertainment. Val explained the situation. Vagandrak heroes. Infiltrating further down the mines. Their mission was to hunt down the intruders. Exterminate them. All except one woman who, cough, Skalg wanted keeping alive for questioning over the recent death of King Irlax, their most exalted leader.

"So," rumbled one warrior, who went by the name of Stitch – on account of his flesh being stitched together so many times he resembled a child's attempt at sewing up a doll after a dog attack – "this is a mission on behalf of the Church of Hate?"

"Not at all," said Val, smoothly. "This is strictly off the record. This is a simple search and destroy, but sanctioned by *no* official body of the Harborym. If we were to be apprehended, then we know nothing, and the Church will not vouch for us."

"Apprehended?" said Stitch.

Crayline leant forward, and whispered in Val's ear. The Slave Warden smiled. "You don't need to worry," he said. "Where we're going, trust me, nobody will want to follow."

They marched. And Val dreamed.

Dreamed of the woman, tall and elegant, with thick braids of hair, and a face that had become his perfect image of any female he had ever met. Down long tunnels they marched, through halls with high arched ceilings, rough-cut by the bloodied hands of ten thousand slaves, their moans and groans and blood and piss and sweat soaked into the rock, a part of the chamber, a part of the mines – the mines Val loved so well.

The mines were not just Val's home, a place of residence, for Val was so committed to his job he never left the mine complex deep within the Karamakkos; no, to Val, who was a twentieth generation miner, just like his long line of ancestors before him… this was not just a home – the mines were in his blood, in his bones, in his soul. Never had he set foot in the cities above the mines. *Never*. Not for Val a stroll down the streets, a visit to a Church of Hate to relieve his soul of its sins; not for Val a night in an alehouse, or a whorehouse, although he had heard such pleasures were, well, *pleasurable*. Val had everything he needed *right here*, and after his sudden promotion to Slave Warden after the untimely death – murder – of Krakka, he was proud to say he had never left the mines. Why would he ever need to?

He had power. Wealth enough. And when the overlander slaves had been brought in, Lillith amongst them, he had found a sort of love.

She was perfect.

He remembered lying with her. Touching her soft smooth skin. Caressing her breasts. Even her trembling had brought an excitement to Val, for with her fear came more power to him; he was in control of this beautiful, gorgeous, voluptuous creature. She was his. He could do anything with her. And after long nights, even her complaints and anger had stopped. She'd attained a dead-eyed understanding of the way things were. And the way things were, was a world where Val was in complete control.

However, as events transpired, and with the interference of Skalg, First Cardinal, that crippled old hunchback, so Lillith had been taken away from him. *Taken away!*

O Skalg, you bastard, how I wish I could have just an hour with you in my torture room. I'd learn you a thing or two. You think you have pain now with you broken spine? Well, we all know about you, about your personal decadences, you're a fucking scandal within the church; there isn't a priest alive who doesn't know about your drinking, your drugs, your rapes, your murders... your legend goes well beyond the Five Havens, and not a single Harborym dwarf would shed a tear if I was to slice off your hunched back, layer by layer by layer, cutting you into slabs to find out what's inside, to find out what makes you tick, you warped and fucked-up feeble excuse for a dwarf...

Val's eyes flickered open. He allowed a deep breath to exhale.

He realised he'd become sexually aroused at thoughts of torturing Skalg.

"One day," he muttered, "one day," as they emerged onto a black granite platform and stopped.

He turned and surveyed the thirty battle-hardened, grim, scarred, battered dwarves. Not for Val new recruits. No. This mission had come from... a special place. A special person. One Val respected above all else. Yes. Even above Skalg, First Cardinal of the Church of Hate.

"This way," he said and the grim dwarves followed Val, dropping down into the cutting and, with weapons drawn, gleaming, headed into the smoky, obsidian gloom of the mine carriage network.

Deeper Underground

Beetrax shook himself, his body and mind stunned, trying to remember what the fuck had hit him.

Dragon beast splice thing.

Chamber?

Fire?

Talon... *burning...*

With a growl, Beetrax stood, trailing dust and debris, and rolled his head on tortured neck tendons. He glanced over at Lillith who was pale and shocked. Jael stood behind her, looking like he was going to puke. Beetrax glanced at Sakora: unconscious. Blood ran from nostrils and mouth. Maybe she was even dead. He felt an incredible raw rage well up from inside him. *How dare it! How dare this cunt kill them after all they'd fucking been through! Well, he, Beetrax the Axeman, he had something to say about it...*

He moved sideways, eyes fixed on the creature that was busy tearing at the scaffolding struts. More and more broke with heavy cracks and snaps, and the whole structure teetered again, making the flames roar higher. Talon was hanging on for his life. He'd lost his bow. His legs were kicking...

Beetrax grasped his axe.

Braced himself.

And screamed, "Come on, you ugly motherfucker, is that really all you've got?"

The creature turned, and its strange elongated face fixed on Beetrax, eyes locking onto him, its brow furrowing.

"You understand me?"

Its lips twisted, but no sound came out, only flames.

"What the *fuck* are you?"

With a wail more filled with pain and sadness than anger, it charged, taking the final supporting strut with it as the scaffold creaked and cracked, and almost in slow motion, collapsed, sending Talon tumbling into the heart of the raging flames...

It charged at Beetrax, who suddenly turned on the barrel, and his axe slammed out, puncturing the wood and iron struts. Again he hit, and again, until a sudden flood of oil gushed out onto the rocky ground before him. The creature came on, growling and snarling, as Beetrax's axe hit the second barrel, puncturing it, sending its black oil contents gushing out over the rocky floor. He turned and ran...

As Talon rose from the centre of the flames, bow in hand, face grim, and sighted down the shaft of an arrow with a flaming, flickering tip...

The arrow flashed, an orange streak across the chamber, and hit the gushing oil surrounding the creature.

There came a *whoosh* of screaming flames as the oil went up, and the beast was caught in the centre of an inferno, its feet and legs soaked, its body burning, its arms thrown up, muzzle lifting to the cavern roof as it wailed and screamed and gnashed its fangs, and fire burned and flames rolled and a thick, black smoke rolled up to fill the chamber with a dense cloud...

Talon leapt across the burning scaffold, patting at his flaming clothing in panic, and then sprinted to Lillith and Jael. Beetrax stood, shoulders braced, axe ready, watching the creature burn.

It fell slowly to its knees, flesh on fire, the scorched stink of burning meat twitching their nostrils and making them want to gag.

Fire roared. Glowed.

The beast writhed... dropping to its knees, voice keening, wailing, ululating a song of desolation to a god of engineered flesh, a demon of the Equiem, who did not care, would never care, because the Old Gods despised everything living in the world of men.

Gradually, the flames died down, the oil burning out, except for a few pools on the scorched rock.

Beetrax strode across to the crumbled, keening creature, and stared down with his hard face, and his hard eyes, and yet couldn't help feel some sympathy for the poor, burned, fucked-up mess.

Talon had helped Sakora to her feet, and Dake had only just recovered, and they moved to Beetrax.

"It's still not dead," said Talon, breathless, face a little scorched in places.

"I can see that, lad."

"Well... shouldn't we kill it?"

Beetrax stared at Talon hard. "It tried to burn you alive, lad."

Lillith touched Beetrax's arm. "Please. End its life. Show some mercy, Trax. Please."

"I agree," breathed Dake, holding his bleeding nose.

Beetrax nodded. "Stand back, then."

Like a man about to chop a huge tree trunk, he stepped back, braced himself, and took a mighty swing. His axe whined, and thudded home. The creature's keening raised in pitch. Beetrax cursed, wiggling his trapped axe free. He took another swing, and another, each time the dying creature's wail of pain increasing, and raising the hackles on all their arms and necks.

"Why won't you die, you fucker?" mumbled Beetrax, taking another seven, eight, nine swings. Until, finally, there came a *crack* and the head finally detached from the body. Fire blossomed out, a sudden heat blast that sent Beetrax skipping back, and then the creature seemed to fold in on itself, and crumble down, and inwards, into scaffolds of ash.

Beetrax gave Lillith a haunted look. "You know what I've

learned about Equiem magick?" he said, his voice hoarse, cracking, as if he might cry at any moment.

"What's that, my love?"

"You magickers can keep it," he said, softly, and turned, and walked away.

It was later.

Much later.

Sakora walked through the gloom, and although she normally spent her life without fear – her decades of training, of suffering, of hardship, of purity, after her hardcore upbringing in the art of the Kaaleesh had made her brave and yet wary – things were now getting too much. She was wary of their predicament. Wary of this foolhardy mission they had embarked upon, and the terrifying monsters that seemed to lurk down in these ancient, twisted halls. She was wary of every single dark corridor, black tunnel, junction, hall and intersection. Sakora hated weapons of violence, indeed, hated violence, and yet her life seemed to be a spiral which went down and down and down... a spiral which had started with her husband, Raka.

The bastard.

She could not even fully quantify her hate. She hated him so much, she could not bring herself to utter his name. To picture his face in her mind made her blood immediately boil. To think of his hands on her... touching her flesh... she shuddered. It made her skin crawl. And she was still confused as to how it had all gone wrong, until she thought about it *very carefully*. And she realised. It was complacency. And boredom. And a realisation that he *did not want her*. He did not want her one fucking bit. It was a one-sided relationship. It was a farce, viewed from the outside as a perfect marriage, but inside, internally, she was boiling, she was breaking down, she was crumbling like a chalk cliff into a violent sea.

But now, several years down the line, Sakora was free. Free of his twisted machinations.

It had taken some gentle persuasion.

One day, he turned up with a cart, smashed his way into her home – which had been *their* home, until he left – and started helping himself to her things. She'd arrived as he was rifling through her underwear drawer, and he'd grinned at her, and it was that grin that sent her over the edge.

Raka should have known better. He knew her history, or so he thought. It was just his base stupidity that allowed him to formulate a plan that meant *ripping her off*. Not that she cared about material possessions – not at all. To Sakora, everything of importance was internal. Flesh and mind and soul. Everything else, all real world-possessions, they were just gravy.

But there was *concept*.

And there was *honour*.

And there was *respect*.

Raka was showing her no respect, and despite him being a big man, and even a modest champion in the Fighting Pits, she decided it was about time he learnt to respect her properly. With care.

"You are in my things," she said, voice quiet.

"Fuck off!"

"I told you not to come to this house again."

"Fuck off, you bitch! I'm taking what I want. I'm taking what's owed to me. I have a new woman now, one who's not so into your spiritual kind of shit, one who I actually *want* to fuck. Not like you. Boring little Sakora. You're not worth the hassle, with your fucking sermons and your healthy living and your meditation. What a boring *cunt*."

Sakora moved fast, hand striking an uppercut to his chin that sent him staggering backwards, tripping over a stool and banging his head on the wall. The underwear he'd been holding landed on his face, lace covering his eyes. He looked quite ridiculous.

"I suggest you stay down, Raka," she said. And smiled at him.

His face turned red, and rage flooded him. He scrambled

to his feet. "Oh you've done it now," he growled. "You want to play big boys' games? You want to come play with daddy? Come on then. If the gloves are off, then the gloves are off."

He charged at her, his bulk terrifying, dwarfing the slim and gently proportioned woman. His fist hummed past her ear, and she twitched, knee coming up to block, as his boot stamped down to break her knee. Then she frowned. That just wasn't *nice*. That was a dirty pit-fighting trick. Her left elbow struck his jaw, and as he went down again, diagonally, her arm came up, fist in the air, and the tip of her elbow slammed down vertically on the top of his head.

He hit the ground hard, and lay there for a while. An elbow strike to the skull was like being hit by a helve. Or it was when Sakora delivered it.

Sakora smiled internally, and took several steps back, waiting for what she knew would follow.

Groggily, he climbed to his knees, and shot her a look so bad, if looks could kill, she'd be in pieces in a bucket.

"I suggest you leave," said Sakora, knowing he wouldn't.

"I suggest I fuck you," he growled, with an evil glint in his eye, and getting to his feet, he charged her, hoping to smother her with his bulk.

Sakora skipped back, legs snapping out, each blow a connection from her shin to his knees and thighs. He howled, but still came on, grappling for her. Sakora ducked and slipped right, slapping a right hook to his jaw, then leaping onto his back, high up, her arm coming up again and tip of her elbow slamming down on his skull, three, four, five times. She rode him to the ground, and he was groaning. She rolled him onto his back, grunting a little for he was a heavy son of a bitch, and then she leapt atop him, straddling him, grinning down.

His eyes fluttered open.

"You bitch," he said

"You bastard," she said.

"I'm going to fucking break you."

"Like this?"

She slammed her hand down, fingers straight, hand like a blade, straight into his septum. Blood sprayed out and his nose broke with a cracking splinter.

His fist whirred past her, then a second punch, which she met square on with her own, what appeared small and delicate, fist. There came a splintering of bone as she crushed two of his knuckles.

He cradled his hand, tears in his eyes.

"I have a suggestion," she said.

He groaned, unable to reply.

"Why don't you pick yourself up, or even just *crawl*, and get out of my house. Never come back. Never contact me again. And we'll both be happy people. I don't want to hear your voice, and I certainly don't want to see your face."

"Urrhhhh…"

She punched him in the cheekbone. Just a light slap. To get his attention.

"Do we have an agreement?"

"Yerrrrhhhhh…"

Sakora stood, fluidly, and considered stomping on him. But she was Kaaleesh, which trained restraint. Kaaleesh was not the art of aggression, but the art of self-defence, the art of channelling energies, of honour, of doing the right thing.

Raka crawled to the door. Sakora followed.

He managed to make it to his feet, and staggered outside to where his cart waited, hitched to a patient donkey.

Sakora smiled.

"Goodbye, Raka," she said, and was half closing the broken, skewed, smashed door when he screamed, and charged back down the short path wielding a mace. It was an ugly-looking weapon, of black and silver steel, the haft about a foot long, the head circular but containing tiny plates of sharpened steel, like mini axe blades. Raka swung for her, and she stepped out into the small garden, skipping sideways as a second blow threatened to crush her skull. One blow from that mace, and Sakora would be dead, skull caved in. Blood and brains leaking to the stone chippings.

"Come on, bitch," he said, eyes glowing. "Let's finish this."

"You really want to?" Her voice was perfectly calm. She lifted her chin a little, and eyed the man she once thought she had loved. *I cannot believe I had such emotion for him*, she thought. *I cannot believe I thought I loved him. Did I? I must have done. But now, he is nothing but a primal insect. I am happy for him to die. I happy for him to be crushed underfoot.*

He charged again, and the mace whirred past her head. She ducked and twisted away, spinning low, not seeking to land a blow – not yet – but instead, weighing up his technique, his tactics, *studying* him. It was part of the art of Kaaleesh. After all, it was an art, not just brutal combat.

"Come on!" he screamed, and she saw the red flush of anger, and this was good. With anger came stupidity. With anger, came foolishness. With anger, came mistakes that got you dead.

He charged a third time, and the mace slashed in a low horizontal arc. Again Sakora danced back, the mace a thumb's breadth from her abdomen, but this time, as Raka came past, she struck him on the neck. He staggered, flailing low, dropping the mace and ploughing his face into the soil.

He groaned, and did not move.

He could not. Sakora had broken his neck.

She moved, and crouched down beside him. "Consider this the end of our marriage," she said, and grinned. His eyes swivelled up and fixed on her. He tried to snarl, but barely managed to curl his lips.

"I'll fucking kill you," he managed.

"I'll be waiting," she said.

Three months later, Raka was dead. He'd received his own dagger in the eye during a tavern argument as he sat in his chair, next to his walking sticks. Sakora felt no sorrow. Only a relief that washed through her like gallons of water, cleansing her system, cleansing her soul, washing her in purity.

•••

The tunnels seemed to go on forever, stinking of oil and grease. Several times the group heard large numbers of dwarves rushing past, be they miners or soldiers, they did not know, and they crouched down in the darkness, or used rocks or abandoned carriages or even the huge chains themselves as cover. They feared another onslaught from a weird, engineered beast. However… they were lucky. There were no monsters. And every dwarf seemed to be preoccupied with something – probably the very real fact that the three dragons from The Dragon Engine had escaped, and the primary source of power in the Five Havens had been, effectively, severed.

"This is shit," muttered Beetrax, as they crouched once again, hiding behind wood and iron wheels. "This is no way to live. Lillith, for the love of the Holy Mother, let's make good our escape *now* whilst we still can."

"We have to think of the bigger picture," soothed Lillith.

"Yes, like our own fucking lives!" snapped Beetrax. "You remember that *fuck* we had to deal with back there? That's not *normal*, Lillith. It ain't natural. It's bad magick. It's dark, and twisted… just *wrong*."

Lillith looked around, at the pale faces of her companions. And she realised – they were all deeply frightened. They had been through a terrible ordeal during these last few months, and now, with her mission of… honour… Lillith was extending it.

"You need to trust me," said Lillith.

"We trust you, but we want to live," said Talon, his voice quiet, eyes narrowed.

"This does feel like a mission of madness," acknowledged Sakora.

"I still believe in you," said Jael, his voice gentle.

"You shut your fucking hole, lad, lest I fill it with my fucking boot," snapped Beetrax.

"You leave the lad, let him be," said Lillith. "He's fragile."

"Fragile? Fragile! I'll fucking give him fragile when I strangle the little cunt."

"What did you expect him to do?" hissed Lillith, suddenly, a rage coming upon her, making Beetrax rock backwards. "You expect him to take the force and skill of a seasoned torturer? You think you could have endured that at his tender age? He did what he could to survive. We all suffered down there, Trax, all of us, in our own different ways. So you back off, I'm warning you, because Jael here will still surprise us, I promise you."

Beetrax clenched his jaw, ground his teeth together, and frowned, but cut off his curt words. He remembered previous arguments with Lillith. He'd lost every single one.

"I'm sorry," said Jael, voice wavering. He half-looked at Beetrax, not daring to meet the huge axeman's stern gaze. "I'm really, really sorry. I never meant to betray you all. That Krakka, he was a brute. He terrified me."

"And I don't?" growled Beetrax.

"Lillith's right, leave the lad alone," snapped Dake. "Who knows what we would have done if we were his age!"

"I wouldn't have fucking backstabbed my friends, that's for sure," said Beetrax.

"Yes, well, we're not all big, tough, terrifying axemen like you, are we?" said Dake, with a sweet sardonic smile in the gloom.

"Much as this conversation is fascinating," observed Talon, his voice dry and biting, "I do fear it may draw attention to our predicament if you *don't keep your fucking voices down!*"

"You there! Come out of the shadows!"

Talon scowled at Beetrax, as if to say, *see you big fat fucker, I told you so.*

"I've hurt my leg, I can't move!" wailed Beetrax suddenly, in his best harsh dwarf voice.

"Hurt my leg?" mouthed Talon. "Are you a village idiot?"

Three hefty dwarves dropped down into the cutting, and moved towards the carriages behind which the heroes crept.

"I didn't see *you* come up with something better," scowled Beetrax.

"Who's there? Show yourselves! We hear more than one voice!"

A shaft whistled from the gloom, hitting the lead dwarf between the eyes, point smashing through his skull and mashing the brain within. He stood, stunned, before physics caught up with him, blood trickled down his forehead, and he toppled backwards in a tangle of limbs and armour.

The other two drew swords, and charged, screaming ancient dwarven war cries. Beetrax took the first, stepping out of the darkness and chopping his head off with an economic short slam of his axe. Dake took the second on the point of his sword, forearm warding off a blow, his blade pushing and twisting between plates of leather armour to slice the heart within.

Silence fell, except for a bubbling sound from one of the corpses.

A few seconds passed.

They waited in the darkness, to see if any other rogue dwarves had heard the short melee.

"See?" snapped Talon, quietly. "Voices to a minimum!"

"We need to find somewhere to rest," said Lillith.

"Why?" said Dake.

"I... I need to show you something," she said.

It was an hour later, in a small side-alcove halfway along a deep tunnel. It had a table and rough wooden chairs, maybe a refuge for train engineers, or maybe just dwarves caught out in the open cuttings. Whatever, it was deserted, and Lillith bid them all sit in a circle.

"Why?" said Beetrax.

"I wish to enlighten you," she said.

"Why?" said Beetrax.

"Because I have lost you all, I think, in different ways. You are despondent, you do not believe in what we are doing. I need to show you what I saw. I need to open your minds and make you realise... these dragons, they are not only three. The threat is much, much bigger than anybody could possibly imagine."

They sat in a circle, and joined hands as Lillith bid.

"Close your eyes."

They did so.

"Breath slowly, to my count, in through your nose, out through your mouth."

She started to count, and the group, intrigued now, did as she bid.

And then... then they were falling through their own minds, through a rush of blinding white, and they were falling through the sky high above the world, and far below lay tiny distant forests, rivers, rolling hills, mountains. The land of Vagandrak. There were villages and towns and cities. There were streams and lakes. To the south was the ocean, and over the high mountain peaks beyond the Pass of Splintered Bones, beyond the vast snaking walls of Desekra Fortress, lay the amber rolling dunes of the desert.

And they spun, and they were all as one, and they were flying, high above the world.

"Relax," came Lillith's soothing voice, as vertigo gripped them.

And their gaze shifted, altered, and around them were dragons, ten dragons, a hundred dragons, a *thousand* of the great wyrms, all black and scaled and spiked, their long, almost equine faces savage and noble and terrifying. They flew in formation, a perfect V with one huge, magnificent beast at the tip. This was the queen.

Below, fires started to blossom. Villages burst into flames, houses smashed and burned and destroyed. Beyond, cities were being torn apart. Houses and civic buildings, churches and towers, all broken to the cobbles, roofs torched, black smoke rolling up into the sky.

And then the scene accelerated in the blink of an eye, and they were flying towards the mountains, rearing high over snowy peaks, then *slam* into the eye of a needle, a long dark tunnel leading down, impossibly *down*, so tight they all screamed as they believed they would crash and crumble and disintegrate. Down, twisting, turning, wings tight behind her back as the dragon suddenly entered a vast, open cavern, a cavern as big as a city, sporting huge stalactites and stalagmites, millions of years old. Jagged teeth spread across the floor and roof alike, making the cavern appear as some huge, vast mouth, sporting a million teeth and waiting to chomp down on the tiny insects who dared invade this huge giant.

They fell, and at the last moment levelled across a great dark lake. It was ink-black, and still like glass. Below, they could see the reflection of their own image – and they could see a dragon, huge and spiked and scaled and terrifying. Wings slapped a *boom*, and ripples pounded across the surface creating huge waves. They... *she*... flew beyond the lake, and into another wide tunnel – so wide, it could have taken a thousand dragons side by side, and it flowed *down* deep into the bowels of the Karamakkos, deep below even what the dwarves had achieved, down, towards *Wyrmblood...*

Beetrax, Dake, Sakora, Talon, Jael, they were dizzy with speed and power and a soaring sense of vastness.

How could something be so big?

And then they emerged, and below them sat Wyrmblood, and the city *shone*.

A world spread out before their eyes. It wasn't just a city, but an underground world, lit by a soft golden light. There were massive square buildings, pyramids, towers with intricate designs, all fashioned from silver, and gold, a vast world of precious metals. There were towers of bronze, arches of silver, glittering roads of golden cobbles weaving through the vast, empty place. There were palaces fashioned from precious stones, which shimmered in different, hazy hues. There was a river, cutting the huge city in two. It flowed with a sluggish demeanour. It was a river of molten platinum.

There were towers of pure diamond, bridges of glowing ruby, each brick a gem bigger than a man's fist. There were huge churches and halls and palaces, each one fashioned from precious metals, from gemstones, from what humans would consider *riches* but the denizens of Wyrmblood had used as everyday building materials.

And they flowed down, suddenly, sinking below this unbelievable show of wealth, down through golden cobbles, down through the river of platinum, down, to a cool dark place, a secret place never before witnessed by human eyes, by dwarf eyes, by any eyes other than the royalty of the Blood Dragon Empire.

And, stretching away to all sides, was a vast chamber.

The floor was covered by a thousand eggs... *ten* thousand eggs.

Dragon eggs.

Waiting to hatch.

Waiting to populate the Empire once again.

Beetrax's eyes snapped open and he gave a short, sharp bark. "What the *fuck*," he muttered, and realised he was holding Dake's hand. He shook it free, as if he'd been holding the diseased paw of a leper.

Uneasily, they looked around.

"They were dragon eggs?" said Talon, gently.

"Yes." Lillith nodded. She was incredibly sombre.

"And they are going to hatch? Thousands and thousands of them?" whispered Sakora.

"Yes," said Lillith.

"What will make them hatch? What's the trigger?" Dake scratched his chin, frowning. "I was under the impression those imprisoned dragons had been slaves to the Harborym for thousands of years. So why didn't the eggs hatch then?"

"I don't know," said Lillith. "But I can... *feel, sense,* that now the dragons are awake, once their initial fury and acts of revenge are complete, they will come back. To their city. To Wyrmblood. And once there are thousands of them, we will never be able to halt their onslaught."

"What are the dwarves doing about it?" rumbled Beetrax.

Lillith shrugged. "Nothing. Or maybe they don't even know. I think they discovered Wyrmblood, and released the imprisoned minds of the dragons, allowing them to escape from the Dragon Engine. By accident, of course. Or maybe by design."

"So let me get this right," snapped Beetrax. "You want us to go down through that city of treasure, find the eggs, and destroy them before the dragons come back and hatch them? Or the world will be overrun by thousands of dragons, and we'll be, like, dragon-fucked?"

"That's about it," said Lillith.

Beetrax frowned. "But we can, like, fill our pockets en route, so to speak?"

"Yes. If that's what you want, Trax."

Beetrax scratched his beard. "And, er, like, if I was to find these fabled and *very expensive* Dragon Head jewels, then they'd be mine?" He looked around. "*Ours.* To keep."

"Yes," nodded Lillith. "And as I said, they have incredible healing properties." She very carefully *did not* look at Dake, who was pale, eyes drooping, body-language that of a warrior in defeat.

"Well, I'm fucking in," growled Beetrax. "If there's one thing I'll risk my life for, not counting saving my friends of course, it's a backpack full of loot." He grinned, showing a cracked tooth.

Lillith looked around the group. Friends. Heroes. Men and women she would fight for. Men and women she would die for. Comrades she'd known for years, whom she trusted with every atom of her life, every breath, every fibre of her soul.

"Let's go to work," she said, with a smile.

The Mountain

Skalg paused, panting, tears running down his cheeks, snot dangling from his nostrils, his face twisted in agony, his limbs trembling, his fingernails bleeding, and his whole frame shaking as if he were producing great racking sobs at the funeral of his mother. He looked up, up the steep rocky slope ahead of him. It was sheer and violent, jagged and uneven, black, speared by mineral lodes of blood red which made the whole thing look like a series of open wounds in a burned corpse.

Skalg let out a sob, eyes blinking away more tears of pain and frustration, for this was frustrating, the most frustrating thing he'd ever been through since that fateful day when the mine collapsed and buried him alive and broke his spine, and he'd lain there, weeping, ruminating about his pointless existence and his lack of money or power or importance, and how now he'd die under the mountain, unloved and nameless and forgotten. For *the mountain gives, and the mountain takes away*. The mountain had taken away his mobility, but by crippling him, it had given him a new hate, a fresh determination to crawl his way to the top of the pile of cockroaches called *The Church of Hate* and tread on every face that looked up in awe at his violent ascent. But here, and now, Skalg had had his power and influence *removed*. His wealth meant nothing in this place of cool air and jagged mountain rock. And he gritted his teeth, his eyes burned bright and he pushed himself onwards.

No secondhand god is going to beat me, he thought.

Ahead, he glimpsed the silver-skinned boy. A peal of childish laughter reverberated down the mountainside, down the rocky spine on which Skalg clung like a limpet waiting for the waves to crash down.

I will not stop.

I will not give in.

I am my own master, now.

On he climbed, waddling slowly upwards, his powerful bleeding fingers clutching at rocks and ridges, hauling himself up, each pull and tug sending spears of pain not just down his twisted spine, but through his trembling arms, his agonised fingers, pounding his knees with sledgehammers of effort, grinding his hips like mashed meat in a butcher's sausage machine.

He stopped to rest, slumping down, then rolling onto his back on the slope. He wedged his boots against a lip of rock, and lay, crooked and disjointed, like a broken corpse. More laughter echoed down from the rocks above. Skalg scowled, fuelled even more by anger and hate than ever before.

With the back of one swarthy hand he wiped sweat from his brow, and he could taste salt in his beard. His mouth was parched, and he would have happily begged on his knees for just a sip of water, but decided he would not.

What, call to that silver worm Mokasta for help? I'd rather die.

His eyes surveyed the plain below. He had made some considerable height, and the land was distant, a platter of black surrounded by jagged teeth. The whole scene appeared as some huge mouth out of which he was making an escape. Skalg gave a wry smile. It was a fitting simile.

Now, he could glimpse beyond several of the low mountains. Far off in the distance he could determine greenery: rolling hills, a forest, a lake. Suddenly, this lifted his heart, for surely it was a nirvana to which he now climbed? Yes, he was suffering now, but his ultimate objective was a place of peace and beauty. It elevated him a little, and he turned, and went to rise but suddenly lost his footing, boot scraping, and he started to slide down the rocky slope, arms flailing, sharp stones digging into his limbs and his twisted back. He bounced, and slid, and rolled, until he slammed with jarring force into a luckily placed boulder – lucky for Skalg, for if the boulder had not been so positioned, he would have sailed out over an abyss and fallen to a bone-crushing death far below, probably to a soundtrack of Mokasta's sonorous laughter.

Skalg lay there, panting, thanking the Great Dwarf Lords for his good fortune. And then he remembered it was *because of* the Great Dwarf Lords he was in this predicament! And so he cursed them instead, vehemently, as pain rioted through his entire body and he wept, tears coursing down his cheeks, as above him, more laughter echoed.

After a considerable time, as his body grew stiff with chill, Skalg finally roused himself.

Fuck you, he thought.

Fuck you all.

Fuck the world.

I'll fucking show you.

I'll not be broken.

I will fucking show you what a fractured cripple can do, you shower of horse shits!

Skalg gritted his teeth, and ignoring the pain, and the cold which seeped through his bones, he pushed himself up, and he looked up the mountain as a breeze murmured across him, and without any further words, moans, grumblings or whimpers, Skalg, First Cardinal of the Church of Hate, began to climb.

Seconds. Minutes. Hours. Days. Skalg did not comprehend how long it took him. There was no passing of day or night here, but then Skalg was used to that, living under the mountain. And as he climbed, and forced himself ever onwards, he kept relaying the same mantra, over and over and over and over: *the mountain gives, and the mountain takes away*. But in Skalg's experience, the mountain gave to those who worked fucking hard for it.

There had been a famous playwright, not that the Harborym Dwarves were big on playwrights or the theatre in general – give a dwarf an ale and pig slab, and he was as happy as a mine donkey when the harness is removed. However, in some more *cultured circles* there had grown an interest in what the dwarves called *The Less Coarse Arts*, and without that umbrella of more mild entertainments than axe throwing and drinking to be sick, came literature, and study, and artistry, and the theatre. Admittedly, many early performances had simply aped the reality of life under the mountain: quaffing, mining, more quaffing. But as the art of the stage developed, so it became more sophisticated. Now, Skalg was reminded of a rather pithy orator and ink scribe, known as Demakkos de Shakkos, who had quipped the most amazing statement (to Skalg's mind) the First Cardinal had ever heard.

Demakkos de Shakkos?

Yes?

You are doing extremely well for yourself!

Why, thank you.

But tell me… aren't you incredibly lucky to have got where you are?

Yes. But the funny things is… the harder I work, the fucking luckier I get.

And now, Skalg realised, the harder he worked, the harder he climbed, the luckier he would get. Because these were the Great Dwarf Lords. The fucking *gods*. And they were testing him. So fuck pain. Fuck anguish. Fuck fear. Fuck everything. Because Skalg wanted to get to the top of that mountain. Skalg wanted to know what was on offer. What the deal was. What was in it *for him*.

Time had no meaning. After pain, after more torture, Skalg slumped exhausted to a rock. He teetered on the brink of unconsciousness. And he remembered. *Remembered* Anya. From before the mine collapse. When life had been

simple. When life had been *normal*. And now, on that
mountainside, with a cool breeze playing across his tortured
flesh, with sweat stinging his eyes, and salt in his beard,
Skalg thought back to Anya, and how they'd met, and how
everything had seemed perfect. But things can quickly
change. Skalg thought he'd been in love, but what is love?
Skalg was poor and lonely and flattered. But it didn't take
long – didn't take long for Anya to show her true colours.
He still remembered, standing there as she screamed at him,
red face with fury, wagging her finger, spittle flying from
her lips. She'd grabbed his hand, tried to force him to hit her
but he'd shied back, pulled away. *I'm not like that,* he said.
And back then, he wasn't. Back then, he'd been...

Skalg smiled, lying on that mountain rock.

Skalg had been *kind*, one day.

Loving, and honest, and kind. As his parents brought
him up to be.

His life with Anya got worse, went from psychopathic
explosion to psychopathic explosion. And then his mother
died. Skalg fell into a well of sleep. And he remembered.
And he dreamed.

*Watching her lying in bed. Weight had fallen from her. Her skin was
grey. She was no longer the stocky, powerful dwarf of his childhood.
No. She had shrunk, and withered, muscles wasting away.*

"I love you," he said, looking into her sad, watery eyes.

*"I know, son," she said, and patted his hand as if he were a little
boy again. Which to her maybe he was. Maybe he'd always been.*

*"I love you so much," he murmured, tears falling down through
his beard, and pattering like raindrops on the tiles.*

*A long moment of silence. Skalg wanted to climb inside her, find
the evil cancers, tear them out with his bare hands, with his fucking
teeth. But that would not happen. Could not happen. For it was an
impossibility, and he just had to accept that she was (shhh)*

...dying.

*He watched her. Watched her rasping breathing. Her eyes had
closed once more, and every now and again her entire body would*

tense, as if a ripple of intense pain was passing through her, like a wave rolling up a jagged shore, like razor blades in her bloodstream.

Suddenly, she jumped, and Skalg jumped. Her hands clenched his, and although the muscles had dropped from her, as if she'd melted in a terrible furnace, her grip was so powerful it made Skalg gasp and cringe.

"Where's Renyak?"

Skalg's eyes narrowed, and he wanted to say, "Renyak knows you're dying, mother, he's known for the past four weeks; but Renyak is a cunt, and not even thought to visit his old dying mum. That is what your eldest son is like – filled with bitterness and jealousy, filled with a fucking pettiness so vast it cannot bridge itself to come and see you, to visit the woman who nurtured him as a babe, suckling him at her breast, wiping his shitty arse, teaching him right and wrong, feeding him, nurturing him, loving him until he could go out into the world and stand on his own two feet. Oh no. Renyak is selfish and petty beyond all fucking belief. Five times I've told him of you lying here, during your final days, your final hours, but he cannot see past his own... immaturity."

Skalg took a deep breath. He bit his tongue. He bit back the acid bile. He clenched his fist. He narrowed his eyes. And he forced himself to say, "Renyak is on his way. He loves you. He will be here."

Skalg's mothered settled back with a small smile, and her breathing was harsh, fast, a hunted deer, a fish without water, lying beside the pond, stranded, flapping, unable to do anything but flap, and gasp, and die.

A blur. Snapshots.

And it was over.

She lay, rigid, face contorted in pain.

At that moment Skalg realised an important fact of life: there is no nobility in death. There is no honour. No glory. There are no weeping fucking angels. There is just pain, and misery, a great sense that the universe is unfair, that the gods mock us, and there is certainly no Heaven.

Funeral.

Renyak.

The Wake.

"You fucking cunt!"

Brawling with him between the tables, punches flying, Skalg kicking him repeatedly in the face, kicking out his teeth, crushing his nose until blood ran like fucking Xashak Red.

Long hours.

Sleeping.

Wishing he was dead, tears like molten metal scorching his cheeks.

It was the early days with Anya. She was there to help him. There to take control. There to put a cold compress on his blackened eyes and his swollen cheeks and knuckles. And slowly, Skalg had come back to the world of the living. A little more bitter. A little more cynical. But with Anya by his side, making him solid, eternal; a rock to which he could cling. Until, after all the arguments, he realised.

Realised what she wanted.

His mother's money.

The. Fucking. Money.

Skalg's mother had not been wealthy, but she'd saved studiously for years. Her money, much of it in small gold pieces and diamonds, so beloved of the Harborym, had been divided between Renyak and Skalg equally. Because that was fair. Even though Renyak was a sulky toddler, an adult with a child's perspective. "She preferred you to me. You were her favourite. That's why I never visited her when she was dying. I was cast aside. She loved you more than she loved me." Bang. Fist in jaw.

But Anya, Anya was better, more intelligent, more sneaky. A real snake-in-the-grass. Waiting for her moment. To rear up and bite… or at least, fill a small leather satchel with Skalg's mother's money, and leave him. There was a note on the table.

I took the money. Because it's mine.
After all the support I gave you.
After all I had to put up with.
You owe it to me.

A

•••

Skalg found Anya three days later, half drunk and sat on a stone mason's lap. She was giggling and buying everybody drinks. Skalg staggered in, eyes wild from exhaustion and filled with a primal hate.

Their eyes met across The Dragon's Fire Tavern, and the smile fell from her face. Skalg stalked over to her, and spat on the stone flags.

"You fucking bitch. You are beyond contempt. You bided your time, waited for my mother to die, and then took her money for yourself. You called my family vultures for what they did, but look at you, you fucking pathetic specimen of a dwarf; you are just like the others: a vulture, feeding off the remains of the dead."

A big fight ensued.

Skalg could not remember it.

He could only remember biting Anya's ear off.

The blood pouring out.

Her screams.

It was the moment Skalg had changed forever. It was that act, betrayed by his brother and his lover, over the death of his mother, that determined he would never play fair again. Everybody around him was fair game. He would use every ounce of cunning and strength and guile and backstabbing nastiness to get what he wanted, get where he wanted, and fuck anybody and everybody who stood in his way.

Because, it was only the mountain that gave, and the mountain that took away.

Everyone else could burn in the Chaos Halls.

Three days later, Skalg was trapped in a mine-collapse, screaming for his life.

After hours, days, what felt like fucking *years,* Skalg breached the final ridge, his bloodied hands clawing the rocks, and he rolled onto his back, and looked back at the vast vista before him. This dark black world rolled out, ominous and alien, and Skalg felt hot tears run down his cheeks, but this time he was congratulating himself; he'd done it, he'd surpassed insurmountable odds and achieved something even most able-bodied dwarves would have found impossible.

He looked at the view.

The world seemed broad and wide and harsh.

There came a cough.

Skalg looked to his left, tearing his gaze from the stunning view, to see three squat, powerful dwarves standing there on the rocky flat plateaux. They had grumpy faces, broad and flat; faces which appeared as if they'd been punched several hundred times. And with a start, Skalg realised...

These were the Great Dwarf Lords.

Not immortal, not gods, but flesh and blood, just like him.

They wore tarnished iron armour, black and battered, and carried a variety of ancient chipped weapons which had seen decades of better use. There was nothing to set them apart from *mortals*. Except, maybe, their eyes. Their eyes were older than the mines, dark and glinting like devil's diamonds.

Slowly, Skalg pushed himself into a seated position and surveyed his three... tormentors. And he smiled.

"It is an honour to meet you, finally, O my gods," he said, and bowed his head, affecting a submissive posture.

He heard a snort. And the stamp of a boot.

"Get up."

"You took your fucking time!"

"We've been waiting fucking aeons!"

"Looks like you crawled up the fucking mountain on your fucking face!"

Skalg smiled internally, and cursed them, but rolled over, and got to his knees, and then gradually, to his feet. He surveyed his lords, his masters, his gods. Those sublime creatures who, as it was enshrined in the *Scriptures of Hate*, had transcended flesh using dark magick after imprisoning the great wyrms to do their bidding. After creating... the Five Havens. After constructing the Dragon Engine.

Skalg took a deep breath.

"I am your slave," he said.

"We know," said one.

"You bastard," said another.

"You think we've nothing better to do?"

"But you waited," said Skalg, calmly, intuition kicking in. "You want me."

"In the absence of any other better hero material, yes, we need you."

And there was that word. And Skalg breathed slowly, calming himself.

Need.

"What can I do for you, O Great Dwarf Lords?" said Skalg, and his lips smiled, just a little. Pain flooded through him, his fingernails were broken, he had two snapped fingers, a broken rib, a twisted ankle, a bump the size of an egg on his forehead, and to make matters perfect, needles of agony jabbed down his spine. It was like somebody had drilled into his back, and was pouring liquid iron into him. The molten fluid spread slowly, like a web, throughout his shoulders and back and spine and arse. And yet here he was, expected to smile and put up with it and that's all anybody ever expected of him. To act like he wasn't in fucking agony all the time because *that made them feel comfortable* and if they knew he was in pain, then *they were uncomfortable.* Dwarves. The way their minds worked. It was fucked up. Selfish, and fucked up.

"We have a mission for you."

"I thought so," said Skalg, coolly.

"You seem distant! What's the matter, mortal? Cower before our omniscient deadly gaze!"

Skalg bit back various sarcastic comments that leapt to mind, and bowed lower. "What can I do for you, O Great Dwarf Lords?"

"You have released the dragons! The wyrms!"

"Me, Lords?"

"Not you specifically, no, but your *kind.*"

"*Our* kind, surely?"

"Yes. Yes yes. Well, they must be stopped. Or destroyed.

Or re-imprisoned!"

Skalg took a deep breath. "Er. Can you not come and do it?" he said, without any irony.

"We have transcended," said one.

"We are in a different level."

"We are on another plain."

"So it's not your problem?" said Skalg, with a smirk.

The voice built up, like a hand-turned generator gathering speed. When the blast came, Skalg thought he was ready for it, but he wasn't. It was like nothing he had ever heard or seen or smelt or experienced...

"OF COURSE IT'S OUR FUCKING PROBLEM YOU TINY FUCKING MAGGOT!" came the scream. It blasted into and *through* Skalg, making his hair and beard stream backwards, and for long moments his smugness and sense of gentle superiority were dissipated as he realised the Great Dwarf Lords did indeed have Power.

There was a long silence.

A cold wind blew.

Skalg's nostrils twitched. He imagined he could distinguish the scent of carrion on a long distant battlefield.

"I chose an eternity of this," he said.

"I will suffer the consequences of this," he said.

"Lead me to the source of your despair."

Skalg stared at the Great Dwarf Lords. And they stared back.

"We have a way forward," said one.

"You can help."

"You can be a saviour."

"And we will be forever in your debt."

Skalg considered this. "You will be in *my* debt?"

"Listen."

"Focus."

"Understand."

"You are crippled. Weak. Broken. Fucked up. A fucking maggot. A rat with a snapped spine. A cockroach with a crushed skull. You are a fucking nothing, Skalg, *First*

Cardinal. Yes, people look at you, and they smile, and they talk, and they talk about what a fucking disgrace you are, what a fucking pathetic specimen of a dwarf, and how can you possibly run the church when you are so ridiculously crippled. What can you offer with your broken body? After all, we are a race of *warriors*. With your kind, we leave you down in the mines to die."

"My kind?"

"The broken ones. The useless ones."

"You discriminate." Skalg's face showed no emotion. It was not a question.

"Yes."

"Why? Do you know how many years I have suffered? How many years I have fought? How many fucking years I have fought *cunts* like you to actually achieve something with my wounded life?"

Skalg was panting with exertion. And passion. And fury.

"Are you angry?"

"YES!"

"Then you will help bring the dragons under control?"

"Why?"

"Untold wealth, power, status. And we… can make the pain go away."

Skalg guffawed, spittle spraying from his furious mouth. He slapped his thighs. Spittle drooled from his lips. "Yes, right, the finest surgeons in the realm could not help me. I am fucked beyond belief. What can you fucking offer, you… you *false idols?*"

And then it happened.

The pain left him.

The pain left Skalg.

For twenty years he had been tortured.

For twenty years, he had been nothing but a suffering mess.

But now.

Now.

The pain disintegrated.

It fell away, like tears from a dying child's eyes.

And Skalg, well, Skalg felt purity flush through him.

He fell to his knees.

Tears streamed down his face.

"I do not believe it," he whispered.

"Believe it," said a Great Dwarf Lord.

"We control you. Like a puppet."

"And we can cure you, like a surgeon."

"Just do as we ask."

"Do as we command."

"Join with us."

"Taste immortality."

"How?" whimpered Skalg, overcome by a feeling of normality so pure he never thought to experience it again. It took him back decades. He was young again. Poor. Worthless. Invisible. Betrayed. But with new thoughts of lust and power and glory. But then, the terrible mine accident...

I was robbed.

No.

You were enlightened.

"We have a mission."

Skalg grimaced. "What do you want me to do? I will do anything you command, O Great Dwarf Lords."

One of them grinned. Then all three grinned. They were shimmering, as if seen through a massive heat haze. They shimmered. As if witnessed from a great distance.

"What would you have me do?"

Again, a long pause. Skalg could hear heavy breathing.

"You will infiltrate a dragon."

"Infiltrate? What the hell does that mean?"

"You will take over its mind."

Skalg frowned. "And do what?"

"You will kill the other dragons."

"You want me to *become* a dragon?"

"Yes."

Skalg considered this. "How?"

"We use the magick contained in the dragon heads."

"Is it safe?"

A laugh. A chuckle. A gurgle.

"You will become the most impressive physical specimen of any creature to ever commit murder across our fair world! You will be stronger than anything else in Vagandrak. You will impale, and slice, and burn your enemies. How can that not be the *safest* place to be?"

"I will *become a dragon*?" said Skalg, eyes wide, in awe.

"Yes."

"Tell me what to do," said Skalg, and his eyes were wide and bright and the concept of throwing off the shackles of his dwarf flesh, crippled for so long, a flesh prison in which his mind had been trapped. Now he would be free.

Yoon's Secret

The tall, elegant man paused in the middle of his speech, and smiled across the Grand Palace Hall to where Yoon was perched on his throne, hands on the rich, ornate, gold-trimmed arms of the throne, face impassive, like a wax mask, long, curly, oiled black hair glistening from the light of a thousand candles and various braziers which burned around the perimeter of the chamber. A hundred maids-in-waiting lingered around the edges of the room, some in extravagant ball gowns, silk glistening in the subdued glow, some naked and seated on cushions, watching the proceedings with drug-eyed lethargy, yet others wearing silken strands that attempted to be items of clothing.

"May I continue, Your Highness?"

"Continue, Duke Sargoth," drawled Yoon, settling back and lifting a heavily-ringed hand to his goblet. He drained half in one gulp, and the red wine stained his lips, standing out against the pale make-up which caked his face. He clicked his fingers, and a young naked lad ran over with a footstool. Yoon placed one silk slipper on the stool, and bade the young lad sit, where Yoon's free hand gently wound its way through the boy's golden curls.

"Well," said Sargoth, eyes alive with his pitch and the drugs which infused his bloodstream. "My engineers did a reconnaissance to the foothills of Zunder, and I think Your Highness would be mightily impressed with the minerals we found there. There were also traces of precious gems, buried deep under the volcanic rock. What I require from you, King Yoon, as I mentioned several months earlier, is not just patronage, but an investment. Give me... ten thousand in gold, and I guarantee within the year, I will triple the amount!"

Yoon considered this, and drained the rest of the wine from the goblet. He stood, and slowly descended the steps from the throne plinth, to stand on the marble tiles of the Grand Palace Hall.

"So," he said, shifting closer to Duke Sargoth, so much so it was almost as if he were gliding. "What you're telling me is you want ten thousand royal gold to finance some kind of dig, around the foothills of Zunder, where you are convinced there is a wealth of precious gems?"

"Yes, yes!" said Sargoth, his eyes shining.

"But I am confused."

"How so, Your Highness?"

"Well, you state you will return my investment threefold."

"Yes, Your Highness!" His face beamed.

"Why not tenfold? Or twenty?"

"Highness?"

"Why not make me a partner on a percentage basis?"

"Er, Highness?"

"Boy, you boy, yes *you*, you fucking imbecile."

"Yes, Highness?" squeaked a small boy in pink silks.

"Go hither. Get yonder silver tray and letters." Yoon flapped his hand.

The boy ran across the hall, returning with a silver tray. Upon it lay various letters in a variety of interesting envelopes. Many would be invitations to dinner parties with the wealthy and powerful, Yoon knew, and even more would be invitations to attend drug parties and orgies, and in these Yoon was more interested. But there was one letter Yoon was searching for specifically, and his ringed fingers sifted through the pile, pushing paper around until he found a stoic brown envelope of the terminally bureaucratic.

"Ahhh," he said.

Duke Sargoth blinked several times. The smile and eager, shining eyes had dropped now, disintegrated, to be replaced by a handkerchief-wringing posture of nervousness. King Yoon was known wide and free across Vagandrak as being a little... unstable. But despite his reported acts of decadence and apparent occasional insanity, he could have moments of lucidity and incredible intelligence. After surviving thirteen assassination attempts, many whilst high, it had to be observed that Yoon was nobody's fool, and took more precautions than was readily acknowledged.

Yoon plucked out the brown envelope.

It was studiously stamped, stencilled and waxed.

He took a long, delicate letter-opener of filigree silver, and proceeded to slice open the top of the envelope. Then from the dour brown object, he plucked a thin sheet of white paper, on which was a handwritten missive. Yoon tapped the letter opener against his bottom lip as he read, eyes travelling from line to line, and Duke Sargoth watched his king with an increasing sense of uneasiness.

What could I have done wrong?

What the HELL could I have done wrong?

Yoon continued to read. And then he stopped. And then, without moving his head, his eyes lifted to fix on Duke Sargoth.

It was not a pleasant look.

Yoon remained like that, until sweat started trickling down Sargoth's forehead, and his cheeks sang red like the breast of a robin.

"Your Highness?" he quavered, finally, unable to take any more tension.

"Duke Sargoth," purred King Yoon, and stood up straight, pushing back his shoulders. He started to speak, quickly, economically, words and sentences clipped as if prepping elite soldiers on a military mission. "You came to me three months ago, proclaiming your misfortune, your divorce, your children leaving you, your loss of monies, your bad business deals, your incurred debts. You specified you were about to go searching for precious gems around Zunder. You asked if I would be interested in investing if such a survey proved to be fortuitous for both parties."

"Yes, yes?" said Sargoth, wetting his lips.

"You then sent out engineers to test the aforementioned site. Is that not so?"

"Yes!"

"So did I, Duke Sargoth. So did I."

There was a pause.

"Oh," said Sargoth, and the wetness disappeared from his lips.

"I have here my engineer's report," smiled Yoon, and to any who knew him, or even any who knew *of* him, that should have been a very, very dangerous sign. Duke Sargoth did not know Yoon, and as such, did not take the hint to run.

"Oh," replied Sargoth, for a second time, frowning.

"Would you like to know what it says?" asked Yoon, never one to miss the opportunity of milking a fellow human's misery.

"Yes. Yes please."

"*My* engineers discovered a very rich lodestone of precious gems around the foothills of Zunder. And do you know how they found this? They excavated in exactly the same locations as *your* engineers. Which means you know what I'm about to tell you."

Sargoth almost choked. In the end, he could not reply. His throat was too parched with fear.

"*My* engineers discovered that for an investment of ten thousand coin, I would not recoup in multiples of three. Or even ten. Do you know how much money I *should* be receiving? Even as a *percentage* of what you would excavate?"

"I don't know," croaked Sargoth.

"Thousands," said Yoon, and any hint of a smile or humour had gone from his face. He turned, suddenly, and squared up to Duke Sargoth – who was actually quite a big man, and wearing sword and dagger at his belt. But Sargoth looked ill. He looked green. He looked like he was going to puke.

"No," said Sargoth. "I swear, I didn't know the extent! I don't know these things! My engineers must have... "

Without looking up, Yoon clicked his fingers again. Sweat danced beads of sweat along his upper lip. He was smiling. He was enjoying the spectacle. He was enjoying the situation. He was enjoying the *drama*.

The far doors to the Great Palace Hall burst open, and two guards, carrying gleaming razor-sharp pikes, marched an engineer down the marble tiles. His boots were half dragging. Blood stained his nostrils. He glanced up, and tried to scramble back, but a guard punched him in the stomach, folding him over, and he went limp, and was dragged towards his audience with King Yoon.

"This is Devander," said Yoon, smiling gently. "He was very cooperative. He told us about his report. He showed us his report. It had your signature of witness on it."

"Noo!" wailed Sargoth, and both his hands came up, pressing against his cheeks. "It's a lie! A fabrication! A plot by my enemies to discredit me!"

"No," said Yoon, moving closer to him. "It is a deceit, it is a conspiracy to rob your king of his rightful profit from an investment. How dare you, Duke Sargoth. I knew your father. We were friends... "

"Until you had him hanged," whimpered Sargoth.

"Acknowledged, until I had him hanged," said Yoon, without breaking stride, "but the fact still remains you *lied* to me. And, as I am appointed by the gods," he preened a little, running a hand through his oiled dark curls, "and in fact, I *am* a god, this is heresy. Blasphemy! So I condemn you to... "

"Yes?" squeaked Sargoth.

"Death!" said Yoon, and even as he spoke the word he was spinning, with the filigree letter opener in his closed fist.

It punched into Duke Sargoth's eye, driving deep into the brain beyond. Blood spurted, and Yoon cackled. And, still clutching the embedded knife, Yoon leapt aboard Sargoth's huge body on its collapse to the ground, riding him as he would a dying stag, and they crashed against the floor and Yoon started to scream, words almost incomprehensible but containing just enough clarity to be understood by the several hundred people present, *"You fucking bastard, thought you'd cheat me, eh? Thought you'd cheat the King of Vagandrak, O you fucking dirty scum, you backstabbing cunt, you motherfucking bitch cunt scumbag commissioning your own fucking report then planning on cheating your very own fucking KING out of monies due to him, well I know your sort, I know them!"* He twisted the makeshift murder weapon, ground it around in the eye-socket, then withdrew it with a *schlup*. He stared at the blood for a while. The corpse slowly deflated. Then with a sudden vicious movement, he stabbed the blade into the good eye socket. Blood welled up around the silver, pooling out over the dead face of Duke Sargoth, flowing down in tiny red rivulets. Yoon tugged out the blade, and stabbed again. And again. And again. He started to stab down violently, randomly, taking the blade by both hands and working himself into a frenzy as he stabbed and stabbed and stabbed, panting and spitting and grunting, blood splashing up over him, into his face and smearing his hands and arms and robes of state. After maybe two hundred blows, when the corpse of Duke Sargoth no longer had a face, just a concave platter of blood, bone and pulped brains, Yoon slumped to one side, lying alongside the corpse, cradling the dagger, and crooning softly, like a child who wants nothing more than sleep or his mother.

"I am surrounded by vagabonds," he said.

"I am surrounded by liars and cheats," he said.

"I am surrounded by the immoral."

Not one person in that chamber moved, or breathed, or made a sound. They'd frozen, watching in horror at the violent outburst of this, their king, their monarch, their leader, appointed by the gods and repeatedly stabbing his victim in the eyes, in the nose, in the face.

Distantly, a door opened. A military man marched in, boots stomping, sword held by his side, face grim above his dark armour. He was a broad man, powerful, and exuded not just confidence but a natural leadership, an intrinsic authority. This was Zandbar, Captain of the King's Guard, and he looked supremely pissed off.

"King Yoon!"

"Yes?"

"King Yoon, get up!"

A hush settled over the chamber. Nobody, *nobody* spoke to Yoon that way. Yoon giggled, then sat up. More blood had pooled out from the corpse and stained his robes, his arms, his legs, everything. Every part of him.

"King Yoon. Please. Compose yourself."

"What is it?" Yoon squinted, and giggled again. "Zandbar! Is that you? Help me up, man."

Zandbar reached down, and in distaste, covering himself with Sargoth's blood, he helped Yoon to his feet.

"How do you feel?"

"Like I need a drink," said Yoon. Immediately a young woman, naked from the waist down, quim shaved and oiled so it looked like polished marble, ran forward, bearing a goblet of Kcrankian White. Yoon supped it noisily, and it left trails through the blood on his chin.

"We have a situation."

"What kind of situation?"

"An extremely serious one."

"It's not the fucking Red Thumb Gang again, is it? I have a mind to exterminate half the city to eradicate those scum. Burn the whole fucking place down! Torch the slums. Burn the poor. I'm sure they won't mind. I bet they have nothing better to do."

"I don't think you'll need to," said Zandbar, voice dangerously soft.

"Hmm? What? Why?"

Zandbar snapped a salute. "King Yoon. I, Zandbar, Captain of the King's Guard, feel it necessary to report that we have a wyrm in the city of Vagan."

There came a long pause.

"A worm?" said Yoon, swaying a little. "We have many of those, my friend."

"No. A wyrm. A *Great Wyrm*. A fucking *dragon*, Your Highness."

Another long pause.

"Surely you must be mistaken?" slurred Yoon.

"Please. Sire. Come with me."

Zandbar, in an unprecedented show of over-familiarity, took Yoon's elbow and propelled the uncomplaining monarch towards the Great Doors. They were big doors. In fact, they were *great* doors. Thirty feet high. Oak and bands of iron. Domineering. Oppressive. Designed to instil awe in bloody poor people. Designed to instil fear in those who feared for their lives. Which was almost everybody.

They burst out into the evening air. The sun was sinking behind the jagged, saw-toothed skyline of the city.

Yoon squinted, turning his head, hand coming up, photophobic after days in the luxury of his palace, drinking, taking drugs and fucking. Oh yes. And killing.

"Yes, yes, this is foolish, there's nothing there but the setting sun." Yoon stared hard at Zandbar, his blood-caked face breaking into a scowl. "Are you failing me, captain? Have you gone simple in the skull? Brain turned to sour milk? Do I need a *new* Captain of the Guard?"

"*Look, Your Highness!*"

And King Yoon looked. And King Yoon *saw*.

It leapt from the Tower of the Moon. There came a mammoth beat of wings, and the black dragon soared, banked, and dropped with infinite grace. Fire roared out, and several buildings went up with walls of raging fire, sending fireflies sparkling up into the heavens, as others were smashed apart by the huge, whipping tail.

Yoon blinked.

The dragon had gone.

"Did I just see that?" he said, tongue darting in and out. "Or was it, you know, part of the noises. The things I've been seeing. Like, mud-orcs and elf-rats." He squinted again, shading his eyes, scanning the horizon.

Nothing.

"It's real," growled Zandbar.

And suddenly the dragon was there, looming up from a narrow street, wings knocking bricks from walls, tail snapping rafters and disintegrating roofs in great striking sweeps. It lifted its head, and the dragon roared, and flames blasted the sky. The tail crashed against the corner of the palace, and pieces of white stone were smashed free, and came raining down, amidst pebbles and stone dust.

A fist-sized stone bounced from Yoon's head.

"Ow!"

And another from his shoulder.

He clutched it, and rapidly retreated to the shadows of the arched doorway. Yoon was frowning now. "A dragon? In *my* city! But... but I didn't give it permission!"

"I have a feeling," snarled Zandbar, "that this creature needs no permission. And I also feel, Highness, that if we don't do something quickly then the Chaos Halls are going to break loose. Permission to assemble the City Guard. And I *mean*, the City Guard."

"Granted. Oh yes." Yoon was dreamy again. He smiled at Zandbar, swaying, as if he was a weak-limbed branch on the breeze.

"Yes?" snapped Zandbar, with efficient military bearing.

"Summon Chanduquar," he said. "I'm going to get cleaned up."

King Yoon led the way, with the small, wizened figure of Chanduquar following closely behind. Then came Zandbar, erect, carrying a hefty pike, and they were followed by another twenty pikemen, all hardened veterans, all aware that where they travelled now was not the safest of places in the city.

The tunnel led steeply down. It had a high, arched ceiling of skilfully placed stones, many of them huge and terrifying – if one were to fall it would crush many men under its sheer weight. The walls were smooth, almost polished, the very finest black granite. The cobbles beneath their feet were damp and slippery, and polished by centuries of use.

"I hate it down here," grumbled Chanduquar, who was renowned for his brash and aggressive behaviour, his constant complaints, and the disrespectful way he spoke to the king. Yoon would have happily had him skewered on a pike, but he was just too valuable an asset.

Yoon glanced back. He studied Chanduquar for a moment. This small, skinny man, with skin the colour of ebony. He wore a short length of black cloth covering his genitals, and black boots, but little else – unless you counted the hundred or so piercings which adorned his scrawny body. He had an over-large skull, yellowed eyes from decades of alcohol abuse, and his lips were tattooed with a delicate script rumoured to facilitate his spells and focus on magick.

"Stop moaning," said Yoon, dropping into the sort of talk he knew Chanduquar understood.

"Well, it's true. It's a miserable and grim bastard place, even more miserable than the main streets of your city, ha!" He grinned, showing small neat teeth.

"Well, we'll get the job done, then you can get out of here, little man."

"Of course we can, fat king."

Yoon stared at him. *I could have you executed in the blink of an eye*, he thought, sourly. *I could have your skin peeled off, your toenails ripped out, hot pokers shoved up your tight little arsehole; I could have your nipples and your nose cut off, which would make an awful mess when you fucking sneezed… I could cut off your fingers one at a time, giving you a day between each snipping to really savour the pain and the proposed disability… I could have your spinal discs crushed with a sledgehammer, one at*

a time, as I pinned down your head with my boot and sang songs
about happiness and wine…

Yoon took a deep breath.

He calmed himself.

No. Not now.

He looked at the little man, the little thorn in his ego, the spear through the skull plate of his narcissism, and yet, bizarrely, also one of his most important tools; his greatest *weapon*.

Not yet, he told himself, and turned away, and continued to march deep *deep* down into the bowels beneath the palace.

During the journey, there had been several trembles in the stone, felt even this deep.

"What's happening above?" asked Yoon, after a while.

Zandbar fixed him with a glass stare. "I don't know, Your Highness. But, from extensive reading in the Great Rokroth Library, I believe dragons can cause quite a lot of damage."

"I'll show it fucking damage," growled Yoon, and for once, and this didn't happen often, Zandbar actually found some respect for the King of Vagandrak. He might be – occasionally – as insane as a Keekum smoker after three bowls, but on occasion he could show quite an amazing set of balls.

As they got closer to the location, to what Yoon had discretely referred to as "The Cells", so a noise started to come to them. It erupted from the deep interior. It consisted of banging, and scratching sounds – like steel against stone. Screeches, long and high-pitched. Thuds. Crumbling sounds. Battering sounds.

Yoon and Zandbar exchanged glances. Chanduquar seemed nonplussed.

The heavily armed soldiers, on the other hand, were visibly twitchy. Several were wiping sweating palms on uniforms, and a few kept dropping pike heads as if expecting some sudden frontal assault.

Tension was running high.

They came to a door. It was big. And, suspiciously, it was not like the usual oak portals they had crossed. This was iron. And when Yoon produced a thick key from around his neck, and inserted it into a well-oiled silent lock, the door swung open revealing the portal to be extremely thick. Thicker than any human or dwarf prisoner could ever expect. Thick enough to make any person entering wonder about the contents of this eerie prison chamber.

Zandbar stopped on the threshold.

Yoon stopped, also, and turned. He smiled, but the smile did not spread to his eyes.

"Have you been doing what I think you've been doing?" said Zandbar.

"And what do you think I've been doing?" said Yoon, voice a croon, without any splinter of fear.

"You've been collecting splice. Rounding up the rogue ones. The ones that got away after Orlana was... " He was going to say killed, but knew it was probably not exactly accurate. In all reality, the Horse Lady had probably been banished to an eternity in the Chaos Halls, alongside the sorcerer Morkagoth. Zandbar shivered with intuition.

"I confess," said Yoon, examining his brightly polished fingernails, "that I do have a certain fondness for the creatures of Orlana the Changer. There is in them a certain... primitive violence. And also an essence of corruptness, of metamorphosis, to which I am greatly attracted."

"King Yoon, they are the demon blendings of man and horse. They're fucking *evil!* In what way could you possibly be attracted?"

"I am attracted to their decadence," growled Yoon, and licked his lips. "Now let us move on."

They came into a long, low chamber. Huge iron posts had been fitted at intervals, each the size of an oak tree trunk. These formed the cornerstones of the prison cells. Between each post was a wall of iron, several feet thick and set on massive, broad wheels dropped in grooves which had been carved through stone.

Beyond, in the cells, came various snarls and crashes. There also came the clanking of huge chains.

"You there," said Yoon, pointing to one guard. "Go and pull that lever." He gestured to a huge iron staff, inserted into the wall alongside many others.

The guard stared, helplessly.

"But, but what will happen when I do?"

"If you do not, your head shall suddenly detach from your body," said King Yoon with a grin, but it was a toothy grin, like an exhumed skull, not the happy smile of a reigning monarch.

The guard stumbled forward, and he suddenly seemed less than threatening, and more like a child charged with a dangerous task.

He looked around.

Everybody stared at him, tense with apprehension.

Beyond the steel wall, something raged.

He pulled the lever, and leapt back as if something might jump out and snap off his head. It was an amazing intuition, for the creature that was revealed was nothing less than an abomination.

It was part horse. Part man. But there, any likeness to either of the host creatures ended.

The *splice*, one of Orlana the Changer's *special creatures, special pets, special killers,* was bigger than a horse, although of different proportions. It was vast, uneven, stocky, with bulging lumps of muscle distending from its torso, seemingly at random – as if flesh and bone had been broken in places and forced back together again under a blind surgeon's scalpel. It was a rich black, glossy, like the finest stallion, and yet the uneven skin was patched with horse hair in segments, as if it had suffered burns from a fire. It hobbled forward on four legs, but the front left did not touch the ground, for it was too short, and bent forwards at a deviant angle giving the creature an irregular, if terrifying, gait.

The beast suddenly leapt, screaming in a high-pitched

voice like that of a woman, although without any discernible clarity of words.

There was a clanging and clanking, and the splice was yanked backwards at the end-trajectory of its leap by the thigh-thick chain which restrained it.

Yoon stepped forward. He was panting.

Everybody else stepped backwards.

"Kneel!" he commanded, and licked his lips in nervous pleasure, as he admired the heavily muscled body, thick horse legs with twisted, iron hooves, uneven chest, up to the head, the great misshapen head that was too large to be right, too twisted and elongated to be living. The head was a broken horse skull, long and pointed, but with the mouth pulled back, jacked open way too far, showing huge yellowed fangs oozing blood and pus and saliva. The eyes were uneven on the head, one green, one blood red and nearly double the size, and from the top of the bent skull curved a jagged horn, easily the length of a short sword and fashioned from yellowed bone.

The splice observed Yoon, and its lips quivered, black and yellow against fangs which could rip his head clean off.

Yoon moved forward.

Zandbar hissed, "*Nooo*!"

Yoon was within the perimeter of the chain now, which lay slack on the floor. The splice looked down at its tether, then up again at Yoon, eyes bulging, throat gulping, as if this vast, distorted creature was starved of oxygen.

It knew. It realised.

It could snap Yoon like a twig.

"Sit down," said Yoon, and his voice was gentle, almost a song, which surprised both Zandbar and Chanduquar. They had never heard Yoon utter such words. Even more surprisingly, the great, tufted monster obeyed and dropped to its front knees, then its rear haunches collapsed, and the head came up, quivering, eyes searching, and it fixed on Yoon and the head tilted, and it...

smiled.

"It's fucking *smiling*," said Zandbar, through gritted teeth.

"Shut up," said Chanduquar.

"What happens next?"

"If the splice gets pissed at something, we're all fucking dead."

Zandbar nodded, eyes saucer-wide.

"Undo the chains," said Yoon, eyes fixed on those differing orbs of the splice. And he moved ever forward, within lunging distance now, and he reached out and gently touched the creature. The splice's great, uneven head tilted to one side, and it started to... croon. It was a sickening sound, like the death rattle from a wounded horse, and it made all present shiver, hairs standing up on forearms and necks, and Yoon was gazing into those eyes like a *lover*.

A guard moved to another set of levers and pulleys, and very slowly, pulled one. The chains on the splice went slack, and now, *now* the creature really could kill if it so chose. But it didn't. It allowed King Yoon to slowly run his hand up its snout, past ridges of broken and mended bone, past tufts of sprouting hair, over ridges and corrugations of burned flesh. And all it did was croon, and blink, the great red eye filled with blood as it gazed adoringly at Yoon.

"What the fuck is going on?" whispered Zandbar from the corner of his mouth. His skin was crawling. His mind was flitting. Every primeval sense he had screamed at him to get the fuck out of the chamber before the splice launched at him and tore him limb from limb.

"It trusts him," said Chanduquar, voice quavering.

Zandbar looked at the wizened, alcoholic old magick man, the priest, shaman, whatever the hell he was. His eyebrows lifted a little. "*Really*?" he said.

Chanduquar met his gaze, and gave a tiny shrug. "Maybe the human part of it *remembers*. Maybe it can recollect trust, and affection, and love. Look closely, soldier man, really fucking *look* at the beast."

And Zandbar looked. The splice, the huge, quivering, disjointed, amalgamated mass of man and horse and whatever demon had decided to jump into the pot, something so ugly – by human perception – that it could never win any genetic design awards, it was *enjoying* Yoon's attention; savouring his touch.

"He commands it," said Zandbar, in awe.

Yoon turned, and all present were shocked to see the expression on his face. For it was indeed a look of love, and they realised King Yoon was not just some mad king, some playful puppet, some dangerous tyrant; no, he truly *was* insane, and he *was* connected in some way to this splice.

"Release the others," said Yoon, voice thick with emotion.

"I have not cast the charms," said Chanduquar.

"We do not need them," said King Yoon, dreamily.

"But… we *need* the Equiem magick… to protect us, Your Highness. If the… the beasts turn feral…"

"We do not need your magick this time," said Yoon.

"What did you do to it?"

Yoon smiled. "I entered her mind. And she entered mine. It has been a long time since somebody stroked her face."

Zandbar looked at Yoon. He felt sick to his stomach. Then slowly he shifted his gaze to the massive, misshapen head, perhaps four times larger than Yoon's, with the quivering black lips, yellow fangs, pointed equine skull, jacked open mouth, jaw longer on one side than on the other, the green eye, the double-sized red orb, and the horn which came from the top of its skull. It was a creature of nightmare. A demon from the Chaos Halls. A mutated unicorn. A creature of mutilation and death.

"*Her*?" said Zandbar, from a mouth drier than any salt plain.

"Her name was Christa," said Yoon, turning back to the splice. "Her husband was a desert warrior. She was his princess. Until Orlana's mud-orcs captured her, dragged her screaming before the Horse Lady and she, like so many hundred others, were merged with broken horses, twisted into something… else."

Zandbar wanted to puke. For now, within the splice's…

within her *frame* he could see distant echoes of humanity. A row of eyelashes. A fingernail, merged with a section of horse flesh. A toe. A woman's toe.

"By the Seven Sisters, how can one person do this to another?" hissed Zandbar.

Chanduquar looked at him sideways. "I don't know why you're so surprised," he said, voice harsh and slick at the same time. "Your race has been abusing itself for millennia," and he smiled a knowing smile.

Your race?

Chains started clanking, as Yoon's instructions were carried out, and along the hall the doors began to roll open on their iron wheels. Snarls and squeals erupted, and Zandbar looked down the massive chamber and realised, in horror, there were not five, not ten, but... twenty prison cells, each housing a splice. He swallowed, and took a step back. But realised too late the guards, in their eagerness to please, or maybe in abject, unthinking terror, had also released the chains...

The splice shambled out from their cells, shaking off, or scrambling from, or scratching free of their shackles and chains. They were a sorry, motley, but terrifying vision to all present. Every man froze, did not breathe, as the twenty or so huge creatures, many drooling pools of thick saliva and pus and blood to the stone flags, shambled out and, very slowly, turned, orientating on the steaming stinking human meat standing helpless before them.

They lumbered forward, and this turned very quickly into leaps as huge muscles, locked away for so long, stretched, and hooves and claws pounded the stone and the beasts launched down the underground prison yard, screaming and growling and spitting forth twisted whinnies... and every man pissed himself, urine running down legs and into boots and forming puddles on the stone flags.

Except for Chanduquar.

He lifted his hand, and closed his eyes, and a calmness flooded the chamber, like a *puff* of warm summer sunshine rolling over a field of bobbing flowers.

The splice slowed, and then stopped. They orientated on Yoon.

Yoon smiled, eyes drug-wide.

They shuffled into a circle, crooning and snarling, and slowly surrounded him. Yoon was smiling, and crying, and reaching out to touch the snuffling muzzles which stretched for him. His hands ran over their equine snouts, up over corrugated flesh, over tufts of hair, ridges of distended bone, over open wounds weeping blood tears, over muzzles and teeth and uneven jaws.

Zandbar was backing away, and his back touched the wall. He stopped with a jerk, like a puppet that's had its strings cut. He was absolutely not ashamed of the piss that stained his trews and filled his boots.

Yoon turned, grinning. "They're beautiful!" he said, and tears were rolling down his cheeks. His dark eyes were filled with them, each tear a tear shed for a lost soul, a soul taken by Orlana and changed into these... *nightmares*... these pitiful specimens of damaged life.

The creatures ambled around Yoon, and he looked into their eyes, and he laughed out loud. "I can see you," he said, voice effeminate. "I can see all the way into your souls!" And he turned, fixing Chanduquar with a stare. "They were human, once. And now I am a part of them. And they are a part of me. We have seen deep inside each other's hearts and minds and souls... and we are a family now. All of us." He looked around at the splice, with their heaving, disjointed bulks, their heavy, twisted muscles, their battered horse heads, their broken legs and hooves and open wounds. They snorted, and crooned, and wept blood.

"Come," said Yoon, "follow me..." and he led them down the corridor, and through the portal, and up towards the distant light.

After a few moments, only the terrified soldiers, and Zandbar and Chanduquar, remained.

"What does he intend to do?" asked Zandbar, voice so low

it could have been the backdrop hum of the underworld.

"He has tamed the splice," said Chanduquar.

"How the *fuck* did he do that?"

The little man raised his eyebrows, a movement that shifted possibly thirty facial piercings. "Maybe he carries some of the blood of Orlana," he said, and gave a little chuckle. "Maybe he made a pact with the demons of the Chaos Halls!" He slapped his knee, and roared with laughter. Nobody laughed with him.

Zandbar stared up the sloping stone corridor, leading up, leading up to the palace and Vagan beyond.

"I think he seeks to save the city," said Zandbar.

"From the Great Wyrm? Aye. Aye. Maybe."

Zandbar looked at the little shaman, then. He watched the man's tattooed lips squirming, but no sound came out. "Can the splice take on a dragon?" he said.

"There's only one way to find out."

Like Wolves to the Slaughter

Dek clenched his short-sword tight in one fist, and glanced back, scowling. Narnok had lifted his axe in both hands, and was spinning the shaft, blades glittering by the light of the sinking sun. Trista carried two knives, although what use they'd be against a *dragon* was anybody's guess. Mola stood, hands on hips, great fists clenched, his eyes fixed on the sky as he searched. And finally, Kareem had found himself a spear, and held the shaft in one huge fist. This group, this party of Iron Wolves, looked mean, and hard, and terrifying. But then, they were about to face a Great Wyrm... so it was going to get real bad, real fast.

"Where is it?" said Dek.

"We can't stand against *that*," snapped Trista. "It's a fucking dragon!"

"Yeah, well it's come to our fucking city for a fight," growled Narnok, single eye squinting. "So let's give it one."

The fire consuming The Fighting Cocks roared, and another roof timber collapsed. Smoke billowed up into the sky, and sparks danced on the breeze like intoxicated fireflies. The Iron Wolves jogged down the cobbles, and stopped, each one searching the sky.

"Where's that fucking thing gone?" said Dek, shielding his eyes from smoke.

And then Volak appeared, with a smash of her wings, and careened down a nearby street, wings outstretched, each wing-tip smashing the roof from a house with concussive booms, boom after boom, roof after roof smashed up into the sky with spinning roof joists, torn windows, flying bricks and huge chunks of mortar. The dragon screamed, and fire splashed the cobbles. There were perhaps thirty people, running down the street, and they were picked up by the blast of fire, propelled forward on a jet of energy, and devoured by the flames.

Dek looked down at his sword. "I don't think it's enough," he grumbled.

"We have to *try*," hissed Narnok.

"Come on, if we all attack together… aim for the soft underbelly as she goes past," said Kareem, dark eyes glinting.

"She?" asked Narnok, raising an eyebrow.

"Well, she's a bitch, ain't she?" snapped Kareem.

"We'll soon find out. She's turned, coming back in to finish off the street!" observed Trista. She looked down at her daggers. *Fuck. What I'd do for a spear right now!*

Volak sang, voice ringing out as she banked, evening sun turning her black scales crimson. A spear came from a rooftop, and glanced from her side, skittering off. From this distance, it looked like an attack with a toothpick.

"It's big," said Kareem, suddenly.

They ran down the street, splitting, crouching in doorways, Dek, Trista and Mola on one side of the street, Narnok and Kareem on the other.

Narnok looked back at Kareem. "Keep a hold of that spear, lad. I think you might bloody need it!"

The Iron Wolves stared down the street. Rubble lay strewn, and timbers lay crisscrossed, flames licking along their lengths.

"She's coming back," said Dek.

Volak came in low, wings tucking behind her, dropping like a missile from the sky and into the channel of the battered street. As she entered, so her wing-tips spread, smashing through bricks and stones once more, windows and timbers, with terrible crashes and bangs which echoed throughout the city. She roared, and fire scoured the street, and as she passed, so the Iron Wolves leapt out, weapons raised, leaping to slice and cut and stab. Narnok's axe-heads missed the dragon's belly by inches, and he landed again, in a crouch, as that great beast smashed overhead. Dek, lighter and more agile, made a higher jump, and his sword slammed at the dragon, grating against scales with such violence the weapon was torn from his grasp and went skittering along the burning street. Kareem's spear found its mark, punching upwards, but again, like Dek's sword, the point grated with rapid-fire cracks along the matt-black scales until the shaft snapped in Kareem's fingers, and he landed, knees bending, staring at the snapped shaft in his fists. He shook his head. "Fuck me, but those scales are hard."

"So much for a soft underbelly," muttered Dek.

"Er... guys?" said Trista.

"Yeah, what?" snapped Dek.

Trista gestured.

Volak had lifted from her attack run, banked in a tight loop, and was coming back.

"I don't think our prodding went unnoticed," she said, face turning to thunder.

"Er... back to the doorways!" yelled Dek.

Volak screamed, the sound echoing out across Vagan. Thousands hid in cellars, sprinting down cold stone steps, bolting doors and wondering what the hell they were going to do.

Volak came back fast. Wings pumped. The Iron Wolves peered from doorways, then cringed as Volak suddenly shot out her wings, checking her speed, and plunged down through a building, sending timbers flying, walls crashing down, bricks spinning off in all directions to smash the windows of other buildings and bounce from walls.

A brick bounced off Narnok's shoulder, and his face went purple with fury.

"That fucking beast," he snapped, surging up, axe

clenched. Kareem grabbed him, and dragged the axeman back.

"Are you *insane*?" he snarled.

Volak arose from the rubble of the building, shaking her head, flames flickering around her snout. Her tail snapped out, and another wall went crashing to the ground. Dust flowered up like a mushroom, engulfing half the street.

Through the temporary fog Volak strode forward, claws crunching bricks, head weaving from side to side.

"Where are you?" she called. "You little people who want to stab at me with their steel. Where are you hiding?"

There was almost comedy in her voice – as if this were a simple game, and there was no chance of her ever losing.

Volak's wing lashed out, the spiked tip crashing into a house. With a twitch, she brought the entire front of the building crashing down. Stones rolled across the cobbles. Wood clattered. Volak's great head was swaying, like a serpent slithering through sand, her black eyes searching the street, the burning timbers, the crushed buildings.

"Where are you?" she said again, and chuckled, and fire flickered around her snout. "Are you in that house?" Flames roared, turning from blue to white, and the whole front went up in a wash of flames, and then the house collapsed backwards, sighing down and in on itself, as stones glowed and floor joists shot up flames. "Or in this one?" Again fire roared, and a pretty, detached house with a turret woven with spider-strands of clinging ivy went up with a sudden roar. Fire screamed and flames danced. For a moment, the house was invisible, trapped within an envelope of fire; and then it collapsed with a sigh, like some huge dying animal.

A woman screamed in the distance. Several dogs barked. Smoke rolled into the sky. The city of Vagan seemed suddenly... *deserted*. A barren place. A ghost town. Of Mola's dogs, there was no sign... he'd bid them *run*. Fighting a dragon was no place for a mutt, even a fighting mutt.

"I think you are playing a game with me, little people," grinned Volak, and took several strides forward. Her head thrashed left, and she peered through an arched doorway – all that remained of a battered house. "I think we're going to have some fun, me looking for you, you, who wanted to poke me with your tiny, shiny sticks of metal... and me, with my raging fire, and hateful heart, and message of bloody revenge." A wall of fire slammed down the street, licking at wood and glass and bricks.

Seven houses down the street, huddled just inside the doorway, Narnok growled, "I'm fucking bloody sick of this bloody foolishness." He shifted, and Kareem grabbed him.

"Whoa, Big Man. Where are you going?"

"I ain't being bloody hunted like no mouse in a house by a big fluffy cat. There ain't ever been an enemy I haven't faced and beaten. I'm going to cut that there fucking dragon's head clean off!"

"*Narn!*" and Kareem was frantically gesturing to Dek. Hand gestures that said, *get the fuck over here!* "Narn, you can't just stride into the street and take something like that head on! Are you crazy?"

"Maybe I am," grumbled the axeman, and stood, and Kareem grabbed at him, but it was too late. Narnok strode out into the middle of the street, perhaps twenty feet away from the towering dragon, and stared up at the wyrm with his good eye.

"You looking for me, fucker?" he roared, and stood there. There came a *clunk* as his axe-blades hit the battered, smouldering stones. Narnok grinned, his one good eye glistening, his crisscross of scars gleaming by the reflected light of so many idle fires.

Volak's head came up, slowly, and her dark eyes fixed on Narnok.

"You have some guts, little man."

"Not so little," said Narnok, puffing out his chest and frowning. "Now then, stop fucking about. Why are you here? What do you want? What can we give you, so youse fucks off?"

Volak chuckled, and took a step forward. Bricks *pinged*

and crushed under her claws. Her dark scales were
crusted with powder, dust and ash, from so much physical
destruction. Even now, dust was drifting and swirling in
eddies, and settling against her scales like so much volcanic
fallout. This part of Vagan now seemed to be suffering a
coastal fog... if only that were the reality.

"You think you can barter with me?" said Volak, eyes
gleaming. Flames flickered around her snout. She lowered
her head a little, serpentine neck rippling, an act accentuated
by the spines along the arch. "Your race is a disease on this
world. Once, this was all *mine*, for ten thousand miles,
everything you see, everything you cannot see, all belonged
to me, belonged to my royal clan, for I am Volak, Queen
of the Wyrms, and I have come to wreak destruction on
you... you *parasites*, you wriggling little maggots, you shit
that squirms under the base of my claws. I will see you all
burn. I will see you all devoured."

Narnok considered this. Then, in a deep rumble, he said,
"You'll have to go through me first."

Volak's peal of laughter rang out across the city, swirling
the dust in the air into violent new shapes. It was genuinely
a noise of humour, made even more bizarre as it came from
the fire-licked lips of a dragon.

"How refreshing!" she cried. "What is your name, tiny
human?"

"I'm Narnok. Don't forget it. It's a name I'm going to
carve on your arse."

Volak laughed again, but the *tone* of the laughter had
changed a little. This time, she was not so amused. This time,
there was a hint of being offended amidst the laughter, as if
one was laughing as if to save face, rather than out of joy.

"You are correct, little man. It is a name I will not forget.
I will remember you for many years to come. I will also
remember how you ended up."

"Oh aye? How's that, like?"

"As ash," said Volak, her voice low and dangerous. She
inhaled, a mighty breath, and in one swift movement

Narnok hoisted his axe, swung back his shoulder, and launched the weapon with all his considerable might. As the axe left his hands, so he dived sideways, back towards the limited protection of the crumbling house... and the axe went end over end, butterfly blades gleaming crimson by the light of the dying sun, and as fire began to erupt so the axe slammed inside Volak's mouth and she stumbled, choking, as twisted streamers of fire erupted around the axe lodged in her throat.

Volak's scream went up, a high-pitched wail full of pain, and her knees bent, wings sweeping back, and with a powerful leap and *slap* which sent a concussive *boom* reverberating down the street, so she took to the sky.

There came several heartbeats of silence followed by a clatter, as Narnok's axe hit the cobbles, haft smoking, blades tarnished by heat.

They peered from the ruined building, from under the leaving, broken arch, where dust trickled down and invaded their clothing. The city seemed suddenly quiet; desolate. Like a tomb.

"Where did it go?" whispered Trista.

"Why are you whispering?" said Dek.

"In case the fucking thing is behind us!"

"Ahh. Good point."

"You see that? You see what I did?" grinned Narnok, grasping his smoking axe to his chest.

"You didn't kill it, is what I saw," growled Dek.

"Yeah, but I bloodied her nose!"

"Narn, if your axe in the throat didn't finish her off, I'm not quite sure what will."

"We need bigger weapons," said Mola.

They turned and stared at him. "Bigger than what?"

"Bigger 'an what we got!"

"Er," said Narnok, and wiggled his axe, as if to say, *fucking wield something bigger than this, my friend!* "You have something in mind, Mola?"

The stocky Dog Man nodded. "I was once part of the
Spear Guard. Many years ago. Before Desekra. Before the
mud-orcs. Before the Iron Wolves."

Dek tilted his head. "Spear Guard? I heard of those. An
ancient clan. Guardians of the City, or something. Charged
with being defenders if ever the city was under attack. Like,
sieged by an army, that sort of thing."

Mola nodded. "Aye. It comes from ancient times, when
there was these marauding raiders, these bastards, the
Vaikaii. They'd sail in, packed in their longships, and raid
inland. Vicious bastards, they were. It was always coastal
to begin with, but then they got bolder, braver. Came with
armies. Attacked cities."

"Is this going to take long?" snapped Trista. "Only there's
a fucking dragon on the loose and I'm guessing she's *really*
pissed off having an axe lobbed in her mouth."

"Calm down, calm down," muttered Narnok. "Let the lad
spin his yarn."

Mola scowled at Trista. "Listen. Point is, there are
periphery towers. Around the city walls. And they're still
armed in case of a city siege. It's written in blood in the
King's Scriptures. They can never be dismantled."

"These towers are armed? Armed with what?" said Dek.

"Big crossbows. Catapults. Siege engine grade – designed
to protect whatever the fuck was attacking the city. They
was well stocked, used to have engineers checking them
weekly. This was part of the Spear Guard's detail. Defenders
of the city, and all that."

"So they have giant crossbows?" said Dek, eyes gleaming.

"Aye."

"And catapults designed to crush siege towers?"

"Aye!"

"What are we waiting for?" boomed Narnok.

There came a reverberating *crash* as Volak hit the street,
and the whole world seemed to shake. Buildings trembled.
Stones fell, crashing against the cobbles. Fire screamed,
and the Iron Wolves dived back as flames splashed past the

arched opening, torching anything flammable in its way.

The fire stopped, and there seemed to be an inrush of cooling air.

"Where is that fucking axeman?" screamed Volak, her voice powerful, musical, but imbued with an anger like nothing the Iron Wolves had ever heard before. Glass shattered. Distantly, a woman screamed. "Where is... *Narnok*?" It came out as a terrible rumble.

"See!" beamed Narnok. "I told you she'd remember it!"

A dog barked, and Mola twitched, listening, then realised it wasn't one of his. He could tell his own dogs' barks from a hundred leagues. He grinned sheepishly. "Sorry. Worried about my bitches, is all."

"*Mola!*" chastised Trista.

"We gotta move *now*!" growled Dek.

Volak came charging down the street, her huge bulk, tipped wings and tail smashing through buildings. Dust and smoke swirled through the air, and the day now turned into a sombre half-night. Fire crackled. Destroyed buildings creaked. Bricks toppled.

"I agree," nodded Narnok, hastily, as they moved back through the building, deeper into its confines, running now, boots stomping through somebody else's possessions. They came out of a back door and stood, looking around. Ahead lay a factory, and Narnok led the way, kicking down the door as behind them it sounded like hell was breaking loose.

More fire screamed, and looking over their shoulders they saw the ignition of yellow flames. Volak charged *through* the house where they had stood, moments earlier. Beams and stones went flying. The stone archway was sent spinning into oblivion in jagged pieces by a twitch of her mighty, black-scaled head and snout. Roof beams were nudged aside. A wall was blasted with flame, and for long seconds it glowed until it exploded.

"How does she know we were there?" hissed Trista, through gritted teeth.

"I reckon she can *smell us*," said Narnok, and he was deadly serious.

"Fuck off," snapped Dek.

"No, really," said Narnok, eyes wide like saucers. "I've read about stuff."

"Yeah, in the *Children's Happy Book of Dragon Fairies*," said Dek.

They sprinted into the factory, and stopped. It was an engineering place, and the whole ground floor was filled with giant, iron machines – presses and industrial guillotines, lathes and stomps. The place smelt of scorched metal and old oil. It was gloomy, badly lit. Above, several massive H-section iron beams hung on thick chains. In various alleys – streets created by the vast machines which stood idle – were braziers full of glowing coals. Steam hissed through pipes, including feeder pipes which ran along the walls, thick as a man's waist. The whole place reeked of hydraulic oil, sweat and scorched metal.

"Where now?" said Dek.

"Spread out," said Trista, eyes gleaming. It was rare Dek had ever seen her so panicked.

"What is this place?" said Kareem, glancing about.

"They make shit," said Narnok, eyes still wide, still freaked.

"No shit," scowled Kareem.

They moved amidst the machines, some as big as a house. Steam hissed from pipes, and oil bled on the floor, like blood from severed arteries. The workers had obviously heard the good news, and fled. Their machines stood idle oozing uselessness.

Dek stopped, hand against a huge black edifice of iron. He turned to look behind, just as Volak came through the wall.

Bricks flew as the great wyrm smashed a dragon-shaped hole where once had stood a door and several windows. A massive pipe was severed, and steam suddenly screamed in Volak's face, and she ducked her huge shoulders, and heaved her way through the hole, averting her eyes from the blast of steam. Any other creature would have been burned to a smoking, trembling cinder; but Volak was impervious. Fire was her trade.

"Where are you, you fuckers?" she growled, flames licking around her snout.

The *fuckers* were making their way stealthily across the factory floor, running from machine to machine, looking over their shoulders, waiting for the next blast of fire.

Narnok gave a short whistle, and the others looked over. He patted his forearm, then signalled ahead. They nodded. Narn had seen something, and they followed on his path, running, heads low, panic now a constant.

Volak strode after them. She charged suddenly at a huge machine, a press for stomping parts out of iron – and she clashed against it, and it did not move. Iron groaned. The ground shook. For once, it seemed Volak had met her match. The press was the size of a small house, and must have weighed several hundred tonnes. It shuddered and groaned, and Volak dropped one shoulder and heaved. Huge bolts the length of a horse were ripped from the ground, shearing with squeals, and Volak shifted, lifting her wings, voice screaming through the factory. The massive press rolled away to one side with a noise like an avalanche, steam hissing from broken pipes, the press smashing through several smaller machines and crushing them down into the ground. For a moment it felt like an earthquake had taken hold of the factory, and everything was shaking, rumbling, and the Iron Wolves glanced up, worried the great roof high overhead would come crashing down. But it didn't, despite thick beams shaking, and disgorging dust. It held. For now.

"Come out!" screamed Volak.

The Iron Wolves ran for it.

Narnok was in the lead, and they all dropped to a crouch, panting, by a wall. It had huge brackets and bolts, and Dek frowned. "You brought us here?"

"Look inside!"

Dek moved around the side of the... tank, and half-climbed up some adjacent steps.

"Oil?"

"For cooling the machines," said Narnok. "I've been somewhere like this once before. This is the storage tank."

"What kind of oil?"

Narnok shrugged. "Dunno. But I bet it fucking burns."

"You want to draw the dragon here?"

"Yeah. You see the bolts? We can collapse the wall of the tank."

"How do we ignite her?"

"She'll do that herself," grinned Narnok.

"Nice place," snapped Trista. "But how the fuck do we get those bolts out? The heads are almost the size of Narnok's arse."

"With this spanner?" said Kareem, and grinned. The spanner was the size of his arm, and he rammed it onto the first of the six bolt heads. He strained at it for a moment, face contorting, muscles standing out on his arms, tendons standing out on his neck. Then the great bolt shrieked, and turned, and Kareem spun it. Oil started to ooze from the wall of the tank.

"If we can get her over here, we can drench her in oil, set her on fire!" said Dek.

"We need a decoy," said Trista.

Everybody looked at Narnok.

"Whoa," he said, as Volak screamed, attacking another machine on the factory floor, and Kareem went to work on the second bolt. "What do you mean, a *decoy*? If I stand here, *I'll* get fucking drenched in oil as well! I'll go up like a bloody fish-oil rag on Dead Lepers' Night! No, I'm not having it..."

"Come *on*, Narn! The dragon's coming!"

"Got you," growled Kareem, spinning the second bolt free. It was huge, black and corroded, and he dropped it to the factory floor with a *clang*. He looked around. "Don't nobody fucking help, why don't you?"

Dek ran over, finding a second huge spanner.

Volak crashed through the factory, and they heard her scream again, fire raging, cutting a hole *through* an iron machine.

Dek went to work, and he and Kareem took out bolts number three and four.

"Look," snapped Trista. "You stand on top of this wall, right?"

"The one we're unscrewing?" Narnok looked dubious.

"You entice Volak over there," she pointed, "the guys take out the last two bolts, you jump for it, I'll light an arrow and fire it into the mess. Volak will go up like a bonfire. What do you think?"

"Sounds dangerous," muttered Narnok.

"More dangerous than a dragon trying to fucking scorch us?"

"Yeah, well, I'm just saying."

"Get up there! Kareem, Dek, how we doing with those bolts?"

"Nearly there," grunted Kareem. Sweat was dripping from his brow.

Trista unslung her bow, and ran up the steps, followed by Narnok, still grumbling. Now the factory spread before them. Some machines still blocked their view, but Trista and Narnok were foregrounded; lit up, so to speak. Trista knocked an arrow to her bow, and running beyond the oil tank, found a brazier. Narnok watched her, and she gestured wildly to him.

"It's a shit plan," mumbled Narnok, and frowning, walked down the narrow wall of the tank, and stepped out onto the side Dek and Kareem were busily unbolting.

"You all right down there?"

"When it goes, it'll go fast," said Dek. "When we've taken out the bolts, there's two flimsy pins holding everything in place. If me and Kareem hit them simultaneously, the whole fucking thing will explode."

"So what am I supposed to do?" scowled Narnok.

"Just don't stand in the middle, all right? Stay near the

side. Just step onto the side wall. You got it?"

"Don't like it."

"Just fucking *do it*!"

"Fifth bolt out," said Kareem.

"Trista! You ready?" bellowed Dek.

"Ready."

"Do your thing, axeman," grinned Dek.

Narnok strode out, clasped his axe in one hand, then shouted, "Oy, you! You fucking pain in the arse dragon! I'm here, me, Narnok, the one what threw my axe into your big wide-open fucking mouth! Sting a bit, did it? Those steel blades eating into your soft mucus tissue? Well, come on over here and have another taste of my blades. They're desperate to get intimate with your vocal chords."

He looked down at Dek. "Is that all right?" he mumbled. "*Soft mucus tissue?*"

Narnok shrugged. "I was improvising, wasn't I?"

Volak heard him. And she stopped. And she turned. Her head came up, and those black eyes orientated on him. She stormed forward, bulk crashing machines out of the way, eyes fixed on Narnok and his single orb, which stared right back, angry, defiant, unafraid.

Volak halted, claws gouging the stone floor, and her wings folded back.

"As I said earlier, you have some balls, little ugly man."

"Ugly, is it? You're the one with a face like a diseased horse."

Volak smiled, lips rippling back over fangs. She tilted her head.

"You are too good to burn," she said.

"Well, come kiss my axe then," said Narnok.

"You... challenge me? That is a sweet concept."

"Come on, bitch! Or are you too used to letting your fucking subordinates do your killing for you?"

Dek was signalling frantically, even as Volak's gaze dropped to study the two men, the two Iron Wolves. Then her eyes narrowed. Pupils dilated, black on black. The

flames around her snout became more intense, more...
agitated.

"Now!" screamed Kareem.

With spanners, they hit the retaining pins and danced
backwards as the wall slammed outwards and down, on
huge iron hinges. There came a muted roar, and oil gushed
out, flooded outwards, close enough to drench the wyrm in
thick black sludge. Oil gushed and roared. Trista took aim,
but she wasn't needed... the pilot light flickering around
Volak's muzzle did the rest. Oil coated the dragon... and
then ignited her by her own fire.

A sheet of flames screamed upwards, touching the high,
vaulted ceiling of the factory, and Volak was lost in a sudden
inferno. Kareem and Dek ran for it around the back of the
tank, using machines as cover as the flames superheated
their backs. Narnok had leapt, and stood on a slippery
narrow wall, axe in both hands now, trying his best not to
topple into the remaining sludge.

Trista shielded her eyes.

In the midst of the roaring inferno, something seemed
to squirm. Like a bucket of dark eels in clouded water, so
Volak writhed in the fire. And a cry went up, a wail like
nothing the Iron Wolves had ever heard; it was a song, a
long, ululating call, a call of pain and anguish and fear. It
reverberated around the factory, a sound so intrinsically
painful it brought tears to all their eyes.

They gathered, up on the raised platform of the tank, and
watched Volak squirming in the furnace.

"I never thought I'd see a dragon burn," said Narnok,
and there was a hint of sadness to his voice.

Dek looked at him. "It fucking torches people *all the time*.
It burns flesh from their faces. It exterminates men, women,
children. Little babies. Don't be feeling sorry for it, Narn. Or
you're dumber than I've ever given you credit for."

"But... listen to it."

They listened, as Volak flapped around in the oil and fire,
her cries getting weaker. And then she seemed to fold in on

herself, compacting into a black ball only half glimpsed in the flames.

"Right," said Dek, "who's for the pub?"

"It burned down The Fighting Cocks," pointed out Trista.

"That *bitch*," said Narnok.

"Come on," said Dek. "Let's get out of this charnel house."

They turned, as a group, and started working their way through the factory, towards the opposite side, where there was less carnage and at least some semblance of normality. Behind them, fire crackled, in pools, in puddles, parts of machines, areas of oil which still burned.

Noise had died down to a minimum. A muted crackle.

Several huge metal machines clicked as they cooled.

The Iron Wolves reached the far door, and turned, looking back. "I actually feel quite sorry for it," said Narnok.

"Why?" scowled Dek.

"Well, we burned her. To death. And she was, if we're honest, a pretty magnificent creature."

"Not magnificent when she's eating your children," scowled Trista.

"Or flame-grilling your parents," said Kareem.

"Yeah, but we killed her. Killed her dead. So we should show a mark of respect."

"You want to fucking *pray* for it?" snapped Trista, staring at Narnok in disbelief. "Is this really the man who drank *two* barrels of ale? *Five* bottles of whiskey? Who endured the torturer's acid eating his eyeball? And now you want to pray for a dead dragon?"

Narnok shrugged. He lowered his eyes. "It's just, y'know."

"We don't know," growled Dek, looking around warily.

"Well, since I were a wee lad, I read all them story books. Dragons were always honest and noble, and flew through the skies and rescued people and shit." He looked around, and scowled. "It's not *my* fault the pissing authors were pro-dragon, all right? It's not my fault I have a bloody soft spot 'cos of when I was a kiddie."

Dek deflated, and laughed. "Great, Narnok the bloody One Eye! He has a soft spot for dragons."

Trista opened the door. Outside, night had fallen, but she couldn't see the stars because of the smoke and the swirling dust. She glanced back. "I think we better get out of here," she muttered. "Before…"

"Before what?" cackled Narnok.

"Before…"

She rose from the mess of oil and broken machinery, and she screamed. Then, in the blink of an eye, Volak shot upwards, sending three huge iron machines tumbling away, to crash through the roof high above. Ceiling joists came tumbling down, clattering on the ground, and then everything became calm.

Dust and smoke swirled in eddies.

Dek and Narnok ran to the door, closely followed by the others.

"It's not dead," said Dek.

"Surely, wounded unto death?" said Narnok, rubbing at his empty eye socket.

"I'm not so sure," mouthed Trista, and peered outside again.

They moved out into the street.

"What now?" said Dek.

"I vote we head for the nearest Spear Guard Tower," rumbled Mola.

Narnok stared hard at the squat Dog Man. He frowned. "You don't think the dragon is dead, then, do you not?"

Mola shrugged. "The way I sees it, she's a creature of fire and brimstone. We hit her with a hard blast all right, hurt her even, but at the end of the day, she fucking *breathes fire*. She's a dragon. You ain't ever going to kill a dragon with fire. She's impervious, she has to be, or she'd ignite herself."

"You could have mentioned this before?" said Dek.

"Why?" Mola shrugged and grinned. "You was all having so much fun! And anyway, it was worth a try. Maybe we hurt her, maybe we scared her away and even now she's flying off to some far and distant dragon land to lick her wounds and try and recover."

"And if not?"

"We'd better get to that tower. There's no answer like hard-forged iron."

The Iron Wolves moved through the darkness, looking skywards continually. Vagan was under a pall of fog, no doubt caused by so many fires raging through the city. They could still hear them, the distant roar of flames, the tumbling collapse of buildings, the screams, the wails, the muffled noises in the murky dark.

They met few-to-no people on the streets. Most were indoors, terrified of the dragon they'd all witnessed rampaging throughout the city. But now, the great wyrm was curiously quiet. As Mola had said, maybe she had gone to lick her wounds. Or… maybe not.

The tower stood unguarded as they reached its foot, and Mola stopped, looking up. The others did the same. It was circular in design, built from red stone and with only the occasional tiny window, and it disappeared off into the fog. This was a tower of defence, not a tourist attraction.

"We're in," said Mola, peering through the doorway. He grabbed a spear from a rack, and tossed it to Dek. Taking another, he passed it to Trista. "Come on. Seems we have the place to ourselves."

"This feels wrong," said Dek, looking about, grasping the hefty spear in his fists. "Where's the City Watch? Where's the King's Guard? Have the fuckers just *run away*? Why's it always come down to us, eh? That's what I want to know. Orlana's mud-orcs, twisted fucking elf-rats, now a fucking dragon – oh, the Iron Wolves'll deal with it, they'll sort out the shit, no worries, no questions asked. Whilst everyone else fucks off and hides in cellars and drinks cider and eats toasted currant muffins."

He subsided.

"You finished?" growled Mola.

"Not even started, mate," said Dek.

"Well, put a lid on your mouth. Because we've a long fight ahead of us, I reckon."

"Oh yeah?"

Mola gave a long, low whistle. And from the fog came three horrific beasts, hell hounds, fighting dogs barely under control – even under their master. Mola knelt on the cobbles, fondling Duke, Sarge and Thrasher; cuddling them, stroking them, hugging them, allowing them to lick his face with tongues better suited to eating demons from the Chaos Halls.

"I always meant to ask… " said Dek.

"Yeah?"

"Where the *fuck* did you get such ugly beasts?"

"I bred them with your mother," grinned Mola.

There was a moment of tenseness. You did not joke about Dek's mum. And, for a moment, in his own heightened tension, Mola had forgotten. Realising his error, he stood, and held up both hands. "Look, I'm… "

"No!" laughed Dek. "No, don't worry. Is a funny joke. My mother. Yes. You only have to look at my face!"

And they all burst out laughing, Trista and Narnok sharing a glance behind Dek's back. Not very long ago, a comment like that would have got you a broken spine. It would seem facing down death with a rogue dragon was enough to chill Dek out. For the present time, at least.

"Come on. Let's climb."

They moved into the tower, and looking upwards, started up the spiral stone steps. They were narrow and curved, and did not lend themselves to climbing. Dek came last, and stopped outside the tower, staring up at the high walls which surrounded the city. They were fashioned from huge blocks of stone which reminded him very much of the walls of Desekra. But whereas that last battle had been a war against mud-orcs, a host created from humans and blood and magick, now, here, this battle was against a solitary foe. A dragon. A powerful, sentient beast with, apparently, her own twisted agenda.

"Let's do this," muttered Dek to himself, and grasping the spear, he entered the dark interior and started to climb.

They stood on the flat summit of the Spear Guard Tower, and looked out across the city of Vagan – or at least, what they could see above the heavy fog. Fire burned in a hundred different places, some still raging, like the Church of Sacred Spires, and some just glowing amidst the fog, like Whore's Quartet and Pig Square Market. Volak had certainly been busy in her little one-dragon mission of fire and destruction.

Mola ran across the roof to a huge contraption. It had six cups, each the size of a large melon, and in surrounding baskets, thick lead balls which could be loaded with much swearing and grunting. Mola lifted one, and dropped it into a cup, then grabbed a huge lever and started to wind it. Clicking reverberated across the rooftop.

"What is it?" said Narnok.

"We used to call it the Decimator. Unbelievable against infantry and cavalry. Fair fucks up anything that gets in its path."

"So you'd fire it from up here?"

"Aye. Not so accurate, but it was designed to carve a big fucking hole in a front line when they're all bunched up together. Forget shields and plate armour, these lead balls would go through ten men before coming to rest."

"This the crossbow?" said Dek, grabbing the huge length of iron and twisting it on its oiled monopod. It was mounted on a ball and socket arrangement that meant Dek could swing it easily and precisely, despite its weight. The siege crossbow itself was easily the length of a horse, and Narnok stepped over, whistling softly as he stopped and grabbed a crossbow "quarrel".

He grunted. It was as heavy as him.

"That's some fucking spear," grunted the axeman, and with Dek's help, loaded the quarrel into the machine.

"Now rotate that, yes, the grey handle." Dek turned the

handle, which clicked on a heavy ratchet. "It'll take three. Load her up. Kareem, help me fill up Old Bessy here."

"Old Bessy?"

"Six balls is never enough," winked Mola, with a disgusting grin.

Far across the city there came an awful, awful wail. It lifted above the smoke, and hung there, a solitary, mournful note, which finally died away and was gone, leaving a resonance surfing across the fog.

Gradually, silence returned.

Only the distant crackle of fire infiltrated the muted city.

"Was that her?" said Narnok, eventually.

"I reckon it might have been," said Dek, loading the third quarrel into the siege crossbow. "And I also reckon, if it *is*, then maybe, thanks to Mola here, we have the weapons to fight her."

"We'll only get one shot," said Mola, then eyed the crossbow. "Well. In your case, maybe three. If the fucker doesn't torch you first."

"You believe these weapons can bring her down?"

Mola shrugged, and knelt, patting Thrasher. The great shaggy beast, more a cross between demon and wolf than actual *dog*, gave a little, half-friendly whine.

Dek smiled at it.

Thrasher growled and bared fangs. That look said, *not fucking welcome.*

With weapons loaded, the Iron Wolves looked out over the city. Nothing stirred. Smoke flowed, undulated, coalesced. Occasionally, a dog barked, or there came a bang, a crash, as some opportunistic looter kicked his way into a shop or undefended house; but other than that, nothing.

No dragon.

No attack.

No fire.

No violence.

Kareem moved to the opposite side of the tower, and stared south. His mind wandered, and he pictured the massive structure of Desekra Fortress. Desekra, four mighty walls with wide battlements and high crenellations, built by King Esekra the Great. Deep within the Pass of Splintered Bones, a place of haunted misery; thus Desekra had grown on the splintered bones of the thousands who had fallen defending the pass against the southern desert tribes. Wedged between towering mountains, Desekra had become a stronghold, a symbol of Vagandrak power, of not bowing to the whims of larger armies and more powerful nations. There were four walls: Sanderlek, Tranta-Kell, Kubosa and Jandallakla – leading to Zula, a huge, stocky keep, black and grim and foreboding, more like a prison than the core of a fortress. Zula meant *peace* in the old Equiem tongue, and it had been here, on his deathbed, that old King Esekra had indeed found peace, secure in the knowledge he had built not just a protective barrier to guard his people of the north. No. It also stood as a monument to the greatest Battle King ever to walk the lands of Vagandrak.

Now, Kareem thought about that king, and his mind drifted to the days of blood, fighting the mud-orcs. Sent by Orlana the Changer, otherwise known as The Horse Lady, the mud-orcs had numbered in their thousands and attempted to storm Vagandrak, aiming for the soft underbelly of the lands beyond Desekra.

But the soldiers of Vagandrak had held a different opinion.

Kareem shivered, remembered knives and spears and swords – steel jutting into eyes, cutting open bowels, skewering livers. He shivered, and remembered comrades vomiting blood on the battlements. But the worst bit had been the screams of those he knew, those he loved; those wounded beyond reach, whimpering, crying, begging to be released from their mortal agony as mud-orcs crouched beside them, drooling and laughing and masturbating, unwilling to let these good men die, unwilling to put them out of their misery so that their cries could taunt the survivors and sap their morale.

"She's playing with us," said Kareem, suddenly, looking up.

"What?" said Dek.

"The dragon. That fire never hurt her. She's testing us. And she's playing with us. Like a cat with an injured mouse."

"Why?"

"*I* don't fucking know," said Kareem. "Maybe it was because we stood up to her. Gave her a fight. I bet she respects that. In us *insects*."

"So what happens next?"

"We wait," smiled Kareem, grimly. "We wait. And our fear grows. And thus she grows stronger."

"Well, I ain't scared," said Narnok, and Kareem looked into his eyes, and he truly believed it.

"Ain't nothing scares you, eh, old man?"

"Less of the fucking old. You're only old when you're sucking soup through a tube and you can't get a hard-on for a beautiful woman who's shoving her erect nipples in your mouth. That's when you call it a day. That's when you beg for your bed, your slippers and your fucking grave."

"I remember you," said Kareem. "On Desekra."

Narnok puffed out his chest. "You do, lad?"

"Yeah. And... I don't mean to sound like I'm kissing your arse, but you were... incredible. Just a killing machine. I've never seen anything quite like it."

Narnok shrugged, and stared off above the distant fog. "Killing ain't really something to be proud of, lad." Somewhere, a bell chimed. It was a haunting, lonely note. "I never asked to be the way I am," he said, voice now soft, not really speaking to anybody, just voicing an internal diatribe which wanted, *needed,* to be free. "I was a good man, once. But every man has his head on the anvil of life, and some get slapped, some get hit with a hammer, and some get pulverised by a sledgehammer. I was the latter. Toughened me up. Made me realise no cunt was going to look after me in this world; no. All everybody wanted to do was take, and so I'd have to look after myself, real hard, like."

Trista moved forward, and sat suddenly, cross-legged. She looked up at Kareem and Narnok. "I agree. I had my whole life, my whole world ahead of me. And my cheating bastard husband took it away. And so I took him away. And I'm still taking him away." Tears were on her cheeks, and Kareem realised she had a razor dagger in each hand. "I wish Kiki were here," she said. "Kiki understood."

"And Zastarte," said Dek. "I miss that dandy bastard, despite his fucking silk and lace."

Trista laughed, and rubbed tears from her eyes. "Yes. Zastarte."

Narnok fished a flask from his pocket, and unscrewing the cap, lifted it. "To Kiki and Zastarte," he said. "Gone, but not forgotten." The others repeated his words, and he took a hefty swig and passed it around. Dek swallowed, as did Trista. When it was Kareem's turn, he choked on the liquid fire, spluttering like a toddler on too-hot milk.

"What the fuck is this?"

"Serendian Fire Water. It'll put hairs on your chest, lad," grinned Narnok.

"Or scars in my gullet."

"That as well."

Distantly, fire blossomed. It rose up into the sky, eating through the fog, and roared for a while, white-hot and terrifying.

"Dragon, or natural explosion?" said Trista, idly.

"We'll soon find out," rumbled Narnok, scratching at one of his facial scars.

"I meant to ask," said Kareem.

"Yeah?"

"The scars… on your face…"

"Yeah?" Narnok turned purple.

"Oh. Nothing."

Trista jumped up, and put a hand on Narnok's heavy shoulder. "He doesn't mean anything. Let it go."

"Well, some people give me no privacy."

"Let it go, Narn."

"I'm just saying."

"Let it go."

The scream echoed through the city of Vagan, and it contained not just fury, but white-hot hatred.

"I reckon this is our favourite little bitch," said Mola, scanning the horizon. It was vaporous and ethereal, fog illuminated by fires beneath. Tonight, due to the dragon attack, no lamps had been lit. Only the fires, the moon and the stars supplied their light on this ghostly scene. It was quite unique.

"When she comes, she'll come fast," said Dek, looking up at the stars. For a moment he felt quite emotional. This might be the last time he ever witnessed them. Tonight, in a few minutes, time could be his last moment in the world. And then he'd be gone, and within a short time nobody would remember the name Dek. No children to mourn him. No children to continue his name – to give him at least a little form of longevity.

"Damn." His eyes shone. "Let's give her a fucking fight."

"Will do," grinned Narnok, and slapped Kareem on the back. "You up for this, lad?"

"Yeah, I am," said Kareem.

"Well, help Mola on the ball thing; me and Dek will operate the crossbow."

They grabbed their weapons, and waited.

When she came, they didn't see her. They only heard her.

There came a *swish* of air, high above. Glancing up, something dark obliterated the stars, and then was gone.

"She's checking us out," said Dek, and swivelled the crossbow around on its monopod, so it was facing up. "Come on you wyrm bitch, give us a clear shot."

"Do you think she knows what we've got here?" said Kareem.

"Well, she'll soon find out. We'll learn her!"

Again, something slammed high overhead, dark against the stars. And they saw her shape flash before the near-full moon. And it was true. Volak, Queen of the Wyrms, was far from dead.

"What's she been waiting for?"

"Recovering, I reckon," said Narnok, grinning. "Maybe we did hurt her."

"Time to hurt her some more," said Dek.

Volak fell from the sky like an asteroid, screaming towards the tower, wings folded back, jets of fire burning in her maw. She turned at the last moment, wings smashing to slow her, and a huge roaring *wall* of fire screamed across the face of the tower, aimed directly at the Iron Wolves, who cowered with wide eyes in sudden shock and fear...

The Harvest Field

It was harvest time. Bales had been gathered, and formed crude straw walls. They walked along a rough mud track, hand in hand, stopping occasionally to gaze at one another. Their eyes shone. Love defined their faces.

"Look," she said, and pointed.

Beetrax turned, and could see the outline of a stone ruin. He frowned. His face was a face created for frowning. "What is it?"

"The old Kelbery Church. Seven hundred years old. It's beautiful. Want to see?"

"You're beautiful."

"No I'm not." She blushed, and lowered her eyes coquettishly.

"Oh but you are, my lady," he said, and stepped in close. Closer. And they stood, like magnets, attracted, pulled towards one another, trapped in one another's orbit. And when you were trapped within another orbit, you were, quite literally, fucked.

"I'm not beautiful," she repeated.

"You are," he said, moving a little closer. He smelled her skin. He smelled her hair. It was subtle, but necessary.

"Did you just smell me?"

"Yes. You smell good."

She didn't know how to respond.

Unconsciously, her hand came up and rested on his hip.

She did not realise what that meant to him. That unbidden instinct. That soul connection. That subtle and yet intimate moment, not designed, not chosen, just a part of natural intimacy.

"I like that," he said.

"I like it as well," she said.

His head lowered. He stared at her. Their lips were inches away.

"Do you realise, you have a love heart of freckles on your cheek?"

"I do?"

"Yes."

"It must be because I'm so in love with you. So kiss me," she said.

And he kissed her.

Their kiss lasted a million years. And then her hands came up, gripping his hips. And slowly, they lay down amongst the bales of hay.

"Kiss me again," she said.

He did. His hands moved over her, exploring, gentle, questing, and she did not complain. Slowly, she removed her skirts, her blouse, her undergarments, and she lay back, naked and pale and beautiful, a perfection doll, motionless amidst the hay.

She gazed up at him, face like the moon, eyes wide and imploring.

He lowered himself onto her, into her, and she groaned, and that primal animal groan fried his blood like no words or golden coin could ever fire him. She wanted him. She *needed* him. She was his, body and soul, and in return, he was hers, body and soul.

They made love in the hay field, under the beaming sun, with the ruined church in the background, a sentinel watching over their embracing of nature, their base merging with the magic of the earth, of this simple, natural joining, of connection, of sharing, of love.

Afterwards, they lay giggling like children. Until

awareness of their nudity prompted them into action.

She dressed, her beaming smile one of hope and joy.

He dressed, mind swimming, watching her, watching her move, every simple elegance a wondrous moment.

"Hey, aye, what the fuck have we got here then?"

Six young men were on the path, watching Lillith hurriedly pull her blouse together. The largest of the youths, Jelgeth, leered at her. "I've been asking you for months, but you'll happily get your tits out for this fucking simpleton!" he growled, eyes narrowed.

"Shut up," said Lillith.

"Why?" asked Jelgeth, looking genuinely surprised. "A whore needs good coin to open her legs. And yet you – why, you do it for free!"

A ripple of laughter circled the group.

"Why, you arrogant, hateful little bastard," growled Beetrax, stepping forward, as a young man rose before him with an old, battered helve, and swung, clubbing him. Beetrax hit the ground hard and fast, blood leaking from a crack in his skull. The youth with the helve smiled, and nodded to Jelgeth, and the circle moved, and closed, and contracted around Lillith, now pale with fear.

She glanced down at Beetrax. The woodcutter was out cold, blood leaking from his head, along his jaw, forming a point on his chin, and dripping slowly into the rich brown earth of harvested stalks.

Jelgeth stepped in close, and Lillith screamed as he leapt forward, grabbing her, and bearing her to the ground, kicking and screaming, his mouth pressing against her face, his tongue licking streaks across her struggling cheeks. Two others were there, each grabbing a leg and pulling her wide open.

And then – calm. Silence.

Jelgeth moved close. "You're a pretty one, all right. And even though that big, dumb bastard has filled you full of his seed, each man here is going to enjoy you. And you know something, pretty one? You'll keep your mouth shut.

But more importantly, you'll fucking enjoy it. Because my father is the Warden of Vagandrak, and I can have your whole family put to death with a single word. You hear that, pretty one?"

"You are scum," said Lillith, spitting in Jelgeth's eye.

He laughed, wiping it away and looking at her fluid. "Well. That'll be a start in getting you wet... if you aren't already..."

Lillith screamed again, and Jelgeth started struggling, tugging at her underwear.

Beetrax rose behind the fixated group, blood pouring down his face, his eyes dark, like pools leading down a tunnel into death. He moved to the man who had hit him with the helve, and punched him in the back of the head. Even though he was unconscious when he hit the ground, Beetrax stamped on his head, twice, and took the helve, weighing it thoughtfully. He wished it was an axe. But here, and now, timber would have to be good enough.

"Oy. Cunts," he growled.

They all turned.

Beetrax smiled.

"Welcome to my rapists' party of pain," and the helve swung, hitting a man in the face and knocking six teeth out with a bloody crunch. His head slammed sideways, expression intense and twisted, and he flailed his way to the ground.

Beetrax waded forward, the helve slamming left and right. Arms came up in defence. Bones cracked. Broke. Poked from skin with piss showers of blood. The helve cracked jaws, breaking them, sending young men screaming to the soil. It cracked skulls. It knocked out teeth. It broke legs and cheek bones. Beetrax waded through them like a scythe through wheat, no fear, filled with a dark hate that burned in his narrowed eyes.

And then they were all down, moaning and screaming and holding broken faces, except for Jelgeth, whose eyes burned and arrogance shone as he turned, still holding Lillith's ankles.

"Don't do anything stupid, peasant," said Jelgeth. "My father is the Warden of Vagandrak! I can have you hanged from the battlements for heresy so easy, it isn't even funny. So let me fuck this bitch, and then you can have a second go, and then we'll go for a few beers. I'll even buy them, to show you there's no hard feelings." He stared hard at Beetrax, and any who knew Jelgeth knew the young man was deadly serious, backed up by a reputation of malice, violence and an abuse of power.

"Well," said Beetrax, rubbing his square chin, "that's a mighty fine offer, from one so highly placed as you."

"Yes?"

"But."

"But what?"

"But I'll have to decline."

Jelgeth stared at the large youth. "Based on what?"

"Based on the fact I'm going to beat you to death, you fucking rapist."

The helve hit Jelgeth in the face, dislodging teeth and breaking his nose.

"No!" gasped Lillith, her hand coming up.

But Beetrax was in a different world, a different time, and he stepped over the bastard and the helve rose and fell, beating his head into a mashed, deformed pulp.

Afterwards, Beetrax stood there panting.

"What have you done?" whispered Lillith.

"I've made Vagandrak a better place."

"But... his father! The Warden! He will never stop hunting you!"

"I've been hunted before," growled Beetrax, and despite his nineteen years, he looked as mean as any wild predator on the hunt. This wasn't fun. This was fucking survival.

Lillith gazed about, tugging together the torn buttons of her blouse. A cool wind blew, shifting her beautiful, rich hair.

"What about the others? They are witness to your killing?"

Beetrax grinned a nasty grin, and as the other broken men were coming round, he moved forward, dropping the helve and pulling free his small skinning dagger. "That's all right. They'll never speak again," he said, as he cut the first tongue from its owner's mouth with a struggle and a scream.

Mallageth, Warden of Vagandrak, walked down the cobbled road, face grim, eyes narrowed, thinking about his debts. Gambling debts. Debts from the whore house. Debs from borrowing money from the Red Thumbs.

"Horse shit." No matter how much he gambled, no matter how much he risked, no matter how good his luck was – well, he always came off worse. And the Red Thumb Gang were starting to take a very real interest in him, despite his rank.

His two guards walked ten yards behind. They were good, alert, hands on daggers, eyes searching. And so it came as some surprise when a large man stepped from the shadows and decked both guards with single punches. Mallageth heard the crunch of broken bones and whirled, whimpering the one defence he had ingrained for moments like this...

"I have lots of silver! Don't hurt me! It can be yours!"

Beetrax loomed from the shadows, eyes evil. "You are Jelgeth's father?"

"I might be?" offered Mallageth, tentatively, his arms coming up.

"I'll take that as a yes."

Beetrax stooped, and pulled a sword from one of the guards. He grinned at Mallageth. "It would seem your parenting skills have been called into question."

The sword lifted, moonlight glinting from the chipped blade.

"What do you mean?" squealed Mallageth.

Beetrax loomed close. "It seems you've raised a rapist as a son," he said, and the sword hacked down, cutting the Warden's head straight down the middle. Mallageth hit the cobbles, and slowly, his mashed brains leaked out, a grey and blue ooze.

Beetrax pushed back his shoulders, and dropped the short sword with a clang. He looked around for witnesses, but if truth be told, he didn't care. Right now, he'd take on the fucking world.

"And if there's one thing I hate," he whispered, "it's fucking rapists."

Rage

Volak's wall of fire screamed towards the Iron Wolves, but fell short by inches, the heat scorching eyebrows and fringes of the shocked heroes who lifted arms to protect their faces. Flames scorched the stone. Volak dropped and twisted, accelerating down the street, demolishing two chimneys into a shower of bricks... and then was gone.

"A warning shot?" rumbled Narnok, voice deep, breathing quickly. "She'll be back, and back quick."

"We know that, donkey dick," snapped Trista. "Just be fucking ready!"

"I'll be ready!" snarled Narnok, as Volak erupted from the centre of the building before them, stones and bricks smashed up and outwards in arcing trajectories, and she hung there before the tower, screaming, as fire blasted out once more, and the Iron Wolves stared at her in horror before suddenly hitting the ground hard and fast as fire washed over their heads and illuminated the night sky and the summit of the Spear Guard Tower and the very world...

Volak's great wings flapped, gave a boom, and she banked, and was gone, accelerating down through the fog of her own creation, to disappear amidst the city chaos.

Narnok climbed to his feet. "It's all right!" he said. "I'm all right!"

"She was *right in front of you!*" yelled Dek. "All you had to do was pull the fucking triggers!"

"Hey!" Narnok brushed some soot from his shirt. "She got me by surprise, all right? I can't be mister-bloody-everywhere-vision, can I?"

Dek scowled. "You're joking, right?"

"Guys! She's coming back!" hissed Trista.

"How can you tell?"

Tris pointed. The smoky haze was shifting, as her flight beneath the smoke dragged patterns in her wake, like a shark in the ocean, creating shapes above.

Volak rose from the smoke, and Narnok screamed, and pulled the trigger on the massive crossbow. A massive quarrel sang, flashing through the night air, to skim Volak's wing as she banked, rapidly, a strangled scream erupting from her dark jaws. Although it didn't penetrate, the quarrel sheared free a line of scales which fluttered like errant iron butterflies for a moment, before tumbling beneath the smoke. Black blood spurted out.

And in a flash, she was gone.

"You see that?" roared Narnok.

Kareem slapped him, grinning. "You cut her up!" he boomed.

"Don't get slack," rumbled Dek. "She's hurting now; she's pissed. She'll be back fast, mark my words. We need to be ready!"

And Dek was right. She came back through the centre of the demolished building, and her eyes were acid, and she breathed, flames flowering like nothing the Iron Wolves had ever witnessed, washing over the tower top and setting fire to the Decimator's huge stock. The roar seemed to go on and on, and it was like the end of the world.

"No!" wailed Mola, lying low, hands over his head, back seared as flames scorched above him. The Decimator's wood burned, and the cups burned, and heavy lead balls dropped to the stone flags with six long, slow thuds.

The fire stopped.

The silence was deafening.

And Volak was gone, leaving a destroyed siege machine in her fiery wake.

•••

Long minutes had passed. The stone tower summit had cooled, but still they could smell scorched stone, burned metal, smoke.

"It's getting cooler," said Kareem, and lifted his nose to a lulling chilled breeze.

The others stared at him, and glanced about.

"Seems fine to me," said Dek, looking up at the moon and the stars. "See? All our favourite constellations."

"No. There's a storm coming," said Trista.

They looked to the west, and huge clouds towered over one another, tumbling as they fell forward, heading east towards the humbled city of Vagan.

"That's good, right?" said Dek.

"Why good?" asked Trista, with a tight smile.

"The dragon... if it's still alive... well, the storm will mask us; make everything harder to see..."

"Or maybe it uses scent? The scent of our blood? Or sound? Or heat? Dek, maybe it has better night vision than we do?"

Dek scowled. "Fuck me, Trista, you're ever the optimist, right?"

They waited, watching the distant storm roll in. The dragon no longer emerged; she had vanished. Deep down in the city, fires burned below the smoky fog, illuminating from beneath. It was spooky. Otherworldly.

"That's creepy," said Narnok.

"Worse than your face?" said Dek, with a grin.

"Yeah. Thanks for that, you fucking cuckold."

The tumbling clouds were blacker than black. Lightning cracked through them, splitting the sky like a ruptured insect egg.

Time rolled back, languorous, as below, the city appeared to sleep.

"Do you think we killed the dragon?" said Narnok, at last.

Trista stared at him. "Do you?"

"We winged it."

"We might have hurt it. But remember the factory?"

"That was oil. The bitch is fireproof – we learned that one today. But this was steel. Cold, hard steel."

"We didn't kill it," said Mola, sombrely. "It'd take more than that. Much more."

A cold wind blew, chilling them. And now they could hear the rain, as the clouds rolled in and gradually covered the moon and stars. Darkness fell, and the world was lit only by the burning fires below.

"And I know that we are lost, and none can help us now," intoned Kareem.

Dek nudged Narnok. "Happy little fucker, ain't he?"

"Leave him alone. I know how he feels."

Lightning broke the sky into triangular segments, thunder rumbled, and the storm came crashing in over Vagan. As the lightning vanished, crackling, so it left blue after-images tattooed against their brains.

Now, they heard the patter of rainfall, which seemed gentle at first. But it was not gentle. It became steadily more violent, slamming towards them in smashing diagonal sheets, and then, with a surge, washed over the Iron Wolves like a great flood, drenching them instantly.

"Are we having fun yet?" smiled Trista, grimly.

"Just keep an eye out for the wyrm," said Dek, both hands on the massive crossbow. "When she comes in, she'll come in fast. I guarantee it. She's biding her time. Waiting for us to drop our guard. I reckon I know how she thinks."

"Yeah, right," scoffed Narnok. "How could you possibly have any clue how a fucking dragon thinks? She's probably a million years old and used to eating us humans for breakfast."

Dek shrugged. "I've just… been watching her. I understand her. She has a natural cunning."

"Yeah. I'll give you that one," said Narnok, and the others nodded, wiping rain from their eyes.

The rain pounded Vagan, and gradually began to erode the smoke. More thunder rumbled, and lightning cracked

out, demolishing the spire of a church in a massive blast of
sparks and fire. Roof slates and stones tumbled, bouncing
down the flanks of the structure. The Iron Wolves watched
with wide eyes, taking deep breaths, then scanning the
horizon again.

"As if Vagan ain't got enough problems," said Narnok,
"without Mother Nature getting in on the act."

"There's another cruel bitch, if ever I've seen one," said
Kareem, wiping a sheen of water from his forehead. He gave
a twisted smile, as droplets pattered from his massive bushy
beard, now a glossy black pelt. His dark eyes gleamed.

"At least she's neutral in her hate and murder. She kills
good and evil indiscriminately," said Dek.

"I've got this great story about my dogs," began Mola.

Everybody groaned. "Please," said Dek, holding up
his hand, his drenched sleeve flapping, "I love you like a
brother, Mo. I'd kill for you, and I'd die for you. But I swear,
one more story about those fucking flea-bitten mutts and
I'll toss you from this very tower myself."

"*Flea-bitten mutts*?" Mola whistled, and the huge beasts
came out of the relative safety of the stairwell, and trotted
to their master, growling at the other Iron Wolves as they
passed. Mola fondled their shaggy pelts. In fact, they were
barely dog; more between dog and wolf. "These bitches have
saved my life on more than one occasion. They are family.
My tribe." He coughed, and seemed to be getting quite
upset. Nobody could see his tears through the pounding
rain. "They're the only family I have left."

Trista moved over to him, but Duke growled. Mola
rapped his knuckles on the beast's snout. Duke subsided.
Trista stepped in close, and gave the stocky man a big, rain-
soaked hug.

"We're your family as well, Mo. Don't forget that."

"Yeah. I love you guys. But you're not the same as my
dogs."

"Really?" She moved back, hands still planted on his
shoulders, face kind. "Explain?"

Mola looked up at the towering black storm clouds which now covered Vagan. The rain was still bouncing from his face, but he was so wet he no longer cared – you could only *get* so wet. Then he glanced off across the city. "People are people. They love, they hate, they fight, they fuck, they have babies, they disappoint one another, they stab each other in the back, they betray and steal and basically fuck one another over without a second thought. Men betray their wives, wives betray their husbands, best friends turn bad, work colleagues try their best to fuck over the others in a scramble to the top of the cockroach cockpile shit heap; it's all a barrel of cheap donkey shit. But dogs. No. No, no. Dogs are loving and kind and, most importantly, loyal. Once a dog has its master, or mistress, that dog is completely loyal. It'll kill for you. Die for you. Protect you over everything else. You can beat that dog with a stick, but it'll still come back. A dog's love is unconditional. It doesn't care whether you're human, dwarf, elf, what colour your skin is, what fucking religion you are. The dog loves the person. The person loves the image, the perception, the package. Change the package, and the deal is off. I knew this guy, had the most loving wife ever, but he got his legs cut off on the walls of Desekra. What did his loving wife do? Ran away with his best friend. Even tol' him, she tol' him she wasn't looking after no disabled. That's people, Tris. People can be real bad deep down inside."

"And dogs can't be?" said Kareem, who'd put down a few rabid specimens in his time. "When dogs turn, they can turn real bad." He said it gently; it was not a criticism.

"But not on their masters," said Mola, smugly. "I know these things."

Kareem opened his mouth to argue, but Trista gave a quick shake of her head. To Mola, dog was god and god was dog. And that didn't even take into consideration his dyslexia.

"I'm going to get more spears," said Mola, face a frown, and disappeared with his hounds in tow into the depths and bowels of the tower.

The rest of the Iron Wolves stood for a while, in silence,

scanning the city. Despite the fog clearing thanks to the torrential downpour, now the clouds had blocked out the moon and stars, and the city seemed even more gloomy and claustrophobic. Some fires had been extinguished, but miraculously, many still burned. These were now the single source of illumination through the entire vast network of streets and alleys. Dark days really had come again.

"Where is she?" muttered Dek, moving the siege crossbow around, as if taking aim. "Come on, you bitch."

"She's biding her time," said Narnok, matter-of-factly. "Either that, or we killed her."

"We didn't kill her," said Kareem, who was like a dog with a bone when an idea incepted.

"I reckon," said Narnok, scratching his drenched, heavily scarred face, "and just listen, before you start putting me down, but I reckon there's a good chance we penetrated her armour, and she's either lying down there, bleeding to death, or fucked right off and away, because she knows she can't..."

There came a *whump*.

"...can't really..."

Another *whump*. The air seemed to shift and alter, as something blacker than the velvet darkness arose from the gloomy chasm.

"...conquer us, like." Narnok turned, as another *whump* made him stagger back, blasted by the force of air from those great, outstretched wings, and Volak was there, big and black and evil. Thunder rumbled. The Iron Wolves stared at one another. Then in sudden panic Dek spun the huge siege crossbow around as Volak breathed in, her black eyes glinting, her lips drawn back over her fangs, fire rolling around her snout, and she prepared to murder with extreme prejudice...

Narnok paused at sentence end, mouth hanging open, like the biggest of village idiots.

Dek hissed.

Kareem drew back his spear...

And lightning crackled from the sky, a great actinic zig-zag, striking Volak with a terrific splash of bright white energy, a strike which split into hundreds of fingers of lightning, crackling through the wyrm's scales, through her limbs, through her body and snout, and spinning her around in a series of tight circles, flames bursting out along her body as she reared, wings folded, and suddenly plummeted to the hard cobbled street far below…

Dek, Narnok and Kareem sprinted forward, leaping up onto the slippery stone battlements. They peered down into the gloom.

"She's down there!" crowed Narnok, triumphantly.

"By the gods, I think it killed her!" grinned Kareem.

"She's all folded up, smouldering, lying still."

"If only we had some big rocks to drop on her," said Narnok, idly fingering a facial scar. He looked around at the others. "What? *What*?"

"Just want to make sure, eh?" said Dek, shaking his head.

"Aye, I've watched her get up too many bloody times! I'd feel a little bit better if we could drop some rocks on her evil twisted hide."

Dek rubbed his chin, and sniffed the air. Again, thunder rumbled from the black, coalescing heavens. He could smell hot metal, scorched iron, cooked flesh. "I reckon that lightning did for her, good. Boff! The power of Mother Nature. So much for your fucking theory, eh Narnok?"

"What theory's that, then?"

"You, moaning about Nature never giving us a helping hand! She bloody helped us out real good this time!"

"Well, about time!" snapped Narnok.

"Never happy, are you? Always moaning."

"Well, it's what happens when you have a happy life, and some cunt cuckolds you, and you end up having your eye put out and horrific facial scars carved into you because of your evil bitch of an ex-wife. That kind of shit makes a man paranoid, you know what I mean?"

"Er, Narnok?"

"What?"

"Shut up for a moment."

"No, fuck you, Dek, I won't fucking shut up for a moment! How dare you, you pugilistic little scrawny bastard. You know how this thing goes, and you know you stabbed me in the fucking back, instead of being a friend to me, and, you know, not fucking my wife. What am I supposed to think of you when you're the one who fucked my wife?"

"*Shut up*!"

"Why the *fuck* should *I* shut up, when *I'm* the one who's injured, eh?"

Dek spoke very slowly, very carefully, his eyes swivelling up to fix on Narnok. "Because," he said, and licked his dry lips, "the dragon is moving."

"Oh." Narnok peered down.

The distant, black, crumpled mess was indeed moving. At first it seemed she was squirming, like eels in oil, or mud-orcs in slime, but this quickly turned into an act of unfolding herself and straightening out her massive, spike-tipped wings.

"Er," said Dek, and met Narnok's gaze. "Now's the time for those bloody rocks!"

"Bollocks! Man the fucking crossbow! I cannot *believe* a lightning strike only slowed her down."

"That's one hardened bitch," said Kareem, shaking his head.

The rain pounded the Iron Wolves, lashing across the city, and Mola appeared from the stairwell carrying as many heavy spears as he could manage. He was red in the face from the climb. "Here." He allowed the spears to tumble from his arms, where they clattered onto the stone tower's summit floor, now awash with sheets of draining water. The gutters gurgled, sending a stream into vertical troughs cleverly built into the very fabric of the tower. They could hear the water gushing down towards street level, and probably the sewers beyond.

"She's getting up!" bellowed Narnok. "Let's be ready!"

The others each grabbed a spear, and readied themselves. Narnok was the only one standing on the battlements, on the treacherous, rain-slippery ledge.

Thunder rumbled. A huge lightning bolt crashed down, smashing up a civic office and spreading the majority of it across a quarter of an acre.

"Fucking bureaucrats deserve to burn," muttered Narnok. Then, "Right lads, she's flapping out her wings, now she's looking up, er, it looks like she's looking up directly *at me*, and that is just too fucking freaky…" He glanced back at Dek, who shrugged.

"Get down here and grab a fucking spear, will you?"

"Wait! Wait! She's… she's unfolding her wings, no, she's folding them up again…"

There came a mammoth, reverberating *crash*. The world seemed to vibrate. There were sounds of tearing wood, beams being stripped into splinters, and a roar of fire that carried heat up to them, even over such a great height.

"Is she coming?" screamed Dek.

Narnok turned and stared at him. His mouth flapped open and closed.

"Narnok, you idiot! Which direction is she coming from? Speak, you bastard son of a bastard's son!"

"Er," said Narnok, and his gaze swept the Iron Wolves.

"What *is* it?" snapped Kareem.

"She's, like, gone inside the tower."

"Which tower?" said Dek, frowning.

"The one on the other side of the fucking city," snapped Narnok, gritting his teeth. "Which fucking tower do you think?"

They stared at one another. Trista hefted a spear.

There came more crashes, terrible rending sounds, and the tortured noise of twisting, screaming iron.

"What's she *doing* down there?" muttered Mola.

Rain lashed across the tower-top. More towering clouds rolled in. The storm was in for the night.

Thunder growled.

Lightning crashed zig-zag streamers.

And yet, despite the noise, the sounds from inside the tower were greater. Volak, seemingly, was tearing the place apart.

Suddenly, the tower shuddered.

The Iron Wolves looked at one another.

"Duke, Sarge, Thrasher. To me!" Even though his voice was low, he still commanded obedience. Mola grabbed the thick, studded collars of his dogs, and frowned. "I don't like this. What's the bitch doing?"

"Smashing things up in a temper?" suggested Narnok. "If I'd just been struck by lightning, I'd be smashing things up in a temper."

Dek scowled. "If somebody spills your fucking *ale*, you smash things up in a temper."

"Now now, lad, no need to be like that," said Narnok.

There came a high-pitched keening sound, a ululation which reverberated up from the bowels of the structure. And then more crashes and squeals of tearing wood, and the crunching of broken stones, crumbled walls, smashed pillars.

"That's louder," said Dek, tilting his head, frowning. Thanks to some sudden inner intuition, he swivelled the siege crossbow around – away from the street – and towards the top of the stairs leading from the tower interior. "Kareem. Jump up on those battlements, tell me what you see."

Kareem did so. "Nothing," he said, eventually.

"No dragon taking to the skies?"

"No."

There came a blast, and a noise like air being sucked through a pipe.

"What was that?"

"A fire blast," said Kareem.

"You saw it?"

"I saw flames coming through a window."

"At ground level?"

"No. About a third of the way up."

The Iron Wolves looked at one another. There was understanding in those looks. It was an uneasy understanding that did not bring happiness.

"Fuck. She's fighting her way up, isn't she?" said Narnok. "Through the bricks and the beams?"

The tower shook again. There came crashing, banging, tearing sounds. The tower trembled, like a leper in a brothel.

A roar screamed through the tower, high-pitched and filled with hate.

There was a *whoooosh* and a sound like a smith's furnace, roaring and roaring and roaring.

"She's higher now," said Kareem. To his credit, he kept the tremor from his voice, but his face was twisted, as if to say, *what the fuck do we do? The fucking dragon's climbing up the inside of the tower? There's no way out!*

Again, the structure trembled. Shook. Rain lashed down. Thunder rumbled. Lighting cracked the sky like a bad egg.

Suddenly, there was a tearing sound. Trista leapt back as a zig-zag of black raced across the floor, crackling, almost like a lightning strike, or a mockery of one. The others stepped back, and shared nervous glances.

"She's going to bring the whole fucking thing down," rumbled Dek.

"Have we pissed her off that much?" scowled Narnok.

"I think *you* have, mate!"

They considered this. Volak, Queen of the Wyrms. A killer of humans. A killer of dragons. Unchallenged. Not only had Narnok insulted her repeatedly, and buried his axe in the soft tissue of her throat, he'd also been instrumental in torching her like a criminal, like a murderer, like a witch.

Was it safe to assume Volak would stop at nothing to see him dead?

Narnok nodded to himself, face pale beneath the onslaught of the storm.

On Volak came, smashing and destroying, and the Iron Wolves readied their spears. Mola's dogs were growling something horrid, big strings of saliva drooling from jaws ready to kill. Only this time, unfortunately, it wasn't another dog, or even a man. It was a beast considerably larger.

Kareem still stood on the battlements, clutching a spear. And he blinked.

"There's something coming," he said.

"Something? King's Guard? Desekra Fifth Infantry? Cavalry? What is it, lad? What is it?"

"I… don't know."

Kareem watched the shapes pounding down the street. The light was nearly non-existent. And the shapes were… too weird, too big, too misshapen.

"They're monsters," he said, eventually, his voice soft with horror and respect.

"What you fucking talking about, lad?" boomed Narnok, and ran towards him. But at that moment there came a scream, and a smash, and stones blasted upwards, went flying outwards, and a head appeared in the stairwell. It reared, like a serpent from the ocean, black, elongated, equine, dark eyes glittering, flames flickering around a snout filled with razor-sharp fangs and a promise of death.

Volak surveyed the Iron Wolves.

"So here you hide," she said. "Like the fucking cowards you are."

Narnok jumped down from the battlements, Kareem's grab missing him, and brandished his axe in both hands, terribly scarred face puckered into some kind of nightmare. "You remember me, *wyrm*?" He made the word *wyrm* sound like *cunt*. In fact, he said it. "You're a dragon cunt. Slick, and ready to be fucked. So bend over. Narnok's going to teach you a lesson."

Volak stared at him. Black pupils dilated in black eyes.

Kareem swallowed.

"Fuck," hissed Trista.

Fire swirled around Volak's snout…

"You want fucking?" said Mola, his voice so quiet and gentle it could hardly be heard around the buffeting and fury of the storm. Then his arm suddenly came back, and he launched his spear with unnerving accuracy. Volak's head, wedged in the stairwell she'd smashed her way into, could barely manoeuvre. The spear flew from Mola's fist, powered by a smouldering fury. *Fuck with my dogs?* he wanted to scream. *Burn my dogs, will you?*

The spear flew, and slammed into Volak's left orb.

It split, like a ripe melon under a sharpened axe.

Volak screamed, head thrashing from side to side, smashing bricks and timbers.

The tower groaned.

More cracks zigzagged across the tower top, splitting the battlement.

Stones tumbled from the tower's summit.

The world seemed to pause… a hush, a sigh, a hiatus in time.

And then, in slow-motion, stones started to crumble. The base of the huge stone tower bowed outwards, sagging like the shit-filled pants of a terminal alcoholic; the tower moaned, and *shifted*. More stones crumbled, popping free of the main walls like lost dice in a game of *Stab the Officer*. Like teeth knocked free by Dek in the Fighting Pits, his left cross and right hook legendary in fighting circles.

The tower *groaned*.

A dying sea creature.

A moaned resonance of desolation from Sayansora alv Drakka. The Drakka. The Sea of Trees.

The *Suicide Forest*.

Where people went to *die*.

Narnok and Dek caught one another's eyes.

Narnok shrugged.

Dek grinned, a tight-lipped grin containing very little humour.

And then, in one titanic mass of stones and beams and dust, with a sound that blocked out the rage of the storm, the rage of the dragon, the very foundations bowed outwards, cracking, the final supporting beams split, and the tower…

…collapsed.

Underworld

Beetrax crouched by the stairwell, and glanced over his shoulder. In one hand he carried a flaming brand, in the other his battered and chipped axe. He scratched his beard with the head of the axe, and scowled as Lillith approached, her face almost serene.

"This must be it," she said, gently, reverently, and her eyes lifted and she surveyed the vast cavern above them. The ceiling was a dome, perfectly symmetrical and formed from some dark rock, possibly obsidian. It was polished. Smooth. Perfect... too perfect. "Look at this place... not once have we seen such a perfection of engineering from the dwarves!"

"So... we're arrived at Wyrmblood?" queried Dake. "The City of the Dragons?"

Lillith nodded. Her face was flushed, lips red, excitement quite obviously her mistress.

"So, what now?" asked Dake, uneasily.

"We enter."

"Down there?" He gestured to the dark portal, a circular opening in the very ground rock itself.

Lillith nodded, and turned, placing her hand on his shoulder. "Trust me, Dakerath. This is our destiny. Without our intervention, the dragons will return. Without our help, the world will soon be a place of scorched rock, barrenness and genocide. They will exterminate us. They will enslave us. They seek to re-establish the Blood Dragon Empire."

Dake nodded, and looked to the others. Faces were pale and gaunt, eyes just a little haunted. These were people who needed to see the sunlight again. And yet, there was strength there, and a determination to do what was right.

"Well fuck it, we're going in," growled Beetrax. "You want me to lead the way, my beautiful lady?"

"Yes," she smiled, moving up close behind him, and slipping her hands around his waist. She moved closer to his ear. "I love you, Trax," she said, and placed her head against his back. "Until the stars go out."

"I know, flower. I know."

It had taken them perhaps a day to find this relatively new part of the mine, and in the end it was only Beetrax and Dake beating the living shit out of a captured dwarf guard engineer that allowed them to find the place. They'd taken the dwarf prisoner, travelling with him for half a day before they found a series of cells, and were able to lock the battered specimen behind thick iron bars, and throw away the key.

"By rights I should cut out his tongue," said Beetrax, as he stood, glowering at the dwarf. "Then he can't talk." But as ever, Lillith's calm and moderation brought Beetrax back from the brink of violence.

"It's not the moral thing to do," she said.

"This bastard would kill us at the first opportunity," snarled Beetrax.

"And that's what makes us different from them. We will show humanity, and dignity, and fair play. No murder. No longer, Trax. I forbid it."

And now they stood by the spiral steps which fell away and down, through the centre of the hall's floor. They were dark steps, dropping away in a wide circle, and Beetrax stepped down, boot clunking, and glanced back.

Lillith nodded.

Beetrax moved down the steps, and they dropped down into darkness which, as they descended, gradually brightened, allowing Beetrax to blink, and *see*. He licked his lips. Beetrax reached the foot of the steps and halted, tossing aside the fire-brand he carried. It was no longer necessary. This place, this underground world, was lit by a soft golden light. It was the place from the vision which Lillith had showed them, a massive city of buildings, pyramids, towers, bridges, arches, sculptures, all intricate and rich beyond any thief's dreams.

Beetrax walked forward, axe coming to rest over his shoulder, as his head turned left and right, eyes wide, surveying the precious metals in such massive abundance. It was a paradise of wealth, greater than any mortal had ever witnessed.

The others had come down behind him.

"I think I'm going gold-blind," smiled Dake.

"There is more wealth than any man could ever spend in a million lifetimes," said Talon, instinctively stringing his bow and checking his quiver.

"Wow," said Jael, eyes wide, innocent face round and open with awe. "I have never seen anything like it!"

"And you never will again, lad," smiled Dake, and placed his hand on the young's lad's shoulder. "This is something men only ever dream about. A place of incredible richness, and a place of dreams. We're not dreaming, are we, Sakora?"

Sakora smiled, her scars stretching. "No, Dake. Unless you want me to pinch you, see if you wake up?" She ran her hand down her baldric of knives, hidden beneath her shirt. They gave her a little comfort.

"I can pinch myself," he said, watching her movements. They made him shiver.

They gazed across hazy squares, and witnessed the molten platinum river which they'd seen in their spirit flight; in the dream-scene of Equiem magick. And each and every person felt a unique awe. Like he, or she, stood on the raw bedrock of a million-year history, and were intruding on a culture they would never be able to comprehend.

Lillith led the way now, and her walk was fast. They

all followed, eyes scanning for possible enemies, twitchy, nervous, but at the same time drifting as if through a dream of smoke and oil.

They passed a huge palace, impossibly ornate, with a huge iron door ten times the size of a normal human door, the exterior surface encrusted with a myriad of precious gems. Beetrax moved over to the door, looking suspiciously about, and after peering inside to see if there were any potential enemies there, but finding only a vast hall surrounded by unlit braziers and intricately carved silver statues, so he returned to the gems, pulled out his dagger, and started working the point behind a ruby half the size of his fist. He finally prized it free of the iron supporting claws, and it sat there in his hand, like solid, glittering blood. It sparkled from the warm light of Wyrmblood. It shone ruby light into Beetrax's awestruck face.

"We are going to be so incredibly fucking rich," choked Beetrax, happily.

"The only problem we've got, as far as I can see," muttered Talon, eyes scanning, mind calculating, "is how we carry as much as possible out of this place."

Beetrax considered it.

"Some kind of winch and pulley system? We could hire a hundred horses. *Five hundred* horses, with baskets. Rig up a big pulley system, haul as much shit out of this place as is humanly possible."

"You think the dwarves will let us do that?" said Talon, with a wry, sideways smile.

"I'll fucking die trying," rumbled Beetrax, and slapped Talon on the back.

"Come on, we need to keep moving." Lillith had stopped, sandals flat against the golden cobbles of the road. Talon and Beetrax exchanged glances, then watched as Lillith trotted off, with Jael close behind.

"Er. Your woman seems a bit keen," said Talon, frowning.

"Yeah, I know. Probably just a little over-excited." He nodded knowingly.

Dake moved to them, and glanced after Lillith. "Anybody fancy telling her we need to take it a little easy? We have no idea what's down here. There could even be *dragons*."

"Ha!" scoffed Beetrax, but then thought about it for a moment. He remembered that huge, black-scaled bitch ripping the roof off the Iron Palace. It had been a truly terrifying sight. How could a mere mortal take on something like *that*?

Beetrax looked up at the huge door. It was a *dragon-sized* door.

Ahh, he thought. *Ahh. Shit. Is that how it is?*

"I think we should maybe catch up with Lillith. Find out what the hell is going on."

"Good idea," muttered Dake.

They jogged down the golden cobbles, boots slapping.

"Lillith?" called Beetrax. "Hey, Lil, wait!" But she did not halt, and continued her fast pace, Jael still in tow.

Frowning, Beetrax put his head down and sprinted forward, leaping in front of Lillith, arms wide, head tilted to one side, face riddled with confusion.

Lillith came up smart, and her head lifted, and her eyes were narrowed, dark, her face not a happy sight to behold.

"We need to get there," she hissed. "Get out of my way."

"Whoa girl, whoa! What's got into you?"

"You can't see it, can you? Any of you? We have to get *down there*, we have to get to the dragon eggs, stop them hatching, stop them growing, stop them taking over the world! They will establish a new Blood Dragon Empire, and we will all be lost, destroyed, turned to ash in the ensuing onslaught!"

"One step at a time," said Beetrax, kindly, slowly, placing a hand on her shoulder.

Lillith slapped his hand away with incredible force. "*Get off me*!" she shrieked. "You may not understand the importance of this quest, but I do."

"So do I," said Jael, lifting his head.

Slowly, Beetrax turned and looked at the youth. "I'd

shut your fucking mouth, if I was you," he snapped.

"Or what?" said Jael. "I watch you, bullying Lillith, ordering her about, moaning at her all the time. The big bad axeman. Oooh. Scary. You've made your judgements about me, the kid, the coward, and I've come to make my judgements about you. I once looked up to you, Beetrax. I thought you were a hero, just like in the story books. Like they taught us in school. But I see something different, here, in reality, in the flesh. I see a thief, and I see a murderer."

"Oh you do, do you?" growled Beetrax, eyes glinting.

"I've watched you kill a hundred dwarves now. I've seen you strike them down, even when unarmed, even when trying to surrender. That's murder, Beetrax. Or, as you would curse, *fucking* murder. And back then, you took the ruby from the big palace door. That's the work of a thief. A dirty, scumbag, shit-swigging, low-down thief."

Beetrax surged forward, but both Dake and Talon were there, each grabbing a shoulder as they tried to drag the big man back. Their boots skidded along the cobbles as they failed, and that big axe came up, notched blades glinting in the warm light, and Beetrax's face was contorted in rage as...

Lillith stepped before Jael.

"No," she said.

"Get the fuck out of the way, woman!"

"You forget to whom you speak."

"You, Lillith, my woman, my lover. But I'm not taking these insults from this..." he eyed the suddenly pale figure of Jael, cowering back, "from this yellow streak of pig-shit. I'm going to teach him a fucking lesson."

"No, you're not."

"Yes, I am."

"No," she held up her hand, and placed it flat against his chest.

Beetrax growled, and dropped his axe with a clatter. "I won't kill him. All right? But he will feel the taste of my knuckles."

"One last time, Trax. *No*."

Beetrax looked at Lillith, really *looked* at her this time. Her eyes had gone dark, and he couldn't swear it, but they seemed to swirl with a black smoke, half-seen, tiny fluttering motes, like the image of a half-remembered dream reflected in the eyes of a dead lover.

Beetrax pushed forward, scowling.

The next thing he remembered, he could taste metal, hot tin, his head was pounding, and he was thirty feet away from Lillith, face-down on the cobbles. He groaned, and the others ran over to him, rolling him onto his back, then staring back at Lillith with wide eyes.

She turned, and started forward, Jael by her side, a faithful puppy.

"What... what the *fuck* hit me?" groaned Beetrax.

"I think you pushed Lillith too far, old horse," chuckled Talon, but it was a sombre chuckle designed to cover his shock.

"Or the other way round," Beetrax growled, and hoisted himself to his knees, then his feet. He swayed for a moment, and looked at her retreating back. "She used..." he savoured the words, like he would a mouthful of rotten fruit, "fucking *magick* against me."

"You were threatening the lad, to be fair," pointed out Dake. Beetrax turned on him, and Dake took a step back, lifting his hands. "Whoa, mate, I'm not the one insulting you, and I ain't the one who's just flung you thirty feet across the street. Maybe you need to go talk to her?"

"I fucking will," he growled, and ran forward, scooping up his axe, and pounding down the cobbles.

Sakora looked at Talon and Dake. She ran a hand down her face, almost as if to cover her scars. It had become a self-conscious action, but nobody had the heart to point it out. After all, who could blame her? Vanity was intrinsic to the human condition. It was part of the shell, the mask, the psychological barrier which stopped one crumbling like a salt pillar against the onslaught of the ocean.

"I think we're in trouble," said Sakora, gently.

"Why's that?" said Talon.

"Lillith has changed. Since we came down here. She's changed, Tal."

"In what way?"

"I don't know. I think it's this *place*. Some kind of ancient magick, an influence of the dragons maybe; the influence of Equiem magick. Listen. We need to go after Trax. We need to sort this shit out."

As they arrived, Beetrax had once more halted Lillith's progress. They were at a crossroads, and a gentle hum filled the air. Sakora looked around, because *everything* felt odd. Something bigger was going down. The world felt suddenly *wrong*.

She moved forward, could see Beetrax talking heatedly, and she turned and looked at Lillith's face. The white witch, the woman Sakora had known for twenty years or more, wore an expression that looked… *alien*.

"What do you think you're doing?" snarled Beetrax. "Using fucking *Equiem* magick on me? Are you sick?"

"You know nothing of which you speak," said Lillith calmly, voice cold, her eyes fixed on Beetrax without blinking. "Now get out of my way, before I do it again. Only next time, you won't wake up for a fucking week."

Beetrax stared at Lillith, mouth flapping. He absolutely could *not* believe what he was hearing.

"Lillith," he managed, finally, as Dake and Talon stood by, helpless, wondering what the hell they should do; does one intervene in a lovers' tiff? In their experience, only one person ended up in the shit, and that was the one sticking their bloody nose in in the first place! And so they watched, and listened, and readied themselves to jump in the middle if any problems occurred…

"Lillith. My life. My love. What in the name of the Seven Sisters are you doing?"

"I am following my destiny."

"Which is what?"

Lillith stared long and hard at Beetrax. "Have you listened to nothing I've ever told you? Have you not realised my path? Yes, we have shared time together, Beetrax, and I have tried to instil in you my love, and faith, my belief in peace and calm... but here, and now, this is not a place for peace and calm. It is a time for action, for doing, because if we do not, then the world will be a very different place. Can you not comprehend the import of why we are here? Why destiny led us here? We have a mission to perform, Beetrax, and although I love you to the core, although I love you to the grave, you *will* get out of my way within three seconds or I'll hurt you so bad you won't walk for a fucking month."

Sakora stepped between them. She'd been approaching, quiet, stealthy, as Lillith ranted. Now, she stood between them, her back to Beetrax, dwarfed by the huge axeman, her scarred and battered face focussed on Lillith.

"This is not you," she said.

Lillith stared at her, dark eyes narrowed.

"Get out of the way, bitch."

"Lillith would never speak like that."

Lillith cackled, then, and tilted her head. "Of course I would. It only depends on a certain set of circumstances. It depends on one realising one's own potential, one's own reality, one's own purpose in life."

"What is your purpose in life, Lillith?"

"We need to reach the dragon eggs."

"Why?"

"To stop them hatching."

"You are sure of this?"

"Yes."

Sakora suddenly struck out, slapping a stinging blow that spun Lillith around, and dropped her to her knees.

"No!" choked Beetrax in anguish, but Sakora turned, and this time placed her own hand against Beetrax's chest. Then, still holding that position, she turned, and frowned, and watched as Lillith looked up.

The white witch seemed different, somehow. Her eyes were no longer as dark. No longer tainted with smoke flecks. She reached up, and touched her own stinging cheek, feeling the handprint there, for Sakora did not pull her punches.

"How you feeling, Lil?"

Lillith tilted her head. She coughed, and climbed to her feet. Then, as Sakora stepped out of the way, she ran to Beetrax and threw herself into his arms. He stood there, like a useless bear, and Lillith's tears stained his shirt and he looked over her shoulder at Sakora.

What? he mouthed.

What the fuck is going on?

Then Lillith looked up. And Beetrax looked down. And Lillith smiled. And Beetrax smiled. And he knew everything was going to be good with the world. Again.

"Forgive me?" she said.

"What happened?" he said.

"It's this... place. It gets into your blood. It oozes... magick. White magick, but also... the dark arts. Equiem magick. The spells are here, in the air, in the gold, flowing with the platinum river. This place is old, Beetrax. Older than anything I've ever experienced. Forget the Harborym Dwarves; forget the Church of Hate and the Scriptures of Hate. Those things are parasites riding on the flesh of a million-year-old empire."

Everybody present was chilled by her words. For she spoke the truth; the truth, which bled from rock and gold and bones and dust.

"The Blood Dragon Empire," she said, and pushed her head into Beetrax's chest.

"But it's gone," he whispered. "All gone."

"Not all gone," said Lillith, looking up at him, then looking round at the others. "The dragons ruled, for a million years. They were unconquerable. And we, men, dwarves, elves, we were their slaves. We were the slave races. They bred us, to build, to grow crops, to farm meat. They were

kings and queens, and we their playthings. But they went
to war against one another..." She paused, and her eyes
drifted distant, and she reached out as if to touch something
that floated in the air... "Three clans, three terrible, violent
clans, and the world was bathed in fire for a thousand days
as dragon fought dragon, clan fought clan, and a war raged
like nothing which had gone before it."

Lillith paused, sagging a little, and Beetrax held her, as
he always would.

"They destroyed themselves," said Lillith, softly. "Killed
one another mercilessly, with hate, and spite, and violence.
Impervious to fire, they tore one another apart, snapping
wings, ripping off legs and tails and heads. It was a war of
sickeningly violent bloodshed... and below it all cowered
the remnants of their slaves. And then it was done. Then it
was over. Only a few remained. And a group of slaves, made
up of the hardiest men, dwarves and elves, they banded
together and slaughtered the few remaining dragons. They
built machines, using ancient Blood Dragon technology,
and with these great machines they captured some of the
old clans, and they destroyed the rest. From this came the
birth of the Harborym Dwarves. From this came the Great
Dwarf Lords. From this came the cessation of the Blood
Dragon Empire!"

Lillith slumped, and Beetrax bore her to the ground,
where she suddenly slept.

He looked up at Sakora, eyes searching for answers.

Sakora gave a little shrug, and smiled. "This place," she
said. "We do not belong here. This is a place of evil. A place
of evil for us, anyway. And... it *knows* it. It knows we are
intruders. It's like a virus invading the human body; the
body then creates antibodies to fight the infection. That's
what we are, here; an infection. Anathema to a million
years of dragon rule."

"And this place seeks to... destroy us?"

"I think so. I think it... kind of took over Lillith, for a
little while there."

"So I just slap her to get her out of it?"

"Do you remember being thrown thirty feet across the cobbles?"

Beetrax nodded. "Aye. That hurt, that did."

"You just focus on killing… dwarves. And dragons. I'll look after Lillith."

Beetrax nodded, with a sad grin, and knelt beside his love waiting for her to waken.

It was hours later, although there seemed to be no time in this place. The same warm glow infused the world of Wyrmblood, and never seemed to change. Lillith had emerged from her short sleep of exhaustion, of horror, of possession, and apologised to Beetrax profusely. But her fixation was the same – to find the dragon eggs she had seen so many times across the tapestry of so many visions.

And so they followed her, more sedately this time, with Jael looking back sheepishly at Beetrax. The axeman studiously avoided Jael's stare, in fear of taking his axe and planting it between the little bastard's eyes.

The city of Wyrmblood seemed to go on *forever*. Endless roads, endless highways, some cobbled, some smooth silver or paved with a million jewels. Their boots trod the roads, their heads turning, surveying the endless, endless empty buildings.

"Millions must have lived here," said Dake, at one point.

Lillith, more herself now, nodded. "Yes, somewhere near that. But not humans. Or elves. Or dwarves. They were down in the slave quarters."

"Slave quarters?"

"Caves. A vast tunnel system, far below the mines of the Harborym Dwarves. It is a miracle the dwarves never discovered them before. The *slaves* would have no luxury from Wyrmblood."

"There's a lot of mountain," observed Dake.

"A lot of mountain to fill with slaves," agreed Lillith, with a narrow smile.

Beetrax strode at the back, now, his faith subtly shaken. His woman, his true love – this place had changed her. And he could not help but blame himself for bringing her here; yes, he'd dressed it up, eventually, as a rescue mission for Jonti Tal, but the truth of the matter had been twofold: greed, and adventure. So much for the adventure! The notion and glamour of adventure soon fades after one is tortured by barbarous dwarves for weeks on end with the aim of breaking a man's will. Driven to the limits of sanity by sheer physical pain, by suffering, by the evil machinations of evil scumbags, living offal. He thought back, to better times, living, laughing, loving, drinking Vagandrak Red, eating smoked sausage and bread and cheese in meadows filled with buttercups. He smiled to himself, and before he realised what had happened, Jael was there, walking alongside him.

Beetrax strode on, eyes fixed ahead, his temper slowly rising.

"I wanted to apologise," said Jael, his voice small.

"No apology needed," rumbled Beetrax, still not looking at the youth.

"No. I *need* to apologise. What I did was wrong."

"It's all right, lad. Now I knows you're a coward, I won't be turning my back on you in a hurry." He gave a tight-lipped smile.

"There is no excuse for what I did, but I want you to know, I will prove myself to you in the future. I will make this right again. I *will* show you I am worth something to you, that I do have courage when it counts."

Beetrax halted, and Jael stumbled to a stop. "Well. Only time will tell. No go on, go walk with Lillith. I'm sure she's missing her little, shitty-arsed pet puppy."

With red cheeks, Jael accelerated ahead, leaving Beetrax alone with his thoughts once more. Dake dropped back to him.

"A little harsh?"

"It's what he deserved."

"Really?"

"Don't you fucking start. Because of him, we could all be dead! *And* I broke a finger."

"Ah. The finger." Dake smiled. "Some things will never cease to amuse me."

The roadway had been heading imperceptibly down, until they passed through a collection of huge buildings, golden cubes, each one as tall as the tallest church in Vagan; and yet these were simply cubic structures fashioned from gold bricks, walls perfectly symmetrical, but with no windows or doors. Their purpose was not clear, but they spread out now, and the overlanders walked between these seemingly pointless monoliths, eyes looking up, necks craning.

Conversation had ceased now, and they travelled in two discrete groups: Lillith and Jael up ahead, leading the way, and a subdued Beetrax, Talon, Dake and Sakora bringing up the rear. Lillith led them on a zigzagging path through what turned into a maze of these huge golden buildings, and soon everybody felt lost; yet still Lillith led them onwards, without faltering, without halting to check her way.

And then, they turned a corner, and it was there.

A mammoth, golden dragon, seemingly carved from one solid block and towering above them. Its wings were slightly outstretched, almost triangular head pointing forward, stretching out as if to attack. Lips curled back over fangs, eyes narrowed, threatening, glinting gold.

"That, my friends, is fucking awesome," said Beetrax, stopping in his tracks. They all stopped. And looked up. And stared in wonder. Never had they seen a statue so big, or so impressive. It could have swallowed ten Vagan churches.

"What is it?" whispered Dake.

Lillith turned, staring back at the group. "It is the embodiment of the Dragon Queen, a merging of every Queen Wyrm that has ever existed down here in Wyrmblood. Every time another Queen dies, so her image is absorbed into the whole, and becomes part of a hive mind, a kind of ruling

conscience which offers advice to the rulers of Wyrmblood.
Every time another Dragon Queen is absorbed, the exterior
alters a little to accommodate her physical form."

They stared at her.

"How could you possibly know that?" whispered Sakora.

Lillith frowned. "I don't know," she said, finally. "I just
know."

They stared for a little while longer, and then without a
sound, Lillith padded forward towards the statue's massive
front legs, claws splayed, each claw bigger than a serrated
longsword. The others followed, staring up once more as
the golden dragon reared above them, silent and glowing
under the strange, ethereal light of this underworld.

Reaching a point beneath the front legs, so Lillith paused,
and closed her eyes, and there came a grinding of ancient
gears, a spinning of cogs, and the floor opened in a circle,
a spiral staircase dropping silently, smoothly, deep down in
a wide shaft that, once again, told the overlanders that this
was not their city, not their world; it was a strange, alien
place, and the staircase was big enough to allow several
dragons side by side.

Struggling, they dropped down from step to step, down
into more warm light. Beetrax counted softly to himself,
but gave up when he hit three hundred. They were deep.
*Deep*er than deep.

Finally, they emerged into a massive chamber with an
intricately carved ceiling; it seemed to be some kind of
language. The walls and ceiling were perfectly smooth, and
plain, and a soft cream in colour. The chamber stretched
off further than the eye could see, and the heroes dropped
from the final step, crunching something underfoot, as they
moved away from the great dragon stairwell and peered
about.

They moved, and each footfall crunched, a seemingly
deafening sound because the vast long low chamber was
so quiet.

Beetrax stopped, boots crackling, and he knelt, rubbing

his hand through the tiny white particles.

"Shells," he said, finally. "Like seashells on a beach."

"Not seashells," said Lillith, and they all looked at her.

She closed her eyes, and lifted her hand. Her lips started to writhe, and the centre of her outstretched palm glowed red. The others looked about, then to Beetrax, who shrugged, face open with his own curiosity.

Suddenly, the world around them seemed to fade. They were in the same place, but the features changed; a mist hung across the ground, but spreading out before them were orbs of cream, nestled in the mist, stretching away into the distance. Each one was a slightly different size and shape, many of them irregular; not one had any form of symmetry.

"What…" began Beetrax.

"Shhh…" came Lillith's gentle lullaby.

More noise, a series of sudden clatters and shouts. They turned, staring back at the stairwell, and from it, like drifting ghosts, spilled the hazy figures of three dwarves, sporting huge beards, fearsome scarred features, each carrying a massive battle axe stained with blood.

"Here!" bellowed one harshly, over his shoulder, and more dwarves spilled into the chamber, and they started kicking the cream orbs, creating a path, as yet more dwarves emerged. They were a rough-looking bunch, many of them wounded, some singed by fire. Many had lost eyes, blood dried on their faces in streamers, and several had lost limbs. They appeared as if they'd just emerged from some violent battle.

"This is it, lads. We have to destroy them all," came one voice, a harsh, guttural sound without any hint of doubt.

They readied their axes, and looked at one another. There was a long pause, as if these dwarves were considering the significance of their actions. Then the lead dwarf, who'd led the way, approached a large oval egg – lifted his axe above his head, and brought it swiftly down. The egg shattered, and inside the embryo of a dragon was almost sliced in two. It squealed, a high-pitched screaming sound, shrill and painful to the ears, the body curling in upon itself, squirming in juices, and a second blow cut it in half, ending the noise. Flames flickered around the shell interior.

"Come on, lads!"

The spell was suddenly broken, and the dwarves waded in, axes rising and falling, boots stamping, crushing the skulls of released dragon chicks. A huge cacophony of squealing went up, but the dwarves were brutal, uncaring, battering and chopping. Yet more dwarves arrived, until they were a hundred-strong, and the ground was slippery with chopped dragon embryos and smashed shell oil… and with roars, the dwarves surged forward, smashing, breaking, slicing, killing…

The scene faded.

The heroes stared at one another, each sick to the stomach.

"It's a slaughter," said Beetrax, eyes narrowed.

"I suppose they're getting their revenge," said Dake, carefully. "And they couldn't let the eggs hatch. Or there'd be a thousand more dragons to fight. We were slaves to the dragons, remember, Trax?"

Beetrax turned on Lillith. "So these are the shells of the slaughtered? It makes me sick. They were babes."

"… that would have grown up into killers," said Lillith.

"You could say that about humans, as well," snapped Beetrax.

Lillith turned her back on the group. "Follow me," she said, and strode forward, each footstep a crackle reminding them of the carnage, the murder, the infanticide.

The others followed, reluctantly.

"What next?" muttered Beetrax, and he'd tumbled into a foul mood. Because of the vision of the dwarves, yes, whom he admittedly despised anyway, and now despised with a need for further murder, but also because of Lillith. Not only did she seem more cold, more distant, she also seemed to be on some secret mission, guided by magick, maybe *misguided* by magick, that she was not willing to share – and, more importantly, not even willing to share with him.

"I couldn't even guess," muttered Dake.

"I bet it's unpleasant," scowled Talon, looking down at each crunching footstep.

"I bet it's dangerous," said Sakora, and they all nodded in agreement.

The chamber seemed to stretch off for an age, and before long they looked back, and the descending stairs had disappeared. Their means for escape had, temporarily, vanished.

"I feel," said Talon, "that the longer we stay here, and the further we descend, the less chance we'll ever have of getting back up to the surface. Honestly, guys, I don't feel like I'll ever see the sunshine again. I don't feel like I'll ever smell the clean air again – just this fucking dwarf stink. And it stinks all right."

Sakora moved close to him, and put her arm around his waist. "Hey, Tal," she said, "you need to try and be more positive. We're going to do this thing. We may die trying, but Lillith is right – it's for the greater good."

"You think there are more eggs that need destroying?" His voice seemed very small. "I don't know if I could do that."

"Me neither," rumbled Beetrax. "Give me an enemy before me any day of the week with a big battered axe, tattooed knuckles and obnoxious breath. But murdering the unborn? That's for men with stronger stomachs and weaker minds than me."

The others nodded, wondering what Lillith was about to reveal – for in the vision, when they had *flown* with the image of the dragon, so they had seen fields of eggs, and these had not been smashed. Had they, by some miracle, survived?

Finally, a wall came into view. It was matte black, and stretched off to either side, disappearing distantly. It was a bizarre sensation. In this place far beneath the mountain, time seemed to have no meaning.

Lillith stopped, and the others gradually crunched up behind her.

"This is it," she said.

"What is it?" asked Beetrax.

"A portal," she said. "A secret place. When the dwarves invaded this sacred place of dragon eggs, laid by the Queen, Volak, over a period of several hundred years, they thought they had destroyed them all. But they never found the second chamber, because they were ignorant and uncouth, and unversed in the ways of Equiem magick."

"So there *are* more dragon eggs?" said Beetrax, voice soft. "Listen, Lillith, we cannot destroy them. *I* cannot destroy them. I swear, I haven't got it in me." He seemed to deflate. "I don't believe these creatures are evil; they were just *dominant*. Like us, now. To kill the unborn… it's just wrong, Lil."

"Just follow. And watch," said Lillith, and turned, and smiled at them. "We don't have to destroy the eggs, we just have to stop them hatching. These are two very different concepts."

Lillith approached the wall, and placed both hands flat against it. She started to whisper, and her lips writhed, and once more her hands glowed. Slowly, silently, the great black wall started to slide away, accelerating as it flowed almost like a vertical liquid stream, to reveal…

A huge, soaring chamber, with a massive, smooth, domed ceiling, and walls covered with tiny intricate machines fashioned from gold and silver, all moving, tiny pistons and cogs, gears and spinning shafts, a hundred machines, a hundred *thousand* of them… and the floor dropped, it was a depression in the ground, and nestled in the vast space were eggs, dragon eggs, but these were different from the ones in the vision – whereas those had been a plain cream colour, these were different, these glittered and gave off a gentle glow, as if each egg was a covered in a tiny, complete covering of active *flame*.

"The dwarves found the room where the bad eggs were stored," said Lillith, and stepped across the threshold. The others followed, moving onto a slick, black, polished walkway which led all the way around the chamber. They looked back, and up, where thousands of tiny machines clicked and whirred and spun and pumped and twisted, like some vast array of clockwork, as if they stood inside the chamber of the world's largest, most complex clock.

"Bad eggs?" whispered Beetrax, for this room commanded reverence.

"Yes, the deformed, the broken, the twisted; those that could never live as dragons if they hatched. The dragons would never leave their greatest prize, these, their offspring, their future, for the dwarves to simply stumble across. No. There was the extra barrier only accessible by magick."

Dake and Talon were frowning.

Sakora surveyed the sea of fire-glowing eggs. There must have been ten thousand. Ten thousand dragons waiting to hatch. A new empire. The next Blood Dragon Empire.

There came a gentle tremble, under their boots.

"Lillith?" said Sakora, and her eyes were wide in her freshly scarred face.

"Yes, my sweet?" Lillith smiled.

"I'm confused. *Why* exactly did you bring us here? *How* are we going to stop this thing from happening?"

"We didn't stop it happening," said Lillith, and she smiled, and it was a smile that should never have belonged on Lillith's face, a smile like nothing Beetrax had ever seen before. He blinked, and a cold chill blew across his heart, and blew across his soul. "We have started the countdown," she said. "The queens. They demand it."

"What?" bellowed Beetrax, leaping forward but Lillith grinned, her eyes glittering black and filled with smoke, and both hands came together, a *clap,* and Beetrax, Sakora, Talon and Dake were smashed from their feet, hurled high into the air, out over the centre of the dragon-egg field to hang, suspended, spinning slowly, amidst the clockwork machinery and beneath a smooth, black, polished sky.

"What are you doing?" cried Sakora, as Jael padded alongside Lillith and knelt, petitely, at her feet.

Lillith's grin widened, and her eyes narrowed. "It was written. It is Equiem. Dragon Lore. It has to be this way." She licked her lips, and dragon smoke oozed from her open mouth. "I'm hatching the dragon eggs," she said, and her eyes glittered black, like the eyes of a dragon. Lillith was no longer in control. Something *older* had taken control of her mind.

Hunter's Gold

Val was pissed.

Not pissed in the sense he'd had a keg full of ale, and was about to decorate the flagstones with his vomit. No. But pissed in the sense he was massively frustrated... because his true love was within reach, and yet he couldn't quite grasp her. Not yet, anyway. *But soon, my love,* he crooned to himself. *Soon.*

As they moved through the mines, so Crayline kept tossing him odd looks. He did not like the looks, even less than he liked the huge array of weapons at her belt. It wasn't just her reputation for extreme violence that freaked him out a little, or more honestly, a *lot,* it was the stories he'd heard about her killing friends, murdering family, torturing employers. She was a cunt you did not trust. If anybody was going to stab you in the back with a serrated dagger covered in fatal poison, Crayline Hew was the bitch to do it.

It was the corpse that sent them in the right direction. Or rather, a series of three corpses. They were well hidden, obviously victims of a sudden skirmish down here in the tunnels. They had been hidden well, but not well enough. Crayline Hew found all three bodies; she seemed to have a particular knack for hunting out the tortured and the dead.

"They came this way," she said, dark eyes narrowed.

"How do you know?"

"Trust me. I have done this sort of thing before."

"Hunted people?"

"Hunted and *killed* people. Well. People. Elves. Dwarves. It's all the same barrel of twisted rotting flesh to me. I don't care what race you are. I don't care whether you subscribe to the Church of Hate or not." Her eyes gleamed, dark and nasty. "All you cunts deserve to die."

Val coughed. "Yes. Well. We are on a very specific mission here," he said, the pitch of his voice just a little too high.

"Yes. You are," she said.

"What does that mean?"

"It means what it says. But we'll let that one go for now, shall we? I wouldn't like to embarrass you in front of the, ah, men."

Val nodded, face pale, eyeing her weapons once more.

It took several more hours to reach the new dig, the new chamber, with the high domed ceiling and the spiral steps leading down. Val was happy to let Crayline Hew take the lead, mainly because he didn't know what the fuck was down there, but also because if the overlanders were waiting with primed crossbows, he was happy to let the bitch take three quarrels in the face, and to hell with it. He'd reached a point of tension where he didn't know whom he trusted least: Beetrax the Axeman, or Crayline Hew, his second in command.

As they descended, each dwarf with axe, sword and crossbow at the ready, licking dry lips, wondering what the fuck they were dropping down into, so the light softened, and increased, and within long languorous moments, like dreams through treacle, they found themselves in...

"Wyrmblood," whispered Crayline, dark eyes shining.

They stood, surveying the incalculable wealth, a city built from tens of thousands of years of dragon rule. But... who knew? Maybe it had been here a million years. How long had the wyrms ruled the planet? How long had humans and dwarves been their slaves?

"We should split up," said Val, taking charge and eyeing his group of hardy dwarves with a mixture of pride and open fear. Val was no warrior, no hard case; he was a Slave Warden, inadvertently propelled to the peak of his career without forethought or any real understanding of his duties. He'd been promoted above his natural ability, and then given a mission fit for a warrior. Val was proud of his accomplishments, but deep down, as all such people did, he really suspected he wasn't up for the fight. Deep down, he knew he couldn't do it, and it was only a twisted sense of pride that forced him to carry on. To step down, to step back, was unthinkable. He'd rather fall on his axe blade.

"In what way split up?" said Crayline, dark eyes locked on him.

Val shifted nervously under that unreadable gaze.

"This place is vast. We split into three groups and carry out a search."

"These men, and women, about whom we speak. They are dangerous, no?"

"Yes."

"So, better to hit them head on? With our full force?"

Val looked around, and swept out his arm. "But *look* at the size of this place! This is no normal city, Crayline. It could take us forever!"

"Well, you let me track, then," she said, and smiled.

"You can track them?"

"How do you think we got this far?"

"Er. All right. So we all stay together?"

"That would seem the sensible option in terms of logistical firepower. And by that, I mean force of crossbow arms."

"Of course, of course," said Val, nodding, and scratching his chin, but secretly thinking *if, if I can pull this off, then Lillith will be mine once more, my woman, my lover, my slave, my hobby, for me to do with as I will. Mine, to have and to hold, to love and nurture, to fuck and abuse. And she will grow to love me, despite the pain. I know she will. I know she will learn to enjoy me.*

Crayline knelt, and for long moments crawled about on the gold cobbles. Then her head came up, and she pointed. "This way," she said, and looked back at Val. "You trust me, right?" She smiled again. The smile of a shark. The smile of a weasel.

"Of course," said Val, and coughed, trying to hide his eyes.

"Follow me, then."

And the group of hardened dwarves set off across Wyrmblood, following the scent of the bastard intruders, those who had no right to set foot in the Five Havens, those who should, at the very *sight* of Wyrmblood, have been executed on the spot.

Because this was the city mentioned by the Church of Hate.

Wyrmblood was cursed in the Scriptures of Hate.

Here, it was, that the Great Dwarf Lords had imprisoned Volak, Moraxx and Kranesh.

Here, it was, that the Great Dwarf Lords had found immortality.

Fire Fight

Skalg soared, and was free.

He cast off the shackles of his flesh.

He left behind his weakened shell.

And… for the first time ever, was *unfettered*.

It was like nothing he could have ever dreamed. Even from being a small boy, he had been physically inferior to his fellow dwarves. In tests of strength, or stamina, or axe fighting, he had always been bottom of the class – the shitty scum under the others' boots which they scraped off with a stick. Not for Skalg any praise and sweet cakes, honeyed wine and fresh dwarf bread. No. Only pain, as the wooden axe cracked his skull, humiliation, as other young dwarves laughed at his lack of prowess, his lack of physical attributes, his natural *weakness*, his natural *cowardice*, his ingrained and very fucking real inferiority. And in shame, with cheeks burning red beneath his young beard, he crawled out of sight again and again and again.

There goes Skalg. What a fucking weakling!

Skalg! Hoi! Wait there, I need somewhere to rest my weary boots.

Ho! Skalg! You fucking dreg. Come back next year when you've grown a pair of real dwarf bollocks.

You say you have five silver? Hand it over. It's mine now.

Pain. Beatings. Humiliation. Even from his brothers and sisters. Even from his parents.

You fucking useless child, why don't you fuck off and fall down the Great Well?

Mama, Mama, Skalg has taken all the gravy again!

What? Take it off his plate!

I will do Mama, after all, it's not like he's going to fight me for it...

And that was Skalg. Weak. Spineless. A coward.

And then... a cripple. Which, bizarrely, changed him. The mine collapse finally showed him what the prospect of death could be like... and Skalg did not want to experience death. He walked the dark side of his own understanding, and realised what it would be like to lose that one tiny precious gift called *life*; he realised that, actually, to get anywhere in the Five Havens you didn't just have to *fight*, you had to have fucking *teeth*.

And he'd done that.

Grown.

Experienced that.

But always, they laughed at him. Not to his face, not always; although those that did had a serious meeting with the Church of Hate's *Educators*. No. They laughed at him behind his back. Because in dwarf society, more than any other society he had studied, the weakling, the cripple, was worthless.

To have a strong back was the epitome of being *dwarf*.

Thousands of generations of miners. Digging. Breaking rock. Searching out precious gems and silver and gold. That was what being a *dwarf* meant. Stocky. Powerful. Able to find the gold to feed his family.

That was the dwarven *way*.

A cripple? With a twisted spine. A hunchback?

One might as well be dead...

But now, now, now, ah...

Skalg soared, he flew, his hazy mind sending impulses as he unfolded his great wings and cracked them against the sky, lifting himself high above Vagandrak and surveying the world below with incredibly powerful and sensitive eyes...

There, a village. Tiny people running, screaming.

Skalg took a deep breath, enjoying the scent of fire which lingered around his nostrils, and he straightened his spine, which crackled softly, tucked in his claws, folded back his wings, and dived towards that bright green-grey world below…

People screamed and shouted and ran, waving their arms in panic.

Skalg felt the most incredible exhilaration he had ever experienced. He felt not just powerful, but as close to god as one could ever hope to get. He was on a higher level than the Great Dwarf Lords, for although they, so they claimed, had transcended the physical realm, become something *more* than *dwarf*, here, and now, Skalg felt like nothing from beneath the stars could ever halt his progress.

Moraxx swept in, inhaled, allowed her glands to relax, and breathed a jet of pure white fire as she slammed down the street, chasing little running people. Several were caught in her blast, and ignited, burning as they ran.

Skalg targeted a woman, a succulent, plump woman with shoulder-length blonde hair and buxom bouncing breasts which wobbled and jiggled as she ran. He caught her in his jaws, lifting now, flapping his wings with a *boom* which he knew made the villagers' ears bleed. He held her gently, and she was in shock so didn't struggle; but then some form of courage, or a primitive need to survive, returned, and she began to struggle violently. So, as he flapped his wings, rising into the sky, Skalg squeezed his teeth just that little bit tighter, and there came a gentle *pop*, and she didn't struggle any more.

Skalg squatted on a rolling hillside. Night was falling. The sun was a bloated orange corpse caressing the horizon.

He looked down at the woman, lying limp and twisted on the grass. She was broken, her spine snapped, but she was not dead. Her eyes followed Skalg as he moved, backwards and forwards, strutting, trying out his new body, testing the muscles, and how his thought impulses made everything work.

"Hel... " she said.

Skalg nodded, dropping his huge dragon head towards her. She shrieked, but could not move. Tears ran down her cheeks. Snot ran from her nose. Blood ran from her anus and vagina, and Skalg's nostrils twitched, recognising the reek, the stink, of human discharge.

Who are you? What are you?

An internal voice spoke, and the words came unbidden from the depths of his subconscious and Skalg frowned, though it was not possible to do so. He frowned *mentally*, at least.

I am Skalg. Who are you?

I am Moraxx.

I am unfamiliar with the name.

I am Moraxx, the killer of humans, the eater of dwarves, imprisoned for thousands of years, my mind churning, burning, disintegrating until I could break free and FUCKING SLAUGHTER EVERYTHING THAT MOVES ON THIS FUCKING PLANET...

Skalg was blasted back by the onslaught, and he realised, suddenly realised, that although the Great Dwarf Lords had placed him inside the mind of a dragon, *Moraxx* the dragon, her mind was also still in there. Displaced, but not dead.

Tricky.

Skalg stalked around the wounded woman on the hillside. The sun was sinking behind the rolling hills, rays fanning out in pretty red streamers. He moved close, dipped his head, and sniffed the woman.

She screamed, and screamed, and screamed.

Bizarrely, the noise hurt his head, so gently, he reached out, nuzzled her, then taking her body in his jaws, he bit her in half. The noise stopped. Two body parts fell. Blood pumped out, staining the grass; staining the soil and infecting the world.

Skalg felt...

Nothing.

He looked up at the sky, saw the infinity of stars stretching out beyond the cool blue yonder. A sudden urge came upon him. He could flap his great wings, leap up into the air, and accelerate until he reached those stars, and became a part of that glittering tapestry; and by doing that, he would live forever... merged, into an infinity of space and time.

The voice, again.

You are in my mind. You are in my body.

I have a mission.

I am MORAXX. You do not have permission!

I am here by the will of the Great Dwarf Lords...

A sneer. *Oh. Those cunts. We WILL catch up with them, sooner or later, and when we do it will be a happy day for the sycophants. For we will burn them hotter than anything has ever burned in this world before...*

Interesting, thought Skalg.

Why interesting?

Because, and Skalg savoured the words, *because YOU are my slave, and I have your body, and you are MY sycophant. I have all the power. The might. The fury. The hate. And ultimately, the fire...*

Moraxx began a reply, but with a scream Skalg sent the mind spinning away. He pumped his wings, leaping up into the dying sky, and powered upwards, eyes seeking out the stars.

Flying...

The land falling far behind.

Distant.

A blue and green pastel scene, tinged crimson by a forlorn and dying sun.

Exhilaration grabbed him. Upwards, he surged.

Onwards.

His dragon shell was vibrating now, each scale shimmering, and as he passed a crescent of the world so the sun came up once more, swinging into view, and crimson light bathed him like a blood shower. He welcomed it. Welcomed the world. Welcomed this, the complete and utter freedom to be all powerful, to do absolutely whatever he wanted...

And the blood of the innocents?

Skalg thought about it.

And his mind went hard.

Fuck them, he thought.

The weak deserve to die.

He flew, heading for the stars...

No. Not yet.

Why?

You are there. For a reason.

I remember no reason.

You will kill the other dragons, then return and destroy the eggs.

Skalg considered this. A tiny spark ignited in his mind. And that great triangular head nodded.

Yes.

Skalg shifted his shoulder, dipping it, dropping it, and listening carefully, he could hear the distant destruction wreaked by Kranesh.

He twisted, and suddenly dropped like a meteorite towards the world of Vagandrak far far below.

Gavi was happy. No, Gavi was *ecstatic.* He toddled across the straw floor, and grabbed hold of the rough-sawn bench by the table. He beamed up at Mama. Mama was busy sewing, her face narrowed in concentration, eyes focussed, and Gavi gurgled up at Mama, giving his biggest round smile as the happiness coursed through him... because he *knew, knew more than anything,* that Dada would be home soon. Mama said Dada had been deep in the forest cutting down the BIG TREES with other men of the village, and that's why he had been so long gone. And Gavi had spent THREE WHOLE DAYS imagining Dada out in the woods with the other men, his big hands clutching his big axe, and swinging it with big powerful strokes to cut down the BIG TREES. The time had gone slowly, stretched off forever, and although Mama did fun things, played games with him, told him stories about the wolves in the forest and the noble dragons in the sky, tales of kings and princesses and witches and magick, of lost treasure and fun pirates, it wasn't the same without Dada there, because although Gavi loved Mama, loved her with all his heart, Dada was a GIANT and Dada was a GOD and nothing in the world would get between Gavi and his Dada.

Mama was busy, so Gavi toddled across the floor to the little stool. Mama had told him never to touch the little stool, because if he climbed on the little stool he might fall off and land on his face, and then he'd have an ugly twisted face like Padda Wa who lived in a cave and threw stones at children. But this time, *this time* Gavi knew it would be all right because Dada was coming home and he wanted to stand on the little stool and look out the window and be the first to see Dada walking down the mud road.

Gavi reached the little stool, and quietly dragged it across the straw floor, which gathered in golden strands around the wooden legs which Dada had carved himself. Reaching the cupboard beneath the window, Gavi carefully manoeuvred the little stool, his face all wrinkled up in concentration, and with maximum effort, climbed onto the little stool. He stood, triumphant, but realised in horror that he was not *tall enough* to see over the edge of the cupboard. Oh *no*! What would he *do*? Dada would be home soon, and Gavi had to be the FIRST to see him! He just had to be.

Gavi climbed down from the little stool and thought long and thought hard. He glanced at Mama, who was still sewing and muttering to herself about something. Come to think about it, she looked quite angry right now. Her brow was creased and Gavi didn't like that because it stopped her being pretty like she usually was.

And then, an idea filtered into his head. And he knew it was *genius*.

Yes, he was not tall enough to see out of the window. But with the little stool, he was tall enough to reach the door latch.

Gavi dragged the stool sideways, gathering more errant strands of straw around the legs, and balanced it near the door. He climbed slowly onto it, and stood there wobbling, having sudden horrible thoughts about Padda Wa. He didn't want to end up with an ugly face and living in a cave and throwing stones at children! No! But he calmed himself, and turned, with little pigeon steps, and eyed the latch. He reached out, and caught the metal prong, and lifted it, pulling the door slightly towards him. Success! He climbed down off the stool and tugged it out of the way, checked to see if Mama had spotted his actions, and she hadn't, but he knew she'd understand because Dada was coming home and it had been sooo*oooo* long since Gavi had enjoyed his hugs and his smell and his wild stories of life in the forest chopping down the BIG TREES.

Gavi gripped the edge of the door in his podgy fingers, and pulled. A cool breeze drifted inside, and the evening light made him squint. When the gap was wide enough he let go, and toddled out into the street, his feet running away with him for a moment before he got his balance once more.

Freedom!

Dada!

He looked down the street one way, but there was no sign of Dada. And so he looked down the street the other way, and there was still no sign of Dada. He looked back at the door, and there was no sign of Mama. So he toddled further out into the street, and looked around at the big world, his eyes wide and his mouth open. Everything was so... *huge*!

Something glittered in the sky.

It was silver.

Is it a star? thought Gavi, and a wide smile took over his face. *Oh by the Seven Sisters! It is! It's a star! It's a silver star flashing with silver light!* He lifted his little hand and pointed.

"Mama! Mama! It's a star! A star!"

There came a muffled curse from inside the stone cottage, and Mama appeared at the door, a look of absolute shock on her face. "Gavi! What are you doing? How did you get outside? Oh you naughty, naughty little boy..."

Gavi was staring at her, with total incomprehension. He

pointed again. "Mama! A star!" and he turned and looked at the silver star getting closer, and closer, and closer, and then his face changed, from awe, flickering through fear, then to a look of excitement. "Mama! A dragon! A dragon!"

Mama looked up, and gave a short sharp intake of breath.

It *was* a dragon.

It was Kranesh...

She was diving from leagues above Vagandrak, and her silver wings suddenly shot out with a crack, as fire trailed vapours from her nostrils and her claws flexed. She hit the street with a *thump* and rattled her wings, her head dropping low and moving close to the little boy in pants and vest, standing there, staring up in absolute open-faced wonder.

Gavi took in the bright silver scales, glinting in the light of the failing sun. The magnitude of the dragon filled his mind with a total confusion. It was just so... *BIG*.

"Hello, Mr Dragon," said Gavi, eyes shining, "have you come to play?"

Mama screamed, and Gavi turned to look at her, and slowly his face dropped from awe and wonder to a look of confusion. And then Mama was there, kneeling in the dirt, her arms wrapped around Gavi, dragged to her breast, tears streaming down her face as her whole body racked with sobs.

"Don't hurt my baby," she said, through snot and tears, looking up at those narrowed, slanted black eyes in a head bigger than she was. She watched lips curl back over fangs, yellow and black, each one a curved dagger. "Please, please, don't hurt my baby!"

Kranesh lowered her head, and a deep-throated rumble emerged as flames flickered around her snout, and her grin seemed to widen.

"Why not?" she purred, and then lifted her gaze as at the end of the street emerged nearly thirty men, carrying spears and longbows and expressions of terror and trepidation. Kranesh transferred her gaze back towards Mama and Gavi.

She was going to enjoy killing these little insects...

Mama must have *sensed* Kranesh's intentions, for she turned then, and looked up in absolute fury. "How dare you," she spat, her lips curling to make her face ugly. "You abuse your power, bitch. You are a disgrace to everything living. I *defy* you."

"You defy me?" Kranesh's laughter reverberated down the street. "That is… interesting."

Mama's gaze suddenly transferred to a point beyond Kranesh, her eyes growing wide, which the great wyrm found astonishing. At the moment of her death, at the moment of her child's execution, something had *distracted* this woman?

Kranesh almost turned. One shoulder dropped a little, her head swayed to one side, but with eyes still locked on the human insect before her, who was *definitely* looking at an object behind the great wyrm…

Moraxx hit Kranesh from behind, outstretched claws clamping around Kranesh's neck, wings still back in a dive. Both dragons slammed forward, narrowly skimming over Mama and Gavi to pound a spectacular spinning path down the street, hitting the road, then a cottage, demolishing one wall in a shower of stones and snapped beams, then the road again, then cannoning into the armed villagers; those foolish enough to remain, stood with opened mouths, rooted to the spot. Men were tossed aside, several crushed, as the dragons slid into them and beyond, into the stone fountain, demolishing it. Moraxx, on Kranesh's back, reared her head and her fangs came down, clamping Kranesh's neck. Kranesh howled, wings flapping, claws gouging the stone flags, as Moraxx shook her like a giant dog with a giant bone. Kranesh's howl rose in pitch until it was a scream, her head thrashing back, and flames erupted, a huge jet of fire that scorched three houses on its shaken, jagged trajectory. Kranesh's spiked tail whipped around, then curled up and over Moraxx, crushing her wings to her body. Now Moraxx screamed, and both dragons flopped about, one biting, one crushing, both ejecting random bursts of fire that shot out, scorching huge sections of the village and igniting thatched roofs.

The remaining village men ran back towards the skirmish, and began launching spears. They bounced off the two great coiling wyrms, and suddenly both relinquished their grips; Moraxx leapt into the sky, with a crash of wings, and Kranesh shook her tail and neck, head coming round, then lifting to follow Moraxx's arc.

She grimaced, ignoring the spears and arrows which clattered from her silver scales. She worked her neck several times, for Moraxx's bite had been powerful and caused some tendon damage.

"Oh, you evil, back-stabbing bitch," she growled, flames flickering, and her wings came back and she leapt upwards, wings beating hard, accelerating fast as she banked in a violent arc and flew in pursuit, a roar echoing from her jaws that deafened the remaining villagers and seemed to shake the world...

Back down on the street, Mama slowly unfolded.

Gavi looked up at her, with tears in his eyes.

"Mama, that was a dragon," he said, lower lip pushing out.

"Yes, my darling," wept Mama, stunned to be alive. "Yes, it was!"

Gavi rubbed his eyes. "I not like dragons no more," he whimpered.

Skalg glanced back as he soared through the skies, wings beating hard. He watched Kranesh leap into the air, roaring with pain and hate, and take up the pursuit. In Moraxx's mind he grinned to himself, and revelled in the power, soaked up the feelings of absolute dominance. *You feel that?* he wanted to scream back at Kranesh. *You feel that sting in the back of your neck? That was me, Skalg, a feeble hunchback dwarf whom the entire kingdom of Harborym Dwarves despises... but now, now I am the same as you, now I have your privilege, and I'm going to bring you down, motherfucking bitch wyrm, I'm going to torch you, and crush you, and rip out your bones…*

High over Vagandrak Skalg soared, and he pumped his wings again, amazed at how he never grew tired, never felt weak. Ahead, the Skarandos Mountains reared, snow on their caps, and between these vast, natural structures, these devil's teeth, lay the weaving, undulating snake, the Pass of Splintered Bones, pointing, like the markings of an adder, towards the four massive, intimidating walls of Desekra Fortress.

Skalg headed for the mountains, and heard Kranesh coming up fast behind… Flames roared, and Skalg put back his wings and dived hard, but Kranesh also dived, following Moraxx down close and fast, fire still screaming to scorch Moraxx's tail…

Skalg dropped into the Pass of Splintered Bones, levelling out only a few feet from the surface, and skimming along with powerful wing beats. Beneath, bones and skulls were blasting from the path to rattle against the rocky walls of the mountains. A unit of marching soldiers broke ranks and fled, spears forgotten, as Moraxx flashed by, closely followed by Kranesh, her jaws snapping at Moraxx's tail.

They reared up over the keep, with a couple of soldiers below shouting and waving, then out over the desert of Zakora. Within moments the landscape had changed, and they swept low over rolling sand dunes, their passage leaving scarred patterns in the sand, until, with a supreme effort, Kranesh launched forward, smashing into Moraxx, and they became entwined and hit the sand hard, spinning and tangling more as they cut a huge groove across a dune, then up towards its summit, where they finally came to a motionless rest, looking out over a great wide valley.

Flames licked idly around snouts.

Both great wyrms lay, stunned.

Eventually, Kranesh lifted herself up, and disentangled herself, huge wings flapping to give her some lift. One wing had damaged bones, and not quite the same power it once had. Kranesh scowled, and took several steps back, claws raking the sand as she gazed with narrowed eyes at Moraxx.

Within seconds, Skalg forced Moraxx's eyes open. He choked for a moment on imbibed sand, then ejected it on a spurt of flame that turned it into droplets of molten glass, falling like crystal tears. His head came up on the serpentine neck, neck spines bristling in anger, brass scales gleaming under the remnants of light from the dying sun, which had recently dipped below the desert horizon.

Skalg turned to face Kranesh, and he forced Moraxx to laugh, her voice musical and deep.

"Are you insane?" hissed Kranesh, flames licking around her muzzle. "By the Sacred Heart of Wyrmblood, what do you think you are doing? We have a mission, we have humans to exterminate, then we have dwarves to kill…"

"Kranesh," said Skalg with Moraxx's voice, "you have grown weak, and feeble, and I no longer trust you."

"You don't trust me?" shrieked Kranesh, and she backed away, flames washing out, a yellow stream that engulfed Moraxx for a moment, but caused no real damage. "What the fuck has changed in your diseased mind? We were locked away for centuries together… now we need to put things right… now we need to *hatch*…"

"But only when our Blood Dragon Empire is safe from threat," said Moraxx, staring into her sister's eyes, black orbs meeting, "and now, here and now, you are the one thing which threatens the future of our race."

"How?"

Skalg attacked, fire roaring out, claws stretching for Kranesh's eyes. They smashed together, claws slashing, fire roaring, jaws biting, and they connected, slammed fifty feet into the air above the desert, their claws scrabbling at one another, heads butting together, fire roaring in one another's faces… before Moraxx suddenly lifted, arms wrapping around Kranesh's neck as Kranesh's tail slashed and punched at Moraxx's belly.

Skalg suddenly powered upwards, rose fast, breaking away, and flipped, heading back towards Vagandrak.

Kranesh screamed and headed in pursuit, but they were both flying at full power now, full speed, and the sister wyrms were equally matched.

Desekra appeared fast on the horizon.

Kranesh suddenly lowered her head under her own belly, and breathed a powerful, screaming jet of fire. She accelerated rapidly, smashing into Moraxx as Desekra fortress reared fast, and the great first wall, Sanderlek, appeared black and solid and unmoving. Locked together once more, the wyrms tried to pull up, but didn't quite make it in time, clipping the top ten feet of wall and sending a shower of stones screaming up into the sky, a fountain of broken castle masonry. The two dragons ploughed through stone, described an arc over Sanderlek, then both went limp, separated, and felt to earth, carving huge grooves along the open grass killing ground which separated Sanderlek and Wall Two, Tranta-Kell.

Silence fell like drifting ash.

Smoke rose from both dragons... but they remained still.

"Sarge?"

"What is it, Nomado?"

"SARGE!"

"This had better be fucking good, lad," mumbled Sergeant Barahim, rolling from his bunk and grabbing his trews and boots. With a weary groan – he'd been running the new recruits *all day* – he pulled on a loose black shirt and opened the door to the barracks corridor, scowling.

"Er, Sarge?"

"Spit it out, lad."

"Dragons."

"What?"

"Dragons!"

"You pissed, lad?"

"There's, er, two dragons! They've just crashed through Sanderlek." Nomado remembered his training, and snapped a salute. Then his shoulders slumped. "Please. Sarge. Just

come with me, right now, none of the lads know what to
do…"

"If this is a wind-up, you'll be dumped in fucking solitary
for a week," scowled Barahim, following the new recruit
out into the late evening air.

The sun had only recently sunk beneath the horizon, and
although the rearing Skarandos peaks darkened the evening,
especially at this time of year, there were quite clearly two
massive dragons laid out on the grass, surrounded by a
detritus of broken stones and cracked masonry chunks,
smoke crawling slow columns from their nostrils.

Fifty men stood around, staring, and Sergeant Barahim
sent out runners. Within minutes, rusting chains the
thickness of a man's arm had been dragged from storage,
and with much grunting and cursing, dragged over the
body of the silver-scaled wyrm.

They began wrapping the chains around the beast as
best they could, as another fifty soldiers mobilised and
began carting rocks from the rock storage area. These were
normally used during days of siege or battle, to drop on
any attacking force from the summit of Sanderlek. Now, an
attacking force had landed in their front yard, so to speak,
so the rocks were being put to a much more unconventional
use.

"More chains for the second dragon!" shouted Barahim,
his parade ground bellow ringing clear across the entire
killing ground.

More chains were dragged from the storage sheds at the
foot of Sanderlek, and then across the grass, cutting grooves
in the soil, to the motionless body of Moraxx.

"Which end first, Sarge?" asked Nomado, looking up
from the dragon and scratching his head. "It's lying funny. I
don't think I can chain it from this end first, I… " He glanced
back at the brass-scaled wyrm.

The eye had opened. It was looking at him.

Nomado yelped, and jumped backwards, dropping the
chain.

"What are you fucking doing, you idiot?" bellowed Barahim.

"It's looking at me, Sarge! It's fucking looking at me!"

"Bollocks, lad. You ARE pissed, aren't you?"

But before any more could be said, Moraxx lifted her head, on her rippling neck, and turned to stare at the soldiers. They yelped, stepping back, as Moraxx got her legs beneath her, and pushed herself up, wings extending, flapping, her head shaking, flames curling around her snout.

She turned her body, and the soldiers were running now to get spears. Moraxx turned and looked down at the chained wyrm, Kranesh, who had just started shaking her head to find she'd been wrapped in chains, some of them weighed down by rocks.

Moraxx strode forward, and stared down at her sister.

Kranesh met her gaze.

"What have they done to me?"

"Secured you. I'm sure if you had a minute you could be free."

Kranesh started to struggle, but Moraxx took a step forward and brought her claws down on Kranesh's head, a massive, sickening blow. Kranesh groaned. Moraxx beat her again, and again, and again, the final blow ending with a crunch. Kranesh slumped down, the chains forgotten, the flames around her snout diminishing.

"THERE! ON THE COUNT OF THREE, SPEAR THE FUCKER!"

Moraxx turned, and eyed the several hundred soldiers now gathered, many hefting spears and pikes, their faces grim.

"Really?" said Skalg, and grinned, inhaling, and screaming out a wall of fire that sent the soldiers sprinting for the second Desekra wall, many with their trews on fire, several crying for their mother.

Moraxx turned back to Kranesh, and Skalg stared down with her eyes.

No, said Moraxx in his mind.

Please, you cannot do this, she is my sister, she is my own flesh and blood, you cannot do this, she cannot die thinking I murdered her!

Leave me to my work, growled Skalg. His mind was filled with laughter, with joy, with an absolute utter and total rush of power. He was the most dominant creature on the planet. He was unstoppable. Immortal. A… god.

Please, begged Moraxx in the caverns of this, their now shared mind. Only Skalg had control, and Moraxx was an unwilling passenger. *Please stop. You must stop. This is unholy. Think of… our babies… our Empire…*

Skalg stared down at the weakened dragon before him. Blood drooled from her maw. Her eyes were still focussed, focussed on Moraxx, focussed on Skalg, and he *knew* that scheming bitch would leap up and rend him limb from limb if she so much as thought she had a chance.

"Time for you to die, Kranesh," said the voice of Moraxx.

"How can you do this to me, sister?"

"How can I not?" said Moraxx.

"But… after all we went through."

"You think Volak would let us live? You really, truly believe when the hatchings are done, Volak will stand by and say, 'Yes, sisters, I trust you not to stab me in the back and take control of our newly built Empire.' You believe that?"

"There may have been arguments…"

"There may have been *murder*!" snapped Moraxx, suddenly.

"And you think murdering me is a solution?"

"Yes," said Moraxx, with Skalg grinning inside the wyrm's skull. "How does it feel to be turned upon by one of your own? And not just one of your own – but your own blood? How does it feel to be stabbed in the back, sister? How does it feel to be utterly and truly *betrayed*. Not good, I expect. Not a pleasant place to be."

Kranesh was staring up at Moraxx from her half-crushed skull.

"You are not Moraxx," she said, finally.

"What?"

"You are not my sister. I do not understand how, but I know my own blood when I see it. So do your fucking worst, because I have been given some redemption; it is not Moraxx who takes my last breath at the final hour. It is an imposter. A weakling. By some twisted magick, it is a fucking *slave*." The contempt in her voice was complete. She oozed disgust. She vomited mistrust. She pissed out *hate*.

"You are wrong."

"Kill me now, imposter. I await death. You are a worm. A slave. A fucking *human*."

Screaming, Moraxx lurched forward and began to stamp on Kranesh's head, time after time after time, until blood oozed from her maw, from her broken eyes, from her nostrils. Slowly, agonisingly, the fire around her snout flickered, and played, and flickered, and finally went out. Bubbles of blood popped from Kranesh's crushed skull. Her great dark eyes had closed.

In a rage now, Skalg breathed in deeply, then ignited his fire glands, and blasted Kranesh in the face. For long minutes he raged against her, fire streamers turning from yellow to white to blue to a colour that was not even a colour, just pure heat.

Finally, exhausted, Skalg pulled back, and Moraxx looked down, and Kranesh's scales were untarnished. Fire could not harm her. A natural evolution had seen to that.

"Fuck it," growled Skalg, as more hate, more rage, swamped him, and stepping forward, he lowered his head, and chewed, and bit, and chewed, and gnawed, and it took him some time, because despite his fangs being razor-sharp, and able to inflict damage on dragon scales, Kranesh was his sister, she was the elite, and she had not been willing to die.

Finally, there came a *thud*, as Kranesh's head fell free of the body. Inside the hole of her neck there raged an inferno. Out of curiosity, Skalg peered inside, and it nearly burned his eye out of its socket.

Slowly, he picked up the head in his jaws, then leapt into the sky.

Darkness had fallen.

A billion stars twinkled.

A few errant spears followed him, *her*, up into the velvet black. All lacked enthusiasm.

Moraxx reached several thousand feet up, where the sky was filled with ice, where the night was ebony, where only the cold hydrogen of space offered any sort of conversation, investigation, contemplation.

Moraxx held out her sister's head, and with a sigh, allowed it to fall back to the grey pastel landscape of the starlight-crusted world below.

Hex

Val crept forward, boots crunching softly on the shells underfoot. He winced with every footfall, cringing, wondering if it would bring a sudden onslaught of unseen violence. But it did not. So, with each cracking footstep, he welcomed the lack of attack, the lack of screams, the simple peace of not having a violent axeman offering a series of axe-blows to his skull.

Crayline, however, was the polar opposite. She smiled as she remembered.

It wasn't that she had been brought up on war or battle; that would be a gross misrepresentation. Basically, she simply hated... *people*. Anything that walked or crawled, from a very early age, she had despised. So, in effect, she despised *life*. She'd killed many people during her years of efficient service, from ministers to poets to politicians, royalty, bureaucrats, doctors, teachers, market traders, stonemasons, miners, and the one common denominator she could see that linked all these chance meetings (*shhhh, chance murders*) was the fact she'd turned them all from the living into the dead.

Of course, it never began like that.

First, she killed animals. Bugs. Cats. Dogs. Pigs.

Just to see what it was like.

Crayline never even blinked, not even during the most atrocious animal slaughter. After all – they were just animals, right?

And then she met a handsome dwarf.

Swept her off her feet.

Romance.

Wedding.

Pregnancy.

Twins.

Twin dwarves, two girls!

It had been a dream for a while, and Crayline had revelled in her new-found role. No more killing. No more murder. No more extermination of innocents. A normal family life, with a husband, and children. Her maternal instincts had come to the fore. Until, one night, for no reason whatsoever, Crayline walked to the kitchen and stood there, listening to the children crying, listening to her husband shouting, *what the fuck are you doing you useless fucking bitch? I need a fucking packed lunch for tomorrow when I'm down the mines, get on it bitch, I haven't got all night…*

She was tired of him. Tired of his petty outbursts. His ridiculous demands. Tired of his small-minded rantings. Just… *tired*.

Crayline picked up a bread knife.

She looked down the length of the blade.

It gleamed, reflecting in her eyes.

"I actually despise you," she said to herself, watching those dark reflected eyes. "You are somebody I helped. Somebody with whom I laughed and joked. I came to the hospital with you. I helped you when you discovered you might be dying. But then – you betrayed me. Snake in the grass. Backstabbing cunt. And I realised; there's a lot of you out there. And you know what?"

The wind sighed, like a discarded lover.

"Some people might call it unnecessary. But I call it retribution."

The cool breeze chilled her skin.

She looked down at the blade.

"Because, if you live by the sword, then you die by the sword. That's only fair, right?"

And she stood.

And she moved through the house.

Her husband was in bed, attempting to get to sleep.

He got it first.

It was messy, as was to be expected.

But necessary.

And then Crayline stood, staring at her two sleeping girls. Their breathing was regular, rhythmical, and yet a shard of glass pierced her heart, and she thought, and she *knew*. She knew she was going to die. So what would their life be like without her, *her*, their mother? So there was only one answer, right? She had to kill her little girls. She had to kill her own flesh and blood. Because nobody else was ever going to have them; nobody was going to experience the ecstasy she'd felt creating her own children.

I created them, she said.

They are mine, she said.

I own them, she said.

So. They are mine to destroy.

She stepped forward, and the blade came down. A hundred years of blood. It sounded like a river. She stabbed over and over. *Over and over we die*, she thought. *One after the other.* And she kept on stabbing. Kept on killing. Kept on murdering. And, although *enjoyment* wasn't the right word, the right concept, it was indeed the necessary word; the necessary concept.

And so she stabbed her little girls.

She stabbed them to death, and watched the deep pools of crimson well up in the deep, wide wounds.

She watched them sigh, and deflate.

Their eyes opened.

Why, mummy? Why did you do this?

And she couldn't answer. They would never understand.

But she knew in her heart.

It was the right thing to do.

Because it was all about *control*.

And here, and now, Crayline Hew had the control.

•••

They moved across the shells, as if traversing a broken shore.

"Everything is dead," observed Val.

Crayline held up a hand, and didn't even qualify it with a patronising *shh*.

The soldiers, warriors, mercenaries, guards, miscreants, vagabonds, they all stopped. Ahead, something glittered. It was intricate. Detailed. Impossibly complex.

"We've found the eggs," hissed Crayline.

"What eggs?" said Val, head tilted to one side.

Crayline smiled. "Don't worry about it. Dwarves, to me!" and she charged forward, boots crunching shell segments, her mind somewhere else, her mission paramount, and behind her came Val, running with a crossbow cradled in his arms, and he couldn't help thinking *what the fuck is happening? I don't understand*, but he realised suddenly this was all out of his control somehow – and he couldn't work out how. He'd been played for a fool, lied to, used, for a greater purpose maybe, but still *used*; passed over in some bureaucratic lottery. His employer had fucked him over by offering reduced information. In all reality, Crayline was in charge. She had been from the start. That fuckbitch.

The dwarves surrounded her, bristling with weapons.

Crayline nodded, as if giving her approval.

"Ahead," she said, voice hard.

Again, the group moved forward, and they could see a chamber, a vast chamber. And there stood a woman. She was tall, almost athletic. Her hair fell in dark braids. She had her hands raised, as if in the middle of some mystical incantation.

Crayline and Val stepped forward, ducking a little under a barrier they could barely comprehend, to survey a world of miniaturised machines affixed to the vast array of walls, a huge vista of machines, they were everywhere, spinning and clicking, shunting and twisting.

Crayline brought about her crossbow.

Val stared ahead, then turned.

"What are you doing?" he said. And he frowned. For in this moment he had no understanding.

Crayline levelled her crossbow. She gave a narrow smile, looking sideways to Val.

"Some reflect," she said, and sighted down the stock. "And some shine."

She pulled the crossbow trigger.

And Val screamed, realisation kicking him in an instant. Because Val, and most of the others, *reacted*. It was a natural response state. One couldn't unload a crossbow in a dwarf's face. That was killing. That was *murder*. Most dwarves could not do that. It had been proved. To *react* was normal. To *proact* was abnormal.

Which is what made Crayline's actions so bizarre and unusual. So unexpected, to the rest of the group.

She stunned them with her immediate action.

Crayline's quarrel left her crossbow, and hummed across the space.

As if sensing the assault, Lillith turned, eyes fixing on Crayline.

And the crossbow bolt entered her chest, blossoming in a shower of red, and punching the white witch from her feet. She flew back from the walkway, and was absorbed by the eggs, by the mist; effectively, she vanished.

Jael held up his hands, cowering. "Please... please..."

"Any other cunts want a fight?" snapped Crayline, scanning left and right. She stepped forward, boots clacking. She could see no more enemies, other than the young lad. "Get in here, you fuckers!" she growled, face breaking into a grin like punctured yolk, and pointed towards Jael.

The dwarves tramped in, crossbows at the ready, and scanned the thousands of dragon eggs, the intricate machinery; silver machines hissed and clicked and ticked and tocked across the walls. It was an ocean of clockwork technology. And yet here, now, it mattered for nothing.

Survival.

Survival was what mattered.

Hanging in the centre of the chamber, Lillith's magick suddenly dissipated. With cries, Beetrax, Dake, Talon and Sakora dropped like stones down a well, and Crayline's eyes went wide as they suddenly entered her vision – then hit the ground, hard, cracking several eggs and sending them spinning off in all directions, before the mist rolled over them.

Jael ran for it, heading for the far side of the chamber, boots slipping and sliding on the polished walkway.

"Kill them all!" screamed Crayline, cutting down with her hand, and the thirty dwarves levelled their crossbows and began firing.

Crossbow quarrels twanged and whined, hissing across the chamber, cutting slits in the mist and punching into objects within…

Two dwarves turned on Jael, sighted down their weapons, and pulled triggers. Two bolts hit him in the lower back, and he folded, slowly, stumbling, then hit the walkway on his face, momentum carrying him sliding forward until he lay, unmoving, blood leaking out onto the slick, black, polished walkway, where it ran to the edge, and dripped down into the chilled valley of the dragon eggs.

Spliced

Dek remembered his first tattoo.

It was just before General Dalgoran summoned the young soldier to his office at Desekra to outline his plans for a new elite squad: the Iron Wolves. Dek remembered that day proudly, stood to attention, spring sunlight spilling through the lead-lined windows across Dalgoran's oak desk; but he remembered it *more* because of the tattoo.

"You have to have one, Dek, old boy."

"I don't know if I fancy it." He'd grinned, sheepishly, his young lad's face boyish and ruggedly handsome, hair close-cropped in the military style, his eyes shining with an innocence of youth.

"Come on," said Brozo, "I'm having one done after the party tomorrow night. You *are* coming to the party, aren't you?"

Dek frowned. "Well, Sergeant Regander is taking me through some boxing combinations. You know I have that fight coming up." He looked around to check nobody could overhear. "Regander has a lot of money riding on it," he whispered, rubbing his chin. "And you know I've been training for this fight for the last three months. It's against that big bastard from Seventh Battalion. Trax, or something, he's called."

"Aye, Beetrax. I've heard of him. Apparently he's incredible with an axe."

"Well, this time he'll have to use his fists." Dek winked. "Reckon I'll give him a black eye or two."

"Still, you can come to the party after your training, right? And we'll nip down to the Ink Barracks, see if Skoffo will put us under the needle."

"We'll end up locked up, if we get caught," said Dek, appearing a little worried.

"Ach, fuck it man, live a little, will you?"

The party was over at Chicken Barracks, so named because one mad soldier there kept three chickens and supplied the other men with fresh eggs to supplement their rations. Cruel jokes were made about Chicken Barracks, and the obvious association with *chickens*, hence cowardice. But one thing was for certain – anybody who got an invite never turned it down, because Hujo Krant was housed in Chicken, and he made the finest illegally distilled vodka anywhere in Desekra. Three times he'd been up on a charge, even done time in solitary, but the bastards just could not find his still – which was a minor miracle. There weren't that many places to distil spirits in a fortress!

Dek and Brozo made their way through the night air. Despite being spring, it was still chilly, and they blew into their cold hands and rubbed them together as they trod the frost-crisped grass of the killing ground, heading for Chicken Barracks. Brozo gave a complicated knock, and a big fucker with a bushy beard and shaved head opened the door a narrow crack and peered out.

"Yeah?"

"Brozo and Dek. We're on the list."

The huge shaved soldier checked his list, peered behind the two men to see if they were being observed, then opened the door to allow entry. They nipped inside, to find all the bunks had been moved away and tables set out with cards and knuckle-dice. Many men were standing around, with tankards of ale or the tell-tale small glasses of neat vodka.

Dek was aching from a hard workout at the fists of

Sergeant Regander, and he still had a sore jaw from a savage right hook, but the young Dek was used to taking his punches, and even more used to giving them, so he didn't grumble, he just peered around the room, nodding at a few friends he knew, until Brozo returned with a glass of Hujo Krant's finest. "Get this down you. It'll put hairs on your chest!"

Dek sniffed the liquor. "I heard about this one guy... Zastarte, his name is, fucking *shaves* his chest! Can you believe that?"

"I heard about him as well. Likes his men, as well as his women." Brozo winked.

"How's that, like?"

"You know. He'll go to bed with men."

Dek stared at Brozo. "Really?"

"Fuck, Dek, are you really the backward village idiot you pretend to be?"

"Well, I ain't experienced no city life, like you, Bro," Dek said, and frowned. "I'm not used to the same sort of people as you!"

Brozo drank his drink, and choked, gagging, eyes watering, his breath wheezing out. "Well you get that down you." His voice had changed, and become husky, as if a fist were inside his lungs. "It's good stuff! Then we'll go get this tattoo done... "

Dek knocked back the vodka. He choked. His eyes watered. "Fuck me," he said, wheezing, "what's he distil it from, fish oil?"

"Come on!"

Ten minutes later saw Dek lying on his belly, chin on his hands, the back of his shirt up, the waistline of his trews lowered.

"Now you sure you want it there, village boy?" grinned Brozo, his words slurring just a little. Four of Hujo Krant's gut-rippers had left him the worse for wear. Dek, also, had drank too much, and he nodded, grinning.

"It's a good place. And an incredible design!"

"What is it again?"

"It's a demon, ain't it?" said Skoffo, streamers trailing from the pipe he smoked. Skoffo had wild hair and a wild beard. He also had wild, mismatched eyes and shaking hands, but Dek couldn't see that because he was drunk and on his belly.

Brozo sat propped on a chair, watching Dek's face. "Go easy with him, Skoffo. It's his first tat."

"Ha," snapped Dek. "How much can it fucking hurt? I've five bare-knuckle fights under my belt, won the lot, took punches from all them lads, jaw, temple, belly, ribs – I'm telling you, I have the highest pain threshold you've ever come across."

"Proud words, son," said Skoffo. "Now keep still. Wouldn't want to fuck it up now, would I?" His shaking hand dipped the thick needle into the ink-pot, and he stabbed it into Dek's flesh.

"Ow, ouch, you fucking son of a bitch!" he snapped, trying to turn.

Skoffo started stabbing at speed, then scratched out part of an outline that fair made Dek want to turn round and break his jaw. Brozo leant over, and patted his arm.

"*How much can it fucking hurt? I've five bare-knuckle fights under my belt, won the lot,*" mimicked a grinning Brozo, looking into Dek's scrunched up face. "You believe me now when I say Skoffo is the quickest in the business?"

"He might be the quickest," said Dek through gritted teeth, "but soon he might just end up the deadest!"

The deadest.

Dek grinned to himself, and then groaned. It was a good memory. A fine memory. What had brought that back? It was pain. Pain across the back of his hips, as if some great weight was pushing down on him.

Where the fuck am I?

What the fuck hit me?

Was it a Pit Fight?

Everything was hazy, blurred, like the morning after the most incredible night out he couldn't ever remember.

Was I drinking? Fighting? What?

His mouth was full of dust, and he spat, and tried to bring his hand up to rub his lips – which was when he discovered he couldn't move his arm. He started to tug, to pull, to flex his powerful muscles, but it was stuck. Panic entered his breast. Shit. Fuck. Was he the victim of some kind of rockfall?

And then flickers of images began to return.

Staccato. Fuzzy. Unreal.

The big, black dragon.

The tower.

A sound like a never-ending earthquake, groaning and rumbling around him.

"Oh, gods," he muttered, "did that really happen?" He shook his head a little, and wiggled his toes. But his back was pinned down, across his hips, pain emanating across that first tattoo which had burned him so bad in those early days. Dek grinned to himself. "By the Seven Sisters, I'm truly fucked here, aren't I?" And he boomed out more laughter, blinking dust from his eyes, *after everything I've ever seen in my life, after all the trials and tribulations, all the punch-ups, sword battles, mud-orcs, elf-rats and now a fucking dragon, to be taken out in a fucking tower collapse… well, that just puts a ridiculous sour full stop at the end of my worthless fucking life.*

Suddenly, there came a crashing sound. Something shifted above Dek, and grunting, two silhouetted figures lifted a stone lintel and cast it to one side, where it clattered down a pile of rubble. Hazy firelight came in, along with rainfall that cooled Dek's face.

"Is that you, Dek lad?" boomed Narnok, his scarred face suddenly coming into focus like some horrific nightmare.

"Aye, it is. What fucking took you so long?"

"You cheeky, cheeky bastard."

Kareem was helping, and they lifted a wooden beam

from Dek's hips, and hauled him out of his hole. Dek
stretched, and groaned, as a thousand aches and pain
prodded and punched him. He blinked, rubbed dust from
his eyes, turned his face to the rain, allowing it to cool his
tongue, then took a second look around. This area of the
city had been demolished. The collapsing tower had seen
to that, wiping out most of the close surrounding buildings,
and decimating many of the others. Fires burned. Down
one square, a group of maybe two hundred armed guards
had gathered.

"I thought I was dead," said Dek.

"So did we."

"Where's Mola?"

"Down there, looking for Trista."

"Fuck! She's still missing?"

"Yes, lad," rumbled Narnok, and his scarred face was filled
with apprehension. "Come on. We have to keep searching."

"Where's the fucking dragon gone?"

"Over there." Narnok gestured vaguely. "Group of archers
took her on, she's chasing them up towards the North Gate
breathing fire up their arses, no doubt." He grinned, a quite
savage look. "Glad we found you."

"Now we need to find Tris."

They started calling her name, and moved down the
rubble pile towards Mola. Mola's eyes were red-rimmed,
and he had the most savage look on his face.

"What's wrong with him?"

"Don't fucking ask!"

"Hey, Mola, what's up with you, big lad?"

"It's my dogs," he said, voice wretched. "I can't find my
dogs. I've been whistling for ages. They're gone, Dek. Gone
and crushed."

Dek bit his lip, wondering what to say. In the end, he said
nothing. He knew how much Mola loved his mutts.

They started calling for Trista once more, occasionally
looking to the sky. But there was no sign of Volak, and after
a while, they busied themselves moving rocks and calling

her name. Until a growl rumbled out from the shadows.

Atop the rubble of the tower, Narnok, Dek, Mola and Kareem straightened from their labour. Narnok still had his axe, but the others had had to scavenge for weapons, either in the fall or in nearby houses. None were happy with what they had found.

"Is that one of your dogs?" said Narnok, carefully,

Mola shook his head. "No. I know their growls anywhere. That," he gestured to the dark insides of a half-collapsed town house, "that's something different."

"It can't be the dragon," muttered Kareem, hoisting a half-rusted short sword that looked too small for his large hands. "She wouldn't hide in a bloody house and growl at us. So what is it?"

"Remember," said Narnok, single eye glinting, "just before the tower collapsed? There were shapes. Dark shapes. Running through the streets. Some across the rooftops."

"I know what I thought," said Dek, and his words were terribly soft.

"What's that, lad?"

"I thought they were splice," he said, eyes fixed on the dark, sagging opening to the house. Something was definitely in there, peering out at them. He could just distinguish a section of outline; it was big. Too big.

"That's fucking impossible!" boomed Narnok, slapping him on the back and making him cough. "Those fucking things died with Orlana the Changer."

Dek shook his head. "No. I've heard stories. About rogue ones, out in the countryside. Rogue *splice*. Gangs of villagers get together to hunt them down. There have been some shocking casualties."

"Dek lad, you're talking a whole load of donkey bollocks... " Narnok grinned, as from the shadows emerged a splice, limping, great rigid muscles tensed and ready to spring, its long head turned away, so the equine muzzle was almost on its side. A big red eye bulged, and open wounds across its face oozed black blood.

The Iron Wolves took a step back, and brandished their weapons.

"Fuck me!" said Narnok.

"I... don't believe it," muttered Kareem, stroking his beard.

"Right," hissed Narnok, eye not moving from the beast. "They're tough fuckers, these ones. We'll have to attack from different sides."

Kareem stared at him.

"What?"

"I was on Desekra," said Kareem.

"Were you?"

"I fought against the mud-orcs, *old man*."

Narnok opened his mouth to retort, as another growl came from the left, where a huge, splintered beam lay propped against a wall. It was surrounded by crushed rubble. Limping sideways, came another splice. Narnok's mouth shut with a clack.

Then, from behind them, a third growl rumbled out.

"Oh, you've got to be fucking joking!" wailed Narnok, and turned slowly as a third creature came from the shadows. And the Iron Wolves realised, with rising horror, that there were more... more splice, crouching in the shadows behind these first ones...

"This is turning into a really shitty day," said Kareem, turning slowly, short sword weaving before him.

"One is hard enough to kill," snapped Dek. "What are we supposed to do against... ten? Eleven?"

They'd stopped, a short distance away, lips curled back, deep rumbles emerging from twisted throats.

"I think we have a problem," said Mola.

"Yes, I can *see* the fucking problem!" moaned Dek.

"No. A bigger problem!"

"Really?"

They all looked up. And saw the dragon circling high overhead. Then she swept down, and something tumbled from her mouth even as she entered the dive. It glinted, silver, and it took moments to realise it was a *knight* in full armour.

Volak landed with a *crash* in Tower Square, and shook out her wings, her head coming up, eyes fixing on the Iron Wolves.

"I confess," she said, voice a musical rumble, "as to being amazed you still live."

"You murdered my fucking dogs!" screamed Mola, taking several steps forward.

"Yes, yes, come to me little fat man. Let us see if your fat can run molten through the gutters."

"I'll cut off your fucking head," he snarled.

Volak chuckled, head turning slightly, to observe the splice. "Interesting choice of playmates," she said. Fire flickered around her nostrils. "They are not born of this world, but carry the stink of the Furnace in their skin. I wonder which demon gave them a stamp of approval."

Kareem shuffled sideways, and nudged Narnok in the ribs.

"Hey! What?"

"Look!"

"*What?*"

"*The splice!*"

And indeed, the group of splice had turned, and their odd eyes and drooling muzzles were facing Volak. Every single one of them.

"They don't seem to like her," muttered Kareem.

"Good! Neither do I!"

"I think..." said Dek. But it was too late. The splice attacked.

One leapt from the shadows, a bound, to land on Volak's back. Jaws snapped down as claws, or rather, a curious combination of claws and broken hooves, stabbed and scraped at her scales as her head reared, she turned to look behind, and backed up several steps and roared.

The others leapt forward, bounding across the ancient stone flagstones of Tower Square. Three more leapt onto

Volak's back, and she reared up suddenly, a terrifying vision, as one splice jumped for her throat. Her claw slammed out, catching the splice and sending it flying through the air, where it hit the cobbles rolling, dug in its claws, leapt up and charged back into another attack.

Flames roared out, setting one splice on fire. Up went its tattered, scarred horse hair, but still it came on, screaming now, jaws chomping, until Volak grabbed it between both claws and ripped it in half. Blood rained down. The great wyrm tossed aside the two body parts with contempt, and looked back again at the four on her back, biting and clawing and stabbing. Her tail whipped up, the great spike lashing through a splice, impaling it. Blood poured from its twisted horse muzzle. Volak's tail lifted the creature high into the air, still wriggling, still vomiting blood, and launched it at a nearby half-collapsed church, where it crashed through a wall and lay still.

Yet more splice came from the shadows, charging at Volak, leaping at her, leaping on her. She realised her error too late, and unfolding her wings, gave a great flap, lifting up from the ground, spinning slightly. But there were ten splice on her back now, doing their best to cause maximum destruction, and the weight alone must have been incredible, never mind the fact they were squirming and fighting. Volak roared again, wings flapping, and lifted perhaps twenty feet off the ground. A splice came from the top of a building, a massive leap, soaring through the rain to clamp jaws on the very edge of Volak's left wing. Volak screamed, fire roaring, as she tipped to one side, started to spiral, and was dragged back down to the ground by the sheer weight of splice…

"Come on," growled Narnok.

"What, fuckwit? What do you mean *come on*?" Dek stared at him.

"Let's go join in!"

"Join in *that*?"

"Together, we can kill it!"

"Together, we can get fucking torched!"

"Come on, brothers!" roared Narnok, single eye squinting, scarred face contorting. He might have looked like a clown, if he hadn't been so fucking lethal.

Volak roared again, and flames washed Tower Square, turning night into day. Rain sizzled. Splice rumbled and spat and growled.

"I agree." Mola stepped forward, boots crunching old stones, and in each fist he carried a battered short sword. "I want to fuck her for what she did to my dogs." Tears still wet his cheeks. "I say we help the splice, although I never thought in my lifetime I would utter such words. We have a common enemy now. An enemy common not just to the city, but the whole of Vagandrak. That dragon needs to fucking die."

"Come ON!" roared Narnok, and sprinted down the rubble, battered axe in battered hands.

Mola followed, with grim long strides, his eyes filled with hatred, his heart filled with vengeance.

Dek and Kareem looked at one another.

"They're mad," said Kareem, twirling his short sword and rolling his neck to release tension. "*Fucking* mad."

Dek grinned then, showing missing teeth. "Yeah lad. But you only live once, right? And you have to live that life to the full!"

With howls, they charged down the scree of tower stones, catching up Narnok and Mola, and all four charged, ducking a random blast of fire as Volak spun around, claws and tail lashing, fire spewing from her angered, triangular head.

Tower Square was a chaos of thrashing limbs, snapping jaws, squeals and growls and bites, random jets of flame igniting detritus lying all around, and even splice, that sprinted away, howling, only to return seconds later, leaping back at the dragon in an attempt to bring her down.

Volak was suffering.

There were two long wounds down her back, where

splice had used razor claws and sharpened hooves to *lever* up scales and attack the unprotected flesh beneath. Dragon blood ran down her matte black flanks, and dripped to the cracked and broken flagstones.

Narnok arrived, with the others, and started hacking at Volak's chest. Her head came down, eyes widening as Narnok's axe flashed up, carving a groove of sparks across her black scales.

"I said I'd carve my name on your arse!" he screamed.

Volak's claw lashed out, a backhand swipe that picked Narnok up and propelled him across the square, to land hard, rolling, axe clattering beside him and damn near cutting his own head from his sorry neck.

Volak's head lifted, and she roared, and her head dropped, and fire screamed from her maw. But the splice pulled her to one side, three on her wing, tearing at her, and she was dragged staggering across the square until her tail snapped round, spike impaling a splice, then sawing it in half with five long, measured movements. Horse guts and human internal organs spilled to the stones, where they glistened like oil.

She whirled about, then, the mighty wyrm, and her tail and claws lashed out, cutting two splice in half simultaneously. Then she leapt, wings beating, but instead of trying to take to the sky, she flipped backwards, landing on the splice which tortured her from behind, crushing them, if not to death, then at least into broken, pulverised bones.

Kareem ran in, sword hacking. Volak's rear leg caught him, smashing him aside where he lay, stunned, wondering if he were dead.

Dek danced backwards as another claw sought him, then he rolled to one side as a blast of fire nearly disintegrated him. "Fuck this," he muttered, and ran to Kareem, helping the stocky fighter to his feet.

"We'll never kill the fucker like this!" screamed Dek.

Kareem nodded, speechless, still dazed from the blow.

Volak rolled over, and using legs and wings, regained her feet. Behind her lay five dead splice, crushed into sacks of flesh-filled bone dust. Three more squirmed, crushed out of recognition but still, amazingly, alive.

Volak roared, and fire painted the skies, turning rain to steam in an instant.

Narnok pushed himself to his knees, still stunned.

And Mola stood, a sword in each fist, eyes defiant.

"Fuck you!" he screamed, and charged Volak.

Volak's head suddenly dropped, eyes narrowing, and with a short intake of breath, she narrowed her lips, and sent an intense blue jet of fire straight at Mola. He was caught in the blast, picked up, smashed backwards, clothes and skin and beard and hair flaming bright until... until the jet of fire whistled and screamed, reaching an intensity of pitch, and Mola slowly disintegrated in that blast, the flesh charred from his bones, his bones burned into ash...

The fire stopped, abruptly.

Two smoking short swords hit the stone flags with clangs, steel turned blue from the heat, their lengths twisted, distorted, bent out of all recognition.

And Mola had gone.

Volak's head came up, and her proud, arrogant, condescending eyes surveyed the remaining men and splice, most of whom were backing away, their fight gone, their bones broken.

"Is this the best you can hit me with?" she snarled, and lowering her head she spat a ball of fire to the flags. "IS THIS IT, YOU FUCKING INSECTS?"

"Er," said Narnok, turning to Dek.

"Fuck," said Dek, turning to Kareem.

"Time to leave?" suggested Kareem, face drawn in shock.

Volak strode forward, and they could see she was injured, with great bloody rents in her back and flank. One wing was tattered, torn, several bones broken. Her one blind eye had turned from jet black to milky white. It made her curiously asymmetrical.

"You cunts are going *nowhere*," she hissed, and lowered her head, to stare at the remaining Iron Wolves.

Narnok brandished his axe.

Volak gave a patronising laugh, and breathed in, deeply, ingesting the air she needed to mix with her fire glands in order to produce an inferno.

There should have been some last words, but Volak was beyond it.

There should have been a miracle, but Volak would no longer allow it.

She breathed in, single good eye narrowed in hate, *to think such fucking maggots had so much fight in them...*

Her ignition caught, and with a roar Volak released the furnace...

Trigger Switch

The taste was something special. He'd never tasted anything quite like it before. He'd experienced every fine wine there was on offer, every gastronomical delicacy the finest chefs could imagine and create. He'd tasted every lip, nipple and quim he could get his tongue on, and he did have a special fondness for the quim, and its wide variety of intriguing flavours. Every quim was different, a flavoursome palette, a subtlety that he was sure his supposed contemporaries overlooked. But not him. Oh no. Quim was up there with the finest wines, strongest brandies, spicy wines, and with the testicles of young piglets, roasted in garlic, and the dry, panting, fear-filled lips of a woman who knew she was about to be raped.

Skalg grinned to himself, revelling in his debauchery.

But… so what? So fucking what?

The world had mocked him, put him down, put him in a hole – quite literally. A mine shaft. A fucking collapsed mine shaft. And now he had risen, through the Church of Eternal Hate, through the ranks, to become First Cardinal… and then *beyond*, to the Great Dwarf Lords themselves, and then further still, to populate this body of a great wyrm, a dragon, the most powerful creature ever to walk the soil of Vagandrak.

And a thought entered Skalg's mind.

His dragon tongue licked slowly across his lips, and

across his fangs. For he could still taste it. Still taste her. Still
taste…

Kranesh.

Her blood. Her fear. Her anguish.

Her *blood.*

But now, *now*, Skalg was in charge.

And the thought taunted him.

What…

What if…

WHAT if…

*What if he never gave the body back. What if he turned on the
Great Dwarf Lords. Fuck them, and their sanctimonious preaching
pile of donkey shit. Who were they to say what lived and what
died? Who were they to say what happened in the world, what
happened in the Five Havens, what happened to dwarves and men
and elves?*

Fuck the Great Dwarf Lords.

Fuck my gods.

I will destroy Volak, and then I will rule.

*I will rule the world, like no crippled hunchback has ever ruled
the world before. Or will again.*

I will rule with omniscience.

I will rule with hate, and fear, and total violence.

I will rule with utter dominance.

His name was Kokar, of the clan Karik 'y Kla, and he was
angrier than any dwarf in the Five Havens. And quite
rightly so. His daughter was dead. His beautiful, precious
only daughter. It had taken days for it to sink in. The
official church letter had told him the facts in cold clinical
ink… accidental death from a high fall. He found it hard to
believe. How the fuck did you fall from the fucking Blood
Tower, of all places? It was church-owned. It had safety
barriers. And Kajella was not a young female dwarf known
for taking risks. She was sensible. She was dependable. She
was *normal.*

Kokar frowned.

His anger increased so much he thought his heart would burst.

By the Great Dwarf Lords, he wanted to get revenge on the dwarf who had done this.

Not only allowed it to happen.

Oh no.

The one who had *done it*.

Because Kokar was armed with *the truth*.

And the *truth* burned him worse than any lies.

You see, it was all about money. At the end of the day, everything is about money. Doesn't matter if you're Irlax's fucking handmaiden, right hand better than the left, or one of Skalg's Educators. Every single dwarf has a lever point. A point where they think, *fuck me, really, how much? Just for a few words?* And the problem with Skalg, Kokar had realised early on in his investigations, the *problem* with Skalg was that had become so fat, so rich, so powerful, he viewed certain people as parts of the furniture. If a young dwarf had come into his chambers to make up the beds and arrange his slippers and wash his silk dressing gown, she no more existed than did the cabinet carrying his bottles of brandy. And, even better, the more ugly a serving wench was, the more Skalg treated her as if she didn't exist, such was his arrogance, vulgarity and superiority complex.

On the night of Kajella's death, one such cleaner had been present.

Ugly. Pointless. Poor. Pathetic. To Skalg, at any rate.

But more importantly, she was *invisible*.

Kokar's payment of five years wages had persuaded her to tell the truth.

And it was a truth that left a bitter, sour, nasty taste.

Kokar was a rich and powerful dwarf. He'd made his fortune some years back, investing in new mine digs. He'd been lucky. Or wise. As the saying went, the mountain gives, and the mountain takes away. In wealth, the mountain had been good for Kokar. It was only evil dwarf flesh that got in the way.

Kokar had employed assassins to murder Skalg.

It had seemed a quick and easy solution.

Only, *only* they failed, because of some Educator bitch who was pretty good with a blade. Money bought witnesses, and Kokar had tracked Skalg to the Cathedral of Eternal Hate. Now, he stood outside the doors, looking up and down the street. The Five Havens seemed deserted now. Gone were the looters and protesters. The escaped dragons had seen to that. It was as if the whole of the Five Havens were in some kind of lockdown; a self-imposed lockdown based on the foundation of fear. The dwarves knew the dragons were going to return, to complete their reign of destruction in retribution for thousands of years of abuse. And instead of fighting, of preparing defences, they knew deep down in their hearts it would all be ineffectual. As a race, the dwarves had pretty much gone into some kind of group withdrawal.

Not Kokar.

Kokar wanted to fight. Kokar wanted to kill. And Kokar wanted *revenge*.

There were no guards outside the Cathedral of Eternal Hate, but that was probably because Skalg had locked the quite incredible, extravagant, ornate doors. Kokar signalled to three of his associates, and they ran forward, placing a box at the front of the doors. One struck a match, a long, evil looking stick, which burned with a foul colour and even fouler odour. He touched it to a taper.

These were chemicals used to blast down in the mines.

There came a bright fizzing. Sparks.

Kokar looked up and down the street again. After the dragons, nobody really gave a fuck.

The explosion rocked the ground. High above, several slates were jostled loose from the cathedral's roof, and fell, spinning silently, to crash and shatter on the street. Kokar looked up in trepidation, but he needn't have worried. This shit was used for blasting rock. In comparison, a cathedral's wood and iron-banded doors were nothing more than hot butter.

Kokar gestured, and his hardiest soldiers entered through the smoking portal, crossbows at the ready, and they found the door, and began their descent.

Down, down towards the Iron **Vaults**.

Kokar had it on good authority **that's where** Skalg would be hiding.

There was a halfway point called the Block. Kokar remembered it, from distant memory. This is where Skalg left his faithful Educators to guard him against any possible but unexpected intrusion.

Now, they were dead, with crossbow bolts in bellies and short black daggers sticking out of eye sockets.

Kokar hadn't lost a single dwarf.

Such was the power of surprise.

They descended more steps. Deep, deep into the bowels of the Cathedral of Eternal Hate. It was cool, down here. Cool, and calm. Especially after the rampage of the dragons. *Such a shame*, thought Kokar, *that the Church of Hate doesn't extend these safety margins to the common people*.

He smiled, a narrow, evil smile, and thought about Skalg.

Dwarves marched through the streets. Irlax was dead. The dragons had escaped. There was no heating. No steam. No power. The dwarves were pissed. They wanted answers. Nobody seemed to have answers. When they knocked on the doors of a Church of Hate, Church Guards and Educators slammed doors, told them to fuck off, were rude and ignorant and arrogant, as they had always been. But now the dwarves were scared. They had seen their world under the mountain grind to a halt. All their social privileges had been suddenly removed. Firebrands burned in fists. Chants started to fill the empty streets. The dragons were gone. They didn't seem to be returning. The dwarves wanted answers. The Crown could not respond. And so, it was down to the Church.

But the Church was silent.

And so the dwarves began a concentrated programme of destruction…

•••

Skalg, First Cardinal of the Church of Hate, was beyond such things.

He no longer inhabited the world of human flesh. His was a world of power, and energy, of dragon lore and feeling like a supreme being. Slowly, he had begun to experience Moraxx's memories as she begged and begged to be released, as she grew weaker in her fight to regain her mind. And Skalg knew, as night turns to day turns to night, that eventually her mind would break, crack open like a fracture-corrupted pebble, and her essence, her *soul* would dissipate. Moraxx would be no more. Skalg would inhabit the dragon flesh fully. Skalg would *be* the dragon.

He slammed through the heavens, wings pumping, high, high above the night-time land of Vagandrak. And his ears picked up the call, the cry of Volak. She was under attack. She was fighting, snarling, her flames roaring out, the deafening sounds echoing through the highest reaches of the thinning atmosphere.

Skalg banked, and dropped, ice frosting his scales, then dropped further, circling, searching. Mountains to the south, the Mountains of Skarandos, a vast jagged line stretching all the way to the Plague Ocean. Beyond the mountains rolled the dunes of Zakora, the desert lands, and as Skalg spiralled, seeking, so beyond the Plague Ocean he saw the vast, forbidding darkness of the Drakka, many leagues deep and stretching all the way north to the Rokroth Marshes.

This openness, even at night, was so bright with stars, so vast, to a dwarf from the mines it was like taking the lid off the top of the world.

Skalg gasped, for maybe the thousandth time, as still these visions stunned him. A billion stars twinkled. Skalg could not comprehend the size of the universe, and his own tiny, microscopic part in it.

More sounds came to him, picked up by his incredibly acute hearing. Sounds of fighting, of roaring, battle cries, snarls. Screams. Animal screams... *almost* animal screams.

Skalg orientated, and saw the storm clouds rolling

towards him from the west, towering clouds disgorging rain and strikes of lightning. From his high vantage point, with his vast vision, it looked like a huge, broiling monster stalked across the land on legs of lightning. Below, trees and buildings lay scorched as the sheer force of nature exacted its revenge on Man.

Skalg powered forward, dropping now to enter the storm. Clouds whipped by, wisps and streamers, and he was buffeted by this incredible force and yet he screamed and roared his laughter into the violence.

I defy you, thought Skalg.

I defy the world.

I defy Nature.

Dropping lower, rain and wind lashed at him, buffeting him hard, making his scales shimmer in the ethereal gloom of the storm. And then he saw it, the city, far below. Vagan. War Capital of Vagandrak. Grim and stark, with areas destroyed, others crumbling, others burning violently.

You have been a busy girl, haven't you, Volak? You have been teaching these horrible little insects a lesson. Well, now, now it is time for us to meet... and I have been waiting for this moment for so long. Treasuring it, in fact. Because when you are out of the picture, the Empire will be mine.

Skalg powered through the storm, and started to lose height, and he heard Volak's roar once more, and his eyes narrowed in Moraxx's face as he plummeted towards the Queen of Wyrmblood...

Volak exhaled, and a stream of fire erupted from her jaws – at the same instant Moraxx hit her hard from behind, smashing into her from a fast high dive, and sending them both crashing along the square. Narnok, Dek and Kareem ducked and squawked, diving away from the two great beasts as the stream of fire whirled about them, turning night to day, sizzling rainfall and then shot up into the sky. The two dragons rolled, entangled, and Moraxx was already biting and clawing, and Volak didn't fight back for a few moments… she was stunned by incomprehension.

Moraxx, disentangled now, climbed to her feet and shook out her wings. A great claw swiped at Volak, tearing a line of scales from her chest and drawing blood beneath the armour.

"WHAT?" shrieked Volak, fire blasting from her jaws as she flapped her wings, dancing backwards. "You attack ME?"

Moraxx grinned at her, black eyes narrowed.

"You look like you've been to war," said Skalg with Moraxx's mouth.

Volak was staring with her one good eye, staring in absolute disbelief. Her chest rumbled, and she clenched her claws, tail whipping from side to side like an irate tomcat.

"Think very carefully about what you are doing, Moraxx."

"I have thought long and hard," grinned Moraxx, taking a threatening step forward.

"We can win this war together. Re-establish the Blood Dragon Empire. Why would you turn on me now?" Volak's head tilted. Her remaining dark eye seemed to glow black. "Only… there's something wrong, isn't there?"

Moraxx said nothing, but took another step forward.

"You have tasted the blood of Kranesh, have you not? I can smell it on your deviant lips."

"I tore off her head with my own teeth," grinned Moraxx, tongue licking her lips.

"Then you really have come to try and kill me. It is a sad day, Moraxx."

"Your time has come, Volak."

To one side, Narnok, Dek and Kareem were on their arses, weapons forgotten, just as *they* had become forgotten. They were breathing fast, unsure whether to stay still – in the hope the two wyrms would think them dead – or to run for it. After all, they hadn't been able to kill one damn dragon – how would they manage to slaughter two?

"What do we fucking do?" muttered Dek.

"Stop fucking talking!" muttered Narnok.

"Will you two *shut up*!" hissed Kareem.

They stared at the dragons. The two beasts seemed very unhappy with one another. They were squaring up, like two pissed-up sailors in a pub. It lacked nobility, but it was the law of the jungle; the nature of every living creature that had ever crawled from the slime.

To fight was to exist.

That was the epitome of life.

"So," said Narnok, frowning. "What do we do?"

That question was answered as Moraxx attacked Volak, who grabbed the wyrm by her throat, and tossed her aside. Moraxx flipped, sliding, to crash into a house, demolishing one wall, stones raining down across her flapping wings, where she squirmed for a moment before righting herself. Her eyes narrowed, and she breathed a blast of fire into which Volak *strode*.

"Your naivety betrays you," said Volak.

"Meaning what?"

"You are not Moraxx."

"Fucking surprised?"

"Who are you?"

"I am your worst nightmare," growled Skalg, and launched a blistering attack. They bit, and clawed, and tails whipped about, spiked tips continually stabbing at scales, and breaking scales. They grappled, as if in some parody of human wrestling, claws slashing out, smashing at one another, at heads and torsos.

Occasionally, flames blossomed. But fire was a useless weapon against another dragon.

They fought.

The Iron Wolves watched, until Narnok said, "This is unproductive. And depressing. I'm going to search for Trista."

Dek nodded. "I'm with you."

"What about them?" gestured Kareem.

"You ever see two dogs fight?" said Dek, scratching his

neck. "You just leave them to it. They work out their own hierarchy. And here and now, I truly do not give a fuck who wins, who loses, or who fucking dies. When their fight is over, if we're still here, we'll have another go. Now, I just want to find my friend."

Kareem nodded, understanding shining in his eyes.

Volak roared, and with a swipe pinned Moraxx to the ground. They had battered one another for an hour, hammering away with tooth and claw. Now, Moraxx was weak, and Volak had flapped her wings, rearing above the other wyrm, and used her bodyweight to slam the bitch to the broken stone flags.

"Yield," said Volak, softly, flames curling around her broken fangs.

"Fuck you," said Skalg, eyes narrowed, scowling up at the more powerful dragon.

"I can destroy you," said Volak.

"Then stop talking and do it, coward bitch," said Skalg, voice full of mockery.

Volak looked down at her sister, and if she'd not been a creature of flame and ash, she would have wept. But that was a physiological act beyond her species. Dragons did not cry. They just screamed.

"I cannot kill you, sister."

"Do it, you spineless cunt."

With a roar, Volak pinned Moraxx to the flags, and her great head came down, and her jaws opened to fasten around Moraxx's throat. She bit, bit hard, and felt the scales crumble, the muscles split, the tendons pop, and her fangs closed around the spinal column and she bit, harder than she had ever bitten any creature in the past...

With a *crack*, Volak bit Moraxx's head clean off. Fire roared from the furnace of her insides, a blast of terrible heat.

And in that instant, Equiem magick was invoked...

The *charm of transference*...

Channelled by the Great Dwarf Lords at Skalg's moment of greatest need.

And in an instant, the blink of an eye, he skipped, from Moraxx's mind, into Volak's – and watched in awe as he bit his own head clean off.

There was a blinding flash of light, incredible pain, and struggle.

An intense struggle of minds.

Volak felt confusion crush her into a ball, and spin her around, and send her crashing down through a dark deep well. She did not understand, even as her jaws closed on the throat of Moraxx, and extracted the very life from her sister with decapitation.

What's happening to me? she thought.

What the fuck is this?

Moraxx's head had come away, flames roaring from the inside of her chest.

And Volak stared, without understanding.

It took minutes to win the battle, to find some kind of stability, some equilibrium. Skalg himself was spinning in the vortex of the mind transfer. He felt the power of the Great Dwarf Lords behind him, powering him on, pushing him forward, forcing him towards conclusion.

Conclusion.

An end to this terrible madness.

What do I do now? said Skalg. Despite his physical prowess, he felt weak and lame.

Now, there is only one.

One is not enough.

You need to hatch the eggs... and choose the strongest.

Then destroy the rest.

We need our Dragon Engine.

We need our dragon slaves once again.

The Great Dwarf Lords demand it.

Volak nodded her huge, black, damaged head. Blood trickled from her in a dozen different places. She turned, and surveyed the Iron Wolves – who cowered, suddenly, expecting to be torched. And she could see they didn't have the strength to fight on. They were done, and finished, and fucked.

"Do it," growled Narnok.

But this was Skalg, not Volak. These peasants meant nothing to him, and he lifted his head, and stared up at the sky. The storm was abating, and rain fell now in a gentle downpour, tickling Volak's snout, cooling her savage wounds. Then she bunched her muscles, her wings cracked out, and she leapt – and began pumping her wings as she shot up into the heavens, and disappeared amidst the reappearing stars... just another glimmering orb, just another shooting star.

Narnok looked over at Dek.

"She went," he said, wearily.

"Where?" said Kareem.

Dek shrugged. "Do you give a fuck? Just... *away*. Away from here."

They considered this, eyes searching the heavens with fear, lest she come back.

"Look at the dead one," said Kareem.

"What about it?"

"Fires still burn on its insides."

Narnok stepped forward, and patted Kareem on the back. "Lad. I reckon that furnace might burn for quite some time. Now come on. Let's find Trista. If she still lives."

"And if she's dead?" said Dek, raising an eyebrow.

Narnok gave a half-shrug. "Well. We'll give her a hero's send-off," he said, quietly.

The sun was coming up over the bruised, battered, scorched city of Vagan when they found a pale hand poking from the rubble of the collapsed tower. Gently, Narnok, Dek and Kareem removed the stones and beams, to find Trista.

Her face was serene, not a mark on her, not a speck of dust, not a smudge of ash. Her blonde curls were immaculate, arranged around her beautiful face as if prepared that way by a professional. In fact, she looked beautiful enough to enjoy her wedding day.

"Tris," said Dek, gently, shaking her.

"She's gone, lad," said Narnok.

"No, no, look at her! She's perfect."

"She's gone," said Narnok, and knelt down beside Dek. He reached out, and touched Dek's arm. Dek turned and looked at him.

"But... look! Not a bruise, not a single injury on her! She *can't* be dead."

Narnok turned, and what Dek said was true. Trista looked immaculate. Perfectly preserved. And yet, still her breast did not rise, and there was no colour to her cheeks, and no living breath in her lungs.

"I'm sorry, Dek," and Narnok hugged him, hugged his brother, and they cried together.

The Mountain Gives...

Sakora lay, stunned. For long moments she had no idea what had hit her. She didn't know where she was, what she was doing, who she was with... but then pain kicked in, and pain has a real way of focussing the mind.

She breathed in the mist which floated above her. She heard the whine and kick, the hiss and rattle of crossbow bolts all around, making her cringe. Confusion tumbled from her mind as she sought something, attempted to fix on a singularity in order to bring herself back to reality. And it was pain that did it. Pain, glorious pain.

The back of her head hurt, as did her neck. But it was her left wrist, shattered as far as she could tell, that sent waves of agony rippling up her arm and into her spinning brain.

Focus.

Calm.

Whilst training in the art of Kaaleesh, Sakora had broken many bones, and now was no different. She breathed, calmed herself, isolated the pain, and started to gradually erode the feelings that panicked her. She analysed the rest of her body. Her left ankle was also in a bad way, so when she got up, and moved, if she had to move fast, she'd have to compensate for her weakened left side, after the... ah...

Fall. Long fall. Lillith. Dragon eggs.

Fall.

She'd landed on her left side.

Dwarves. With crossbows.

Isolate.

Focus.

Isolate the leader.

Slowly, she reached down with her right hand, and pulled a dagger from her right boot. These movements hurt her, and she realised her entire body was battered from the impact after the fall. *Thanks, Lillith*, she thought, and gave a narrow, tight-lipped smile.

It took between six and twelve seconds to reload a crossbow, depending on factors such as competency, technique and panic. Sakora did an internal estimate, and sat up from the mist, surrounded by shattered dragon eggs – which had saved her by taking the brunt of the crossbow quarrel assault, and she *focussed*.

There were thirty mean-looking dwarves, caught in the process of reloading their weapons. And there was Val, weasel face ruptured in the middle of a screamed command. But no. Sakora's gaze travelled, to the pale, haughty, arrogant bitch whose eyes had just settled on Sakora with a calm coolness, a calculated authority, that marked her out as the *leader*.

Sakora's hand snapped back, then forward.

The dagger flew through the humming air, and plunged into Crayline's left eye socket. The female dwarf screamed, and staggered back, but did not fall. Sakora climbed to her feet, sagging on her shattered left side.

Crayline's hands came up, and gently fondled the shaft. Incredibly, she did not go down. Did not die. Sakora pursed her lips in annoyance. Crayline touched the shaft of the dagger in her own head, her own face, no-doubt puncturing her own *brain*... and she screamed again, dropping to one knee.

A second dagger flashed past her face, and embedded in the throat of a dwarf behind. He gurgled, clutching the weapon, and dropped to both knees, vomiting blood onto the smooth black walkway.

The other dwarves glanced up.

Sakora moved her shirt to reveal her baldric. It carried upwards of twenty daggers. The dwarves saw her movement. Recognised its inherent threat. They worked faster to reload their crossbows... but then Sakora went to work. Her left wrist was shattered, but she zoned out the pain and drew two daggers, both arms came back, daggers hissed, spinning. One entered an eye, another through an open, shouting mouth. Two dwarves dropped, blood pooling out.

Two more daggers, thrown with unbelievable accuracy. One entered a throat, another was deflected by a raised arm – but it still entered the dwarf's flesh, making him scream, and add to the rising chaos of the suddenly accelerating scene on the platform.

Another dagger, another eye socket. The dwarf made a meal of it, going down, kicking and screaming, spinning around on his side, begging his comrades to take away the pain – which one did, with an axe blow to the head.

Five dead dwarves in as many heartbeats.

Sakora grinned at them.

They ran for cover, sprinting from the chamber, all except Val and Crayline, who looked at one another, then down at the dead guards around them.

"You have... er... a dagger in your eye," said Val.

"You think I hadn't fucking *noticed*?" screamed Crayline.

"But... er... you're not dead?"

Crayline glared at Val, blood streaming down her face and dripping from her chin like the ticking of a clock.

"You think, cunt, that maybe I hadn't noticed that as well?"

Val giggled, on the edge of hysteria. "Crayline Hew! Not even a dagger in the brain can kill her! Roll up, roll up, and talk to the hard-as-a-coffin-nail bitch!"

Then he turned and stared at Sakora.

Slowly, from the mist, rose Talon. His face was twisted in pain. Pain, and fury. Gone were any doubts which had lingered for long days, long weeks, after their capture and torture. Now the man from the walls of Desekra was back. Here was Talon the archer, scourge of thousands of mud-orcs. And he was pissed.

He pulled free his longbow, and knocked an arrow to the string. He was ready to kill.

Dake crawled to his knees, still stunned from the fall, and stared around. Then he climbed to his feet and unsheathed his sword. This was Dake Tillamandil Mandasar, former Sword Champion of King Yoon's Royal Guard, hero of the Second Mud-Orc War and heir to the Lordship of the House of Emeralds, Vagandrak's largest ruling family. Nothing mattered to him anymore. His wife was dead, gone, lost. And a man without hope is a man without fear. His fear fled like ice melting under tropical rainfall, and he faced Crayline, and Val, and the other dwarves cowering in the adjoining chamber. And he realised with sour humour that he was never going to leave this fucking mine. He was never going to leave this fucking mountain. He would die here. Die here, and be with Jonti. And that was just fine by him.

A crossbow quarrel whined, and hissed through the air. Dake's sword flickered up, smashing the bolt from the air. Talon drew back, paused, released his breath, and let the arrow fly. It spun lazily, and punched the dwarf shooter through the centre of his mouth. The dwarf staggered back, dropped his crossbow, crossed his eyes, and sat down on his arse, groping blindly for the shaft emerging from his skewered tongue. Then he lay down on his side, and bled a little.

Talon notched another arrow. "Would anybody else care to taste my shaft?" he said, and smiled, eyes glittering, and Dake patted him on the shoulder.

"Yes, brother?"

"It's nice to have you back."

Talon looked him in the eye, and saw the strength there, the comradeship, the... *life*. "You also, brother," he said, and grinned. "Now let's kill some fucking dwarves."

"Wait."

The voice came from beneath the mist, which swirled around the hundreds, the *thousands*, of dragon eggs.

Dake and Talon looked at one another. Sakora shrugged.

Beetrax sat up, and shook his head, and scratched his beard. His face was the epicentre of a summer storm. His eyebrows were stormclouds. His eyes were lightning. His grin was the grin of an evil god intent on absolute revenge.

He turned to look at his friends.

"You ain't killing no fucking dwarves without ME!" he boomed, and climbed to his feet, wincing, and lifting his battered, chipped axe. And then he remembered. He remembered the crossbow bolt connecting with Lillith. The spray of blood. Her disappearing under the mist. And his head came up. And he stared at Crayline. And he stared at Val. "Oh, you cunts," he said, voice barely more than a whisper.

A dwarf appeared, and loosed off a crossbow bolt. Talon's arrow hit him in the throat, leaving him scrabbling on his knees, vomiting blood.

Beetrax looked around for Lillith, but couldn't see her...

And impending death was a more pressing priority.

"We doing this?" said Trax.

"Let's do this," said Sakora.

They set off, and broke into a run. Another crossbow quarrel, whining past Beetrax's ear. Sakora's dagger took the dwarf in the eye, and he fell amongst the other dead dwarves creating a pretty plateaux of death on the walkway.

Crayline drew her sword, and stood, lips curled back, snarling, her face a bloody mask, the handle protruding from her eye like an obscene erection. Hers was a stance of absolute defiance. Utter arrogance. Total superiority.

To Crayline, every other living creature on the planet was an amoeba.

Several dwarves came out from hiding, and grasped battle axes in both hands, their faces grim. One appeared with a crossbow, and Talon fired a shaft through the bastard's eye. He grinned. "It's nice to level the playing field," he said, as they reached the walkway, and leapt up onto the slick black surface.

More dwarves spilled out, to stand behind their leader, Val, or in reality, Crayline. Because Val was fooling nobody, and every dwarf present was in fear of Crayline, even more so now, with a dagger protruding from her face, almost proving her immortality. She was like a golem. Made from clay. Indestructible.

They might have laughed about it afterwards in the tavern. *Little Miss Face-Fucked. The Bitch of the Undead, not even a dagger through her fucking brain could bring her down. Or what would no doubt be the favourite in these drinking games, this tavern brouhaha, Crayline Hew, Cock Face.* But here, and now, there was no laughter, no banter, for she was *there* and she was, to all intents and purposes, *terrifying.*

Beetrax stood, facing Crayline, but he turned his eyes on Val, and his lips curled back. To his left stood Sakora, to his right, Talon and Dake. Dake twirled his sword, thinking back to the years of practice, the years of duelling, and the very real fact that his one love, his true love, was now dead; buried in the rubble of a dragon-destroyed palace.

"You want something from us?" growled Beetrax.

"Only your lives," smiled Crayline, and the smile cracked the drying blood on her face to give her a crimson lightning mask.

Sakora stepped forward, and smiled. "You need to come take them, then," she said, rolling her neck and presenting a fighting stance.

"I can do that all right, bitch," hissed Crayline, and gestured to the dwarves. "Kill them," she said, and leapt at Sakora.

With battle cries, the dwarves attacked, and Talon drew his sword, standing back-to-back with Dake.

"Time for blood," he said.

"Just like the old days," nodded Dake.

"Just like the old days," agreed Talon.

Beetrax leapt at Val, but a huge dwarf shifted between

them, his axe coming up, blocking Beetrax's stroke. Trax's axe bounced off, and the dwarf attacked, his axe whistling as Beetrax moved left, then right, dodging the blows, and grinning. "You bastard," he said, and slammed his axe in the dwarf's head, blade cutting through the steel helmet to crush the skull within. Another dwarf charged, but a backhand horizontal cut sliced his throat in a shower of droplets, and Beetrax was there, in front of Val.

"Remember me?" said Beetrax.

"I could never forget the bad breath."

"Lillith. She is my woman."

Val smiled then, a slimy, toothy grin. "Really? I reckon my seed is still inside her. I reckon she could be bearing my child."

Beetrax's face dropped. He went beyond fury, beyond rage, to another place of utter, total calm. "I'm going to kill you," he said.

Val held a sword and a long knife. He smiled again. "I'd like to see you try."

Beetrax's axe slammed forward, and Val twisted, knife lashing out to open a shallow wound across Beetrax's cheek. Blood oozed out, staining his ginger beard. Beetrax's axe slammed out again, then reversed, cutting backwards and turning into an overhead sweep that would have split Val from crown to crotch. Val dodged the blows; he moved fast, no, *fucking fast*, and a second slice of his knife cut the lobe from Beetrax's left ear.

"Ow! You cunt!"

"I'm going to carve you up, piece by piece," said Val, licking his lips, spreading his arms apart and crouching a little in a fighting stance. "You think I learnt nothing being dragged into this miserable fucking life on the streets of Janya? As a child you had to kill to survive. Well, I survived, and I survived by stabbing my enemies in the back. So I'm going to cut you up, lover boy, then take your bitch and fuck her again until she squeals. Whether she's alive… " he feinted and Beetrax blocked, "or even if she's dead."

Beetrax screamed and attacked...

Talon and Dake fought back-to-back, swords a blur, stabbing, slashing, deflecting axe and sword blows. They were hard to get near, and five dwarves had fallen at their feet already, dwarf blood making the walkway slippery...

Sakora and Crayline fought, Sakora with dagger and fist, Crayline with a short sword and dagger. It was a dance; a dance of blood, a dance of death. They spun, attacking and defending. A dwarf ran at Sakora's back, but she twisted, dagger inserting neatly into his windpipe, then back to defend a sword-strike from Crayline, all in the blink of an eye. They moved so fast they were a blur, and all the while Sakora kept thinking, *how, how are you still on your feet with a fucking dagger in your eye? In your brain?* But Crayline fought on, like some kind of monster, like some kind of clockwork machine... a demon that could not possibly be mortal.

Beetrax and Val fought, exchanging blows. Or rather, Val dodged and defended, and his dagger lashed out, cutting Beetrax again, this time on the side of his neck.

Beetrax stepped back, chest heaving, and stared at Val.

"I'm going to fuck you," he snarled, eyes narrowing.

"That's what Lillith used to say. Every. Fucking. Night."

Beetrax growled, his fury white hot and beyond redemption. And yet there was a hint of panic there; because Val, despite appearances, was an incredibly talented fighter. He might look like a weasel that'd had its head bashed in with a mallet, and he might have a streak of cowardice that made him run more often than fight, but with a blade he was damned accurate. And he was cutting Beetrax up. Beetrax was just too slow and lumbering for the speedy little fucker.

Trax attacked, axe slamming down, but Val dodged and sparks screamed from the walkway. Another dwarf attacked from behind, and Beetrax's axe cut his head clean off, where it sailed across the void, to land, nestled amidst the dragon eggs, face contorted into a morbid comedy look of shock.

Val attacked, and Beetrax stumbled back, barely able to

ward off the blades.

And then, he knew.

He was too old, too weak, too injured, too broken. The fire had gone. His will had gone. He'd seen Lillith fall, and in his terror, he was flailing like a madman, trusting his strength and size and experience, when in reality, he just needed his woman back. His fucking *muse*. Or at least, to know she was still alive. To know he had something worth fighting for.

Val was far too skilled.

Normally, Beetrax would have had him by now. But he was a broken soldier. He was kicked down in the gutter, and there was little he could do to crawl back out again.

From the mist, Lillith rose like a goddess. Her clothing was splattered in blood, her hair drenched in blood, but her face was serene and her eyes held raging fire. She stood, hand clutching her chest from the crossbow quarrel impact, but her eyes shifted and she gazed across that expanse of mist and those mystical orbs fastened on Beetrax.

I love you, that look said.

I love you.

Val screamed, and came in for the kill. Beetrax welcomed him, feinting, allowing Val in close, then taking Val's dagger in the guts with a grunt; allowing him the blow. The pain was incredible, unbearable, white fire raging through Beetrax's flesh as the knife drove in deep. Val was there, in his face, grinning like a village idiot.

"I have you now, axeman," he grunted, and jabbed the knife further.

Beetrax's axe clattered to the walkway.

His fingers clenched and unclenched.

His gaze met Lillith's.

She nodded.

Kill him, her eyes said, giving him the permission he sought.

And she smiled.

Beetrax looked into the face of Val, the Slave Warden,

the torturer, the rapist, and he smiled a smile so profound Val's eyes opened in shock, even though his blade was deep in Beetrax's guts.

Beetrax's hands came up, and grasped Val's head.

"What are you doing?" he shrieked.

"You stabbed me, lad."

"Yes, yes!"

"And I agree, you're better 'an me with a blade. You got me foxed there." Beetrax's face fell into thunder. It was the centre of a death storm. "But you got too close, you dumb, arrogant cunt." And his hands began to squeeze, and Val began to scream, his hand falling from the blood-drenched dagger in Beetrax's belly, both hands coming up and grabbing Beetrax's powerful arms and hands, slapping at them, pulling at them, as Beetrax started crushing Val's skull between his great bear paws.

Hearing the cries, a dwarf ran at Beetrax. Beetrax was oblivious in his totally focussed hate.

Talon's arrow took the dwarf through the eye, emerging from the back of his skull on a shower of blood and eyeball jelly.

Beetrax moved his face close to Val's. He stared into his eyes. He stared into the dwarf's soul, as his immense hands and powerful muscles exerted a bone-crushing pressure on the struggling Slave Warden.

"When she screamed," growled Beetrax, "did it sound like this?" He pushed harder, and there was a *crack* of skull, and Val screamed, long and hard, wailing, hands once again pulling and pushing and grabbing and slapping and clawing.

"Stop, stop, please stop," he wailed.

"I'm sure that's what Lillith said to you," whispered Beetrax, straight into Val's face. "But you didn't, did you, you fucking little rapist little cunt fucking maggot. Well, you want to know something, pretty boy? You controlled her. And you controlled me. And now I control you. And guess what? My control manifests in the way I crush your fucking rapist's skull."

Veins were standing out on his arms, his neck, his forehead, and Beetrax's hands shifted around and his thumbs pushed into Val's eyes, pushed through his eyes, and into his brain, and with a final, awesome exertion of pressure, he broke Val's skull and ended his life.

Beetrax let Val fall with a *slap*, and stared down at his bloody hands, almost in wonder.

He staggered back, panting, face purple with exertion.

"If there's one thing I hate," he whispered, "it's fucking rapists."

Dake and Talon were fighting as a team, and wreaking bloody havoc on the attacking dwarves. Crayline and Sakora were equally matched, and this galled Sakora. After her decades of training, to find this dwarf bitch who equalled her... and with a fucking *dagger* in her eye socket!

They exchanged blows, and a kick sent Crayline's sword clattering across the walkway. Sakora hit her with a left straight, a front kick, then a side kick to the chest that sent her staggering back. Crayline bent over, gasping, and so Sakora leapt in for the kill, right hand coming down to...

Crayline shifted, subtly, and her hand suddenly struck out, fingers forming a point, a blade, which hit Sakora in the throat. Sakora's own blow struck Crayline's shoulder, without effect. Crayline followed with a second blow to the throat, in the same spot, and Sakora staggered back, hands coming up, choking, and dropped slowly to her knees...

Crayline dismissed her, turned, and with dagger in hand, ran and leapt on Beetrax's back. He let out a roar, and Crayline drove her dagger into Beetrax's neck. There came a spurt of blood, and Beetrax spun around, dropping his axe, his fist lashing up, hitting Crayline in the nose. But she held on, driving the dagger deeper into the space between neck and clavicle, and Beetrax cried out, dropping to his knees, Crayline still riding him like a dying horse...

Sakora, face now purple, also dropped to her knees. She could not breathe. Her windpipe had been crushed.

Talon rushed to her, but two stocky dwarves got in his way, their axes swinging, and he began a savage battle for survival, sword dancing, stabbing, deflecting, as all the time he watched Sakora keel over, face purple, grappling with her own throat. Talon ducked, stabbing out, drawing his blade across a dwarf's femoral artery; blood washed down like a torrid waterfall and the dwarf screamed, all interest in battle suddenly forgotten. The second dwarf leapt forward, onto the point of Talon's sword, snapping it half way down the blade. Talon let go, and ran to Sakora.

But she was still. Eyes fixed. Motionless. Dead.

Jael remembered sitting in the forest, listening to the trees. It was as if they spoke to him, and him alone, whispering his name, and whispering their secrets. The smell of the forest filled him, like some rare perfume, and he'd always felt as if he belonged. This was his place, his time, his sanctuary. Nothing could touch him here. Nothing could hurt him. It was a place, a world, of gentle tranquillity. A place where bad things didn't happen.

And as Jael grew up, he believed it. Believed in the innocence. Believed in the concept of his own private Haven.

Until the robbers came, and murdered his family, and set his life on a very different and savage path.

When Beetrax and the others had rescued him from torture, it had been, quite literally, a dream come true. Here were the heroes from his history books in school, but more, here was Beetrax, Beetrax the Axeman, a legend amongst him and his friends. In the school field they used to re-enact Beetrax's finest moments, the tale of single combat on the Greggan Field; the rescue of Princess Emilia Ladine when she was but a child, from a horrible mud-orc kill squad; but more than ever, the tales of heroism on the walls of Desekra Fortress fighting the mud-orcs and Orlana the Changer, the Horse Lady, from the Furnace. In the school field, they'd always argued as to who was playing the part of Beetrax the Axeman.

And then here he was!

On an adventure… with Beetrax the Axeman!

Only, he had crumbled at the first sign of danger. Of torture. And Beetrax, being Beetrax, had turned on him.

Jael whimpered, and shifted slightly, gloss black swimming before him. *Where am I? What's happening?*

His eyes flickered open.

He could hear the sounds of battle. Steel on steel. Shouts. Cries. Wails. Thuds, like impacts in flesh.

And for once, he was not frightened.

His hand reached behind him, to his lower back. He was bleeding, but both bolts had entered through his thick leather belt. And although they stuck in his flesh, and the pain burned him like nothing he'd ever felt in his entire life, the leather had acted as armour – and saved a deeper penetration of steel.

Jael rolled over. Tears ran down his face. One leg twitched, and wouldn't work right.

He could see figures, shimmering through a haze. He pulled out his dagger. Nobody would call him a coward this time. Nobody would call him a coward ever again!

Jael crawled to his knees, then his feet, and gripped his dagger tightly. Sakora had given it to him, and it was perfectly balanced steel, razor sharp. As his vision cleared, so he saw Sakora go down, choking. Talon was fighting two dwarves. Dake was being pushed back towards the dragon eggs. And Beetrax…

Jael watched, in disbelief, as Crayline leapt on his back, and stabbed downwards, her dagger entering Beetrax's neck.

"No!" he screamed, staggering forward.

Beetrax punched her, but she clung to him like a parasite; unshakeable. And Jael saw Trax's strength fade in an instant with that stab wound. His eyes shifted. He saw another stab wound in Beetrax's belly. And yet still the giant axeman wouldn't die.

His axe was on the platform, battered and bloody.

Jael stumbled forward some more, and looked at his own dagger. Then he reached for Beetrax's axe, stooped, lifted it with a grunt, and lifted his head. Beetrax had spun around. Crayline was right there, before him, hanging on to her dagger, driving it deeper into Beetrax's neck and revelling in his agony, in his grunts and gasps.

Jael hefted the axe, stepped forward, took a mighty swing and planted a blade in Crayline Hew's back. She stiffened, suddenly, went rigid, and then fell away from Beetrax to lie, quivering, bleeding, on the platform.

Beetrax, on his knees, turned his head and looked at Jael. Pain twisted his face, but he forced a smile.

"Thanks, lad," he said, and keeled over onto his side, where he lay still.

Jael looked down at Crayline. She was trembling, her spine split, her legs twitching, her bladder opening. Urine trickled out, smelling acrid.

Jael stepped forward, looked down at the bitch who had shot an unprotected Lillith in the chest. He grimaced, lifted Beetrax's axe, and brought it down with a thud, planting it securely in the centre of her chest.

Crayline Hew dribbled blood, and lay still.

Talon and Dake killed the last of the dwarves, and a sudden, bleak silence fell over the chamber. The machinery across the wall still twisted and turned, clicked and clocked and spun, and Lillith walked through the mist, which parted, as if to offer her a reverent pathway. She climbed onto the walkway, and surveyed the carnage. Val was dead. Crayline was dead. Even as she watched, Jael fell to one side, and passed into a state of unconsciousness. Lillith moved to Sakora, and knelt for a moment, but the Kaaleesh expert was gone; her soul fluttered away on angel wings.

Finally, Lillith moved to Beetrax, and as Talon and Dake looked on, speechless, Lillith reached down and cradled his face.

"I love you," she said, leaning over him, and blood from

her own wounds fell on him like a gentle, crimson rain, staining his face, staining his beard, running into his eyes, and running into his mouth; into his still, lifeless mouth.

"I'll love you until the stars go out," she said to the dead body of Beetrax.

And beneath their feet, the ground started to shake.

Intensity

"I love you," she said.

"I know," he said, and gave an impish grin.

She punched him gently on the chest, then snuggled closer, moved into him, her cheek against his shirt, against his chest, then lifting slightly, nose nuzzling up below his beard.

"You washed your beard," she said.

"Of course," he said. There was a pause. "I knew I was seeing you tonight, didn't I?"

She giggled, and it was so pure, so innocent, so beautiful, he felt his heart melt and fall down over itself, again, and again, and again.

Candlelight painted the walls with gold.

Below them, the university library, closed now due to the late hour, seemed to sigh, and settle, a million years of gathered knowledge, gently coated in dust, a billion words of learning, all waiting to be discovered.

Lillith was Head Librarian at Vagandrak's University Library. High above the shelves, above the gathered knowledge, was an office. One had to ascend by ladder, and it was reasonably inaccessible to the uninitiated; but it was there, a well-kept secret passed from Head Librarian to Head Librarian, down through the centuries. There was a table, two chairs and a low bed of oak struts, with a straw-filled mattress which had seen better decades. Lillith suspected the hideaway was for the occasional night the Head Librarian got carried away with his or her studies, or duties, and sought a brief slumber before returning to acts of librarianship. She, however, had other plans.

On the floor stood a half-finished bottle of Vagandrak Red, candlelight glinting from ruby depths. On a circular wooden platter were a selection of cured hams, salami, a variety of cheeses, and thick slices of buttered bread. All were untouched, however, as Beetrax sat, his chest naked, his boots kicked into a corner, gazing at his love.

"This is a special place," he said.

Lillith nodded, and she kissed his chest, one hand working its way through the curled hair she found there.

"I like it here."

"I like it here, also," she said, and gave a little bite to his nipple. He made an inward hiss through his teeth, huge muscles tensing, then relaxing a little. "Come. Why don't you lie down?"

"Er. If you're sure?"

"I'm sure," she said, smiling, one hand brushing aside her long, thick plaits of hair.

The oak struts creaked. Straw prickled Beetrax's skin, poking through the mattress like tiny needles. But he did not mind. He did not care. He was smashed away, as if hit by a helve. His senses swam. The world didn't make sense any more. The world didn't work. His logic was broken.

She kissed him.

Her kiss was soft, and sweet, and tender. Realising he could be an oaf, Beetrax responded with gentility, not wanting to make a donkey of himself, and he learnt an amazing fact in that long, lingering moment of candlelit intimacy. The more gentle he was, the more passionately Lillith responded.

She pulled away. Handed him a wooden cup of Vagandrak Red. Instead of guzzling, as he normally would have in the drinking piss pits he frequented, he sipped the wine, as he had seen men in fine top coats with silly hats do. The need was still there, to chuck the wine down his neck in one, but he controlled his hand, watching Lillith over the top of the carved oak cup.

She reached for the platter, took bread, placed salami and cheese on the buttered slab, and handed it to Beetrax.

"Eat," she said.

He took the food. "I'm not sure how hungry I am," he said, voice just a little husky.

"But I need you to keep up your strength."

"Ahh." He reddened, even in the candlelight.

"Not for that, you oaf," she smiled, punching him on the bicep. There came a dull *thwack*. "You said you'd help me move those fifty boxes of books. Over by the rear doors, by the tomes on *Ye Anciente Magick*."

"Ahh. Yes. So I did." He deflated a little, and took a bite from his slab of food.

"That was a joke," she said, moving closer, fast, her breathing coming in short gasps as she straddled him and he dropped his food to the floor, spilt wine down his chest, and laughed as she rode him backwards, and his head hit the straw pillows, and she was on him, kissing him, her hands stroking his face and neck and chest and arms. He kissed her back, more passionately this time, and long into the night the candles burned low, and they made love several times, each time slower and longer and with more deeply ingrained intensity, until Beetrax knew that he knew her, knew that she had melted and flooded into his soul, knew that, insane as it seemed, for those long moments when he was inside her, they had become one, become a part of the same creature and that creature would last forever. It had to. Because of the intensity of their love.

Memory Echoes

Chaos had come to the Five Havens. A breakdown in law and order, a breakdown in church rule, the arrival of anarchy. Dwarves ran through the streets, hacking at one another with axes, looting shops and houses, setting fire to churches.

"Where are the Great Dwarf Lords?" the people would scream.

"Where is our Dragon Engine?"

"Where is King Irlax?"

"Where is the Church of Eternal Hate when you fucking need it?"

"Where is First Cardinal Skalg?"

Nobody could give them answers, and so chaos beat down the door and began a savage party, with only destruction, fire and death as companions.

At the doors of the Cathedral of Eternal Hate, a crowd had gathered, bearing arms and firebrands. A chant went up. "SKALG SKALG SKALG SKALG!" as if the illustrious leader of the church, the First Cardinal, could give them answers, could give them forgiveness, could offer them some form of hope or repentance or saviour. But he could not. He was locked down in the Iron Vault with the Dragon Heads. And his mind was in another place.

Volak slammed through the skies, heading north and east, her great wings smashing the air as if it were an enemy. Inside her head there raged another battle, as Volak screamed and thrashed, attempting to retake control of her body. But Skalg was wielding powerful Equiem magick, and despite the pressure he felt from Volak's thrashing mind, he retained control, and headed for the Five Havens, Wyrmblood, and the dragon eggs far, far below the mountain.

I know where you are, my sweets.

Fuck you, cripple dwarf, give me back my body...

No.

When I am free, I will hunt you down and give you the longest, slowest death I have ever dealt. You will take years to die, you fucking insect. I see you, I can see you even now, crouched in the Iron Vault below the Cathedral of Eternal Hate. I know EXACTLY where you are. I can smell your fear, your piss, your shit, you spineless fucking worm.

The irony being, Volak, that now YOU are the spineless fucking wyrm... for I control your spine, and I will use your discarded shell to murder your unborn babies in their hundreds, in their thousands. You are fucked, Volak. Your reign is over. You'll be imprisoned, back inside the Dragon Engine, and you will serve the Harborym Dwarves once more.

Skalg felt himself shiver. He felt Volak crawling around the inside of his mind, rifling through his memories. How? *How could she do that? HE was supposed to be in total control!*

You lie, said Volak, her voice calm.

No, I will destroy the hibernating remains of the Blood Dragon Empire!

And then you will keep my body, said Volak. *I can see it. In your mind and in your soul. You would seek to BE me, to rule the dwarves, to rule the world. You have become corrupted, Skalg, you have become obsessed with power and physical prowess. Go back to your crippled shell, do it now, and I may spare you when I riot through the Five Havens destroying every fucking dwarf that walks or crawls.*

No, said Skalg, and Volak's single remaining black eye

gleamed. *I will do what I please. I will do what I will. For I am no longer Skalg, First Cardinal of the Church of Hate. I am Volak, Queen of the Blood Dragon Empire.*

The scene to him was the most painful thing he had ever experienced, and he'd experienced many. The death of his father, when he was just fifteen, from a heart attack. Seeing him lying there on the wooden floorboards, face contorted, eyes closed, unable to do anything, unable to bring him back. That had been hard. One of the hardest moments ever, and the sense of frustration at this kind of loss was still with him.

Then there was his mother, a beautiful, noble woman, taken before her time as cancers ate through her bones and left her a shell of her former self. Sitting with her, holding her hand, praying for her, reading to her from the Scriptures of Hate whilst he squeezed her hand and wept at the pain coursing through her; at her clenching and contortions. That had been harder than his father. For this time it had gone on, and on, and on; and there's nothing quite like witnessing prolonged suffering to really put a dwarf's life into fucking microcosmic perspective.

But seeing the body of his daughter, Kajella, after taking her high dive from the top of Skalg's home, the Blood Tower, had been the nadir of his entire life. She'd been crushed, broken up, her face distorted and almost unrecognisable. Lying in an open casket in the church, Kokar had choked, tears streaming from his eyes, and reached out, taking hold of his daughter. He'd inadvertently grabbed one of her arms, not realising she'd been *so* broken up on impact with the hard ground many storeys below, that the mortician had had to arrange Kajella's body and limbs – including detached limbs – in such a way as to appear normal. The poor mortician had not expected a grieving father to grab at her body, or rather, her arm, thus detaching it from its place of rest, and waving it in the air as his wails reached the high, vaulted, expensively gilded rafters of the church.

It hadn't just been the knowledge of her violent impact which had shaken Kokar so badly. After he'd discovered the real means of her demise, it was the fact Skalg had used his... *his* fucking name, *his* position as High Born, *his* clan name Karik 'y Kla, to coerce Kokar's sixteen year-old daughter to his bed, with the Great-Dwarf-Lords-only-knew-what fucking promises. Skalg had raped her. Skalg was scumshit of the lowest order.

Slowly, Kokar walked down the steps, his boots thudding. He halted at the bottom, and pushed open the door.

By the altar, knelt Skalg, head bent, covered in his own piss and shit, and stinking something horrid. Before him glittered three huge gems. The Dragon Heads. They glittered in the chamber, their light threatening, creeping and eerie.

Kokar turned, and reached out, and his friend and comrade, Echo, passed him a mace. It was a hefty weapon, with a brutal, spiked head. Kokar weighed it thoughtfully, and then peered around the chamber, looking for traps, tripwires, hidden crossbows, or any other threat which might leap out and turn him from a living Kokar to a dead Kokar. Amazingly, there seemed to be nothing. Which, now, was almost irrelevant. Kokar's fury had reached such a pinnacle he would have waded through a thousand rotting corpses, swam an ocean of sharks, fought a battalion of mud-orcs in order to get to Skalg's worthless, rancid fucking body.

Kokar strode forward, aware he was treading a path for Echo.

Echo followed softly behind, his footfalls silent.

Kokar stopped, and kicked Skalg hard. Skalg murmured.

"Oy. You fucking rat. Wake up."

Skalg's eyes flickered open, and for a moment panic fleeted there. His lips writhed wordlessly. Then he focussed, and yet was distant. Incredibly distant.

"I've come to kill you," said Kokar, who wasn't one for mincing words, especially when it came to revenge regarding his dead daughter.

"Eh?" Skalg focussed a little more. "Who are you? I have money. And power. More money than you'd know what to do with…"

Still, he was distant. As if processing an internal monologue.

Kokar shrugged, hoisted the mace, and stared down at this wretched specimen of dwarf-kind before him. "You raped my daughter, Kajella. You let her fall from the Blood Tower. By all the powers vested in me, by the nobility and authority of the clan Karik 'y Kla, I sentence you to death."

Skalg frowned. "Wait, wait!" he said, holding up both hands.

The mace slammed down, brushing aside his hands like leaves in an autumn breeze, and connecting with his face. There was a thud. Skalg screamed. Kokar hit him again, pulverising his cheek bone, then his nose, then his forehead. In a fury, Kokar beat Skalg until he was a corpse, with hardly anything left of his bloody, broken head.

A terrible silence fell on the Cathedral of Eternal Hate.

Echo stepped past Kokar, who was panting, covered in blood, his eyes alive, alight, and triumphant.

"That murdering bastard will rape and kill no more," he said.

Echo nodded, slipping the three Dragon Heads into a velvet bag.

"You certainly showed him the fury of your revenge."

"Yes! I did, didn't I?"

Kokar beamed, and wiped his hand on his jerkin, leaving a smear of blood.

Echo walked towards the door leading from the Iron Vault. Then he turned, and lifted his crossbow. "But it's such a shame it had to end like this." The crossbow clicked, the quarrel hissed, and the bolt took Kokar in the throat.

Echo watched him fall, his eyes compassionless, and then weighing the Dragon Heads thoughtfully, he stared at the corpse of Skalg. And he thought about his own sister, so similarly abused.

"Maybe now your shade will rest," he said, and smiled, and left the chamber filled with blood and murder and revenge. He slowly climbed the steps leading to the Five Havens and the riot of chaos and violence above.

Descent

Volak entered the mines at an incredible velocity, soaring up into the sky, into the thin, freezing air, then dropping like a comet, straight into the black descent, a wyrm tunnel which led from the uppermost reaches of the Karamakkos, the Teeth of the World, straight down into the heart of Wyrmblood.

She plummeted, wings folded behind her, her mind a rage as she battled Skalg. But then, like some miracle, he became distant, unfocussed, and for long seconds Volak regained control and her jubilance filled her with an ecstasy she didn't believe possible. Skalg withered and shrunk, his power diminishing, folding in and in and in upon himself, until he was just a tiny screaming voice... but then he started to come back, and Volak, weaving in her supersonic descent, screamed, fire lashing out, scorching the vertical tunnel walls...

Skalg's strength returned tenfold, and Volak withered, relinquishing control once more.

How can he be so powerful?

What channels him?

What motivates him?

And then she realised. And it chilled her soul.

The Dragon Heads.

But the Dragon Heads were mis-named, for they had nothing to do with the dragons themselves, but more to do with Equiem magick; the old, dark magick, the magick of the land, the magick of the shamathe. They were powerful beyond all mortal comprehension, and Volak feared them completely, for they had the power to scorch the earth, to cleanse the world, to kill every living creature on the entire fucking planet.

Just as Skalg's power could increase no more, just as Volak had been pushed into the tiniest cell of her own mind, with no chance of ever escaping, so he was suddenly gone. Skalg was gone. Utterly, totally, completely.

What happened?

And it drifted lazily into her mind.

Knowledge.

Volak knew exactly what had happened.

Skalg was dead.

Thunder rumbled, and she realised, it was not thunder.

It was the beginnings of an earthquake.

An earthquake, deep down under the mountain.

She plummeted, a black, falling star, towards the core of Wyrmblood, where her babies waited for her, softly calling...

Lillith was panting, the bolt in her chest a metal parasite, eating into her. The pain was incredible, like nothing she'd ever felt, but it was all for nothing, and she did not care, because there, before her, her true love, the love of her life, her rock, her anchor, her lodestone, had died.

Beetrax's heart had stopped beating.

Lillith's tears, and her blood, fell to mix and mingle, covering his face in a bloody mask.

"No," she wept. "No..."

Echo ran through the streets of Zvolga, his footfalls light, a dagger in one hand, the velvet bag tucked deep inside his shirt. The dwarves were rioting, and a thousand fires burned through the city, including every single Church of Hate. A dwarf staggered into his path, bearing a massive double-headed battle axe. He growled, and swung at Echo, who leapt over the axe swing, dagger cutting out neatly to slice the dwarf's throat. Echo landed in a crouch, motionless, and glanced back. The dwarf folded over, and lay, dying quickly on the cobbles.

The ground shook.

High above, a grand, carved gargoyle detached from the top of a building, tumbled, and smashed onto the cobbles to Echo's right.

He set off again, increasing his pace, down an avenue lined with iron trees, their iron leaves reflecting the glow of a hundred burning buildings which roared, like burning demons, announcing the end of the world.

The ground shook, more violently, and this time it kept on shaking. Buildings started to collapse, and Echo dodged a tumbling, cascading wall which vomited stones at his feet. The rumbling increased in intensity until Echo could hardly run, such was the violence. All around fires burned and dwarves screamed. Echo's gaze snapped up. High up, a massive, arched stone and iron bridge, built ten thousand years ago by the Great Dwarf Lords themselves, jiggled, and shook, and then slowly, folded downwards, detaching, describing a broad arc as it began to break apart, falling through the darkness to decimate a thousand houses, churches and civic buildings far below.

For a while, it seemed it was raining stone and iron.

Echo ran for it... as the mountain slowly, lazily, began to reclaim Zvolga as its own.

The floor was shaking, the walls were shaking, and a gradual rumble increased in volume and intensity. Everything was vibrating, including the dragon eggs, wreathed in mist, which danced and swirled, creating crazy patterns...

"We've got to leave!" screamed Talon, sprinting to Lillith. He grabbed her shoulder, but she spun, pushing him away. Her eyes were wild, her chest soaked in blood.

"I'm not going anywhere," she hissed.

Talon glanced to Dake. "*Help me*!" he screamed.

Dake ran over.

"He's gone, Lillith. And the mountain feels like it's about to collapse around our heads. We need to *get the fuck out of here*!"

But Lillith wasn't listening. She was leaning over Beetrax, chanting, lips writhing, and the palms of her hands were glowing red, and she felt the energy of the entire fucking *planet* beneath her knees, swirling with energy, swirling with the meshed elements of order and chaos... and her blood dripped, into Trax's eyes, into Trax's mouth, and he drank down her lifeblood, and her hands moved, and she dragged up his blood-soaked shirt, and placed her hands over the wound in his guts. Heat poured out, and the flesh ran together like molten wax. Slowly, as if in a trance, as the whole world around her shook like the mountain itself was collapsing down and down in on itself, so her hands rose to Beetrax's neck, and she covered the wound and prayed, and sang, and invoked the Old Gods, the Ancients, her mind opened and knowledge poured into her, the dark arts, from the elder days before elves and men and dwarves... Power surged through her, and she looked up, looked around, and she could *feel* Hex, feel the group mind of all the dead wyrm queens that had ever existed. They were watching her. And yet there was no hate there, no anger, just a cold and calculating observation.

I can see you, she said.

Yes, said Hex.

I never wished the dragon eggs any harm, she said.

We know. You were a victim of circumstance.

What shall I do?

Heal him, and leave this place. You are not welcome here.

I will do so, she said.

Lillith closed her eyes, and her hands glowed with a golden light. The wound in Beetrax's neck closed, blood running backwards as a localised area of *time* ran backwards, and Lillith continued to pray, to invoke, her lips writhing, smoke pouring from her mouth – like dragon smoke.

Beetrax sat up, screaming, hands clawing his own flesh.

Lillith toppled to one side, face pale, eyes rolled up to show only the whites.

The rumbling increased, and then, smashing through the domed ceiling, came Volak, the Queen of Wyrmblood. Pieces of black stone rained down, as her mighty wings outstretched, and she landed with a *thud* amidst the hundreds of dragon eggs. Flames broiled around her snout, and her single eye orientated on the overlanders, kneeling amidst so many corpses on the polished stone platform.

Volak breathed, and fire rumbled. Then she looked around, at the intact eggs, and looked up, as the whole chamber shook and the shock of the earthquake increased.

"You have spoken with Hex?" she intoned, voice almost musical.

Talon and Dake looked at one another, and climbed to their feet. They brandished their weapons.

"There's no fucking way we can kill *that*," hissed Dake.

"But we'll die trying," said Talon, voice bleak.

Volak strode forward, head weaving, neck rippling like a serpent. "Hex has spoken with your witch," she said, head swaying from side to side. She came close, and closer still, and Talon and Dake both took a step back. Beetrax, both hands above his heart, suddenly became *aware*. His head turned to the right, slowly, to face Volak, Queen of the Wyrms.

She lowered her head, until they were only inches apart.

Beetrax swallowed.

"Er. Lads? Need some help here, lads?"

Volak blinked, her one good eye, multi-faceted in black, fixed on Beetrax's face. Slowly, carefully, she said, "You have my permission to leave."

Beetrax considered this. "All right! Come on, lads! Let's get the *fuck* out of here!" He stood, and picked Lillith up, cradling her unconscious body to his chest as he would the most precious of babes. The ground was shaking, the walls shaking, the tens of thousands of tiny machines whirring faster and faster and faster.

Dake knelt by Jael, and checked for a pulse. Then he stood, dragged the lad up, and threw him over his shoulder. Finally, Talon lifted Sakora in his arms, staring down into her face. Suddenly, she began to cry, and Talon's heart fluttered, hope filling him. But then he realised it was his own tears filling her eyes and running down her cheeks, and he wept all the more.

Lillith's eyes flickered open. She stared at Volak. And she smiled.

"Look after your babies," she said.

Volak nodded her huge head. "I feel that one day we will meet again, Lillith."

"I am sure of it," she said, and curled into Beetrax's massive arms and chest, a child again, Beetrax her protector.

Slowly, as the rumbling and violence increased, so Beetrax, Talon, Dake, Jael and Lillith left the chamber of the dragon eggs; of the wyrms.

They moved through the adjoining chamber, boots crunching on old dead shells, and Talon said, "I can't help feeling we should have stayed, and maybe destroyed the eggs."

"No," said Lillith, gently. "It is already written in stone."

"What is?"

"The death of the Blood Dragons," she said.

The mountain vented its fury. The mountain shook, and the world shook, and the tens of thousands of tunnels, and caves and hollows, of mines and pits and chambers, all had, for millennia, carved a fracture in the infrastructure of the mountain's bowels. Now, with a simple application of tremor, the whole internal warren came collapsing and screaming down. Dwarves ran wailing as high ceilings and bridges collapsed. Houses and towers folded in upon themselves. The earthquake rioted through the Five Havens. None were safe. It lasted for a week, and above, in the open air, amidst the forests and mountain flanks, amidst the snowline and the peaks of rock, so the mountain settled, and shifted, and slowly hunkered down upon itself. Great fissures opened up, only to crack and crumble and fill themselves in once more.

Because…

The mountain gives.

And the mountain takes away.

It took them a week to escape the mountain. And for long stretches of that, it felt like the mountain was taking care of them. They traversed long lost tunnels, travelling upwards, always travelling upwards, and they walked over crumbling high bridges, through chambers that could swallow a cathedral, a village, a city. After the insanity of the main earthquake, so the mountain had settled, and hunkered down, hitting them with many aftershocks but always managing to preserve their route to freedom.

After three days, both Lillith and Jael had been able to walk for themselves. Which was good for Beetrax. He complained of a bad back, moaning long into the night.

On the seventh day, they crawled up a long, thin tunnel, the roof too low to allow any of them to stand.

They could see a circle of bright, white light at the end, and increased their pace, finally emerging with gasps and sighs and tears onto a rocky hillside, dotted with conifers, a view opening up before them, a view that took their collective breaths away.

They looked out over valleys and rolling hills. It was morning, and the spring sun was climbing in a cold, brittle blue sky.

Beetrax breathed in deep, revelling in the fresh air entering his lungs.

Talon, tears streaming down his face, turned and hugged the axeman.

"Tastes good, doesn't it, lad?" grinned Beetrax.

"It's good to be alive," nodded Talon.

Dake gently lowered Sakora's body to the ground, and they stared at her scarred face, a tapestry of the horrors they'd endured in the realm of the Harborym Dwarves.

"We need to bury her," he said.

"Yes."

"Somewhere beautiful."

"Yes. She would have liked that."

They glanced back at the tiny tunnel opening. Even now it was shrouded by trees and bushes, almost invisible to anybody passing. A random vent hole. An escape passage from the world of the Harborym Dwarves.

Under their boots, the mountain trembled.

"She's still upset," said Talon.

Beetrax grunted. "Aren't we all?"

"It's a miracle we're alive," said Jael.

"A miracle is the right word," nodded Beetrax, and looked over at Lillith. She was standing, her back to the group, gazing off at the amazing, panoramic vista which presented itself to them; a vast, rolling, pastel landscape. Something so beautiful it transcended language and thought. It just *was*.

Beetrax saw that her shoulders were shaking. He moved over to her, and wrapped his arms around her from behind.

"Hey," he said.

"Hey you," she said.

"You in pain?"

"Yes. But more in my head than in my flesh."

"You, er, saved my life back there. Well. More than that. Dake says you brought me back from the dead."

"Let us just say the experience of Wyrmblood has opened my mind."

"Equiem magick?"

"Yes."

"You said it was evil!"

"No. I said it was part of the dark arts. But even the dark arts can be used for the cause of good."

Beetrax turned her around, and looked into her face. Then glanced down at her blood-soaked shirt, dried now, but the image still made him wince.

"So, Talon sewed you up?"

"Yes. I did want you to do it…"

"You know I can't stand the sight of blood," he said.

"Really?" She raised her eyebrows. "*Really*?"

"Well. Your blood. It just makes me queasy."

"Why's that, Beetrax?"

"Because I love you so much," he said, simply, and smiled.

An hour later, they had found a small glade filled with flowers. It was bordered by rocks and trees, and was a quiet, solitary place, protected from the wind and bathed with sunshine. They dug a grave, taking their time to remove the rocks, and then laid Sakora out, arranging her hands, folded across her chest. Lillith straightened her clothing. "She was always fussy about the way she dressed," she said, and smiled.

As the sun set, so they slowly filled in the grave, covering Sakora's body first, and then finally, her face.

They piled the rocks they'd collected on top of the grave, as a marker, and to stop any scavenging wild animals.

"Sleep well, princess," said Talon, and his tears fell into the soil, onto the rocks, as he bent over Sakora's final resting place.

The wind sang a song through the wild places of the mountain.

"What now?" said Beetrax, rolling his neck, and glancing over to observe the setting sun. A deep red glow filled the world. It reminded him of blood. It reminded him of dragons.

Lillith looked at him. And she smiled, a kindly smile, filled with warmth and love.

"We go home," she said.

Epilogue
THE COCKS

The insanity of violence and bloodshed which followed, well, it all started because of cock.

"More ale!" cried Beetrax, well in his element, grinning as he wrapped his arm around Dake's shoulders and leered into the man's face.

They were seated in the main tavern room of The Battered Cock. Beetrax had been adamant they drink at The Fighting Cocks, but when they'd arrived they stood, staring in horror and absolute disbelief at the smoking, charred remains.

"It's just a fucking shame," Dake was pontificating. "I mean, *burned to the ground*!" He took another hefty swig. "It's a travesty. That's what it is. We should do something, raise some money, have her rebuilt, that's what I reckon."

Beetrax nodded drunkenly, and slapped Dake on the back. "My very thoughts exactly. I mean, how can we go through life without the bloody Fighting Cocks? 'Twas an institution, is all I'm saying, and, in my humble opinion, the very *best* of the Cocks."

Dake nodded, and beamed as Talon returned carrying large tankards of ale. He was trailed by Jael, who was looking a little sheepish.

"I'm sorry," he said, wincing, and glanced at Beetrax. "I spilled some."

"Hey!" beamed Beetrax, who was feeling extremely amicable; he was alive, his woman was alive, and he wasn't being tortured by a dwarf. Damn them fucking dwarves. "I needs to teach you a few lessons, lad. Right. When you're in a tavern, the rule is, never moan about a bit of spilt ale."

"Why not?" said Dake. "You do."

"I don't."

"You fucking do!"

"I fucking *don't*!"

"Guys, will you keep the noise down?" snapped Lillith, who was seated at a nearby table, a glass of water by her side, poring over an ancient manuscript. Her eyes sparkled, and she winced a little, every now and again, as her chest pulled tight on the stitches over the crossbow bolt. She still carried the iron inside her. She didn't want it removed. She said she needed it, needed the pain, needed the *weight* of iron as a constant reminder of the hell and chaos she'd experienced.

There was a commotion at the tavern entrance, and three big men piled in. One was huge, broad and muscular, with a ridiculously large black beard and dark, twinkling eyes. The second was broad of shoulder, narrow of hip, and carried himself like a natural pugilist – which he was. The final one was a big lad, with a bushy beard, one eye and a savagely scarred face. They staggered to the bar, and ordered drinks too loudly, as other patrons stepped neatly away.

Back at the table, Dake nudged Beetrax. "Hey. Don't we know them?"

Trax squinted, and belched. "I don't think so."

"Yeah. That ugly fuck. That one, there." He pointed, just as Dek turned and stared at him.

"Oy. You. Fuck. What you fucking pointing at?"

Dake stared at him, mouth open, words failing him.

Dek strode to their table, closely followed by Narnok and Kareem. The two groups eyed one another warily, until Dek pointed at Beetrax, and said, "I fucking know you."

"You do?"

"Aye."

"You want a fucking badge for that, laddie?"

"A badge? Are you taking the piss?"

"Taking it? You're fucking giving it away," snapped Beetrax.

"Wait, wait, wait," said Lillith, gliding between the two groups. She looked at Beetrax, then turned and stared at Dek. She smiled. "Yes. You two do know one another. Beetrax, this is Dek. Dek, this is Beetrax. You were supposed to have a fist fight oooh, twenty, twenty-five years ago? But Dek got whisked away by General Dalgoran, and Beetrax went off to train as an axeman, and so it never happened."

"Well it can fucking happen right now," snapped Beetrax, surging to his feet.

"Any fucking time, grandpa," scowled Dek.

"Who're you calling old?"

"You, you old cunt."

"At least I don't shag my best mate's wife."

The atmosphere fell into ice.

"You see!" snapped Narnok. "Every bastard knows about you and your cheating ways."

"Will you give it a fucking rest?" growled Dek. "Or I'll break another fucking finger."

"You reckon you can?"

"I can if you don't shut your fucking hole."

"Gentlemen, gentlemen." Lillith held up a hand. "I think you need to calm yourselves."

"Oh aye?" snapped Narnok, and Beetrax glared at him, fist closing around his axe.

"You show the woman some respect," he said, "or I swear, I'll fucking gut you like a fish."

"Trax, it won't be necessary."

"Why's that?"

"I fear we have a common enemy once more."

"We do?" Beetrax frowned. "Who?"

Lillith sighed, a sound like breeze teasing through dry, auburn autumn leaves. "It would appear Orlana the Changer, the Horse Lady, has escaped from the Furnace," she said.

The mountain screamed, moaned, grumbled, rumbled. It shook with the violence of an earthquake. It shook like it was the end of the world. Rocks fell. Columns collapsed. Tunnels imploded, crashing down, rock and dust screaming outwards in great geysers of debris. The Karamakkos groaned and trembled, and inside the vast depths, chambers collapsed, bridges fell, towers tumbled, and the mountain wept like a virgin on her wedding night.

Pure ice-hot hate swamped Volak.

The very world had turned against her and her kind.

She strutted through the field of eggs, roaring, screaming, fire blasting from her maw in an act of raw defiance, as the ceiling began to collapse. Huge chunks of rock fell, smashing eggs and dragon embryos into splattered smears.

The roof collapse accelerated.

And Volak could *hear* the destruction of Wyrmblood, outside, up above the dragon eggs; huge buildings of precious metals were toppling, towers came crashing to the ground, the platinum river broke its banks and spread like a silver platter across the walkways and roads of Wyrmblood.

Stone and rock fell like rain.

Volak moved to the centre of the chamber, and hunkering down, she gathered ten or twelve eggs together, pulling them protectively under her belly. She could feel how warm they were, fire licking delicately over their living shells.

Volak spread her wings, then brought them in like a shield, as she lowered her neck, lowered her head, tucking it underneath herself to observe her eggs; her offspring; her babes.

"I will protect you to the end," she said, her words a gentle tickling of fire, as above, the mountain screamed and the entire city of Wyrmblood came tumbling down.

Acknowledgments

This has been *the* hardest book I ever wrote, for a myriad of reasons – and thus, these acknowledgements are extremely heartfelt!

First, a big hug to Marco at AR for being so understanding of my sorry ass. You deserve a big kiss, and if you're extremely unlucky, you'll get one.

Next, thanks to my boys, Joseph and Oliver, who are totally awesome and keep me going with bright firebrands to illuminate the darkness. You really do not understand what you mean to me; maybe one day you will.

Super, wonderful, magical thanks to Marie, for breaking her back (and eyes!) test-reading and proofreading and editing my shit. I owe you so many chocolate bars (and fish!) it isn't even funny: thank you.

A big thundering axe-blow to Kareem Mahfouz, for being so supportive, offering his help unconditionally, and for the test reading and enthusiasm. Cheers, whiskey dude!

More big thanks go to Roy Young, for always being there, and for his amusing abusive voicemail messages! "For fuck's sake…what's the point of having a phone… " LOL.

Thank you to Rob Shedwick, my musical maestro and good friend, for long conversations when I really needed them, for his intuition and strength and help, and for allowing me see some light from the bottom of the fish tank.

Thanks must also go to Jake, Kev and Ralphy – old friendships renewed! A big "Yo!" to the good guys of the Branston Crew (but not the scum). And a final sloppy kiss to all the friends who've stood by me through some very dark days.